1 942586 21

KT-465-696

Renfrewshire
Council

The library is always open at
renfrewshirelibraries.co.uk

Visit now for library news and
information,
to **renew and
reserve** online, and to
download
free eBooks.

Phone: 0300 300 1188
Email: libraries@renfrewshire.gov.uk

JUST ONE
MORE DAY

For more information about Jessica Blair visit
www.jessicablair.co.uk

JUST ONE
MORE DAY

Jessica Blair

piatkus

PIATKUS

First published in Great Britain in 2015 by Piatkus

Copyright © 2015 by Jessica Blair

The moral right of the author has been asserted.

All characters and events in this publication, other than those
clearly in the public domain, are fictitious and any resemblance
to real persons, living or dead, is purely coincidental.

All rights reserved.
No part of this publication may be reproduced, stored in a
retrieval system, or transmitted in any form or by any means, without
the prior permission in writing of the publisher, nor be otherwise circulated
in any form of binding or cover other than that in which it is published
and without a similar condition including this condition
being imposed on the subsequent purchaser.

A CIP catalogue record for this book
is available from the British Library.

ISBN 978-0-349-40269-7

Typeset in Times by M Rules
Printed and bound in Great Britain by
Clays Ltd, St Ives, plc

1 3 5 7 9 10 8 6 4 2

Papers used by Piatkus are from well-managed forests
and other responsible sources.

MIX
Paper from
responsible sources
FSC® C104740

Piatkus
An imprint of
Little, Brown Book Group
100 Victoria Embankment
London EC4Y 0DY

An Hachette UK Company
www.hachette.co.uk

www.piatkus.co.uk

For Jill

and

the men and women who fought

and those who waited

RENFREWSHIRE COUNCIL	
194258621	
Bertrams	11/02/2015
	£19.99
ERS	

1

Seventeen-year-old Carolyn Maddison glanced at the clock on her bedroom wall. Ten minutes to eleven. She put down her copy of Daphne du Maurier's *Rebecca*, rose from her chair and stood looking out of the window.

The garden of the detached house in the tiny village of Nunthorpe on the outskirts of Middlesbrough, where her father practised as a solicitor, looked pristine under the care of their gardener. Carolyn loved the view from her bedroom; especially when the summer colours were beginning to acquire the tints of autumn. The seasonal cycle seemed to her a sign of permanency, something which would always be there for her. But even as that thought occurred to her, she realized that in a few minutes' time she might hear that her world was to be turned upside down and her future become uncertain.

Up to now she, her brother Alastair and their mother Sally had lived very comfortably. Her father's solicitor's practice did well and besides that Guy Maddison's great-aunt Maud, with no children of her own, had left the bulk of her fortune to him. Carolyn's father had invested it wisely after consultation with his wife, and when the time came there had been money to pay boarding fees for their son Alastair at

Ampleforth and for Carolyn at the Bar Convent in York, where her mother had been educated.

When he was eighteen next month Alastair would be making a new life for himself away from home and already his mother was beginning to feel the loss. Still, she would have Carolyn for another year before her daughter too took her first steps into the wide world beyond.

But in a few minutes all that could be changed.

Carolyn gazed for a moment longer at the garden. Was she trying to impress the tranquil scene on her mind for ever?

She stepped out on to the landing. Almost at the same moment Alastair appeared from his room.

'Is this it?' she asked her brother.

His answering grimace told her he felt sure it would be.

'What will you do?' she asked.

'If it happens, I'll volunteer for pilot training in the RAF.'

They walked down the wide curving staircase side by side and crossed the hall to the sitting room. Alastair opened the door for his sister and followed her in. Their mother gave them a nervous smile. Their father turned away from the wireless, which he had just switched on.

Carolyn went to her mother, kissed her on the cheek and pressed her hand reassuringly, then joined her brother on the settee.

The hands of the clock on the mantelpiece neared 11.15 a.m.

Silence seemed to hang heavily in the room even though the wireless was on. The family felt helpless to influence the announcement they were about to hear – yet still they hoped it would be not what they feared.

'... *This morning, the British Ambassador in Berlin handed the German government a final note, stating that unless the British government heard from them by eleven o'clock that they were prepared to withdraw their troops from Poland, a state of war would exist between us. I have to tell you now no such understanding has been received, and that consequently this country is at war with Germany . . . '*

When the Prime Minister finished his announcement, Guy rose from his chair without a word and switched off the wireless.

The date 3 September 1939 was one they would always remember.

'The poor man,' said Sally quietly with a catch in her voice.

'Well, that's that. We're at war,' said Guy.

'I'm going to volunteer for flying duties with the RAF,' said Alastair firmly, believing it was best to announce his decision now. He registered his parents' stunned silence and added, 'Please don't try and stop me. I'd rather do this now and have a choice how I serve than wait and be conscripted and sent anywhere.'

'Alastair, you don't know what you're saying!' his mother protested, with tears coming to her eyes.

'I do, Mother. I've been giving it some thought ever since I learned war had become inevitable.'

'But you're only . . . ' The words caught in her throat.

Her husband came to kneel beside Sally and take her in his arms. He whispered for only her to hear, 'Give him your love. Support him.'

She gave a little nod and held out her arms to her son. As she held him she said, 'I'll always be here for all of you. Whatever lies ahead we'll get through. You have my blessing, Alastair. God go with you.'

The next day he headed for London.

3

2

Carolyn stretched out in bed and flung her arms wide to embrace the new April day hoping it would be warm and sunny. She had a fortnight's holiday remaining before she must return to York for her last term at the Bar Convent.

She had promised herself that when that time came she would volunteer for service in the WAAFs. Although she had already hinted to her parents that this was what she wanted to do, they were withholding their approval, at least for the time being: 'Wait and see if you still feel the same when you finish at the Convent.' But she was certain she would not deviate from her desire to join the Women's Auxiliary Air Force and emulate her brother's success in the RAF. Alastair's natural flying ability had brought him praise and his pilot's Wings in short order. He was swiftly commissioned as a pilot officer. Though his parents were proud of his achievements they were anxious when they learned he would be moving south from Acklington to join a front-line squadron flying Spitfires, and were reluctant to sanction Carolyn's desire to emulate him by entering the women's branch of the service.

She swung out of bed and prepared herself for the day ahead, turning over various ideas. She had only herself to please; her mother and father were in Newcastle visiting her mother's sister and would not be back for a couple of days.

She enjoyed her breakfast while sitting by the window overlooking the garden. Judging the weather to be settled, Carolyn decided she would enjoy a bike ride into Middlesbrough to visit her gran. On being widowed, Guy Maddison's mother Mary Jane had worked hard to give her son a good education. He had appreciated that and had rewarded her many sacrifices by qualifying as a solicitor. Though he and his wife had wanted Mary Jane to live with them when they moved to the village of Nunthorpe, she had refused their offer: 'You have your own lives. You are near enough if ever I want you. My friends are all around me here and I have my niece Irene next door. She'll keep her eye on me. I'll be all right.'

She'd kept to that policy even after the outbreak of war and remained undaunted even at night. Whenever the sirens wailed across Middlesbrough her niece would go in to ask her: 'Are you coming to the shelter tonight, Aunt?'

'Nay, lass. If them Germans want to kill me, they can kill me in my own bed.'

Carolyn washed her breakfast plates and a few minutes later was pedalling away from Nunthorpe. She had been woken during the night but the bombing had sounded so distant she had ignored it, telling herself the bombs would be aimed at the industrial complexes and shipping towards the mouth of the River Tees. She hoped the bombers had been unsuccessful in finding their targets and that no one had been killed.

She hummed happily as she enjoyed the ride, but fell silent when she turned into the street where her grandmother lived. Mary Jane's house and those of her neighbours were no longer there, replaced instead by a chaotic mountain of bricks and stones through which twisted metal reared dark against the sky.

Gran! The name rang through Carolyn's mind. She knew her grandmother's policy of staying out of the public shelter. But maybe last night ... Eyes filled with concern and hope, Carolyn scanned the busy scene. People in dungarees, overalls and steel helmets were working busily everywhere she looked. Two lorries and a fire-engine, their jobs done, were parked close by a huge hole in the road. Around it were piles of broken bricks shrouded in a melancholy deposit of grey dust. The front wall of a nearby house had been blasted away. Patterned bed-sheets flapped in the breeze beside a wardrobe hanging precariously from what remained of the floor. Furniture smashed by the bomb blast lay scattered on the ground, a pathetic reminder of what had once been a comfortable, treasured home.

Carolyn jumped off her bike, pushed it to one side and rushed forward. 'Gran!' She must find her! Please God, let her be safe!

'Sorry, miss, you can't go through there,' said a policeman standing by a tape drawn across the road.

'It's my grandmother! She lives there!' cried Carolyn, on the verge of tears, not wanting her worst suspicions to be true.

Moved by her anguish the policeman asked gently, 'Is that her, over there?'

Carolyn glanced across the scene of devastation, hope sending her heart soaring. A fireman who had obscured her view moved, and relief coursed through Carolyn. Her beloved gran was alive! But how could she have survived this devastation?

6

'Come on, lass, I'll take you over to her.' The policeman lifted the tape and, as Carolyn slipped under it, signalled to another officer to take his place.

'Careful how you tread,' he warned. 'There's glass everywhere.' He led the way through heaps of bricks and mortar. 'Mind this wood, lass, it's lethal,' he added, indicating the jagged pieces as he inched past a waist-high pile.

'Missus, your granddaughter's here.'

Mary Jane was gazing down at a framed photograph clutched in her hand. Tears streaked her cheeks. 'Carolyn!' The relief she felt on seeing her granddaughter was touching.

Carolyn took her in her arms. 'Everything's going to be all right, Gran.'

'But look, those Germans tried to destroy my photograph,' sobbed Mary Jane. 'It's that nice one of you with your Granddad.'

Carolyn glanced at it and recalled seeing it standing on the mantelpiece in her granny's 'best room'. They had been in the garden at Nunthorpe when the photograph had been taken; she remembered being asked to give her gran a special smile.

'Give it to me, missus,' said the policeman, gently taking it from her hand. 'I'll be back in a few minutes.' He looked at Carolyn. 'Your grandmother has been checked out. Can you take her home with you?'

'Yes,' replied the girl firmly.

'Good. I'll get some transport for you.' He called to a nurse and in a few moments they had an ambulance organized.

'Thank you,' said Carolyn. 'What happened to the people who lived next door?'

The policeman drew her to one side while the nurse came

over to her gran. 'They and the other people in the shelter are being checked out. No serious casualties, thank God. Your grandmother was dealt with first because of her age. She insisted on coming back here to see the damage. She's done very well. The nurse will have a word with you. Now for that photograph.' He smiled and went off.

The nurse introduced herself and started to note down where Carolyn's grandmother would be living for the present.

When this had been done the nurse concluded, 'Your granny is a tough lady, but there could be a reaction when what has happened starts to sink in. Will you be on your own with her?'

'Today and tomorrow. My parents are in Newcastle, due home the day after tomorrow.'

'Good. I don't think there is any need to worry them now. I will give you details of where to contact me and visit on the evening of your parents' return, if that is convenient?'

'Of course.'

'The ambulance will be here shortly. There'll be two orderlies to see you home, and they'll put your bike in the back.'

'Thank you.'

As the nurse hurried away to instruct the orderlies, the policeman returned.

'There you are, missus.' He held out the photograph, neatly restored to its frame.

'Oh, thank you.' Tears of relief at having her beloved photograph returned to her streamed down Mary Jane's face.

'There's plenty of glass about, missus,' said the man with a sympathetic smile. He leaned forward and kissed her on the cheek. 'You take care and do as your lovely granddaughter tells you.'

Within ten minutes the ambulance was on its way to Nunthorpe. Mary Jane clutched her photograph in one hand and Carolyn held the other.

'Gran, what happened when the sirens went? Were you not at home?' Carolyn's curiosity could not be restrained any longer. She had to know how her grandmother had survived the bomb.

'No, I was there. Irene came in as usual to ask me to go to the shelter. I was on the point of saying I'd stay in bed, but something made me change my mind.' She thought about this and added, 'I think God didn't want those Germans to kill me. Maybe He still has a purpose for me to fulfil.'

Two days later Carolyn and her grandmother were enjoying a cup of tea while sitting in the lounge with the French windows open to the sun. Carolyn was pleased with the way her gran had coped with the shock of the bombing and losing her home, but had no doubt that the experience would have left its mark. Her thoughts were interrupted by the opening of the front door.

'We're home!'

'Mum ... Dad. They're here, Gran!' Carolyn jumped to her feet and rushed into the hall. 'Welcome back,' she cried, and hugged and kissed them both. Then she linked arms with her parents, saying, 'Come with me, I've something to show you.' She guided them towards the door to the lounge. 'Someone's here to see you.'

Guy and Sally gasped at the unexpected sight of Mary Jane.

'Gran will be staying with us a little while,' explained Carolyn as her parents and grandmother said how delighted they were to see each other.

'What's happened?' asked Sally, a little suspiciously.

Although she knew her mother-in-law liked to visit them, she usually gave them advance warning. 'Are you ill?'

Mary Jane gave a little chuckle. 'No, I'm fit as a fiddle, but that stupid man Hitler tried to kill me!'

For a moment there was a stunned silence then Guy said quietly, 'What did you say?'

'Gran was bombed out.' Carolyn explained.

'What?

'Two nights ago,' added Carolyn. 'A direct hit on her house.'

Knowing her mother-in-law's attitude to air raids, Sally was astounded. 'Weren't you in bed?'

'When Irene came in as usual, I decided to go with her to the shelter.'

Sally sank back into a chair, staring in disbelief at her mother-in-law. 'Thank goodness you did.'

'A miracle,' agreed Guy. 'It's a miracle. Someone was certainly looking after you, Mother.' He sat down, saying, 'Now tell us everything.'

'A cup of tea for you first?' Carolyn enquired.

'No,' said Sally. 'We can't wait, tell us what happened.'

Between them Gran and Carolyn explained.

When they had finished, Sally said, 'Thank goodness Carolyn was here.'

'She's been a gem,' her gran agreed with an appreciative smile. 'Now I'll get that cup of tea for you. Then, while you two get unpacked, Carolyn and I will prepare a meal.'

Sally started to protest but her mother-in-law interrupted. 'I'm not going to sit around like an invalid. Let me be useful.'

Knowing it was Mary Jane's habit to always keep busy, and judging it would be good for her to keep occupied, Sally agreed. She went to kiss her mother-in-law then. 'You do know you are welcome to come here and live with us, don't you?'

Mary Jane patted her hand. 'Thank you, Sally, I appreciate that. We'll see.'

The bombing was mentioned again over the meal.

'You really should come and live here permanently, Mother,' said Guy. 'Things are not going well for us in Europe; the Army is having little success. If things get worse, goodness knows what will happen.'

'I know what I want to do,' put in Carolyn. 'What happened to Gran has made me even more determined to join the WAAFs. I'm going to volunteer as soon as I finish school.'

'Not now, Carolyn,' said Sally. 'We agreed this subject would be left until then.'

'Mother, my mind is made up. That is what I want to do and will do, as soon as I'm finished at the convent. I'll be old enough then.'

Sally tensed, recognizing that Carolyn saying 'Mother' instead of 'Mum' showed that her daughter was determined to have her way.

'But, Carolyn, so much can happen in a few months,' put in her father. 'Let's wait till the summer.'

'It's already happened,' she replied. 'Gran's been bombed out and Alastair is serving with a fighter squadron. That's sufficient motivation for me.'

There was a moment's silence. Gran seized her chance to speak.

'Please don't think I am interfering with what I am about to say, but it is my firm belief that if parents support their child in what he or she wants to do, then the child is more likely to succeed and be a credit to them. And, more importantly, they will always keep that child's love.'

11

The wisdom of this observation was palpable. Carolyn was tense; she was sure her future hung on how her gran's words were received. Guy and Sally knew there was a lot of truth in what Mary Jane said. He glanced at his wife. Each read the other's thoughts the moment their eyes met.

'All right, Carolyn, your mother and I will support you in what ever you want to do, when the time comes for you to leave school,' Guy declared.

'Oh, thank you!' She jumped up from her chair and was round the table in a flash to kiss them both and then her gran. Recognizing the important part her grandmother had played, Carolyn whispered, 'Thanks.'

Pleased to see her granddaughter happy, Gran replied quietly, 'Now I know why God performed that miracle!'

But she began to wonder if He had no miracles left when the news turned blacker in the next few weeks.

'I have every sympathy for the Prime Minister,' she commented on hearing of his resignation on the tenth of May.

'He was a weary man,' commented Sally.

'Having to take the country to war overwhelmed him,' Guy put in. 'Maybe Churchill can rally everybody. He has a certain tenacity, though he is not popular with some MPs.'

But gloom deepened and spread with the news that the Army was falling back to the beaches of Dunkirk. There was an appeal for every sort of vessel to come to the rescue of the stranded British Expeditionary Force.

'We need another miracle,' commented Gran.

'Indeed we do,' agreed Sally. 'Do you think we should bring Carolyn home, Guy?'

'No. She is so near to finishing school. Let her do so.'

By the time her exams were out of the way the miracle

had happened. Many more men were snatched from the beaches of Dunkirk than had been expected, though the figures for the dead, wounded and those taken prisoner were huge.

Europe had been overrun by the German war-machine. Only a twenty-mile strip of water lay between Britain and invasion.

3

'Alastair!' Sally gasped when her son walked into the kitchen unannounced. She rushed to him, her embrace expressing all the relief and joy she felt. Still holding his hands she took a step back. 'Let me look at you.' His mother's keen eyes studied him. 'You're pale and tired ... worn out in fact. I can see it even though you're trying to hide it.'

He gave a little laugh. 'Can't escape a mother's anxiety, can I?'

'A mother's privilege.' She linked arms with him and led him into the lounge, calling out as they crossed the hall, 'Gran, Carolyn, there's a surprise for you.'

Curiosity brought Carolyn hurrying from her bedroom where she had been sorting out some clothes. Her gran followed from her room and together they entered the lounge. They gulped with surprise to see who was awaiting them.

'Alastair!' Carolyn screamed with delight and flung herself into her brother's arms. 'I can't believe it! I just can't.'

He kissed her on the cheek and then stepped forward to greet his gran. 'You look as radiant as ever. Glad to see Hitler couldn't break your spirit with his bombs.'

'It would take more than that,' she retorted, defiance in her voice.

'We need more like you, Gran.'

'How long are you here for?' asked his mother.

'Four days,' Alastair replied, and added teasingly, 'if you'll have me?'

'Hang on,' called Carolyn. 'Let's make a cup of tea and then Alastair can tell us everything.'

Within a few minutes they were all seated with their tea and slices of fruit cake.

'This is a bit of a luxury, isn't it?' commented Alastair, and bit into his slice of cake.

'Some fruit I had left over from last Christmas, and we scrimped the other ingredients from our rations,' explained Sally.

'You manage all right then?'

'As soon as rationing came in early in the year Gran and I got our heads together to work out the best way of stretching supplies by combining them with things that aren't rationed. But it's not easy. A weekly six ounces of butter, eight ounces of sugar, two ounces of tea, three eggs and so on is not a lot to get by on, but we manage. Your father's contribution is turning some of the flowerbeds into vegetable plots and he's studying the best varieties of potato to grow. But how goes it with you? How have you managed to get four days' leave?'

'The whole squadron has been stood down ... we are all a bit weary. We've been in the air every day for goodness knows how long. It seems a life time. We gave cover for our troops over France and during the retreat to Dunkirk, and air cover for the beaches during the evacuation. You may hear reports that we weren't over the beaches, but a lot of the action was taking place miles away to prevent enemy planes

15

even getting there. Inevitably some did, though.' Alastair took another sip of his tea and savoured it. 'The best cup I've had for a long time, and that cake is out of this world.'

'How did you get here?' asked Sally. 'No, wait, let's get you settled. Your father said he would be home early today – two o'clock-ish. You can tell us more then.'

'Good idea, Mum.'

'Come on. You and I will see if your room is ready for you. And then no doubt you'd like to freshen up?'

'Yes, I would,' he agreed.

As they went upstairs together Sally felt worried for her son, though she kept that to herself. He looked so tired. Lines of stress furrowed Alastair's face; he had lost his youthful glow. It was as if he had lived years in the months he had been away from them.

'Oh, just as I left it,' he commented as he walked into his room.

'Well, more or less. I tidied up a bit,' said Sally.

'That bed looks comfortable,' he said wistfully.

She smiled tentatively. He looked so drained.

He caught the unease behind her expression, came over and hugged her. 'Don't worry, Mum. I'm all right, just tired.'

'Have a lie down until your father gets here.'

'No, that would mean wasting precious minutes I could spend with you all.'

She was grateful for his thoughtfulness.

When she went downstairs and into the kitchen, Sally found it a hive of activity. 'You both look busy,' she commented.

'Gran suggested she and I should serve up the fatted calf this evening,' Carolyn explained.

'And how are you doing?'

'You'll see,' said Gran. 'When Alastair comes down again, you spend some time with him,' she went on in a voice that demanded to be obeyed.

When Guy came home shortly before two, he was astonished and delighted to see his son.

'How did you get here?' he queried

'I was lucky, our squadron leader brought me,' explained Alastair. 'He runs an MG. Don't ask where he gets the petrol but he does. Ask no questions, hear no lies. He's married; his home is in Corbridge. He offered me a lift and will pick me up on the way back.'

'He dropped you at our door?' asked Sally with surprise. 'You should have asked him in.'

'I did but he wanted to get home. I'll get him to say hello when he picks me up.'

'See that you do,' said his father.

Chatter flowed throughout the rest of the day, particularly during the meal when Guy produced one of the bottles of wine that he had laid in when hostilities seemed inevitable. Tonight they would celebrate; they were together as a family once more. Who knew when the next similar occasion would be?

Before they retired for the night, Guy sought a chance to have a word with his son when the others were out of earshot. 'Do you think Hitler is going to invade?'

'Who knows? I thought he would have done immediately we left Dunkirk, but there are no indications of it. Whatever happens, we in Fighter Command are ready.'

'But have we sufficient men and planes?'

'We'll make the best use of what we have,' Alastair replied. 'That's all I can say, Dad.'

His father knew better than to try and ask more.

*

The next day, when Carolyn got her brother on her own, her questions were far less restrained.

'I'll be leaving school at the end of June. I have always said that when I do, I will join the WAAFs. With the situation as it is, do you think I am right in pursuing that idea still?'

'Have Mum and Dad said yes?'

'More or less.'

'Then go ahead. Nobody knows how things will turn out, but I am of the opinion Churchill will be doing all he can to keep this country alive and kicking. Yes, join the WAAFs if that is what you want to do.' Alastair saw the relief on his sister's face and knew that he had given the answer she wanted to hear so he went on, 'If you do, I would advise you to set your stall out and do your very best in your paricular trade – aim at getting a Commission. It will give you something to work for and ensure you of a better life within the RAF – not that that should be your principle aim. Try and serve your country to the best of your ability. I believe that you will best achieve that through taking a Commission.'

Carolyn smiled and kissed her brother on the cheek. 'Thanks for that. Now my mind is made up, I'll go ahead.'

The squadron leader halted his MG outside the house in Nunthorpe very promptly. Alastair glanced at the clock on the mantelpiece. 'I told you he was a stickler for timekeeping.'

'Invite him in,' said Guy.

In a few minutes introductions had been made and the senior officer was relaxing with a cup of tea. Once he had finished it he looked at his watch. 'This has been very enjoyable and I'm pleased to have met Alastair's family,' he said, rising to his feet. 'He is a credit to the squadron.'

'You see you look after my grandson,' said Gran seriously when she shook hands with him.

He smiled. 'I'll be sure to do that, Mrs Maddison.' He kissed her on the cheek, 'There, that's a promise.'

'Sealed with a kiss,' she chuckled.

As they watched the car drive away Sally was sad to think that soon she would be waving goodbye to her daughter also.

4

But that did not come about as soon as she had expected. July moved into August, which gave way to the cooler weather of September.

'I've volunteered. I should have been called up before now,' Carolyn moaned once more at the breakfast table. 'Don't they want me to win the war for them?' she added peevishly.

An hour later she had to withdraw those remarks when the post arrived and she was able to announce with excitement in her voice, 'I've to report to the Air Ministry a week today!'

Though the parting had tugged at her heartstrings, Carolyn had fought against shedding a tear. Her mother had put on a brave face and her father had masked his feelings with a forced smile and a wink as the train started to steam out of Middlesbrough station. Her mother reached out. Carolyn, lowering the window in the door, took her hand and squeezed it as she mouthed the words, 'I'll be all right, Mum. Love you.'

'Look out, Carolyn!' The sharp tone of her father's voice startled her but she realized why he had warned her when she saw a young RAF officer come running on to the platform and make straight for the nearest door, which was hers. Carolyn stepped back hurriedly. The young man grasped the handle, turned it, hurled himself inside, tumbling into her as he slammed the door behind him.

'Sorry!' he gasped as he straightened up and dropped his kit bag.

'That's all right,' replied Carolyn automatically. Then her own politeness struck her as funny and her face lit up in a broad smile. 'At least you caught the train.'

'Only just.' He moved to one side. 'Come back to the window. You were saying your goodbyes.'

'Thanks.' She leaned out and saw the incident had eased the strain of parting. Her parents were as amused as she was by the near miss.

Carolyn waved until they were out of sight then straightened up and struggled to raise the window.

'Let me.' The officer smiled as she turned out of the way. As he closed the window she noticed the two blue rings around his sleeve and the ribbon on the breast of his tunic – a flying officer with a DFC. She was in good hands. His manner was self-assured; he had confidence without being overbearing.

'Your parents?' he asked, eyes bright with interest.

'Yes.'

'First time away from home?'

Carolyn nodded, 'Except for boarding school.'

'Thought so,' he replied. 'I know what it's like.'

'Does it get any better?' she asked, feeling drawn into conversation with him but not regretting it.

He shrugged his shoulders. 'I don't suppose so,' he replied. You just get used to it and learn to hide your feelings. My mother always grieves when I'm leaving. It's only natural; she's a widow and I'm her only child. We're close, but she never complains or voices any regrets that I'm a pilot, even though I know she's wondering whether she will see me again.'

'I suppose I have noticed the same thing in my parents,' Carolyn replied with surprise in her voice, 'though I've never really thought about it before. My brother's in the RAF too. He's a pilot officer.'

'Yes, that sounds very likely then.' He gave her a knowing look. 'I think we'd better change the topic, don't you, or we are going to have a morbid ride? I always say, take what comes and never look back. Live for today because who knows what tomorrow may bring?'

Carolyn thought how lucky she had been to be standing where she was when this good-looking young man had jumped on to the train. Although the tiredness of war had lined his face prematurely, she was drawn by the friendly sparkle in his eyes mellowing his guarded scrutiny of her.

He too was having thoughts about his luck. To find himself beside a pretty girl, who had taken no offence at his unorthodox arrival, was a bonus at the start of his journey. He liked the amusement in her eyes and the laughter on her lips, reading in them a bubbly energy and desire to get the best out of life.

'Do you want to try to find a seat?' he asked.

'I think it might be hopeless, the train looks pretty full. I don't mind standing. It's not far to Darlington.'

'And where then?' he asked

'London.'

He pulled a face. 'You might have to stand all the way. Trains get fuller every day. The one we'll be catching will be coming from Newcastle ... well, Edinburgh really.'

'You know this route then?'

'Yes, I've used it several times, though that might not be the case in the future, I'm expecting a posting when I report in London.'

'And you can't tell me where, I suppose?' said Carolyn. She saw his lips tighten, and laughed. 'My brother is always wary of such questions.'

'Where's he stationed?' No sooner had the question come out than the young man started to laugh as well. 'Now you've got me doing it.'

'I think both of us are being over-cautious.'

'So do I,' he chuckled. 'I reckon we'd better introduce ourselves, seeing as we'll be travelling to London together.' He added quickly, 'Oh, dear, I suppose I'm being presumptuous, saying that?'

'Not at all,' replied Carolyn. 'I'd be pleased to have your company. This is all completely new to me.'

He smiled and held out his hand. 'Charlie Wade, at your service.'

'Carolyn Maddison.'

Here she was, only a few minutes after leaving her parents and already chatting to a stranger. Take care; be wary of the company you keep ... She could hear her mother saying it now. But a handsome RAF officer had leaped into her life and it dawned on Carolyn that she was totally free to deal with this chance meeting in any way she chose. Here she was, making the first completely independent judgment of her newfound freedom.

'I'm pleased to meet you, Carolyn Maddison.' He seemed to enjoy saying her Christian name. 'Carolyn. Nice name.' Charlie pursed his lips thoughtfully. 'I don't know of any other girls called that. Makes you unique.'

She put on a hurt expression. 'Only my name?'

He grinned and said with a teasing note in his voice, 'I'll

tell you that when we get to King's Cross. So now I'd better start getting to know you. First question – I think we'll be allowed these questions – why are you going to London?'

'To join up.'

'WAAFS, no doubt?'

'Yes.'

'The glamour of the uniform? Or maybe because your brother . . . ?'

'A bit of both. But I was determined to volunteer as soon as I was eighteen.

'And that is what you are doing now?'

'Yes. I was accepted and told to wait at home. I got the buff envelope last week telling me to report today.'

'At the Air Ministry?'

'Yes.'

'Then perhaps you would like to accompany me there?'

'That would be wonderful, if it isn't going to be out of your way?'

'It won't be. I'm due there too.'

Carolyn couldn't believe her luck. She had been worrying about finding her way in the metropolis. Or maybe it wasn't luck. Maybe this was another of Gran's miracles.

As the train slowed coming into Darlington station, Charlie leaned closer and said in a low voice, 'Be ready with your suitcase. There'll be a lot of people already on the platform and then there'll be another trainful, all heading south. Stick close and follow me.'

She nodded. Whatever he had in mind, Carolyn found herself trusting Charlie's judgment.

The train clattered and hissed its way to a shuddering stop. Doors swung open, people were out of the carriages quickly, seeking the station exit or the platform from which

24

their connection would leave. There was bustle everywhere, civilians mingled with servicemen and women, all purposefully searching out trains or seeking information about their onward journey.

Charlie darted through the milling crowd, constantly making sure that Carolyn was close and had not been left behind among the throng. Concentrating on keeping up, she asked no questions, though she did wonder why he was going so far along the platform designated as the one from which the London train would leave. The crowd was largely left behind. Only a few stragglers remained when Charlie dropped his case.

'We should be all right here,' he said.

'Why here?' Carolyn asked with a puzzled frown. 'I thought you were walking me to London.'

He laughed. 'You'd soon be moaning, and that wouldn't be my idea of fun. No, we're more likely to get a seat from here. First-class carriages are always at the front of the train. This is the track running south so First Class will be stopping about here.'

'Oh, my goodness,' she gasped. 'That's no use for me. I haven't a first-class ticket.' As it dawned on her, Carolyn felt a surge of annoyance that he had not mentioned this before. 'Of course you have a first-class ticket, being an officer and all. You might have told me!' She scowled and started to pick up her suitcase.

'Leave it!' Charlie said firmly.

'Don't you tell me what to do!' Carolyn snapped at him indignantly.

'Just leave it. Pick it up when the train is approaching and then stick close behind me. I can't have you standing all the way to London.' Meekly she put the case down again. Whatever he had in mind, she sensed it was to her advantage.

The train appeared, slowing down as it ran alongside the

platform. Once again doors were thrown open, and new arrivals mingled with those trying to step off the train. This was a much more orderly scrum, however, because fewer passengers had paid the extra fare to travel in the first two coaches. Carolyn felt her own second-class ticket like an extra weight in her handbag.

'Come on!' Charlie roused her from her reverie.

Startled, she muttered an apology but he was already at the door to a carriage. She stepped quickly after him. As she climbed up he said, 'Turn left. There are two seats a few yards down the aisle on the left-hand side.'

She automatically obeyed and within a few moments was settled comfortably with him beside her. He said nothing more, nor did she question him. What would happen when the guard came to check their tickets she did not dare contemplate. All she could do was leave it in the hands of the gods. Or more likely Charlie.

It was soon after leaving Darlington that the guard appeared.

'Give me your ticket,' Charlie ordered quietly.

Carolyn fished in her handbag and handed over her ticket. A few minutes later the guard stopped by their seats. 'Tickets, please, sir.'

Charlie handed over his RAF pass. The guard gave it a cursory glance, punched it and handed it back to Charlie, who then gave him Carolyn's ticket, saying, 'The young lady's with me.'

'Yes, sir.' The guard paid no heed to examining the ticket, merely punched it and handed it back to Charlie.

Carolyn could not be sure but she felt certain that there had been some sleight of hand in the transaction. She guessed that a ten-shilling note or maybe more had put that smile on the guard's face.

26

'Have a pleasant journey, miss,' he said with a friendly twinkle in his eye.

As he moved out of earshot Charlie leaned closer to her. 'Always pays to get on the right side of railway officials,' he said quietly.

'It would appear so,' she commented.

Guessing she was about to offer to pay whatever extra was necessary, Charlie raised a finger. 'Say no more. Enjoy the journey and prepare to be introduced to the Big City and the Air Ministry.'

5

Passengers, recognizing they were close to King's Cross, started to stand up and retrieve their cases, duffel bags, and whatever belongings they had stored on the luggage racks. Carolyn began to move but Charlie laid a restraining hand on her arm. When she glanced enquiringly at him, he gave a slight shake of his head and winked at her.

The train slowed, hissed, jerked, and gave one final sigh of steam, as if relieved that its journey was over. Civilians were outnumbered by soldiers, sailors, airmen, and women in a variety of uniforms, all pouring out on to the platform where they joined the human tide flowing toward the ticket barrier, or headed for the Underground, or sought the right platform for their onward travel.

When the last two passengers in their carriage had reached the door, Charlie stood up. 'Let's go,' he said. He led the way on to a platform that by now was markedly less congested. Nevertheless he urged, 'Keep close.'

Carolyn did not reply. By this time she had come to have faith in the RAF officer who seemed bent on looking after her. Reaching the station exit she gasped, 'Look at the length of that taxi queue!' She wanted to complain that he'd held them up but held back the criticism.

'Round here.' She followed him without a word and stifled her surprise when she saw a lone taxi parked unobtrusively close to a side wall a short distance away.

'Ah, Fred's on the ball again,' Charlie observed with relief.

'You knew this taxi would be here?' Carolyn made no effort to disguise her surprise.

'Fred's never let me down yet.'

'So you've done this before?'

Charlie smiled. 'Yes.' He forced himself to look more serious. 'Well, yes as regards telling Fred to wait here, but I'm not in the habit of picking up pretty girls on trains. You were the exception because of the gracious way you accepted my apology for bumping into you. Then, when you announced you were joining the WAAFs and obviously didn't know London, what else could I do but offer to look after you?'

'But how does Fred fit in? How does he know when you'll be arriving in London?'

'Tell you inside,' offered Charlie, seeing the driver emerge from the taxi. 'Good to see you, Fred. Been waiting long?'

'Five minutes. Checked the arrival time. No delay so it worked out well.' He glanced at Carolyn. 'Good afternoon, miss.'

'Good afternoon, Fred.'

'This is Miss Carolyn Maddison,' said Charlie. 'I bumped into her on the train and found that she is heading for the Air Ministry too. Couldn't leave my charming companion standing in that awfully long taxi queue, could I?'

'Nor could I, sir.' Fred grinned, picked up her luggage, opened the taxi door and ushered Carolyn in. He grabbed Charlie's luggage then. As he was stowing it safely in the front of the taxi, Charlie enquired, 'Was the bombing bad last night?'

'Not too bad up here but the East End caught it.'

As they headed for the Air Ministry Carolyn was shocked by what she saw on every side. The devastation she had witnessed in the street where her grandmother lived had not prepared her for the wholesale destruction she saw on this short ride through London; and this was only a small part of the great city. She knew that there were daily attacks by German bombers. Now she wondered how people managed to live through them without being driven to breaking point by Hitler's desire to bring Britain to heel. But life was still flowing through the city's veins. People were still going about their daily lives in as normal a way as possible She saw defiance in their drawn and weary faces and felt that she must live up to this example. Not to do so, not to play her part in the war effort, would be to let down these people and her beloved grandmother.

Seeing the distress in Carolyn's eyes, Charlie tried to draw her attention away from the scenes of destruction. 'You asked how Fred knew I would be arriving?'

'Yes.'

'I plan two days ahead, and send him a telegram with the time of my arrival. He checks for any delays. It works well, as you have seen.' Having drawn her attention away from the bombing damage he went on, 'No doubt you are wondering what takes me to the Air Ministry? Well, all you need to know is that after I had finished my last tour of operations I was on a spell of leave when somebody, somewhere in the depths of government, had the bright idea that it would be good for morale if three or four people like myself, who had seen action, toured the country explaining to the workforce how their efforts were helping towards defeating the enemy. So, in my case, I visit factories building aircraft or making instruments or bombs ... anything, in fact, connected to our flying missions. This entails reporting back to the Air Ministry on a regular basis, hence the frequent rail journeys. After I realized I was going to be held up by taxi queues on reaching London, I took it upon myself to make friends with Fred and put a proposition to him. He was all for it because it did not interfere with his normal schedule by keeping him on a rank. You've seen our arrangement in action today.'

'I have indeed,' Carolyn smiled at him. 'I'm so grateful you tumbled into my carriage in Middlesbrough. You've made my journey much easier and eased the strain of leaving home for a new and unknown life.'

'You'll do well.'

'I hope so.'

'I *know* so. You must tell me how you get on.'

'I don't know where I'm going to be.'

'I'll find out.'

'More string-pulling, no doubt?'

'That's no bad thing sometimes.' Charlie grinned at her.

Fred brought the taxi to a halt outside the Air Ministry and was out in a flash to see to their luggage. Carolyn waited to one side while Charlie paid the fare.

'Best of luck, miss,' Fred called as he went back to his driver's seat, 'You too, sir.'

Charlie raised his hand in acknowledgement and Carolyn called her thanks.

As the taxi drew away they picked up their luggage. Charlie paused and looked at her. 'Welcome to your new life. It begins here.'

'That's nice of you, Charlie. Or should I start saying "sir" now?'

'Charlie will be fine, unless there are other service people within earshot then we'd best make it official.' He grinned at her. 'Come on, let's be official inside.'

'Yes, sir,' she said smartly, and fell into step beside him as they entered the building. The guard at the door sprang to attention.

Carolyn was taken aback when she went inside. This was not at all what she had imagined.

As she had expected everyone here was in RAF uniform, but the hustle and bustle surprised her. There appeared to be no order to the scene at all; it seemed everyone there was not where they wanted to be, if you discounted the three WAAF officers, each with an aircraftwoman in attendance, sitting at three tables. Theirs was the only part of the room where nothing appeared to be happening.

Charlie saw the curiosity in Carolyn's expression. 'It's always like this here, but I can assure you that things are getting done and those folders and sheets of paper you see everyone carrying will reach their rightful destination, and the majority of them will be important.'

'Where do I want to be?' asked Carolyn, somewhat bewildered.

'With one of those three WAAF officers at the tables. Come on, I'll introduce you to Section Officer Paula Burns, the prettiest and youngest of them.'

'Hi, Paula,' said Charlie on reaching the nearest table.

The officer looked up from the list of names she had been checking and a broad smile chased away her frown. 'Charlie, are you back with us again?'

'Here I stand,' he replied with a grin. 'But I hope someone's going to put an end to my travels soon and sit me in a cockpit again. Have you heard anything on the grapevine?'

'You know it doesn't work like that, Charlie. You'll hear soon enough when you report in . . . and you know that's not at this table unless you are re-mustering to the WAAFs?'

'Now there's a thought!' he grinned. 'But I do have a

young lady here for you. She called Carolyn Maddison. I picked her up at Middlesbrough Station and persuaded her to come with me and join up.'

Paula shook her head at him and addressed Carolyn. 'He has the liveliest imagination around here, but there is often a grain of truth in his stories. So what have you got to say for yourself?'

'It's true, he did pick me up . . . after nearly knocking me down while trying to get into the carriage.'

'And then I brought her safely here, just for you, Paula.'

'Luck was with your intuition,' she replied. 'Carolyn's name is on my list.' She put a tick on her sheet of paper. 'Carolyn, you need to go through that door over there.' She indicated a door in one corner of the room. 'You'll find more newcomers in there, awaiting further instructions.'

'Thank you,' Carolyn said, and turned back to Charlie, 'And thanks for the escort.'

'I can help a bit more.' He directed his attention to Paula, 'Put in a good word for her. Or better still, get it on the rec-ommendations sheet – I think she would do well as an intelligence officer on a Bomber Station; she has a sharp mind and a voice that returning aircrew would love to hear while they are being debriefed.' Charlie started to turn away but stopped and looked back at Carolyn. 'I'd like to keep in touch . . . hear how you get on. If you would like that?'

'I would,' she agreed.

'When you find out where you are going, let Paula know. She'll find out what is happening to me and I'll find you. Cheers for now. Thanks, Paula.' He winked at the WAAF officer and hurried away to the stairs, heading for the next floor.

'You were lucky to meet up with Charlie,' said Paula. 'He's longing to get back to flying. I hope for his sake he gets clearance this time, then he'll be happy. Did he tell you what he's doing now?'

'A little. But is there anything in what he recommended I do – Intelligence work?'

'It's a possibility. If he comes across anything or anybody who might fit into a certain slot, he'll put in a recommendation and it will always be looked at. It is the same with we three officers who greet new arrivals; we're always on the lookout for anything special about any of the new recruits and we note it down in our reports. I will give you a note now. Present it when you go into the room I indicated to you, and take it from there.'

'I had hoped to be near some action,' said Carolyn.

'Charlie mentioned debriefing bomber crews – that's the nearest you will get to actual action, but you'll hear a lot and may even see things you'll later wish you hadn't. The authorities are recruiting newcomers for Intelligence work and are beginning to expand the role to front-line squadrons. I agree with Charlie – Intelligence work could suit you. There'll be a lot to take in but you are the right type, unless you forgo a Commission and opt for training as a radio-telephone operator specialist to work in flying control rooms inside air field control towers; those positions do not carry a Commission. As well as that we are looking for young women who have already had experience of radio work in civilian life. But I would strongly recommend you, based on what I have seen and learned in our short conversation, and from Charlie's comments, to aim for a Commission in Intelligence. You could be a real asset in that job and could do well. Would you like me to recommend you for this work?'

Carolyn hesitated, weighing up the alternatives. Then, remembering Alastair's advice, she said, 'Yes, please do.'

Paula handed her a piece of paper on which she had made short notes against various printed questions. 'You've struck a quiet time but any moment now we are expecting an influx of new recruits from East Anglia.' She scribbled on another piece of paper. 'I am more than sure that Charlie wants to know how you get on; he does like to hear about any recommendations he makes. That is the address at which you can reach me. Drop me a line when you know where you are posted and I'll see he gets your address.'

'Thank you,' replied Carolyn.

At that moment young women started pouring through the main doors looking bewildered and curious and all talking at once, while several leading aircraft men were trying to direct them to the three tables.

'I think I'd better get out of the way.' Carolyn smiled. 'Thanks for your help and advice.'

'A pleasure,' replied Paula. 'Best of luck.'

Thankful for having hit a quieter time, Carolyn headed for the door in the corner.

When she entered the room there was a low buzz of conversation among the three groups that had formed in the room. A lance-corporal looked at the paper Carolyn gave her and then directed her to the middle of the three groups.

The sergeant who was in charge of that group checked her name against the list attached to a board held in her hand. 'Good, now my list is complete, we can move out. We are going on a short walk to a block of flats, which were completed but not occupied before war broke out. You will be there for four days, for full registration, documentation, inoculation, uniform and clothing issue, and a certain amount of assessment. Any questions?' Nothing was forthcoming from any of the twenty girls in the group. 'All right, I'm Section Officer Turnbull and this is Sergeant Whitfield. We will be in charge of you during your short stay here. Any queries, come to either of us. This is the start of a big change in your lives. How it pans out for you is in your own hands. Let's go.'

'I'm glad I travelled lightly,' said Carolyn to the girl beside her as they picked up their small suitcases. Some of the girls with them were straining to carry heavy luggage.

'So am I,' came the immediate response from the red-haired girl, she'd addressed whose smile was friendly. 'Lucy Gaston,' she added. 'Might as well start on the right foot.'

'Best idea,' Carolyn approved. 'Carolyn Maddison. I'm from Middlesbrough ... well Nunthorpe actually, a small village just outside.'

'I know it,' replied Lucy. 'I'm from Ripon. Must be instinct that's drawn two Yorkshire lasses together!'

Carolyn laughed. 'Too true.'

'Might as well stick together as long as we can,' Lucy suggested.

'Why not?' returned Carolyn, pleased by the other girls easy manner that did not disguise Lucy's air of self-confidence and almost hidden touch of sophistication that enabled her to wear a trench coat with collar turned up and belt tied casually.

Her eyes were alert, assessing everyone nearby but were never intruding. Her love of the outdoors was evident in her rosy cheeks; it was not hard to imagine her slim but well-proportioned figure enjoying the sun's caresses. She felt that she had already met someone she could get along with.

'Come on,' said Lucy. 'Wonder what comes next?'

Her curiosity was soon answered when they were led through a double door, guarded by an LAC suitably armed with a rifle.

'Are we going to be protected all night?' queried Lucy, raising her eyebrows at Carolyn.

A WAAF sitting at a table called out their names. When she was satisfied that all the names on her sheet of paper had been ticked off, she said to the section officer, 'All present and correct, Ma'am.'

'You'll be sleeping on the first floor, two to a room. The conditions will be basic; palliasses on the floor, each bathroom shared by four girls. The kitchens for the flats were not finished before war broke out. You will eat in the building that stands directly opposite yours. Mealtimes are displayed on the board in the hall as are other directions and times for you to follow. Your evening meal will be in,' she paused and glanced at her watch, 'one hour. Get yourselves settled in. There is a communal room downstairs. You are not allowed out this evening. You will be turned back if you attempt to leave the building.'

'By the LAC with the rifle,' someone added quietly.

But the remark was caught by the section officer. 'Yes, and by anyone else who is on duty during the night. If there is a raid you must evacuate your rooms and make your way in an orderly manner to the air-raid shelters outside. I and my staff will direct you. It is almost certain the sirens *will* sound, but at the moment the bombers seem to be concentrating on the East End. More rules and regulations and off duty times will be explained in the morning. Breakfast will be served from seven-thirty to nine o'clock. First parade will be called at nine for nine-thirty. Don't be late. I am a stickler for promptness. Now all that remains is for me to say: Welcome to the Air Force, and have a good night. Sergeant Whitfield will be on duty here until ten if you have need of any clarification or help. Beyond that there will be two WAAFs on duty throughout the night. Any questions?'

None were forthcoming.

'Right, carry on, Sergeant,' said the section officer crisply.

'Yes, Ma'am.' Sergeant Whitfield came smartly to attention, made a brisk salute and remained where she was until Section Officer Turnbull had departed. Then she said, 'Listen up everyone. You've been allocated your rooms. Get settled in. Your stay here will be brief but let's make it as pleasant as we can.'

In a state of bewilderment, Carolyn and Lucy stood on the threshold of their room a few minutes later.

With hands on hips, Carolyn suggested, 'If we aren't going to be here long, I reckon we shouldn't bother ourselves with this. Just keep it right to satisfy the powers that be.'

'That's OK by me,' agreed Lucy. 'The sooner we are out of London the better. I don't like towns. Ripon is big enough for me.'

'I agree. I was thankful Mum and Dad decided to move out of Middlesbrough to Nunthorpe six years ago.'

They set about making their room acceptable. The meal they ate then was basic but well cooked. The banter between strangers was convivial enough, with cliques already being formed, but Carolyn and Lucy did more listening than chatting.

'Keep some warm clothes handy in case those damned Germans decide to pay us a call,' Lucy advised as they prepared themselves for the night.

'I've got it organized already,' replied Carolyn, 'but this palliasse is a bit hard.' She struggled to get more comfortable. 'I don't think I'll have much sleep.'

Her prediction turned out to be correct. The sirens sent out their warning at ten minutes to midnight.

Half asleep, they tumbled off their makeshift beds to be

brought fully to their senses by shouts throughout their floor as the duty WAAFs urged them all to the air-raid shelters. Moaning and groaning, complaining and cursing, the new recruits assembled in the shelters. A roll call was taken by the WAAFs in charge, and Section Officer Turnbull showed up to report, 'Looks as if they are after the docks again.'

'Hope it remains like that,' someone called.

As if on cue, a loud explosion brought shouts and wails from some of the girls.

'Thought you said they were after the bloody docks!'

'I did, but that doesn't mean they don't offload their bombs elsewhere. Just calm down.'

'Calm down? That's a joke.'

'Get a hold on yourselves!' yelled one of the duty WAAFs. 'Give us a song!' She started singing, '"There'll be bluebirds over the white cliffs of Dover . . . "'

'If you reckon there are, then get me there!' someone shouted, while the picture the words conjured up set some of the less robust girls sobbing.

Carolyn and Lucy joined in singing the new Vera Lynn song that was sweeping the country, and held hands tightly while they did.

Dust sifted down from the roof of the shelter as the bombing gradually receded. The all-clear sounded after four hours.

As the girls started to leave the shelters an announcement was made by Section Officer Turnbull. 'You've done well tonight. Now get what sleep you can.'

'Do we get a lie-in?' someone called.

'No. You'll cope. We have a lot to get through before your posting out of London.'

'The sooner the better!'

'Then let's get some sleep,' ordered the section officer.

*

Although on succeeding nights their sleep was disturbed by more bombing, the following three days were hectic – uniforms were issued amidst laughter and ribald exchanges as some girls struck provocative poses that made Carolyn and Lucy realize they had much to learn from the more 'streetwise' among them. No one was openly critical of anyone else as they all wondered what was going to happen to them next. Medical examinations, dental checks, lectures on elementary WAAF procedures, behaviour in and out of uniform, form-filling and initial assessments, kept them fully occupied. Time flew by until a brake was put on the activity during the fourth day when they were assembled by Sergeant Whitfield. After making roll call, the Sergeant told them, 'Section Officer Turnbull will be with us in a few minutes. Until she comes, stand at ease.'

Immediately speculation ran through the group with some trying to glean information from the sergeant, who would not be drawn.

Then: 'Squad – attention!'

The girls straightened. The section officer walked briskly into the room, acknowledged the salute from the sergeant, and then told everyone to be at ease.

'On the assessments that have been compiled, and from what we know of each of you at this stage, you are being split into two groups. When your name and destination is called, those for Oxford assemble on the right, those for Harrogate on the left.'

Carolyn and Lucy glanced anxiously at each other, both knowing that they hoped they would go together, and preferably to Harrogate.

'Once the allocation has been made you will have two hours to pack, eat a meal and assemble at the two buses that will be parked outside. Then you will be off on the next stage of your WAAF career. During those two hours Sergeant Whitfield and myself will be available if you have any questions. The obvious one I will answer now. No matter which group you are in, the next part of your training will consist largely of drill, discipline and RAF and WAAF procedures, as well as physical training to get you fighting fit. At the same time assessment will continue so that the people in charge at Oxford and Harrogate can decide the best way for you to serve your country in this time of war.' The section officer turned to her sergeant. 'Let's get it done.'

Names were called out, answered, and on hearing her destination each girl moved to the correct group.

Carolyn and Lucy, standing next to each other, waited anxiously. Numbers dwindled. Carolyn ran her tongue over her dry lip.

'ACW Maddison!'

For a brief moment it seemed she hadn't heard. Then she started and replied, 'Ma'am!'

'Harrogate!'

'Ma'am!' Carolyn stepped out, managing a hopeful wink that expressed delight at her posting and hope that Lucy would be joining her there.

The next name was called, then another, and another. Time seemed to be against the two friends. Then, 'ACW Gaston!'

'Ma'am!'

'Harrogate!'

Relief swept through them both. They had to suppress the impulse to shout for joy but there was no mistaking the delight shining in their eyes.

The bus left with its full compliment of twenty girls. They were to take the train to Harrogate, which would be convenient for home visits. How lucky was that? Would the same luck bless the rest of their service life? They didn't dwell on the answers. For now, Carolyn and Lucy were happy together in their new-found friendship, looking forward to experiences that would shape their lives in ways they could never have envisaged when a weary Prime Minister made his declaration of war.

6

On reaching King's Cross, enquiries about their departure time elicited the information that there would be a delay of two hours.

Though irked by the prospect, Carolyn was determined to make the most of it. 'Come with me. We'll dump these bags,' she said decisively

Lucy did not question this. In their short time together she had realized Carolyn was a born leader, who would always have a purpose for everything she did. It would be easy to hang on her apron-strings but that was not Lucy's way; she had her own path to forge but was happy to do so in parallel with Carolyn, so that they had a chance of serving together.

They quickly found the taxi rank and for one moment felt deflated by the length of the queue. But then Carolyn strode to the head of it where a smartly dressed middle-aged civilian was awaiting the first in a line of taxis coming on to the concourse.

'Excuse me, sir,' she said brightly. 'May we share your taxi? We have an important appointment at the Air Ministry. If we have to wait in the queue we'll be late and end up in trouble.'

Though a little surprised by the request, the man gave them a fatherly smile. 'Certainly.' He glanced along the queue. 'I don't know what the rest of the travellers will think, but who cares? I reckon they won't begrudge me helping two attractive WAAFS serve their country. In you get.' He opened the door for them. Carolyn and Lucy scrambled in. 'Air Ministry, first stop!' the gentleman ordered.

Soon they were scrambling out again, making their thanks to the gentleman, who refused their offer to pay.

They watched the taxi draw away.

'That was a bit cheeky, jumping the queue,' Lucy observed.

'Needs must.'

'What are we back here for?'

'You'll see.'

Carolyn led the way with an air of assurance, to impress the guard who asked for identification.

'ACWS Maddison and Gaston,' replied Carolyn briskly as they produced their identity cards. 'Here to see Section Officer Burns.'

'Report at reception just through that door.'

'We're in luck,' said Carolyn quietly, spotting a familiar section officer. She led the way quickly to the table behind which the woman was sitting. They came to a sharp halt in front of her and made a smart salute. The section officer looked up and recognized Carolyn. She acknowledged the salute then said, 'Back again? That's rather a quick return. I don't think we have any detail about you.'

'You won't have, Ma'am. We are on our way to Harrogate. Two hours to wait for our train so I thought I would pop in and see if you had any news of Flying Officer Wade?'

'I have, but I can tell you no more than that he has been posted.' Seeing Carolyn was about to press her, Paula Burns raised her hand. 'Don't ask for any more. You know I can't divulge his whereabouts. What I can tell you is that when he reported here with you, he was called to the CO's office to be told he had been promoted to flight lieutenant and posted back to a squadron.'

Carolyn's eyes widened as she gasped, 'Promoted! Good for Charlie.'

The section officer gave a weak smile. 'I don't know if you'd class it as good. He'll likely be making one of those vapour trails we see every day over London. The Germans are hell-bent on destroying us.'

'Charlie won't let them do that,' said Carolyn confidently. 'I must write to him. Please give me his address.'

'No. You know I can't.' The officer's stern tone told Carolyn not to push it. 'Leave your address, or forward it to me here when you get settled, and I will pass it on.'

Carolyn's lips tightened with regret but she knew Section Officer Burns would not be swayed. 'Thank you, Ma'am. Can you at least tell me if he is OK?'

The section officer smiled. 'Charlie seems to have struck a chord with you?'

'He was very kind to me when I was new here.'

'Then I can tell you he has got what he hoped for, and that it has brightened his life.'

'Thanks, Ma'am.'

'Let me have your address when you know it. It will be one of Harrogate's hotels, I expect.'

Carolyn made her thanks again. They both saluted, turned and left the building.

'Back to King's Cross,' said Carolyn. 'Sorry to have dragged you here, Lucy.'

'No need for any apology. It was better than hanging around the station.' She eyed her friend. 'You're flying high already – hob-nobbing with flight lieutenants. Mind if I tag along for the ride?'

'I wouldn't have it any other way.'

When the train pulled out of King's Cross they were relieved to be leaving a devastated but defiant London.

Six hours later they were pleased the slow journey was at an end. They walked into a rather imposing hotel that had been commandeered by the RAF for use by WAAFs starting out on their new-found employment.

With rooms allocated the two girls found themselves sharing again, which helped them settle quickly.

After a meal and before leaving the Mess, the group was addressed by a section officer. 'My name is Section Officer Johnson. I will also be in charge of another group of twenty. Both groups will follow the same patterns of training, but at different times. You will continue with the fitness courses, drills, et cetera that you started in London but these will be tougher. Alongside them there will be lectures about the various aspects of life in the WAAF, with introductions to onward postings so that we can make a pretty good estimation of the path you should follow. With that in mind, a list of trades we are currently recruiting for has been put on the two noticeboards. Have a look at it before we assemble tomorrow at two p.m. and come with some ideas for what you might like to do. If you have need of any further information about the particular trade you fancy, see either my sergeant or my corporal: Sergeant Munroe and Corporal Tenby.'

The noticeboards were quickly perused.

'Well, what do you fancy?' asked Lucy.

'I want to be near the action, and after what Charlie and Section Officer Burns said, I'm going for Intelligence. I'll

46

aim for a Commission and a posting to an operational unit; to me that means Fighter or Bomber Command, preferably Bomber because Charlie recommended it.'

'Thought that would be it,' said Lucy, with a smile.

'What about you?' asked Carolyn.

'We said we wanted to stick together so I'll give it a shot too.'

During the mid-day break, Carolyn penned a quick note sending her address to Section Officer Burns at the Air Ministry.

A week later she received a reply from Charlie and immediately wrote back.

Dear Charlie,

Nice to be in contact. I am settled in at Harrogate and am pleased to be with my friend Lucy. We have both applied for the course which, hopefully, will lead us to the job you told me about. Your recommendation must have percolated through the system. Thanks for that.

I'm interested to hear that you are at Acklington (not too far from here) and that there is a possibility we might be able to meet. I will look forward to seeing you again.

My best wishes for your success and my prayers for your safety.

Carolyn Maddison

'Carolyn, snap out of it, maybe there'll be a letter tomorrow. Don't slide down in the dumps and affect your place in the order of merit. You've been doing so well.'

'Four weeks and no word from him,' muttered Carolyn grumpily.

'You're expecting too much, too soon,' Lucy admonished. 'Charlie has other things to think about. Don't forget, promotion always brings added responsibilities that generate more work.'

'I suppose so,' Carolyn admitted reluctantly.

'Then you and I should get on with our lives. We have an objective in view: don't let's miss out on it. Charlie wouldn't want that.'

'I know but ... '

A week later a letter arrived for Carolyn. Interviews to expand individual assessments were taking place. She had just been interviewed when she collected her letter. She did not recognize the writing on the envelope. A sudden premonition came over her. Staring at her own name written in an unfamiliar hand, she hesitated. She was glad that Lucy was still waiting to be interviewed, leaving Carolyn on her own. She hurried to her billet, anxiety mounting with every step. Once in their room she threw her hat on the bed and, with shaking hands, tore the envelope open. She withdrew a sheet of paper.

Dear ACW Maddison,

It is with the greatest regret that I have to inform you that Flight Lieutenant Charles Wade, DFC, did not return from a North Sea patrol and is listed as Missing Presumed Dead. There appears to be no hope for his survival because he was seen to go down by two other members of his patrol, which was giving protection to a convoy heading for the Tyne.

He died a brave man.

My condolences,

S/O Paula Burns

The world became still. Carolyn sank down slowly to sit on the edge of her bed, still staring at the letter. 'Oh, no!' Her words were hardly audible but the feeling behind them rocked her. Then they were drowned in a stream of tears. 'This damned, bloody war!' she said aloud. 'Gran bombed out. Charlie killed. Who will be next?'

Lying on her back, staring up at the ceiling, Carolyn brushed away the tears. She didn't feel like meeting anyone but knew she must. She had to get a grip on her life. She reminded herself that she had barely known Charlie, but that didn't ease the pain of what might have been. He had been kind to her; she had looked forward to meeting him again, but ... She pushed herself up from the bed. I must not let thoughts of what might have been get to me, she told herself. She went to the bathroom, dabbed cold water on her face, dried it and looked closely at herself in the mirror. She applied a little make-up, pinched her cheeks, combed her hair, pulled her uniform straight and smoothed it with her hands.

She heard the outer door open and Lucy call cheerfully, 'Are you there Carolyn?'

'In here!' she replied. 'Coming.' With that she went out to be met by her friend's broad smile. 'My interview went well. Did yours? I thought you'd wait for me?'

'Yes, my interview was good too. I didn't wait because I had this to read.' She held out the letter to Lucy who took it with a look of concern.

She read the letter, her face paling. 'Oh, Carolyn, I'm so sorry.' Lucy held out her arms to her friend.

Carolyn did not move but looked pleadingly at her. 'No, don't hug me. It will only start me weeping again and I don't want to do that.'

'There's nothing wrong with grieving.'

'I know, but please understand.'

'I do, but always remember – I am here for you.'

'You're a good friend, Lucy.'

'And I hope I always will be. Now, we'd better get off to our lecture.'

'I think I'll skip it.'

'You can't do that. You mustn't. As I see it, this talk could be vital to your next allocation. I believe Charlie wouldn't want you to miss out. I never met him, but from the way you have spoken about him, I think he would be disappointed and feel let down if you diverge from the course he judged to be right for you.'

Carolyn nodded. 'You're right, Lucy. Thanks,' she whispered.

'One other thing. Remember, you have your whole life before you. Charlie would not want you to waste it, mourning for him. He died doing what he wanted to do. If you loved him, you should respect him and ...'

'I've had time to think and I don't know if I really did love him. Maybe it was just gratitude for his kindness to me, for making me feel singled out. Or maybe something would have grown from it. I'll never know now.'

'We'll focus on the future together. There's a job for us to do.'

The first decisive step along that road came at the end of the training course in Harrogate. Carolyn and Lucy passed with joint top marks, which put an end to any doubts they had had about their ability to go further, and their egos received another boost when they were called to see the squadron officer.

She eyed them critically as they marched in, came to attention and saluted smartly.

'Stand at ease,' she ordered, and laid her hands on two folders set before her. 'I have your reports here. I have to say, they are exemplary. Your marks in all sections do you credit and show you have a desire to do well. I hope that never leaves you.

'I see that your aim is to serve in Intelligence on an operational station. That is a very demanding and responsible job, needing exceptional care and keen focus. You have to be sure the information you assemble for the use of aircrews setting out on a raid is as accurate and as up-to-date as possible. You must also be able to elicit information from returning crews, who will be weary after long flights that have most likely been fraught with danger. They will have seen comrades shot out of the sky, maybe have limped home, themselves wondering if they were going to make it. I needn't go on except to add that, you have to understand what these men's moods might be and be able to cope with any adverse reactions you encounter.' She paused. Afterwards, both Carolyn and Lucy said they thought that pause was when she made her final decision. 'One more question. Do you still want to serve in Intelligence at a Bomber Station?'

Without hesitation they replied together, 'Yes, Ma'am.'

'Good.' She leaned back in her chair. 'It will mean more training and then eventually a posting to an operational unit.' She saw their eyes brighten and knew she had made the right decision about them. 'Very well, I now have to tell you that I am putting you forward for consideration for Commissions. I hope you will accept because I am of the opinion that you will make good officers of the type we require.'

'Thank you, Ma'am,' they chorused, without hiding the surprise and delight in their voices.

'I haven't the authority to make that final; you will have to go before a selection board. The responsibilities being taken on by WAAFs are widening.' She gave a little smile as she added, 'It is believed that pleasant female voices will be welcomed by aircrew returning to base. So, would you like me to recommend you for interview by a selection board?'

'Yes, Ma'am,' both of them said together, with expressions of eager anticipation.

'Good. I'm sure you will impress the interviewers. Any questions?'

'Yes, Ma'am,' said Carolyn. 'When and where is the interview likely to take place?'

'I'm afraid I can't help you there. I am not privy to the selection board's schedule. But just be patient.'

'Thank you, Ma'am,' they said again.

Once outside they laughed and hugged. Then, as they headed for their room, strode out with an extra military swing to their step.

Five days later two letters arrived for Carolyn.

Dear Carolyn,

It was with the greatest delight that we received your news. Congratulations on being considered for a Commission. You must have worked hard and impressed your superiors. Having an objective in mind and striving to reach it always pays off.

Keep up the good work but make sure you also enjoy life.

Do give Lucy our congratulations – we are pleased for her too.

Love,
Mum and Dad

*

The second letter also brought her much pleasure.

Dear Sis,

This is tremendous news. I am so pleased for you. CONGRATULATIONS! You are sure to be granted a Commission. That will bring changes to your life. Intelligence! Now that is a responsibility, but I know you will cope if you are accepted. But you know that too so I'll not go on about it.

I'm sorry we have not been in touch more often but you know letter writing never fitted easily with me. I'll try and do better.

A move for me too is likely but I hope it doesn't take me away from my beloved Spitfire. When I climb into the cockpit I feel we are one. Maybe one day I'll find the opportunity to put down wherever you are.

Congratulations to you again, and of course to Lucy. Glad you have such a good friend. Any boyfriend in the offing? You must have plenty around you to pick from.

Love,

Alastair

Lucy and Carolyn were determined not to let their families down and both committed themselves to seizing this opportunity that had been given to them.

Their chance came in March 1941 when they received instructions to report for interview by the selection board that would be sitting at the WAAF Officers' School at Bulstrode Park, a large country house near Gerrards Cross. The interview would be on 10 April. They should come prepared to stay.

They met on the platform at York station, thankful for the

issue of greatcoats as the cold wind whistled through the station.

The train ride was no warmer and they were grateful when they were met at the station by a bus specially hired to transfer the WAAF arrivals to the country house. Once inside they found they had stepped into a little luxury after the Nissen huts of previous postings. Proper beds and comfortable mattresses helped to temper their concerns about facing a formidable array of interviewers.

There were another ten candidates for interview and it was inevitable that anxiety crept in as they waited to be called before the board the next day. After the last WAAF had faced a barrage of questions, the interviewees were assembled together. Four were told to return to their units, the remaining six plus Carolyn and Lucy were informed they had been granted Commissions 'as of now'.

The officer who announced this went on to tell them, 'You will follow the basic WAAF Officers' course plus other training considered applicable to you from the reports we have received. Take the rest of the day off to find the accommodation that has been allotted to you for the duration of your stay here. Generally it lasts for two months, after which you should be able to take your place in the WAAF order of things with confidence and dignity. You should also have sufficient knowledge of the trade you have chosen to follow.

'You all have a great opportunity here. See that you take it and make the most of it. For this new intake there will be a special celebratory meal this evening – nothing out of the ordinary, rationing precludes that, but the cook generally keeps something up her sleeve for these occasions. Finally, you will be issued with new identity cards, and a note authorizing the local ladies' outfitter to issue you with your new uniform. See that you complete all of that. The day after tomorrow your training begins in earnest.'

When they got to their room, Carolyn and Lucy did a little jig. 'We're on the way,' they sang in unison, and collapsed on their beds in laughter.

Together with the other newly created officers they enjoyed, with much hilarity, their visit to the outfitter, getting settled in and growing accustomed to their new life.

That joy was marred later that week by reports of German successes in Eastern Europe, but Carolyn countered that with news of Alastair who had survived what had begun to be termed the Battle Of Britain, in spite of having to bail out twice, had been awarded the DFC and been promoted to squadron leader of a unit training fighter pilots, where his combat knowledge would be invaluable.

In the next two months Lucy and Carolyn crammed in so much information that at times their heads were reeling. They knew they were under close scrutiny, and like everyone else avoided complaining or putting forward negative questions. The result was a series of good reports, and for Carolyn and Lucy this helped them on to the first rung of the ladder that would take them closer to their ambition of serving on an operational station.

Learning that Lucy's parents, regrettably, would not be at home during her next leave, Carolyn invited her friend to spend the time at Nunthorpe.

Carolyn's mum and gran immediately took to Lucy, who was not shy in coming forward to help in the house, and Guy tapped her knowledge about growing vegetables, acquired from her father. They spent half a day looking round the shops in Middlesbrough and combined this with a visit to the cinema to see Joan Fontaine in *Suspicion*. The highlight of their stay was when Alastair surprised them all with an overnight visit.

'I'm looking into a possible use of Thornaby airfield for training some of our fighter pilots. I can't say more than that so don't ask. I knew this visit was in the offing, and when Mum said in her last letter that Carolyn was coming on leave and bringing Lucy, I thought I would make use of the chance to do my job at Thornaby – and also see if I approved of Carolyn's friend.'

'Don't you dare say you don't!' Carolyn reprimanded him as she threw a cushion at him and scored a bull's-eye.

'Wow!' he praised amidst the laughter. 'Seems to me you should be in Bomber Command.'

'That's where we aim to be,' said Lucy with marked confidence.

'Then I envy its aircrews,' replied Alastair.

'Here we go,' grinned Lucy as they settled down in their first-class compartment as the train pulled out of Middlesbrough. 'That was a wonderful leave. I enjoyed meeting your family ... especially your brother. Thanks so much for asking me. Now we're on our way again. What we want is almost within our grasp: the final part of the training that should take us into Intelligence work. Hold on tight for the ride over the final hurdle!'

'There's one thing I've vowed,' Carolyn said then. 'I'm not going to get close to anyone until this war is over.'

'What?' Lucy looked shocked. 'You can't be serious?'

'I am.'

Her friend gave a little shake of the head. 'I don't believe it. You, an attractive girl, are probably going to end up on an airfield heavily outnumbered by men.'

'I know, but there will always be the thought of Charlie and I don't want to end up losing ... '

'Don't say it. Don't even think it. If you do, your

judgment could be undermined and you can't afford that to happen.'

'All right.' Carolyn gave a little smile. 'You're sounding like one of our instructors.' The smile vanished then and she said firmly, 'Lucy Gaston – I am NOT going to get emotionally involved with anyone.'

7

At the end of the course they were given a week's leave and issued with passes and travel warrants, with orders to report for further training at an establishment that specialized in newcomers. Here they would be recording and disseminating information to imaginary recipients; mastering the techniques and abbreviations in use, and doing it speedily. Such work required keen concentration. In war conditions, accuracy and speed were essential; anything else could have disastrous consequences. At the end of a tense four weeks, Carolyn and Lucy felt they had acquired a measure of the deep concentration required to be on top of their game as Intelligence officers. They were pleased to be granted another week's leave, with orders to report to 5 Group Headquarters at St Vincent's, Grantham at the end of that time.

'This is a bit imposing,' commented Lucy as the RAF vehicle slowed to a halt at the main entrance, which was dominated by a round tower with a spire on top.

The corporal driving them was quickly out of the car, opening the door for them. 'I'll be waiting here, Ma'am, Ma'am.'

Lucy was swift to temper her initial surprise and say confidently, 'Thank you, Corporal.' As they stepped towards the entrance, she murmured, 'He must have to take us some-where else. He knows more than we do.'

When they opened the front door they found themselves in a spacious hall in which the only furniture visible was a large desk and three chairs. A flight officer sitting behind the desk looked up at them.

'Ah, Section Officers Maddison and Gaston, no doubt?' She smiled and held out her hand. 'Right on time, that's splendid. I'm Flight Officer Newbauld. You are here to see Group Officer Pearson.' She saw their surprised expressions. 'You did not know?'

'No, Ma'am.'

'Someone's slipped up. But never mind, you're here.' Then as an afterthought she added, 'But you have come treating this as a posting, I hope?'

'Yes, Ma'am. Our belongings are in the car which is wait-ing outside.'

'Good, good. Right, I'll take you to see Group Officer Pearson.' She headed for the grand staircase.

At the top they followed her along the passage to the right. She knocked on the second door and, after a call to enter, opened the door and announced, 'Section Officers Maddison and Garston, Ma'am,' then stepped to one side.

Carolyn and Lucy marched smartly into the room to halt in front of the Group Officer, who was sitting at an enor-mous desk positioned so that light from the tall sash window fell across it from the left. They each made a sharp salute looking straight ahead.

'Stand at ease,' said Group Officer Pearson, and then thanked the flight officer who saluted and left them, after informing her superior that the new arrivals had been given no information about why they had been called to meet her.

'Sit down.' The Group Officer indicated the two chairs facing hers.

It gave them a chance to observe the woman whom they judged to be about forty years old, with dark hair trimmed neatly above her shirt collar. Her eyes were an intense blue, giving the impression that they were taking in a lot about whatever or whoever they were observing. Nevertheless the two section officers both felt that behind the severity lay a sympathetic person.

'I'm sorry you were not given any more information as to why you have been brought here, but we will soon get that sorted out.'

Carolyn and Lucy detected that they were sitting before a woman who, though naturally kindly, would not suffer fools gladly and had the determination to get things done.

'With the rapid development within the WAAF, various trades are expanding in order to keep the liaison between the RAF and its female counterpart second to none. That of course means cooperation on both sides. I want to see that in this top echelon of Bomber Command, any suspicion that we WAAFs cannot tackle the jobs formerly occupied by men, with the exception of aircrew, is unfounded. Because of inbuilt prejudices we will never fully achieve that goal but we can get near to it. If we take over more support jobs, men will be released to do what we can't. I know, for instance, there are men serving as Intelligence officers who, having completed a tour of duty in Bomber Command, want to get back to flying, but it is inevitable that some will have to continue in Flying Control duties because there are no Commissions for WAAFs in that department. I see from your records that was your aim, and I take it you chose what you thought would possibly take you to a Bomber base, but Intelligence will also do that and I

60

believe you have the makings of exceptional Intelligence officers.'

'Yes, Ma'am, that is our aim,' confirmed Lucy.

The group officer glanced at the two folders she had in front of her, studied some items in them for a moment then looked up and ran her sharp eyes over the two younger officers. Carolyn felt a little uneasy but resisted the desire to shuffle on her chair.

'I see you have been together ever since you volunteered.'

'Yes, Ma'am.'

'And your results on all your courses are almost identical, as are the assessments by your tutors and examiners. That leads me to wonder: is this coincidence or are you really as close as these reports indicate? I am casting no doubts on your abilities but the main question in my mind is how each of you would cope if left to work on your own? Could you handle responsibility if the other one wasn't there to back you up?'

'I'm sure we could, Ma'am,' said Carolyn firmly.

'That is easy to say because you have never been tested to that degree. Now, before you say any more, let me put you in the picture. Reorganisation has made me review the best way to use the increased number of WAAFs who are coming through in all trades. I have a little time at my disposal to assess the best use of WAAFs in Intelligence sections and want to test the waters. I am therefore proposing to split you up for a month.

'Section Officer Maddison, I am going to post you to a Heavy Conversion Unit just down the road from here at Swinderby. It will match as nearly as possible the work of an Intelligence officer on a squadron. You, Section Officer Gaston, can take two weeks' leave and report to Swinderby at the end of that time to take over from Section Officer

61

Maddison, who will then go on leave. At the end of that two weeks you will both report back here to me.'

'Yes, Ma'am,' they replied.

'This is an unusual way for me to make a final assessment, but I'm willing to take the risk of its being frowned on by higher authority in order to have two exceptional Intelligence officers filling posts that will be vital to this group. Have you any questions?'

'Ma'am,' said Carolyn, 'you make this all sound very intriguing. You seem to indicate this is a special group. May I ask in what way?'

'Much of our work is classified but I will tell you 5 Group is being developed as a special group in Bomber Command. There will be times when it operates outside the main bomber force to attack special targets. Every squadron within the group needs a strong and capable intelligence section, but I want to develop Waddington's as the hub for the receipt of information relating to these special missions and its distribution to the group's squadrons. I don't need to go on. All will be made clearer if I decide you are capable individually of fitting my requirements. I have every faith that you will, but go out and prove it to me.' As she finished speaking she rang a bell. In a moment the door opened and Flight Officer Newbauld came in.

'I've made a slight change of plan for these two section officers,' said the group officer, and went on to explain what that was. 'Please see they have the necessary travel warrants.'

Carolyn and Lucy were surprised by the speed with which everything was made ready for them, and realized that Group Officer Pearson packed considerable clout.

The corporal made his first drop at Swinderby. While he took Carolyn's luggage inside the Officers' Mess, the two friends made their goodbyes.

'I'm going to miss you, Lucy,' said Carolyn. 'You're a good friend.'

They embraced.

'So are you, Carolyn. I'm sure there is more behind this separation than we've been told. Why the particular interest in us?'

'Let's carry on doing our best then perhaps all will be revealed in due course. If 5 Group is an elite group, then who knows what we shall have to do or see?'

'Some handsome aircrew, hopefully,' commented Lucy, smiling.

'I've told you, not for me.'

Their conversation stopped when the corporal reappeared. 'Right, Ma'am, we have a train to catch. We should just make it,' he told his passenger.

'See you in two weeks,' called Lucy as the car drew away. She settled herself comfortably on the back seat and smiled. Two years ago who would have believed that Lucy Gaston would ever be a WAAF officer, driven in a staff car to a railway station to go on leave? War had given her a new life, new experiences she had never thought she'd have. She was determined to make the most of it all. She wondered what her parents' reaction would be when she walked in unheralded.

'We've made it, Ma'am,' called the corporal as he drew the Humber Hawk to a halt in the station forecourt. He was quickly out of his seat and opening the door for her.

'Thank you, Corporal,' said Lucy, and hurried into the station. She showed her travel warrant to the inspector on duty at the barrier. Seeing it was for York then onward to Ripon he said, 'This platform, Ma'am. Change at York.'

'Have I time to get a paper?'

He glanced at the station clock. 'Just, Ma'am. Train is running five minutes late.'

'Thank you.' She wove her way quickly through the passengers awaiting the train and was pleased to obtain the last newspaper for sale in the booth.

As the engine slowed she noted the first-class carriages were to the front and hurried along the platform, reaching them almost before the train stopped, with loud clanking and hissing noises. She found a compartment with three vacant seats. Two Army officers cast a casual glance at her as she settled in her seat.

Lucy soon became engrossed in her newspaper. She regretted that the German war-machine was making good progress in its advance to Moscow but drew hope from a report that Soviet opposition was stiffening and the coming winter, if severe, could play a decisive part in the outcome. Closer to home, she read that there was a strong possibility that before 1941 was out Parliament would have introduced a National Service Act, calling up unmarried women between the ages of twenty and thirty for war work. Lucy was thankful that she had volunteered when she did because she'd been given a choice as to which service to join, whereas under the proposed Act there might be no choice and recruits could be directed to the areas of greatest need, military or war work.

The paper kept her engrossed until York where she had to change to catch her connection to Ripon. She chose not to open her paper again; instead she took in the passing panorama of a countryside with which she was familiar. It was good to see it apparently untouched by war; it stretched peacefully ahead and seemed to tell her that some day the whole world would be just as tranquil, in spite of what she had been reading in the paper.

As she walked to the exit, she cast her eyes over the other passengers who had left the train but there was no one she knew. Shouldering her gas mask and gripping the handles of her hold-all, she covered the half mile to her home at a steady pace, enjoying the fresh tangy air of late summer and savouring the thought of the surprise she would give her mother and father when she arrived.

Their house stood in a row of six detached properties that had been built in 1936; a speculative venture undertaken by a builder who had purchased a field that was good for little else. He'd had no trouble in selling them all and had gained a nice profit from his customers, who were delighted with their new homes.

The back door was unlocked as Lucy expected, in accordance with her father's 'we've nowt worth pinching' philosophy, though he was always meticulous in calling to his wife, 'Just locking up for the night, luv.'

Lucy walked straight in.

Her mother, thinking with a little irritation, Who's arriving right on tea-time? swung round from the gas stove where she was frying some potatoes. Her testiness disappeared in a flash to be replaced by a broad smile of pleasure. 'Lucy! What are you doing here?' she gasped as she came to her daughter, arms held wide.

'Mum!' Lucy fell into her mother's embrace.

'Oh, it's so good to see you,' said her mother, eyes dampening with joy. 'How long is it for?'

Lucy laughed. 'The inevitable first question. Two weeks, Mum.'

Mrs Gaston's eyes widened with delight. 'That long?' As her daughter nodded, Sylvia Gaston opened the kitchen door and shouted, 'Kevin!' Then she added, looking at Lucy, 'He's repairing a tap. Kevin!'

'Can I have five minutes?' he shouted.

His wife answered that with, 'Surprise for you!' She winked at her daughter. 'That'll bring him.'

65

Almost on cue came the sound of footsteps crossing the landing to the stairs.

'What is it?' Kevin Gaston called before he reached the kitchen. Any further questioning was cut short when he saw his daughter.

'Dad!' Laughing, Lucy fell into his embrace.

'My goodness, this is a surprise. Here, let me look at you.' He released his hold and stepped back to view his daughter critically. 'You look well. Service life must suit you. And you have the figure for that uniform. Heads will turn. People will see you're a WAAF officer and think, She's doing well.'

'No more than anybody else,' put in Lucy.

'Better than many,' replied her proud father.

'These potatoes will soon be ready,' interposed Sylvia, looking back at her pan. 'Off you go, Lucy. Your room is always waiting for you. Don't be long. The baked beans are in the oven. I'd have tried for a fatted calf if I'd known you were coming.'

'I know you can work wonders with our rations but I think a fatted calf would have been a problem even for you,' quipped Kevin.

'It will be lovely, whatever it is,' called Lucy as she went up the stairs.

By the time they were seated Sylvia had waved her magic wand, bringing to their plates, as well as the beans and potatoes, an egg and a slice of bacon.

'How did you manage this, Mum?' asked Lucy as she savoured her mother's cooking.

'We are living outside Ripon, remember, not too far from a farm. Now ask no more questions about what appears on this table while you are here.'

*

When they had settled down for the evening Kevin asked the question most fathers ask, especially in wartime: 'What are you doing now?'

'Dad, don't ask more than I can tell you. I'm still in training to serve as an Intelligence officer. When I've finished I'll probably end up somewhere in Lincolnshire. That is all I can say.'

Kevin nodded and said, 'Nice county, Lincolnshire. Good deal of low-lying country but a lot of it is not as flat as people think.'

'I didn't know you were familiar with it?'

'In my young days, before I met your mum, I did a lot of cycling. I got to know it then.' He continued to impart his knowledge of Lincolnshire until Sylvia seized on a little lull.

'What do you want to do, these two weeks?' she asked her daughter.

'Relax and enjoy being at home.'

'Well, that's easy enough,' commented her mother. 'You'll want to visit friends?'

'I could do but I expect most of them will have enrolled in one service or another.'

'Damian is still at home.'

Her speed in passing on that information and the sharpness of her tone told Lucy that her mother still had hopes that a childhood friendship would develop into much more.

Sylvia went on, 'Mr Brimstone got his son into a reserved occupation. Don't know how but he did, and Damian jumped at the chance.'

'Typical,' muttered Lucy to herself but her mother had sharp hearing.

'Don't deride that young man, Lucy. We don't know all the circumstances. Anyway, better to take the chance of staying alive than face the possibility of a horrible death.' Her mother went on to say, 'You and he always got on well together when you were growing up.'

'Mum, I've grown up while Damian's seen nothing of life beyond his self-imposed boundaries. I have. The war has changed me. Oh, I'm still your daughter and always will be, my love for you and Dad won't change, but please realize this war has allowed me to look to other horizons. There is no altering that fact. Trying to step back in time is impossible. Please give me your love and support and I will always be a credit to you and this will always be home to me.'

Lucy was pleased that these exchanges had taken place and that her mother had accepted her view, especially when a family visit to the Brimstones' showed Damian was glad of his father's role in procuring for him a place in a reserved occupation. He clearly had no desire to take part in any form of military service, and Lucy realised she could never respect a man with this attitude.

She was thankful to find a different attitude prevailing among other families whom they met, either formally or casually. 'Good to see you doing so well, Lucy.' 'Glad we have people like you, willing to do their bit for their country.' 'Wish I was young enough to join you.' The compliments were frequent and Lucy was secretly pleased that they directed her mother's thoughts away from a possible match with Damian Brimstone.

The time sped by quickly. Although she enjoyed every minute of it, by the end of two weeks Lucy realized she was ready to return to Swinderby.

8

When Carolyn watched the car taking Lucy on leave disappear, a feeling of being all alone struck her. She walked slowly to the Mess. The sergeant steward on duty greeted her pleasantly. 'Good day, Ma'am. Welcome to RAF Swinderby. I understand you are here for two weeks, maybe more, so I have put you in room two, hut two. Second on the left as you go out of this block. My apologies for what seems to be an airfield in chaos but changes are being made here as quickly as possible. They are not as yet complete, with the result that some sections are overcrowded, but it will all come right one day. Would you like a cup of tea, Ma'am?'

'I would kill for one, Sergeant. It has been an unusual day.'

'I'm sure it will soon settle down for you, Ma'am. The tea will be brought to your room in a few minutes.'

'Thank you, Sergeant.'

Soon a knock on the door heralded the arrival of a young WAAF carrying a tray with milk, sugar, cups, a small teapot and a plate with two biscuits on it.

'Good day, Ma'am,' said the WAAF as she placed the tray on a table beside the window. The room was spartan but adequate; the iron bedstead had recently been made up with issue blankets and sheets, but it looked comfortable enough. Apart from one straightbacked chair, there was an armchair, a wardrobe and chest of drawers. 'I'm ACW Beryl Tose and will be your batwoman for your stay,' said the girl. 'If there is anything you want, just let me know.'

'Thank you, Beryl. There is one thing: where do I find the adjutant? There is so much going on here that I'll only be able to find my way around by the time I'm leaving.'

Beryl smiled. 'We are in rather a state at the moment. When you go out turn left, go to the fourth building, and you'll find the admin sections in there.'

Carolyn enjoyed her tea and afterwards went to make herself known to the adjutant. She was welcomed by a middle-aged man with the rank of flight lieutenant, who filled his uniform rather well. He had a WAAF flight officer with him, but when Carolyn apologized for interrupting them he waved her in. 'You'll be Section Officer Carolyn Maddison,' he said, rising from his seat. 'You've arrived at just the right time – you're killing two birds with one stone. This is Flight Officer Chadwell and I am Flight Lieutenant Hargreaves.'

With introductions over, the relaxed atmosphere was pleasant though Carolyn felt herself to be under scrutiny, especially by Flight Officer Chadwell, as she said, 'I have received instructions from Group Officer Pearson about the detailed assessment she wants at the end of your stay so I'll see you have plenty of time with our Intelligence officer. You'll need to learn how things are going in that branch of the service. She also said she would like you to spend some time in Flying Control.' The flight officer saw the look of curiosity cross Carolyn's face. 'That will be because there is more and more interaction between Intelligence and Flying Control – so much so that some station commanders are turning over a room for use by the Intelligence section in the Control Tower. It enables the Intelligence people to get some idea in their minds about the way an operation has gone before returning crews are debriefed face to face. A little foreknowledge is helpful in deciding which path to take while conducting questioning. Though we are not an operational station at the moment, there are people here who have served on them. But I'll introduce you around this evening.'

'Thank you, Ma'am.' Carolyn rose to go.

The adjutant twitched his lips and shot a glance at the flight officer. 'Carolyn, a word. Keep the right side of this witch here and you'll be all right. Cross her and you'll be whisked away on her broomstick.'

'Don't take any notice of him, Carolyn. I'm no harridan. I run a tight ship so my WAAFs know where they stand, and they understand I'm fair in my judgments. Enough of that. Your stay here is short. Make the most of it and enjoy it.'

That evening Carolyn was introduced to many members of the Officers' Mess, in particular those relevant to her purpose for being here. Among them was a squadron leader whose handsome features were lined by the strain of an active war to which the DFC ribbon on his tunic bore witness. As they left the dining table, which Carolyn had shared with five RAF officers, the squadron leader drew her aside.

'As you probably heard, I'm Jim Ashton.' He held out his hand in a formal greeting. She felt warmth in his strong thin fingers and noticed he wore a thin gold band on a finger of his other hand. In a strange way, after what she had said to Lucy, Carolyn felt relieved to see it.

'Carolyn Maddison, sir,' she introduced herself with a smile.

He returned it with a little shake of his head. 'No such

formalities, please, when we're off duty. I understand you are only here for a short while at the behest of the group officer. Some notes have come through to me as head of Flying Control. She wants me to introduce you to what happens in there. Let me get you a drink. We'll find a couple of chairs in a quieter part of the room and have a little chat.'

When they were seated, he went on, 'You'll no doubt be seeing our Intelligence officer in the morning. She isn't in the Mess this evening. I suggest after you've seen her you come to the Control Tower in the afternoon and we'll take it from there. Now we'll forget all that and relax.'

Carolyn knew that she was under close scrutiny from all the departments she had to deal with. Realizing their detailed reports and assessments would be on the group officer's desk soon after her stay at Swinderby was over, she determined all those reports would be good.

Her contacts with Squadron Leader Ashton were among the pleasantest of her encounters and it was with a feeling of regret that she visited the tower on her last day.

'Ah, Carolyn,' he greeted her. 'First take-off will be at two-thirty and we will have a fairly busy time until six this evening. Two new crews will be doing circuits and bumps, both on Stirlings for the first time. Two more crews will be doing their last cross-country flights, taking them north to Scotland via the east coast and returning by the west coast as far as Anglesey before turning for base.'

'Those two will be pleased to get back and be able to move on, I don't doubt. From what I have heard, the Stirling has a bad reputation. Is it really as temperamental as it is made out to be?' she asked.

'Well ... I didn't really like it; it was too underpowered for my liking. It always seemed too big and cumbersome, but there were those who thought differently.'

She knew Jim Ashton had completed a tour of thirty missions, after which, because of injuries, the details of which she did not know, he had opted to move into Flying Control until such time as he was cleared to return to operational duties.

'There are rumours going round that there is a new bomber in production,' Squadron Leader Ashton went on, 'but apart from that I know nothing. Anyone more in the know is being tight-lipped about it.'

The growl of an aero-engine starting up drew their attention. They moved to the window, which gave them an uninterrupted view across the whole airfield.

Another engine started up, then another and a fourth.

Two corporal WAAFs came into the control room from the rest room on the ground floor. The squadron leader and Carolyn acknowledged their arrival.

The corporals glanced at the blackboard on the wall opposite the window and saw that the plane with its engines running was the first of the two faced with the cross-country route. The second would follow in half an hour leaving the aerodrome clear for the two crews engaged on circuits and bumps. The corporals took their places at the telephones on the long desk from which they could view every take-off and landing. They would be in touch with the aircraft, and when the squadron leader made the necessary connection any communication would be relayed via the loudspeaker for all in the control room to hear. While the squadron leader was in sole command, he knew Carolyn had slotted in so well while training with the team that she could unofficially take over any job if required.

Carolyn strolled out on to the balcony that ran round three sides of the control tower. She breathed deep on the clear Lincolnshire air as if to purge her head of everything but the coming activity. Movement caught her eyes. The second crew for the cross-country flight was beginning to assemble, to carry out pre-flight checks on the Stirling allocated to them.

She silently wished both crews a good flight and wandered back inside. The clock showed two-fifteen.

The squadron leader flicked the switch that would bring an open connection between controllers in the tower and the crew in the plane.

The connection crackled into life. The squadron leader nodded and one of the WAAFs made the necessary call to the pilot of the Stirling, to check that the connection was loud and clear. Procedures were followed according to the book until finally the pilot was given permission to taxi to the runway in use. Carolyn watched the huge bomber move slowly from its dispersal and, under the guidance of its pilot, continue round the perimeter track to the end of the runway in use. There it stopped.

The pilot made his final check; a flash of green from the control van at the end of the runway signalled his clearance for take-off. The engines were given more and more power until, at the appropriate moment, the brakes were released. Slowly the bomber moved off, and as more power emanated from the four engines the aircraft moved faster and faster down the runway until, at the right moment, the pilot took it into the air. Everyone in the Control Tower breathed a sigh of relief, but still concentrated on watching it start its ascent.

A few moments later a voice exclaimed: 'Get her up! Get her up!' The urgency in the squadron leader's command sent a tremor of alarm through the room. 'Up! Up!'

Everyone's eyes were now fixed on the plane struggling to gain altitude.

'Oh, my God, he'll not clear that wood!' There was so much conviction in the squadron leader's voice that everyone stiffened with alarm. They stared in disbelief at the scenario that was happening before their eyes, one they were powerless to prevent.

The bomber struggled to gain height, then, as if a huge hand had prevented it from doing so, it sliced off branches, tore trunks out of the earth, while all the time the trees' clawing fingers were dragging it to the ground.

'Alarm! Ambulance! Fire Brigade! Rescue Team!' The squadron leader's voice rang through the Control Tower even as the Stirling and its crew tore through the remaining trees in their path and plunged into the ground with a shattering explosion that reverberated across the airfield.

There was an instant response to the squadron leader's calls. Everyone knew what was wanted.

Carolyn grabbed a phone and called for ambulances to rush to the crash site. Fire-engines raced towards the rising pall of smoke. All units were alerted and all flying was cancelled.

Action had kept her mind off the horrible tragedy she had just witnessed but once every possible help was in place the shock hit home. She sank on to a chair beside the WAAFs who had kept communications open, ever ready to pass messages on speedily.

'You all right, Ma'am?' asked another WAAF, who had appeared in the doorway.

Carolyn gave a weak nod. 'I've never witnessed . . . ' she muttered. She knew she must keep a grip on her feelings; it wouldn't do for her to lose control even though the pallor of her face betrayed the shock she felt.

'I'll make a cup of tea for us all,' said one of the WAAFs, pleased to find something to divert her attention from the appalling tragedy that illustrated the dangers awaiting air-crews even in training. She left the control room and went downstairs, to return a few minutes later with tea for every-one. They all took it with a quiet word of thanks.

A silence charged with the horror they had witnessed pressed down on everyone until someone said inanely, 'It's amazing what a cup of tea can do.'

No one commented until the squadron leader rose slowly to his feet, went to the window and, as befitted his authority, said, 'What has happened has happened. We must put it behind us; we must not let it prey on our minds. We cannot stand still. I'm sure the CO will order flying tomorrow as usual. It is the best thing for morale. I will remain on duty here in case there are any diversions from other 'dromes. I would like one volunteer to remain on duty, the rest of you can stand down.'

As one they all volunteered.

The squadron leader gave a small smile of appreciation as he thanked them. 'Maybe it's best if we all stay. Better that than be left alone to our own thoughts.'

So they busied themselves with secondary jobs that were awaiting attention until their satellite airfield assured Squadron Leader Aston that services there would be able to cope with any emergency and was brought to stand-by alert. Once the station CO was satisfied, he ordered the station closed until noon the following day, giving those dealing with the crash site time to remove evidence of the tragedy.

As they left the Control Tower the squadron leader said to Carolyn, 'Let me walk you to the Mess. I think a strong drink is called for.'

'Thank you, sir,' she said. And recognizing his concern about how she was reacting to the crash, added, 'I appreci-ate the offer.'

'Thought you might like some company, with Section Officer Gaston on leave. Back this evening, I believe?'

'Yes, last bus from Lincoln. She cancelled the staff car to give herself a few hours longer at home.'

'Good. It would not be wise for you to be alone tonight.' He noticed a flash of alarm in her eyes and gave a little chuckle as he said, 'I am not hinting at anything else, but I think after what you have witnessed today you could do with some companionship, so how about we dine together this evening and await Section Officer Gaston's arrival?'

'Thank you, sir.'

'As we are to be table companions I think we should drop the formalities. I instituted Christian names when we are working in the Control Tower because it is clearer to whom we are speaking and avoids any confusion as to whom I'm directing an order. I think we need a more relaxed atmosphere this evening too.' As he left Carolyn near her billet he said, 'I suspect you are in need of advice. If that is so and you want help, I am a good listener. At least, that's what my wife says.'

When she closed the door of her room behind her, Carolyn felt a mood of heavy gloom descend. Alone in the silence, the throbbing in her head turned into the roar of aero-engines. She grimaced and clamped her hands over her ears, trying to stifle the noise. As the sound faltered and lost power she buried her head in her pillows, trying to shut out the memory of an aircraft fighting for altitude – and failing. Tears burst from her and flowed until they had wiped the picture away. She lay still, letting numbness invade her body and mind.

Finally she sat up, glanced at her watch and realized she should move. She swung from the bed and speedily swamped her face in cold water. Make-up was quickly applied, precious silk stockings carefully rolled on, and her neatly pressed best skirt and tunic adjusted to her liking. Finally she viewed herself in the mirror, grabbed her hat and headed for the Mess – a question born in the aftermath of this afternoon's scene of devastation still at the forefront of her mind.

She left her hat in the WAAFs' cloakroom near the front door and walked into the ante-room, to be met by the almost overwhelming buzz of conversation and laughter made by officers having a pre-dinner drink. A little shock ran through her. How could they carry on as if nothing had happened? Seven men had died today right on their doorstep and yet here were their comrades acting as if nothing had happened. She felt the crew who had perished were being betrayed.

Her thoughts were soon interrupted. 'Hello there.' She was startled by the pleasant voice and the compliment it uttered. 'Carolyn, you are looking charming this evening.' The smile Squadron Leader Ashton gave her was one of undisguised pleasure.

'Oh!' Looking embarrassed, she added, 'Thank you, sir.'

He leaned forward and reminded her quietly, 'We are off duty. You know my name – Jim, please.'

Carolyn blushed and nodded.

'Come along.' He led her to the bar and ordered two single malts and was pleased when she did not protest.

The two whiskies came with a small glass jug of water. Jim picked up the jug and glanced at Carolyn. 'Water?'

'Just a dash,' she replied.

He poured a splash into one of the glasses. 'That OK?'

'Just right, thank you.'

Jim raised an eyebrow. 'A connoisseur, I see.'

Carolyn laughed. The ice was broken. 'Hardly, but my father taught me that that is the right way to have whisky – just the smallest of dashes. I'm not in the habit of taking whisky but when I do that's how I have it.'

'I must remember that.'

Carolyn made no comment but wondered if that was a hint for the future. But she dismissed the thought – he was a married man. Guardedly she asked, 'What is life like on an operational Bomber Station?' Then quickly added, 'Don't answer that if it brings back bad memories.'

He gave a faint smile. 'It doesn't. Oh, yes, there are bad times. You see worse things than we witnessed today. You have to forget them and get on with life. We have a job to do and we have to do it to the best of our ability.' He paused and added, 'Let's continue this over our meal.' He rose, and as he escorted her into the dining room said quietly, 'I asked the steward to keep me a table for two. It might raise a few eyebrows but ignore them. My reputation is intact.'

When they were settled he approached the subject again. 'To me the comradeship of a crew is second to none, especially when you all gel together. In my experience you become closer than brothers. Each member of the crew depends on the efficiency of the others. If trust goes then it's a recipe for disaster.'

'How does it work with a crew made up of different ranks?'

'I have known instances when the captain of the aircraft has insisted that ranks remain in use even in the air, but in a good crew once airborne all ranks disappear. You are as one. In my experience it makes for recognizing you depend on each other and so you work for each other, aiming to do your duty by doing a good job and remaining alert. That way everyone survives. Life on a squadron is second to none. Everyone, no matter what their rank, is in it together. There has to be discipline otherwise the whole structure would disintegrate, but no one resents it. A good CO makes for a good station.'

'Would you go back to ops tomorrow?' Carolyn asked cautiously.

'Like a shot.'

'What would your wife say?' she asked, but quickly added, 'I shouldn't ask that; it's too personal.'

'Carolyn, I realize there is a reason for that question and I know that anything I say in reply will go no further.'

Her nod of agreement satisfied him. She knew that today had been a turning point in their relationship. Prior to this it had been on an official basis but now there was a friendship between them in which delicate exchanges could be shared.

'Jean, my wife, would not want me to do a second tour. She was thankful that I survived one. Her prayers had been answered.'

'She is a religious person?'

'Not overly so. She believes in God and in prayer and puts her trust in Him. She will continue to do so. But she would never try to persuade me to forget a second tour, as much as she would dread it. You know, our wives and girlfriends probably suffer more anxiety than we do. We know what is happening and when, while they don't. When they hear the morning news – "Last night Bomber Command attacked Hanover. Ten of our aircraft are missing" – they must be on a knife-edge. I don't know whether I am making any sense to you, nor if I am answering your query.'

'You are being a great help. That crash today shook me. It was the first I had witnessed. I immediately wondered if I had done the correct thing in applying for a position on a Bomber Station, where I might see much worse. I know, now I should not reel away from the horrors of one crash. You are putting much more at stake than I ever will. I believe I am right in wanting to serve with a Bomber Squadron.'

'I'm pleased to hear that because, having worked with you, I know you will always do a good job. You have the temperament. The way you handled yourself and the situation today sealed my good opinion of you. There is one other thing ... you have the sort of voice we flyers appreciate.'

'You are the second person to tell me that.' She gave a little smile and told him about Charlie.

'A very perceptive man. It is sad that you never met him again, but that is war. Think about his observation. I'm sure that turned your mind to Bomber Command. If that and what I have said has helped you make up your mind about your future direction, and that involves serving on a Bomber Station, I hope I am there to have you debrief me.'

'You have given me something to live up to.'

'You'll do well wherever you are.'

'It's kind of you to say so.'

'I really mean it,' he said firmly. 'It would not be right to give you false hopes.'

They fell into easy company and conversation as the night wore on until the door to the ante-room opened and Lucy looked in.

'Ah, here she is.' Jim stood up and welcomed Lucy, who hid her surprise at seeing her friend in the company of a senior officer. 'May I get you a drink?' he asked the new arrival.

'Thank you. A lemonade, please.' Lucy slipped out of her greatcoat.

Jim ordered the drink and when it had been brought to Lucy, said, 'If you'll excuse me, I'll leave you two to chat.' Leaning towards Lucy, he said quietly, 'Look after your friend. It has been a rough day for her.' He turned to Carolyn then. 'You'll be all right now?'

'Yes, thank you. And thank you for being so kind.'

81

A gentle smile touched his lips as he dismissed her thanks. 'It was nothing. Good night to you both.'

When the door closed behind him, Lucy turned to Carolyn. 'What's all this about? You and Squadron Leader Ashton ... Look after her ... ? What's happened while I've been away?'

'It's not what you're thinking,' replied Carolyn, with a faint smile.

'Well, what *is* it? I'm all ears!'

Carolyn quickly related all the events of the day, which immediately changed Lucy's perception of the situation she had walked into.

'Oh, you poor thing. It must have been devastating for you. I should have been here.'

'It was horrible, but there was nothing you could have done.' Carolyn's voice faltered.

'I could have listened to you,' said Lucy, sliding her hand across the table towards her friend.

After a few minutes more, during which Carolyn gripped Lucy's hand and fought to steady her feelings, she said, 'Let's go back to the billet.'

When they had walked a few yards from the Mess building they both stopped at the same instant. Neither of them spoke. They were transfixed by the wonder of the night. The heavens were ablaze with glittering stars set in a black canopy that knew no bounds. The air was still. Nothing moved. Neither of them knew how long they had stood there before Lucy whispered, 'Listen, you can hear the silence.'

'There's magic in the air,' said Carolyn quietly, as if it was important not to shatter the enchantment of the moment. The terrors she had witnessed only a few hours ago were expunged from her mind by the healing balm of this wondrous night.

The silence seeped into them both until it was broken by the drone of an aircraft's engines.

Neither of them spoke.

The sound grew louder only to fade again, but before it was lost completely it slowly rose. It faded again, then strengthened. Its rise and fall continued, coming near then receding, as if it couldn't decide where it wanted to be.

'That's a Wellington,' said Lucy in a hushed tone.

'How do you know?'

'I once stayed with an aunt and uncle who lived near an RAF station from which the two-engine Wellingtons were flying. I got to know the sound. They are mostly non-operational now. That one is most likely from a training unit.'

They stood listening as the pattern of the aircraft's flight continued.

'He's lost,' said Lucy.

Carolyn queried her statement.

'He's flying back and forth. He wouldn't be doing that if he knew where he was,' Lucy pointed out.

They stood listening, anxiety mounting as the repetition continued, until the sound gradually faded and disappeared completely, with no sign of returning.

'He must have found his bearing,' said Lucy, with a touch of relief. 'I hope he gets home safely.'

'So do I,' said Carolyn and offered up a silent prayer for the crew. She shivered. 'Come on, let's get inside.'

Little did they know that the Wellington bomber that was off course that night would have a profound effect on their lives.

9

'Pilot calling Navigator.' Rick Wood's tone came firm and sharp over the intercom of Wellington JA466N, flying on a night cross country exercise out of Bruntingthorpe.

'Navigator here, Skipper,' twenty year old Sam Horn replied, somewhat hesitantly. He knew what was coming and needed an answer, but he hadn't one.

'Where the hell are we, Navigator?'

'Er ... keep flying this course, Skipper.' Sam tried to sound confident but there was a catch in his voice.

'That isn't what I asked. You've had me flying this box course for the last twenty minutes. Something has to be done. We need to be back on the ground before we run out of fuel. Now, get your finger out!'

The rest of the crew, twenty-one year old Bomb Aimer, Pilot Officer Peter Wilkins, twenty-two-year-old Wireless Operator, Sergeant Gordon Barton, and twenty-two-year-old Gunners, Sergeants Tim Myers and Bob Jeffers, tensed at the tone of their Captain and Pilot, twenty-one-year-old Rick Wood, but they knew Sam was not coming up to the standard that Rick required. It was obvious from their first meeting at OTU that Rick would be a stickler for efficiency and their gelling together as a crew. He approached command in what appeared to be an easygoing way, but everyone soon realised that he expected his crew to know their own jobs thoroughly, and to know something of what their fellow members had to do as well, in case they had to deputize in a combat situation.

Now it was becoming obvious that Sam was a weak link. He was a nice enough bloke but he wasn't on top of his job. This was the third time he had lost them on a night exercise – and that was over Britain. It had begun to create unease in their minds. What would happen if he lost them over enemy territory?

The Wellington flew on.

The minutes were stretching towards eternity.

Even the engines seemed to be mocking their plight.

Rick knew it was no good cajoling the rest of his crew. He was certain they would already be on the look-out for anything that would give them a clue as to where they where. It wasn't a pleasant experience to be lost for a third time at night. The engines continued to play their tune, but for how much longer?

'Skipper, Bomb Aimer here.' Peter's voice, coming from his position in the nose of the aircraft, was sharp with confident expectation. He did not wait for acknowledgement from Rick. 'Red flashing beacon just came on. We're passing over it now. It's flashing the letters RA.'

'Thanks, Bomb Aimer. Got that, Navigator?'

'Yes, Skipper.' Sam was flicking over the notes he had been given prior to take off. He felt relief when he saw RA was operating tonight at a position that he quickly found on his map. He speedily worked out a new course that would take them from the beacon to their base. Twenty minutes later they were climbing out of their aircraft at Bruntingthorpe, relief evident in every line of their bodies.

No one commented on the dilemma that had faced them, but in the crew room, as they shed their flying gear, Rick got Peter to one side. 'You are the other officer in the crew so I'm seeking your opinion first. What would you do about Sam?'

'He's pleasant enough but now I'll always be uneasy with him in the crew. I'd try to have him replaced, if I were you.'

'Thanks.' Rick nodded. 'My feeling too. I'll sound out the rest of the crew in the morning.'

'I hope this means we'll have good weather,' said Lucy, looking out of the window as she headed for the bathroom. She stopped at the foot of Carolyn's bed and yanked the covers off her. 'Up! Bathroom will be free in a few minutes.'

Carolyn moaned but she knew her friend was right – it was time for her to be up. They were on duty together at eight o'clock.

'I wonder if that Wellington got down safely,' Lucy called before she started brushing her teeth.

Carolyn rolled out of bed and grabbed her dressing gown, drew it round her and glanced out of the window. She agreed with her friend that the weather looked good.

'If you hurry we could call in at the Intelligence section and see what flying news there is for last night.'

They had a quick breakfast in the Mess and then headed for the Nissen hut that housed the flying reports.

'You two are early,' said the section officer in charge this morning.

'We wondered what flying there was last night,' said Lucy. 'We heard a plane, sounded to me like a Wellington.'

'He seemed to be stooging around as if he was lost,' added Carolyn.

'And you were concerned?'

'Just wondered.'

The section officer shuffled some papers on her desk and extracted one. As she was doing so she said, 'I can tell you there were no operations over the Continent – the weather was too bad. We escaped that and the sky was clear over Britain. Even so, flying was restricted to three cross-country flights by trainee crews.' She glanced at the papers in her hand. 'Reports state that all three flights were safely completed.'

Lucy and Carolyn looked at each other with a feeling of relief and thanked the Intelligence officer.

Before the two friends parted, Lucy for the Control Tower to report to Squadron Leader Ashton and Carolyn to take her two weeks' leave as arranged, they wished each other well.

'Hope there are no flying troubles for you while I'm away,' said Carolyn.

'Forget that part of the past,' Lucy advised. 'What's done is done and can't be put right. You enjoy yourself. And, remember . . . if you can't be good, be careful.'

Carolyn laughed and aimed a playful blow at Lucy, who dodged it, saying, 'Love to your mum and dad, and hope you have good news of Alastair,'

At about the same time Rick Wood was making his way to the adjutant's office at Bruntingthorpe. He was relieved that he had managed to have a word with the rest of his crew individually without Sam knowing. Confident that he had the backing of his crew, he hoped the adjutant would sympathize with him and afford him a meeting with his commanding officer.

His request was fielded by a sergeant who had served the adjutant since coming to Bruntingthorpe four years ago. He consulted an appointments diary.

'You are early, sir. The adjutant hasn't arrived yet, but

should be here any time now. He has half an hour before his meeting with the CO. I'll see if he is willing to see you as soon as he arrives.'

'I'll be grateful, Sergeant. This is a matter that I want to get settled as soon as possible.'

'Please take a seat, sir.'

Rick had been seated only a few minutes when the door opened and a middle-aged man, smart in his RAF battle-dress bearing the shoulder stripes of a squadron leader, walked in. Hair that was greying at the temples, alert eyes and an upright stance gave him an impressive aura, which was emphasized by the Wings and ribbons, including the DSO that adorned his tunic.

As soon as Prime Minister Chamberlain had announced that Britain was at war with Germany, George Raby had volunteered to serve his country in any capacity whatsoever. His experience was valued and he was quickly assigned to duties with the RAF. He was a kindly, fatherly figure, who took no offence when the young flyers called him Pop. He knew none of them would use that familiarity at an inappropriate time.

'Good morning, Rick.' George showed surprise that the young man was waiting for him so early.

'Good morning, sir,' replied Rick, rising smartly to his feet.

'Flying Officer Wood requested an urgent interview with you, sir,' said the sergeant. 'I thought you might fit him in before your appointment with the CO.'

The squadron leader nodded. 'Very well. Come along in, Rick.'

The younger man followed him into his office and closed the door.

'Sit down. Now, what can I do for you?'

'I'm troubled, sir. I want my navigator replaced.'

The adjutant expressed surprise. 'This is unusual, but not unknown. First, for what reason?'

'Lack of skill, sir. He is not up to the job. On our last three night cross-country exercises he has lost us. The first two he recovered but last night he did not. The situation became more serious. He had me flying a box course but did not know where we were. If it hadn't been for my bomb aimer we might have had to bail out. Peter spotted a beacon that we learned afterwards was only switched on at irregular intervals. He read the flashes and that gave us a fix and we made it home. But it was no thanks to our navigator. The confidence of the crew is undermined by his errors.'

The squadron leader had listened attentively to this. 'I can see it is of serious concern to you,' he commented.

'And to the rest of my crew, sir,' Rick put in quickly.

The adjutant nodded. 'You are sure there is no other reason? No personal differences between him and any crew member?'

'No, sir. If it was like that I believe I could handle it, but this is different. I cannot do anything about his inability to be on top of his work. Because there is this weakness in Sergeant Horn, I felt it was my duty to the rest of the crew to apply for him to be replaced.'

'Very well. It will be a matter for the CO to decide, of course, but you have given me a strong case for the situation to be investigated and solved, one way or the other.' The adjutant glanced at his watch. 'I'm seeing the CO shortly. If you will wait, we'll see if he can deal with this before his next meeting. He might be able to instigate action immediately. He doesn't like problems lying around unsolved.'

'I'll wait, sir. The sooner I know if a replacement can be made, the better for the morale of my crew.'

The adjutant nodded, rose from his chair and went to the

sergeant's ante-room. Rick heard him say, 'Get me the file on Sergeant Horn, Navigator.'

In a few moments the sergeant clerk appeared and placed a file in front of the adjutant, saying, 'The file you required, sir.' He left the room.

Without making any comment the adjutant perused the file quickly, pausing now and then to reread an item.

Eight minutes later they hear footsteps come along the corridor. There were muffled voices, then a door opened and closed and a chair squeaked as someone sat down.

The adjutant glanced at his watch. 'Good, he's early. That might be a help.'

Rick made no comment, his nerves jangling. He was going to try to argue his case before a man with the power to silence him utterly. Rick had met him once briefly when, like all good COs, he had welcomed the new arrivals to the Officers' Mess and had made sure a similar welcome was given to the Sergeants in Rick's crew.

After five minutes the adjutant rose from his desk, knocked on the adjoining door and, with Sergeant Horn's file in his hand, entered the CO's office. A buzz of words that he could not make out reached Rick. The door opened again. The adjutant reappeared. 'Flying Officer Wood, the CO will see you now.'

Rick sprang to his feet, crammed his hat on his head, stepped quickly into the next room, came to attention in front of the CO and saluted smartly, keeping his eyes fixed straight ahead.

'At ease,' said the CO. 'George, sit in on this, it will save time. Be seated, both of you.' He waited until they were settled then looked probingly at Rick. 'I hope this is a matter of genuine concern.'

'It is, sir. I would not take up your time with it otherwise.'

'I gained that impression from the adjutant and he has given me all your reasons for requesting a replacement. You are right in bringing this weakness in your crew to my notice. I will have Sergeant Horn put back in training and bring in another navigator for you.'

'Thank you, sir.' Though he tried to disguise the emotion he felt, Rick knew he had not been successful when the CO said, with a little smile, 'That looks like it's a relief to you.'

'It is indeed. There is one more thing I would like to do, sir. May I break the news to Sergeant Horn myself and instruct him to report to the adjutant?'

The CO nodded. 'That is a considerate gesture, Wood. I admire you for taking that responsibility. It won't be easy.'

'I know, sir, but I would prefer to do it myself.'

'Very well. Do it right away so that everything can be settled quickly. Let the adjutant know as soon as you have seen Horn.' He turned to George. 'In the meantime we need a top class navigator for Wood. We have to have a solution quickly so that his crew is not held up. There'll be a new set of aircrew coming through the day after tomorrow. I studied their qualifications yesterday. One navigator stood out in my mind, a Sergeant Don Westwood. From his results so far, he should fit in well with Wood's crew. Have him sectioned out before any crewing up takes place.'

'Very good, sir,' replied George. He pushed himself to his feet and left the office.

Rick had sprung to his feet too but the CO signalled him to wait. 'When you speak to Horn, reassure him that this is only a temporary set-back in his training. I'm sure with a little more diligence and hard work he can become a good navigator. Reports from his training in Canada are all good. His ability has slipped since he resumed training here. I've seen it happen before but, more often than not, these men recover ground and become a credit to Bomber Command. I'm sure you will benefit from getting the top navigator among those reporting in the day after tomorrow. Good luck, Wood.'

'Thank you, sir.' Rick snapped to attention, made a smart salute and left the room.

He hurried to the Mess and was pleased to find Peter there. 'It's done, Pete,' he announced with some relief. 'The CO was very agreeable and is convinced it is the best thing for us and for Sam. More than likely we'll get the best new navigator, a Sergeant Don Westwood, from the bods who will be coming in the day after tomorrow.' He grimaced. 'Now for the worst part, I said I would like to break the news to Sam myself.'

'Want me to come with you?' Peter offered immediately.

'I'd appreciate a bit of moral support. It's not as if I've done something like this before, but I felt I should do it. I want to reassure Sam we have nothing against him as a person and that it's not the end of the world.'

'Come on,' said Peter, heading for the door. 'Let's look in his billet first.'

They were approaching the Nissen hut which Sam shared with five others when the door opened and he came out.

'Hi, fellas,' he greeted them lightly, but there was no disguising the troubled expression that crossed his face when he added, 'Looking for me?'

'Yes.'

'Thought you might be. You're not usually seen around here. It's about last night, isn't it?'

'I'm afraid so,' said Rick reluctantly. 'We just can't go on. Getting lost once was not good, but three times ... and last night was the worst. With the rest of us in mind I had to do something about it.'

'You've seen the CO?' asked Sam anxiously,

'Yes.'

'He's kicked me out?' Sam's voice rose a little.

'No, he hasn't,' replied Rick firmly. 'But what he has done is drop you back a course or two for more training. I'll get a new navigator. He said this sort of thing has happened before and guys come out better for the extra training and go on to be a credit to Bomber Command.'

'So neither you nor he chopped me?'

'No, of course not. You'll do great. But we as a crew cannot be hanging about waiting for you.'

'Not kicked out!' There was relief in Sam's voice and his whole body lost the air of tension that had gripped it. 'I couldn't have gone home if I had been. My father would have labelled me a failure and I couldn't have borne that. So thanks for not coming down too hard on me.'

Rick stuck out his hand, which Sam took with thanks and a smile for Peter as the bomb aimer slapped him on the shoulder. 'You're an OK guy, Sam. All will be well. This is just a little hiccup for you.'

'Thanks, Pete, and thanks for spotting that beacon last night. You most likely saved my bacon, as the saying goes. Do the rest of the crew know I'll not be with them any more?'

'Not yet. I wanted to see you first,' replied Rick.

'Thanks, Skipper.' Sam paused then added, 'I'll miss calling you that.' He turned quickly and walked away.

Rick tightened his lips and gave a little shake of his head. 'I didn't enjoy that, but ... ' He let his words hang a moment then added, 'Thanks for your support, Peter.'

'I did nothing.'

'Oh, yes, you did. You were there and it showed Sam that I must have the approval of the rest of the crew; that I was not doing this off my own bat even though, as Skipper, I have every right to do so. There are those who would have done it that way, but that is not for me. At times I may appear harsh, but it's only because I believe what is best for the whole crew must come first.'

'I know they will understand, but let's go and find out, shall we?'

They found their wireless operator and two gunners in their billet, supposedly lazing on their beds, but the two officers instinctively knew these men had sensed something was happening and wanted to know how it might affect them.

'Something you need to know,' said Rick. Tension came into the atmosphere. 'I have just asked the CO to replace Sam, and he has agreed.' The strain lifted; Rick and Peter saw relief come over the crew members. 'You did the right thing, Skipper,' said Gordon Barton. His statement was backed by Sergeant Tim Myers, who occupied the mid-upper turret. Sergeant Bob Jeffers, the rear-gunner, said nothing, leaving Rick wondering why. He quickly dismissed that in the wake of Tim's question: 'When do we get a replacement?

'Immediately,' replied Rick. 'The CO put that into operation while I was with him. He does not want to hold up the rest of our training. The adjutant will see that the leading navigator among the aircrew who are due in the day after tomorrow is immediately assigned to us.'

Faces brightened. 'So we come out of this smelling of roses,' commented Tim.

'Looks like it,' said Peter. 'Then we only need an engineer to complete our crew, and we'll get him at Heavy Conversion Unit.'

Two days later the adjutant introduced Sergeant Don Westwood to Rick Wood's crew and left them to become better acquainted.

10

'Where are you from, Don?' asked Rick.

'Redcar, on the Yorkshire coast, near the mouth of the Tees,' he replied, busy making up his mind about this tall, fair-haired pilot who cut a confident, imposing figure.

'What were you doing before you joined this lot?'

'I was working in a boat-yard making cobles.'

'Cobles?' Rick looked mystified.

Don laughed. 'That's made you wonder! They're flat-bottomed, clinker-built, three-oared fishing boats used in coastal waters, particularly in the North-east of England. Grace Darling,' he changed tack. 'You've heard of her?'

Rick nodded. 'Rescued some sailors shipwrecked up your way in a storm.'

'Spot on,' said Don, becoming more comfortable with him. 'In 1838, to be precise.'

'So why join aircrew when you had connections with the sea?' Rick asked

'I figured I'd be called up sometime and probably be pushed into something I wouldn't like. Flying fascinated me, so, with my wife's agreement, I volunteered for the RAF.'

'So you're married?'

To the best girl in the world,' said Don proudly. 'I'm a lucky man.'

'Any family?'

'Not yet.'

'And your wife has no qualms about you being in aircrew?'

'No! Not at all. She knows what the consequences could be but never mentions them. She knows it helps me to cope.'

'She sounds like a fine person, Don. I'd like to meet her sometime.'

'I'm sure she would love that.'

'I think we might have a crew get-together with wives and girlfriends included some time.'

'A good idea, Skipper,' agreed Don, feeling established with this crew already. If the rest of the members are as amiable as the pilot, I'm on to a winner, he thought. 'You had to change your navigator,' he commented then. 'Nobody told me why, nor why they pushed me forward.'

'Our navigator was below par so I pressed for a change and it was granted. He will join a later course. We struck lucky getting the top navigator from the new arrivals.'

'I don't know about that,' replied Don, embarrassed by the praise.

'Ah, but I know what the navigation officer and adjutant both told me. We are pleased to have you with us.'

The others chorused their agreement when Rick introduced their new navigator. Rick, however, noticed that their rear-gunner, Bob Jeffers, was quieter than usual. As they headed for their billets Rick sought an opportunity to have a word with him. 'You OK?' he asked.

Bob was startled. 'Er ... yes.'

'Are you sure?'

'Yes. Just feel a bit off colour.'

'Report to the MO if you're unwell. A crew must be fully fit to fly – at least mine must. I don't want our effectiveness undermined by anything.'

'I'm OK.'

Rick noted the snap in Bob's voice but made no comment.

Don slotted in well with the crew and after four cross-country flights, each of two hours' duration, when he never once had to question where they were, their confidence had soared again.

After finishing their course they were given a week's leave. As they parted to go their own ways Rick noted that Bob was quieter than the others but could not put a finger on why this might be. He hoped that spell of leave would solve whatever it was his rear-gunner had on his mind.

Bob shouldered his bag and walked out of Colchester station. A bus was already waiting. He started towards it only to stop after a few strides. The last person in the queue of eight got on the bus. Still Bob hesitated.

'You coming, mate?'

He started when he realized the question had been directed at him.

'Er ... no ... next one will be better.'

The conductor looked at him askance but said no more. He rang the bell. The driver gave the idling engine more power, released the brakes and allowed the bus to move slowly forward. Bob watched it go. He tightened his lips, shrugged his shoulders and muttered, 'What the hell?' heading for the nearest pub.

An hour later he emerged on to the street, not sure if the five pints of bitter he had downed had given him Dutch courage or not.

He got unsteadily on to the bus, paid his fare without acknowledging the conductor's admiration of his air gunner's brevet, and flopped on to a seat. Six stops later he left the bus without a word. He paused a moment as the bus drew away, leaving him staring down a cul-de-sac lined with four detached houses either side of the road. They had been built in 1938, and when he and Rowena had married in 1940, aged twenty, he'd thought the world had opened up for him when his mother-in-law had bought a house and given it to them as a wedding present. Bob saw this as his escape with the girl he loved from the tyrannical uncle who had reluctantly brought him up after Bob's mother and father had died. Life had seemed idyllic then even though there was a war on and he knew that one day he would be called up for military service.

But the house had become a millstone round his neck, and now, as he walked down the cul-de-sac towards it, he remembered how he'd had the shock of his life when he came home from work one day and Rowena had announced, 'Mother has sold her own house and is moving in with us.'

'What? Why the devil didn't she ask us first?'

'She did, and I said yes.'

'I married you, not her. I'm your husband! You should have ... ' The hurt in his voice betrayed Bob's true feelings for his mother-in-law. She had never taken to him, at times making it obvious that she considered her daughter deserved someone better, but he had always bitten his tongue for Rowena's sake. 'I wish she would stop trying to buy her way into our lives,' he muttered.

'She isn't,' his wife contradicted him sharply. 'It's her money, she can do what she likes with it.'

'Maybe, but buying this house does not give her the right to move in. She gave it to us. It's ours.'

'Apparently not. There's something in some document or other by which she has the right ... '

'The bitch!' exploded Bob. 'She's had this all planned. She has the cash from the house that she sold and now you tell me she has rights to this one too. And the worst of it all is she'll be living with us.'

'Don't you call my mother names! She's done this for our good.'

'Her own good and no one else's!'

The hostility at home worsened until finally Bob could stand it no longer. One day he came home earlier than usual from the office where he worked and announced, 'I've signed up – volunteered for aircrew duties as a gunner.'

'You can't!' gasped Rowena.

'You're crazy,' snapped her mother, glaring at Bob.

'I can, and I'm not crazy. I did it two weeks ago, gave my office address so any communication for me would go there. Papers arrived today telling me to report to Saint Athan on Thursday.'

'Two days' time?' gasped Rowena.

'That's right. Then I'll be away from all this bickering.'

But that prediction proved to be wrong. In fact it grew worse, not only when he came home on leave, hoping in vain each time that his life would get better, but intensified by carping letters, obviously dictated by his mother-in-law. He'd hoped that separation would solve his marital problems, that the love he still had for Rowena would surmount them and prove the adage 'absence makes the heart grow fonder'. He was still hoping.

With his gunnery course finished Bob, along with the rest of the men who had qualified to fly as gunners, was sent to the OTU at Bruntingthorpe to crew-up. Strangers depended on instinct to help them find others with whom they would be compatible. Bob liked the look of a tall fair-haired pilot with the rank of flying officer and was delighted to find he was looking for a rear-gunner. Bob thought life must be moving his way when he settled in easily with the rest of the crew and the criticism in Rowena's letters had been toned down. Was his mother-in-law finally accepting his decision and realising that he had a mind of his own?

But there were always doubts hovering. Facing the dangers of wartime flying, as he did, was Rowena aware that his feelings and desires should be paramount in their relationship as man and wife? Not wishing to create any hostility he had never queried if she was aware how disturbing her mother's influence could be and that his leave had not been the rosy time he craved.

Such questions that kept cropping up were insidiously affecting his capabilities of reaching the high standards expected by Rick and his crew.

With the crew-training completed and their leave over, Rick's outfit had moved to the Heavy Conversion Unit at Swinderby, where the day after their arrival they completed their crew when Sergeant Phil Stevens joined them as flight engineer. He was a stocky individual, bronzed from spending so much time pursuing an outdoor life as a cricketer, footballer, and cross-country runner. The crew soon realized that he was a man on top of his job and that he loved engines.

Three days into their course Rick was designated for a session of circuits and bumps with a flying instructor, to familiarize him further in the use of four engines as opposed to two. Though it was not necessary on this occasion for the rest of the crew to fly with him, he insisted that they did so in order to get used to working together. He said nothing at the time, when he overheard Bob grumbling to Tim about, 'unnecessary flying', but he noted it as another example of Bob's negative attitude, which had begun to concern his skipper.

*

Late one afternoon, with flying over for the day, Peter and Rick headed for the Officers' Mess. 'Fancy going to Newark?' Peter asked.

'I think I'd rather relax here with a pint or two,' Rick replied.

'Suits me,' his friend agreed.

'I'll get them in,' said Rick as they entered the Mess. 'You find a couple of chairs.'

Peter headed for the ante-room to find the chairs while Rick headed for the bar to order the drinks. He was surprised to find the only other person at the bar was a WAAF section officer whom he had not seen there before, or for that matter, anywhere around the station.

'Good evening,' he said, and to be polite he added, 'You're new here, aren't you?'

The WAAF gave a little smile. 'Well ... ' She drew the word out.

With laughter in his eyes and his voice, he said, 'You sound doubtful? Surely you know?'

'Yes, I do, but I'm not sure how to answer you.'

'That sounds mysterious. Are you on a secret mission or something?' he asked in a mock sinister tone.

Lucy's laughter was full of amusement at the image this raised. 'Hardly that.'

'It seems to me there is more to you than you are telling me. I'm with my bomb aimer ... would you care to join us? The steward will bring our drinks over.'

'I'm expecting my friend Carolyn. She's been on a fortnight's leave and should be arriving soon.'

'Well, come and join us for now, and then she can too when she gets here. She'll make up the foursome.'

'OK,' replied Lucy, thinking maybe this handsome officer would demolish Carolyn's resolve not to get involved in any romance until after the war. Lucy had already noted the bomb aimer and smiled to herself as she thought, I prefer him, so the way's clear for us both!

Having placed his drinks order Rick led the way over to Peter who, knowing what Rick had said about females and flying, was surprised to see he had a WAAF section officer in tow. Peter sprang to his feet politely.

'I think introductions are called for,' said Rick. 'My bomb aimer is Pete Wilkins and I'm Rick Wood.'

They shook hands as she said, 'I'm Lucy Gaston. My friend, when she arrives, is Carolyn Maddison.'

Two more chairs were pulled over to the low table handily placed for their drinks.

The three officers fell into easy conversation that was interrupted when Carolyn appeared.

The two flyers sprang to their feet and, with introductions over, Peter went off to place an order for more drinks.

'Did you have a good leave?' Rick asked.

'I did, but I was ready to come back after two weeks.' Carolyn added quickly, 'That does not imply any criticism of my family. Mother and I are close and my father spoils me.'

'But having tasted freedom, you began to feel stifled after a fortnight, as nice as your parents are?' said Rick. Carolyn nodded. He went on, 'I know how you feel, it's the same for me when I go on leave.'

'You are a trainee crew?' queried Lucy.

'Yes,' replied Peter. 'What's your role here?'

'We trained together as Intelligence officers,' replied Lucy. 'We completed our training, passed out with top results, and that's led to us being sent here to assimilate more of what the atmosphere would be like on an operational squadron.'

'So that's where you'll end up?' queried Rick.

'More than likely, but we have been told little about our ultimate destinations. It seems the powers that be are making yet more assessments.'

'Have your courses involved handling and communicating with men engaged in operational duties?' asked Rick.

'Yes, to a certain degree. If we serve on a Bomber Station one of our duties will be the debriefing of aircrew, and that means we have to be aware of the psychological influences of dangerous missions on those men.'

Rick nodded, looking thoughtful.

'Is something wrong?' Carolyn tentatively put in.

'I hope not,' replied Rick, 'but I'm a little uneasy about my rear-gunner.'

'Do you think he's not good enough?'

'No. I had that problem at OTU and had to get my navigator changed, but this is different. Bob is a good gunner. I wouldn't want to change him.'

'So what is wrong?'

'I don't think his heart is in the job. He's morose at times, at others he grumbles, and yet he can be very enthusiastic too. It's puzzling.'

Have you tackled him about his attitude?'

'I've asked him if there is anything wrong. He denies there is. I've told him if it's medical to see the MO, but he says he is perfectly all right. I could approach the CO about him but I don't want to do that unless something drastic is bothering him.'

'Rick, you've got to get to the bottom of this. It could affect the performance of the whole crew. You can't afford to have anything undermining their capabilities. Lives could be endangered,' Carolyn stressed.

'I know, it's my responsibility to get to the bottom of his

topsy-turvy attitude. I have to for the sake of the crew, but how do I do it? A confrontation with him could upset the way we all work together.'

'I'm by no means a psychologist, but as Lucy and I indicated we have touched upon psychological techniques in debriefing returning crews. I'll have a word with your gunner at the first opportunity, if you would like me to?' Carolyn offered.

'Would you?' Rick asked, brightening at her willingness to help.

'Of course.'

'You are an angel from heaven!'

Carolyn smiled. 'Hardly that, but I'll do my best.'

'Thank you. And, please, not a word to anyone.'

'Of course not.' She turned away from him then and saw the smiles that Lucy and Peter were exchanging. 'Hi, you two, I think we'd better get something to eat.'

They all agreed and made their way to the dining room.

'Have you heard anything about Jim?' Lucy asked Carolyn as they sought places at one of the tables.

'No. Just the note he left when he moved on, wishing me luck.'

'Didn't he even give you a hint where he was going?'

'No. All he put at the end of his note were three words – "Flying job; delighted".'

'He'll be happy.'

'He certainly will.'

As they sat down, more drinks appeared with the compliments of their companions.

The easy rapport continued between the four of them, born of the knowledge that they were 'here today but would be gone tomorrow' – and no one knew where.

11

During the late summer of 1941, the crew's course progressed at HCU. The special relationship between its members strengthened, both in the air and on the ground, which Rick encouraged to counteract any thoughts of what life on an active squadron would bring: constant danger, with cannon-firing enemy fighters prowling the night seeking out the intruders with the aid of searchlights, and anti-aircraft guns pounding the sky with shells in the defence of German cities and military targets, to send enemy bombers crashing to earth in fiery explosions. Rick also reminded them that work was going on to improve and widen the use of radar in defence and attack. Huge progress had been made before and during the Battle of Britain, and knowledge gained then was developed to aid Bomber Command attain greater accuracy and provide safety for returning crews.

If Rick Wood's crew ever contemplated what might lie ahead for them they never spoke about it, but kept their thoughts to themselves and lived for today. They relaxed together, and made close friendships. They headed for the cinemas, dance halls and pubs of Newark or Lincoln or the friendly hostelries of local villages.

The rapport between Rick, Pete, Carolyn and Lucy expanded beyond the Mess and spilled over into the Lincolnshire countryside where they walked the lanes and fields, enjoying teasing banter and silent companionship.

On one of these occasions Rick put forward an idea to the other three officers.

'At the end of our course we will get ten days' leave. What do you say to having a crew get-together with wives and girl-friends invited? We could have a couple of days in Lincoln, possibly at that hotel opposite the station. It's handy for everyone. If we have it at the start of our leave, we could travel on with wives and sweethearts afterwards.'

'Good idea!' they all agreed enthusiastically.

'I'm sure the rest of the crew will be for it,' said Pete.

'And it will be a good occasion for Lucy and me to put on dresses for once,' said Carolyn.

Pete looked hard at Lucy. 'I've only seen you in a uniform. I wonder what you'll look like in a dress?'

'I'll get my mum to raid my wardrobe,' said Carolyn.

Rick winked at his bomb aimer. 'I've raised some rivalry here, Pete. I think I'd better forget the idea.'

'You'll do nothing of the sort,' chorused the two girls.

'That idea was as good as a promise,' put in Lucy sharply, 'and you should never go back on a promise.'

'Seems we're stuck,' said Pete.

'Reckon so,' agreed Rick. 'So we'll go ahead with it?' Following their unanimous vote of approval, he added, 'As soon as I know the date of our leave, I'll get things moving with the hotel.'

'And warn the crew beforehand,' urged Lucy, 'let them get organized and look forward to it. I hope everyone is as enthusiastic. It will be good to meet their wives and sweet-hearts. Have you ever met any of them before, Rick?'

'No. As you know, Don, Phil and Bob are the married ones. Who the others will have in tow, I don't know.'

'This is going to be fun,' said Lucy.

The following morning Rick was able to ascertain when their course would finish and their leave begin. In the afternoon, when they had completed the checks on their aircraft, ready for bombing practice at Wainfleet range, situated in the Wash close to the Lincolnshire coast, Rick put forward his idea which was received with general enthusiasm. During their flight, though, Bob had second thoughts. What would Rowena think? Would she be influenced by her mother? If she refused to come, what would he tell everyone? What would he do?

Two days later there was no flying so Rick and Pete took the opportunity to enquire early if there was any transport heading for Lincoln. Luck was on their side and they were walking into the hotel at twelve o'clock. With the transport returning at four they decided they would test the hotel by having lunch. Satisfied with everything there and the way their proposed booking was handled, they made the reservation for seven rooms.

Back at Swinderby they soon spread the word to the crew that the hotel was booked for two days from the start of their leave.

Letters were quickly written and posted.

A few days later Carolyn and Lucy received parcels which were ripped open by two young women eager to see what their mothers had sent in reply to their requests for dresses.

'That's a tricky number,' Lucy observed as Carolyn held up a yellow dress against herself to show off the wide shoulders tapering to a narrow waist from which the skirt flared slightly to knee length. 'That front panel of red catches the eye,' said Lucy. 'It'll certainly make Rick stare.'

'He can stare all he likes,' said Carolyn. 'Staring will get him nowhere.'

'Spoil-sport,' Lucy reprimanded her.

'And you behave yourself, my friend. Come the day I'm ordering a taxi to take you and me back to Swinderby, don't you try and disappear.'

Lucy held up her arms in surrender. 'OK, my friend, I know you have my welfare at heart. Thanks for reminding me that I shouldn't ruin it.' As she was talking she had unpacked an attractive pink blouse and a beautifully tailored gored skirt. 'Not quite what I had in mind for a party, but I think there's something else here.' She brought out another package, removed the tissue paper and held up a dark blue dress with silver pleated yokes at the waist and on the shoulders.

'Slip that on,' urged Carolyn.

Pleased to do so, Lucy smiled as she pulled the dress into shape.

'That's stunning,' Carolyn enthused, letting her eyes run down the buttoned front to the calf-length hem.

'I reckon you and I will dazzle a few eyes,' said Lucy. 'And no one's more than Rick's when he sees you in that gorgeous yellow dress.'

'Don't start that again,' warned Carolyn, with a flicker of a smile in which Lucy read that her friend enjoyed her banter, but she also knew that her friend, while enjoying herself, would draw up barriers.

Bob waited apprehensively for a letter. When it came he hurried to his billet to read it.

My dearest one,
    I'm going to have a baby! The result of the last time you were home. I hope you are pleased.
    Love,
    Rowena

Taken aback, he stared at his wife's message as all manner of thoughts vied with each other until his mind was filled with pure joy. He grabbed a pencil and paper and wrote:

My darling,

This news is so wonderful. I hope you think so too. A family – something I've never really known. What joy this can bring us. I look forward to a lifetime together with our – dare I say children rather than child?

This will have to be short; I have to be airborne in half an hour.

Take care of yourself and our child, my darling. We will celebrate at the party.

My love is yours,
Bob.

Four days later he stared at another letter from Rowena with a feeling of mounting disappointment. 'This is unbelievable,' he muttered to himself as the words he read tore into his mind, destroying all the dreams he had recently begun to harbour.

Dearest,

I am so happy you are pleased by my news. Like you, I look forward to a life-time together – the three of us.

I sat looking at those words for a while after I wrote them and I wondered if they would come true? I believe we can make them do just that if you shorten my chances of losing you by you resigning from aircrew. I know this might not suit you, but mother says you now have responsibilities, which you should take seriously and leave nothing to chance.

The letter went on in this vein. Bob's lips tightened further with every word he read. They were obviously prompted by his mother-in-law. 'The bitch! The bitch!' he said aloud. Finally he grasped a pencil and paper and wrote to his wife: '*NO! NO!*' In the way those two words stood out, stark with meaning, there was no mistaking that he refused to consider her request.

But that was not the end of the matter. Letters from her came day after day, pleading with him to reconsider.

I don't want to be left alone with a child to bring up. I need you here NOW, without the worry of what might happen to you . . .

I don't care what the other crew think of you. It's you I want safe and sound for the sake of our child . . .

If you don't resign, Mother says she will write to your Commanding Officer disclosing the circumstances and telling him you need to stop flying.

Bob stared at the stark words of this last letter. He knew with a heavy heart that he had lost. His mother-in-law would certainly carry out her threat and no doubt cook up a story that did not reflect well on him. He knew the CO would have to take her seriously and, even if Bob denied that he wanted to leave, the damage would be done. The CO would not allow a man with personal problems to threaten the safety of his crew.

In a daze Bob left the Sergeants' Mess where he had picked up his mail. He walked on, not sure where he was going until a voice trilled merrily, 'Good morning, Bob.'

He started. 'Oh. Sorry . . . good morning, Ma'am.'

Carolyn jumped off her bike. 'Goodness me, you are formal this morning.' She glanced around. 'There's no one else in sight. Besides, you know I don't stand on ceremony where Rick's crew is concerned. We're all friends, aren't we?'

'Maybe, but not for much longer,' muttered Bob.

'Hey, come on. You look like a dog that's lost its bone. What's wrong?'

Bob shrugged his shoulders.

'Let me help if I can?' offered Carolyn.

Bob stopped. Could this woman be a help? Was this the one person he could turn to? He had no family of his own to advise him. He had been dreading approaching Rick or any of his fellow crew.

He handed her Rowena's latest letter. Carolyn read it quickly then looked at him with sympathy in her face. They walked together, she pushing her bike as she listened to Bob unburden his soul.

'What should I do now?' he asked in a pleading tone.

'No one can really tell you that,' she said. 'You are the only one who knows the circumstances and the people concerned. All I can do is point some things out to you. If your mother-in-law takes this to the CO then everything will come out. He will have to take it seriously for the sake of morale, not only of your crew but of the whole station. If he judges that your resignation is required, he will certainly want to play it down – I don't think he would command a parade for the whole unit to witness you being stripped of your sergeant's stripes and aircrew brevet. Those days are gone.

'You will be shipped quietly away to a unit that deals with these sort of problems. You may end up doing menial jobs around some RAF unit or you may be sent to work down the mines. You will be stigmatized by many as Lacking Moral Fibre. Whatever you decide, you'll have to cope with what happens. I can't see you side-stepping in any way the dilemma you are in. Your mother-in-law has you well and truly in a cleft stick.' Carolyn gave a grimace. 'I hope I have

111

helped by talking so frankly. I'm sorry I can't be more positive than this.'

'I have no one else to turn to. I'm glad you happened to come along. You have a sympathetic ear and you have helped. I know now what I will say to Rick. Please don't mention this to him, will you?'

'Bob, I won't say a word. This is between you and him. But he should be told before anyone else.'

'We are due to fly at three this afternoon, high-level bombing practice. I could be excused as it has nothing to do with gunners but I'll go up for one last time with the crew and store up some memories of what might have been with a grand set of lads.' Bob's lips tightened, and then he said, 'Thanks, Carolyn.'

He walked away and with a sad heart she watched him go, lamenting the way he had been manipulated by his mother-in-law but admiring his love for Rowena, which she hoped would strengthen him against the humiliation he would inevitably have to face.

Shortly before three o'clock Rick Wood, from the cockpit of the Stirling bomber that had been retired from front line duties to serve at the HCU at Swinderby, called up each of his crew members in turn. Each replied promptly that they were in position for take-off. He brought more power to the four engines and, when the instruments showed the correct figure, released the brakes that were holding back the Stirling. The aircraft began to roll forward.

From the outside balcony of the Control Tower, Carolyn watched the aircraft gather speed. Faster and faster. She gripped the iron railing until her knuckles showed white. These were the most anxious moments. Lift-off. The Stirling gained height as Rick adjusted his flight. The aircraft banked to port, climbing steadily. Carolyn relaxed. 'Enjoy your last flight, Bob Jeffers,' she said to herself, and then continued silently to wish him well through the troubled time ahead.

One hour later Rick made a perfect landing and taxied to the hard standing reserved for this aircraft. Just before the plane came to rest he called his crew on the intercom. 'Hang around when you get outside, I want a word with you all.'

Wondering what this was about, they scrambled out of the Stirling. Bob was nervous; had Carolyn spoken to Rick?

'OK, chaps, gather round. First of all, you'll all be pleased to hear that our training is officially over.'

Cheers rang around the little group under the shadow of the Stirling's wings.

'What now, Skipper?' asked Tim Myers.

'Leave. The party's all fixed, then home. Posting to a squadron when we report back here.'

'Which one, Skip?' asked Gordon, the wireless operator.

'We'll learn that when we return.'

As they headed for the crew rooms, Bob said quietly to Rick, 'Can I have a word, Skipper, please?'

Detecting a nervous tremor in Bob's voice, Rick looked questioningly at his rear-gunner. 'Sure, Bob.' They drifted away from the rest of the crew who took no notice of them; it had happened to them all on different occasions with different queries while under training.

Bob had decided to come straight to the point, but even so the words were out almost before he realized what he was saying. 'Skipper, I'm resigning from aircrew.'

Rick froze in mid-step. He stared unbelievingly at his rear-gunner. There were times he had seen unease in Bob but he had never thought it would lead to this – and on the day they were finished at HCU, with squadron life so near. He couldn't let this shattering declaration stop that.

113

'I'm sorry, Rick. There is nothing I can do about it.'

'What the hell do you mean? Of course you can do something about it! You're a good gunner, you fit in well with the crew, and, though I have detected some unease in you at times, I always took your word that all was well. I don't believe you are lacking in moral fibre. What has happened, Bob?'

The rear-gunner explained his situation as quickly and as clearly as he could. He concluded by saying, 'I have spoken with Section Officer Maddison about it. She's been friendly with the crew and when I met her this morning, shortly after I received that last letter, I just poured my heart out. She did not persuade me one way or the other but talking with her led to my decision. She let me see that I was in an impossible situation and that this would be the least harmful way out for everybody.' He went on with his explanation and finished with a heartfelt, 'I am so sorry, Rick.'

He nodded sympathetically and took matters over. 'We must see the CO immediately. If possible I want this solving before our leave. Come on.'

They hurried towards the admin block where thankfully they found the adjutant. A quick explanation brought an immediate reaction. Knowing his CO was on the telephone to Group Headquarters, the adjutant scribbled a few words on a piece of paper, entered the CO's office, placed the note in front of him and left to return to his own office.

In less than two minutes the connecting door burst open and the CO, brandishing the adjutant's note, stormed in. 'What the devil's this about, Sergeant Jeffers?' he demanded, furious that this last minute problem had been thrust upon him. 'Has a yellow streak come out?'

Bob was stung by the implication. 'No, sir,' he answered sharply. 'I am no coward!'

The CO brandished the note. 'Resign from aircrew when

114

you are on the point of joining a squadron? It looks like a clear case of LMF to me.'

'Sir,' put in the adjutant quickly, 'I think you should hear Sergeant Jeffers's explanation.'

'Get on with it then! Time is in short supply – and now you land this problem on me.'

But as Bob explained his dilemma, he could see understanding and sympathy in the CO's expression.

'Very well, Jeffers, if you want me to confront your mother-in-law, I will do so.'

'No, sir, that will only make things more difficult for me and my wife. I think it wisest if you accept my resignation.'

'Do you fully understand what this will mean for you?'

'Yes, sir, loss of my stripes, loss of my aircrew brevet and status, menial jobs at some no doubt remote RAF station . . . or sent down the mines and branded a coward by many.'

'And you are willing to accept all that?'

'Yes, sir, reluctantly.'

'Then you are a brave man.' He gave Bob a curt nod which betrayed mingled annoyance and pity. 'You'll be posted out of here today. You'll have no contact with any aircrew. You'll be sent to a disciplinary unit instantly to await your fate.' He turned to his adjutant. 'You know the procedure. Get Jeffers off the site immediately. '

As the adjutant marched Bob out of the room, the CO picked up the phone and instructed the operator to put him through to the gunnery leader.

In a matter of moments the call came in. 'Tommy, have you a spare gunner available?' he asked.

'Yes, sir. A month ago a crew went missing over the Hebrides. The rear-gunner, Sergeant Mark Jardine, was ill and had been stood down. He's been here since he recovered, hoping for a vacancy in another crew. '

'Good. Get yourself and Sergeant Jardine down here right away.'

'Yes, sir.'

The CO looked at Rick. 'Are you happy with this, Wood?'

'I'm not happy that Jeffers is leaving us, sir. He is a good gunner. But if that is how he wants it, I accept his decision and am perfectly happy about having Jardine join my crew. I've heard talk about him from my mid-upper gunner, and it's all been good.'

'Are you happy with the rest of your crew?' the CO asked as they awaited the arrival of the gunnery officer and Sergeant Jardine.

'Yes, sir,' replied Rick. 'They're a good bunch.'

The CO glanced at a piece of paper on his desk. 'I see you have just completed your training. You'll have your leave and then you'll be moving on.'

'Yes, sir. May I ask which squadron we will be joining?'

The CO gave a light smile. 'You may ask, but although I know the answer, I cannot tell you; that's an order passed down from Group HQ. You'll have to wait until you come back off leave, and even then you might be waiting here until clearance is approved. Sorry I cannot tell you any more.'

'Thank you, sir.'

The conversation was ended by a tap on the door and the appearance of the adjutant. 'Everything is underway regarding Jeffers, sir. And Gunnery Officer Squires and Sergeant Jardine are reporting.'

'Good, show them in.' He glanced at Rick and said quickly, 'Keep mum about Jeffers. Say he's been invalided out.'

'Yes, sir.

The adjutant brought the gunnery officer and Sergeant Jardine to the CO.

'As of now, Sergeant, you will be a member of Flying Officer Wood's crew.'

'Yes, sir,' said Sergeant Mark Jardine with a smile.

'That seems to please you, Sergeant?'

'It does, sir. I don't like hanging around as a spare bod. If any crew is short of a gunner, I'll take it!'

'Good man, you should fit in well with Flying Officer Wood's crew.' The CO gave a little nod of dismissal but indicated to the gunnery officer and the adjutant to wait.

Rick and his new crew member sprang to attention, saluted smartly, and with the CO's final words ringing in their ears – 'Good luck to you and your crew' – left the office.

Once outside the Admin block, pilot and gunner shook hands.

'Welcome to my crew, Mark. You're joining it when we're about to go on leave.'

'That's a good start for me.' He grinned.

'And you've hit a crew party to start our leave.'

'Even better.'

Rick explained what had been organized. 'So in four days' time we'll meet at the hotel. Where are you from, Mark?'

'My family have moved around due to the nature of my dad's job: inspector of works for a large electrical company that was expanding when war broke out. It was switched to war requirements. My dad wanted to jack it in to go into the RAF but his work was deemed essential to the war effort. Don't ask me what he does. His lips are sealed on that topic.'

'Must be vital war work,' said Rick.

'I suppose so. His desire to be in aircrew is being fulfilled through me. I hope I don't let him down.'

'I'm sure you won't.'

'What happened to the bod I'm replacing?'

'Illness. That's a closed shop, Mark. Leave it at that.'

'OK, Skipper. To finish my potted biography, at present Mum lives in Coldstream in the Scottish Borders. I have two sisters, Jean who's sixteen and still at school and Maisie who's eighteen and applying to join the WAAFs.'

'Have you any girlfriends?'

'No one steady, though I have been seeing a girl in Lincoln since I got stuck at Swinderby, Joan Franklin.'

'Bring her along to the party.'

'Can I, without you meeting her first?'

Rick laughed. 'Hey, the love-life of those who fly with me is their own affair. So long as it doesn't interfere with the crew's effectiveness.'

'OK, Skip, I'll bring Joan along.'

'Good. Let's go and find the rest of the crew and get you introduced. They're going to get a surprise when I bring you into the fold.'

'They don't know?' Mark showed genuine surprise.

'No. They won't have an inkling that Bob has left us. It all blew up after we landed today.'

Rick and Mark found the rest of the crew in the locker room awaiting their skipper's arrival, as was their custom after any flying.

'Listen up, fellas. Bob has left the crew due to illness. Mark Jardine here will be taking his place.'

This unexpected information brought gasps of disbelief and expressions of shock. Questions began to fly.

'Hold on, hold on!' shouted Rick. 'I cannot go into details ... just accept that we will see no more of Bob. A new gunner, Mark Jardine, was allocated to us immediately. We are fortunate that Mark has been acting as a spare bod, due to losing his crew when he was not flying with them. I know

118

there will be questions in all your minds. Just forget them and accept the change as it stands. That is where the future of this crew lies. Mark is part of us now. You can get to know him better at the party; he will be there with his girlfriend, Joan Franklin, who lives in Lincoln.' Rick held up his hands. 'No more questions, please.'

'Just one, Skipper, nothing to do with the surprise you've just sprung. Have you learned which squadron we will be joining?'

'Sorry, I haven't. We have to wait until we return from our leave. First, the party in four days' time.'

12

'Get word to Swinderby that I want Section Officers Maddison and Gaston here in my office at two-thirty tomorrow afternoon. Say nothing about anything else.'

'Yes, Ma'am,' replied Flight Officer Newbauld in answer to Group Officer Pearson's order.

'Section Officer Vera Williams will be arriving from training at Medmenham today. Have all her reports, and those of Maddison and Gaston, since they joined up, on my desk by eleven this morning.

'Very good, Ma'am.'

When they received the order Carolyn and Lucy raised their eyebrows at one another.

'I hope it means something is in the offing for us, said Lucy. 'It's three weeks since we completed those individual assignments.'

'It was very nice having two weeks' leave,' said Carolyn, 'but I wish we knew what she has learned from separating us. It might give an indication of what we will be doing next.'

'I think that's why she wants to see us. There's something in the wind.'

'I wish it would blow hard enough to send decisions our way.'

'It's no good speculating,' said Lucy. 'Nor about what's up with Rick's crew.'

'Hmm,' agreed Carolyn. Though she had a shrewd suspicion she already knew. They can be as tight as clams when they want to be.'

'It might be their posting,' said Lucy. 'I'll miss them when they go.'

'Especially Pete, I suppose?' said Carolyn.

'Won't it be the same for you with Rick?'

'Of course not. He's attentive and he's fun but . . . '

'Oh, come off it, Carolyn. He wouldn't look at you the way he does if he weren't smitten and you hadn't encouraged him.'

'I've never encouraged him,' protested Carolyn.

'I don't think he sees it that way.'

Carolyn waved her hand dismissively. 'He'll be posted some time and that will be that.'

'We'll see. A posting doesn't have to mean the end of a relationship.'

When they met Rick and Pete in the Mess for their evening meal, Rick had a quick word in private with Carolyn. 'Thanks for speaking to Bob. It turned out for the best, though I'm sorry for him. We got a replacement right away. Mark and his girlfriend will be at the party.'

'Good. Put it behind you, Rick. It mustn't affect your flying.'

He gave her a little smile. 'It won't. But thanks for the thought.'

As they settled for their evening meal at a table for four, Lucy commented, 'There are rumours running wild around Swinderby.'

'Don't you two look so innocent . . . it's a giveaway that

you know something,' pressed Carolyn, eyeing the two men with a challenge in her eyes, trying to draw information from them.

Rick and Pete exchanged conspiratorial glances and a little nod of agreement passed between them.

The two of them leaned forward, glancing around to make sure there was no one too near. Rick lowered his voice. 'I suppose it will all be out tomorrow. I'm surprised it hasn't been bandied around already.' He glanced at Pete who nodded. 'We have a party to attend and are going on leave after that.'

'And?' put in Carolyn sharply.

'That's it.'

'Come on,' rapped Lucy. 'You have more to tell us than that.'

Rick looked at Pete who pulled a rueful expression.'

'Honestly, Lucy, we haven't,' said Rick, with all the seriousness he could muster. Then he added, 'It's true, believe me. We won't know any more until we return from leave.'

Carolyn eyed him and then said, 'Lucy, I think he's telling the truth.'

'Would I lie to the two most charming WAAFs on this station?' he asked.

'I sincerely hope you wouldn't,' said Carolyn.

'So leg-pulling is permitted?' asked Peter.

Lucy gave him a cuff on the shoulder. 'All right, let's eat.'

As they settled in the ante-room with their coffee, Lucy looked at Carolyn and said, 'Should we tell them our bit of news, but straight from the shoulder – no leg pulling?'

'I suppose we should,' Carolyn agreed.

"Well?' prompted Pete when they still hesitated.

'We've been summoned to Group Headquarters tomorrow.'

'What for?'

'We were just told to report to Group Officer Pearson.'

'Must be important.'

'I think we've served our time here so it could mean a posting.'

'If it does, avoid moving before the party if you can,' said Rick.

'We'll be there, don't worry. After all, we wouldn't want to disappoint two handsome RAF officers, would we?' quipped Lucy

'I hope not.'

'If we are all moving on, we must keep in touch,' added Rick. 'It's been great sharing time with you.'

'It sure has,' agreed Pete. He leaned closer to Lucy and whispered, 'Walk you home?'

She smiled encouragingly. 'It's not far to my billet.'

'How far?' he asked, the twinkle in his eyes teasing her.

'As far as we like to make it,' she replied.

'Then let's see how far that is.'

'See you sometime,' said Lucy interrupting the other two's conversation as she got to her feet and left with Pete.

A silence fell between Rick and Carolyn. There were only two other officers left in the Mess and they were fast asleep. The wireless had been left on low. The tune ended and a moment later Bing Crosby's voice floated gently across the room. Rick sang quietly with him:

Do I want to be with you?
As the years come and go?

Rick slid his hand into Carolyn's. She did not pull away as the tune went on.

'Nice,' she whispered dreamily.

'And for me it's true,' said Rick, with feeling in his voice.

As he leaned towards her he cast a quick look at the sleepers then he kissed Carolyn, letting his lips linger on hers for a few seconds.

She still held his hand even as she said, 'Rick, you're a nice man. I have loved sharing time with you but we are soon to part. After losing Charlie and seeing that crash, I don't think I could go into a serious relationship. Our lives hover on the brink of the unknown. Let's just keep in touch and enjoy our friendship.' She could see disappointment clouding his eyes. 'Please, Rick,' she put in quickly before he said any more.

He gave her a tender smile as he said, 'Who could refuse anything to such a wonderful person as you?' He kissed her again, more passionately this time. 'Remember me. And pray for my crew.'

'You needn't ask that. Of course I will.'

He rose from his chair then and held out his hand to her. 'I'll walk you home.' Then he added, 'I'm still hopeful I might change your mind one day.'

It was a very thoughtful Carolyn who lay down to sleep that night, with Rick's and Bing Crosby's words still in her mind.

Lucy hugged herself when she snuggled down in bed, recalling Pete's kisses, hoping that their postings would not place them too far apart.

As the Humber Hawk left Swinderby for St Vincent's at Grantham, Lucy commented, 'What's in store for us if we are getting this treatment?'

'We'll soon know. Group Officer Pearson's not one to beat about the bush.'

'I have persuaded the powers that be to let me establish, among other things, an Intelligence section devoted solely to

5 Group because its bomber force is likely often to operate independently of the main force,' the group officer told them. 'Part of my reorganization will be an Intelligence section of our own, concentrating on the group's demands. We will gather our own information for the operations this group will pursue independently. If necessary, intelligence would be exchanged between us and Bomber Command.' She left a little pause. 'I am impressed by the reports of your progress throughout your training. Now I want you both to reorganize the Intelligence section along the lines I will discuss with you, but I also want your individual inputs for the betterment of the section, which will ultimately be for the benefit of all the crews within the group.

'You will both have immediate promotion to flight officer with a review of the situation in three months. You will have two leading aircraftwomen under your command, one corporal and one sergeant. You will also have a section officer who has been trained as a specialist in photographic analysis. All of them have been vetted for work in Intelligence. Now, have you any questions before I introduce you to Section Officer Vera Williams who, incidentally, will carry the same rank as you when she is promoted at the same time.'

'Ma'am, I thank you for this wonderful opportunity,' said Lucy.

'And I echo that, Ma'am,' added Carolyn.

Group Officer Pearson rang a bell. The door opened. A petite section officer walked smartly in and made an immaculate salute. She wore her uniform as if it was made to measure and with an air of self-assurance she had adopted when she gained her commission. Even at five foot four she seemed to fill the room with her presence, well aware that she could beguile men just by being herself: an attractive, well-presented twenty-two year old, with a mesmerizing smile, sparking eyes and enticing lips.

Carolyn and Lucy rose from their chairs and the group officer came out from behind her desk to make the introductions.

'Williams, these are the two officers with whom you will be working. You will be promoted to flight officer along with them, with immediate effect. You will all be posted to Waddington where I have had extensive alterations made to your living quarters and workplace. I want you installed and ready to work by the week after next. The time between now and then is yours, to get settled in and take some leave. Flight Officer Newbauld will issue you with travel warrants.' She rang the bell and moments later Flight Officer Newbauld came in.

'Newbauld, you are authorized to issue travel warrants if any of these officers require them. I will sign one in the name of Squadron Officer Newbauld.'

'Yes Ma'am' ... ' The word fading on her lips, she looked with astonishment at her superior.

The group officer smiled at her. 'You heard correctly. Your promotion is as of now. Your replacement will be reporting here in an hour for you to familiarize her with my methods. Your role from now on will be to act as my liaison, based at Waddington with these three and the staff I am installing. To all four of you, I say: make this work. It will be a great asset to the Group. Now go away and report back to me at two-thirty, two weeks today.'

They all came smartly to attention, saluted and left the group officer.

In Newbauld's office congratulations were exchanged all round and she said, 'The office next door will be empty for the next hour so, let's go in there.'

They made themselves comfortable at one end of the oval table that occupied the centre of the room. Several photographs of RAF bombers were hanging on the recently painted walls between the three windows.

As senior squadron officer, Newbauld took charge. 'I think, since we are going to be working closely together, it would be a good idea for each of us to say a little about our life. And it will make for easier relationships if we use Christian names amongst ourselves.' She glanced round them, received no dissent and added, 'Then I'll begin. I am Kate Newbauld, twenty-eight, from Norfolk. My family have an estate near Burnham Market. I had a comfortable life and my parents encouraged me to take an interest in the estate along with my brother Roddy who is two years older than me. When war broke out, he was off to sea. At the moment he is serving on destroyers, protecting North Sea convoys. I wasn't going to be left behind, so here I am. I came into Admin and I moved around until Group Officer Pearson picked me out to serve as her secretary, and that has led to where I am today. May I add, as I finish, that she is a stickler for people being on top of their jobs and won't tolerate any slip-ups unless they are unavoidable. You'll find her fair and understanding otherwise.' She glanced at the others. 'Now you, Carolyn.'

She gave her potted biography succinctly, as did Lucy.

'Now you Vera,' said Kate.

'I am twenty-two and come from Garstang, a small village near Preston in Lancashire. I'm the youngest of four children. I had a happy childhood until I was fifteen when my father left my mother. We were devastated because he had, to all appearances, been devoted to her, but there were undercurrents we knew nothing about. My mother struggled to keep the situation from us but when I was fifteen she realized I was old enough to be told. My eldest sister was eighteen and my brothers, Dane and Scot, seventeen and sixteen. Then the war came and we saw we could relieve Mother of much worry by volunteering for military service. Here I am.'

'Which occupations did the others choose?' Lucy asked.

'Rhoda chose the Wrens, Dane and Scot the Navy.'

'And you were the only one to choose the WAAFs,' commented Lucy.

'Yes,' replied Vera, and added with a smile, 'I thought the uniform looked the smartest.'

'There are those who would disagree, said Kate, 'but I think you are right.'

The others added their approval.

'And with a bit of unofficial titivating, our officer's uniform can look really attractive,' said Vera.

'I didn't hear that,' said Kate in a superior officer's tone accompanied by a mischievous twitch of her lips. 'Right, what do you all want to do now?'

'I'd like to go to Waddington, give our billets and the station the once over, and then maybe take some of that leave,' said Carolyn.

Lucy and Vera agreed.

'Right,' said Kate. 'That suits me. I'll see if I can lay-on transport for us, with a call at Swinderby to pick up necessities for a stay at Waddington. We'll have to be back here in two weeks whatever we do. I'll see if transport will play ball.' She got up and headed for the door. 'I'll be back in a few minutes.'

She was as good as her word and reported, 'They were a little reluctant to oblige at first, but as soon as I mentioned my request was in conjunction with orders from Group Officer Pearson they fell over backwards to organize it.

There will be a car here in ten minutes. I've popped in to tell the group officer what our plans are.'

As they were preparing to leave St Vincent's, Lucy took a moment for a quiet word with Carolyn. 'Do you think we ought to ask Kate and Vera to the party?'

'Why not? The more the merrier. But be aware that Vera's competition.'

They left St Vincent's, made a call at Swinderby, picked up the minimum requirements and went on to Waddington, where Kate was quickly in contact with the WAAF admin officer, who welcomed them.

'We have been working to carry out Group Officer Pearson's requirements for three weeks. Your billets are ready so you can use them whenever you like. Are you intending to stay on now?'

Kate explained the situation and their plans for the next fortnight.

'Very well. But while you are here I'll show you your quarters.'

As they walked she explained, 'As I thought you were to be a conclave on your own, I had one of the billets converted for your exclusive use. It is the hut type with four individual rooms. It had six but I had two knocked into one so you could also have a communal room, should you need it. The ablutions are at one end. Two batwomen will look after you.'

They were nearing the hut when Carolyn spoke up. 'There seems to be a distict lack of aircraft for an operational station.'

'Interesting you noticed,' returned the admin officer. 'Normally we have a full complement but there've been comings and goings lately. We might even have more crews than aircraft at the moment. Bombers are being flown in, and then after a little while flown out by a scratch crew. I've no idea what is going on. It's a situation where rumours can generate but I ignore them. They are very rarely right, and everything will doubtless come out in the wash.'

After she had shown them to the billets, she said, 'So, welcome to RAF Waddington. 'I hope you will be happy with us here. Just one more thing. We are very near Lincoln. If ever you are travelling on, it's always worth checking if our transport section has a vehicle going into town. Make yourselves at home.'

They quickly sorted themselves out, commenting that their rooms were better than expected and the beds, though of the standard iron issue, comfortable enough.

'The only thing is, it'll be cold in winter. They've been good enough to put the old cast-iron stove in the communal room, but I'm going to bring an extra blanket or two from home,' said Vera. 'I feel the cold.'

When she was sure Kate and Vera were in their rooms. Lucy knocked gently on Carolyn's door, tentatively opened it, and slipped quickly inside.

'What's your feeling about Vera?' she asked.

'She's very pleasant but we haven't seen enough to form an opinion yet,' replied Carolyn.

'True, she oozes charm and doesn't hold back, does she? Those sultry dark eyes,' Lucy observed. 'As my mum would say, "She's all there with her hat on."'

'I agree she has an attractive sparkle about her but all that concerns us is her effectiveness. She's been brought in as a specialist. So as long as we gel together, that's all that matters. Now, are you ready for something to eat?'

'Raring to go. Give the other two a knock.'

The four of them headed for the Mess, got some drinks at the bar and took them into the dining room. When they had settled with their meal, Carolyn broached the subject of the party.

Immediately the invitation was made, Vera enthusiastically agreed. 'I feel part of you and this crew already. Thanks a bundle.' She added quickly, 'Are you sure it will be all right with the crew?'

'We wouldn't have asked you if we weren't,' replied Lucy. 'Besides, Carolyn can twist the pilot round her little finger.'

'Oh, do I smell romance here?' queried Vera with a twinkle in her eye.

Carolyn gave her friend a sharp glance of annoyance and said, 'Lucy's good at reading things into situations that aren't there. This crew are at Swinderby where we got to know them. They will be moving on after their leave, so our paths will diverge.' To stop any more query and conjecture, she turned to Kate. 'What about you? Are you a party person?'

'I love them but these dates won't suit. Group Officer Pearson had already arranged for us to attend a gathering of Group bigwigs before these latest developments were put into place. I can't get out of it. Another time, if you'll ask me.'

13

Squadron Officer Kate Newbauld shrugged herself into her greatcoat, looked in the mirror, adjusted her hat and picked up her briefcase in which she carried her notes and personal requirements for a three-night stay at St Vincent's. She went out into the corridor and knocked on three doors.

'I'm off,' she said when Carolyn, Lucy and Vera appeared. 'Have a good party. I want to hear what I've missed when I'm back. And best of luck to the crew. Maybe our paths will cross sometime.'

The three WAAFs wished her well, and when one of the batwomen opened the hut door and announced that a staff car was approaching everyone went outside and gave Kate a royal send off.

As they trooped back inside Lucy said, 'What now?'

'I'm going to the Mess to see if the mail is in. I'm expecting something,' said Vera.

'May as well come with you, though I'm not expecting anything,' said Carolyn.

'Nothing for me,' moaned Lucy, when they reached the Mess.

'You can't grumble. You got three yesterday,' Vera pointed out.

'Nothing for me either,' declared Carolyn. 'You're the lucky one, Vera.'

She was ripping her envelope open. 'Yipee!' she yelled. 'Mum's come up trumps!' She brandished something in her hand. 'Clothes coupons!'

'For the party?' Lucy queried.

'Yes. When I rang Mum and asked her to send me one of my dresses for the party, she said to leave it to her. Come on, let's see what Lincoln has to offer. You can help me choose something. I'll treat you to lunch, or we can make a day of it ... have something more substantial and take in the cinema.'

'We'll decide as the day goes on,' suggested Lucy.

The other two agreed.

Their luck was in. They reached the airfield gates just as an RAF transport vehicle had to stop for the barrier.

'Going into Lincoln, Ma'ams?' the driver, a middle-aged corporal, called out.

'Thanks, Corporal,' Vera replied as they all squeezed in beside him.

'Have you been at Waddington long, Corporal?' asked Carolyn as they set off.

'Three years, Ma'am.'

'You'll have seen a lot of changes then.'

'I have, Ma'am. None more so than what is going on now.'

'A lot of building.'

'Yes, and that tells me there's going to be big intake of personnel.' He shot the three of them a quick glance and could tell they were hanging on for more information. 'Are you new here?'

'Yes, Corporal, some of those new buildings must be for us.'

'If so, you must be starting a permanent posting. Maybe in connection with the new runways they are putting down instead of the grass, and from my experience that would indicate heavier bombers than the Hampdens we have had here.' Realising he might be saying too much, he allowed the conversation to drift. 'Are you ladies staying in Lincoln long?' he asked when he pulled up near the station. 'If you want a lift back to base, I'll be leaving from here at five o'clock.'

'Thanks, Corporal,' said Lucy. 'Our day isn't planned but we'll bear that in mind. Don't hang around if we aren't here at five. We'll find our own way back.'

He picked up a card from a holder in the door. 'You can always get a taxi if you ring that number.'

As they walked away from the station, Vera called out in a cheerful tone, 'Dress shops, here we come.'

Two hours later she said, 'Hey, I'm spoiling your day. I should make up my mind.' Then added with a sigh, 'I think I still prefer the first dress we saw.'

'Then let's get back and see if it's still there,' cajoled Lucy.

'Hello again,' greeted the assistant in the dress shop. 'I thought you might be back.'

As she was talking she lifted a hanger from a rack and held it out at arms length to show off the dress that had attracted Vera. The light green rayon crepe with a yoke of fuchsia sequins and a cyclamen coloured sash dazzled her once again. So she went to try it on.

'Is it for an RAF party?' queried the assistant as they awaited Vera's grand entrance.

'Yes, some of us are moving on,' replied Carolyn.

The curtain was pushed back and Vera stepped out and did an exaggerated twirl, smiling expectantly for their approval.

'Wow!' gasped Lucy.

'It's just you,' said Carolyn.

'You'll send the RAF boys into a spin!' commented the assistant.

The deal was done and Vera insisted they should celebrate with the best tea they could find.

On waking early the following morning Vera looked out of her window to see an early-morning mist lying across the silent airfield. She gave a satisfied nod. This would clear and leave a fine day, the perfect prelude to the party. Excitement sparked between the three friends throughout the rest of the day, heightening at lunchtime when, on entering the Mess, the steward informed Carolyn, 'Ma'am, there was a phone call for you. Would you ring this number?' He passed her a piece of paper. She glanced at it and immediately went to make the call.

'I have ordered a taxi to pick the three of you up at Waddington at five o'clock,' Rick informed her. 'I've also persuaded the hotel manager to give the ladies in our party exclusive use of one of the Ladies' Rooms, so you'll have a changing room and your dresses won't get crumpled in the taxi.'

'Oh, Rick, thank you. That is so thoughtful.'

'I wanted you to look your best. Must go, things to attend to. See you later.'

The girls were waiting in the guard-room at the main entrance when the taxi arrived promptly. On the journey into Lincoln they bubbled over with excitement, speculating about the crew's wives and girlfriends. With late passes signed by Squadron Officer Newbauld in their pockets, they arranged with the taxi to collect them at one-thirty in the morning.

As they entered the hotel Rick was there to greet them.

'You are nearly the first,' he told them. 'Tim and his girl-friend arrived about ten minutes ago. Your changing room is on the first floor.'

'Thanks, Rick,' they chorused, 'we'll not be long.'

Excited banter criss-crossed the room as the girls changed, helped with adjusting dresses, and sparingly applied their almost unattainable make-up until they felt ready to present themselves.

Peter was crossing the hall, heading for the lounge, when they appeared on the stairs. He came to a sudden wide-eyed halt. And gulped.

'Who are you?' His words tumbled out.

'Carolyn ... Lucy ... Vera.' They each announced their name, one after the other, as they reached the bottom of the stairs.

'No, no.' He shook his head. 'They're WAAFs, not ... '

'You'll have to take us as we are,' laughed Lucy.

'I'll certainly do that. You all look gorgeous.'

'Where's Rick?' asked Carolyn.

'He went to check something with the manager.'

Lucy noted a glint of disappointment in Carolyn's eyes, but almost immediately it was gone when Rick walked in. He stopped to view the scene. 'Goodness me, we've got our own film stars here.'

The three girls each struck an exaggerated pose then broke down into laughter.

'Come on, meet Tim's girlfriend Zoe,' said Rick. When Lucy linked arms with Pete, Rick arched both his arms and announced, 'I'm the lucky one. I have two dazzling beauties to escort.'

When they entered the lounge they were greeted by a round-faced, rosy-cheeked person whose complexion needed no make-up. Her wine-coloured dress swept off the shoulders

136

to a tight waist then flared a little to calf-length. An attractive marcasite brooch in the shape of a lizard became a talking point as they learned Zoe was working in the Land Army in North Lincolnshire. Her friendliness helped to set the tone for the rest of the evening as the remainder of the crew arrived with wives and girlfriends. Everyone introduced themselves and mingled happily.

Rick found an opportunity to sound out Peter's opinion. 'Happy about how the party's going?'

'It's splendid,' he returned. 'Everybody's in the mood. They are all getting on well. Bringing in wives and girl-friends has made us all so much closer. Now we know how everyone ticks, we can stop worrying.'

Rick looked relieved to hear this.

Conversation flowed, jokes were shared, and the convivial atmosphere continued during the meal, the variety of dishes surprising everyone considering there was rationing.

As they were drifting away from the dining room, music started to filter through from the next room.

'Ambrose!' Someone identified the band-leader's noted tempo.

'Records for dancing,' called Pete.

As Rick took Carolyn's arm, she said, 'Before you ask me to dance, can I have a word?'

'This sounds serious,' he countered.

'The party is a great idea, the atmosphere is terrific, but before we get swept away by it all I want to clear up matters between us. I think a lot of you, Rick, but I don't want you to expect more from me than friendship. You know how I feel about getting serious and why, so please don't crowd me on this.'

The serious, deliberate tone of her voice brought dis-appointment to his face. He bit back the sharp retort that had come to his lips. Harsh words could not be taken back. Rick did not want this conversation to go on. This was not the place. He did not want the party spoiling for everyone.

'If that is the way you want it then so be it,' he said coolly. He began to turn away but stopped. 'The posting will be taking me away anyway. Who knows what lies ahead? Maybe your attitude is for the best. Wherever life takes you I wish you well.'

He went through to the bar and ordered a large whisky. After drinking half of it in one mouthful he wandered miserably over to the dance floor where a record of Lew Stone's band was in full swing with a foxtrot.

Dresses swirled in a colourful kaleidoscope, but Rick stared morosely into his glass.

He felt a gentle touch on his arm. 'You can't stand there alone, looking like that. Dance with me.' Vera's sultry voice held promise and her smile threw out a challenge.

There could be only one answer. 'It will be a pleasure.' He drained his glass, put it down on a table, and, with Vera in his arms, glided across the floor to the rhythm of the music.

'You're not a bad dancer,' she murmured in his ear.

He rose to the praise and eased her closer. She moulded herself to him and they danced as if they could go on forever. The rhythm of the music surged through them. They pressed closer still. Vera wanted to be sure Rick would remember this dance.

Carolyn, who was talking to Phil Stevens and his wife Myrna, was aware of Vera and Rick, flirting and laughing together. She felt a little surge of jealousy but chided herself for that. After all, she had warned Rick not to expect anything but friendship from her.

A waltz started.

'Phil, I'm sure Carolyn would like to dance,' prompted Myrna. She looked at Carolyn, 'Although I say it, he is a wonderful dancer.'

Phil smiled at Carolyn. 'You've been shanghaied into this.' As they moved on to the floor he added, 'You are no novice either from what I've seen earlier this evening.'

'I don't know about that, but I have always liked dancing, and I have a brother who would always partner me from a young age.'

'Then you were fortunate.'

They did not speak for a few moments. Phil sensed a dance-floor partnership. He gave a little smile. 'Let's show them a step or two!'

Her answer was a little nod. Within a few moments he had tested her ability to follow him through two or three intricacies and, knowing she would match him, put on a performance that had others stopping to watch them. As Carolyn floated past Rick and Vera, she felt dagger glares from Vera, who had been quite happy to parade Rick in front of her. When the record finished everyone clapped and enthused about the performance.

'Can we beat that?' said Vera, her words heavy with challenge.

'Sure we can,' Rick laughed, and immediately as a quick-step struck up he was crossing the floor with dazzling footsteps.

Phil was tempted to compete but instead leaned closer to Carolyn and said, 'I don't think we had better show the skipper that he's not in the same league as us.'

She said, 'I think you're right. Let's leave things as they are.' She fell into conversation with Myrna, and Phil with Peter, who had brought Lucy to join them.

Rick had thrown off his thoughts of what might have been

with Carolyn and believed he had found a new beauty, someone of his own opinion who would live for today and let tomorrow take care of itself.

As the evening settled down, Lucy noticed that Carolyn and Rick had not danced together. Taking an opportunity when Peter went to replenish their drinks, she had a word with Carolyn.

'You haven't danced with Rick. Is everything all right?'

'Yes, Lucy, I've had a word with him, that's all. Told him I don't want to get serious. Please let's leave it at that.'

As Lucy went to rejoin Peter her thoughts were on her best friend; she wanted the future to be bright for Carolyn who, it seemed to her, was letting the past influence her unduly.

Nobody wanted this party to end, but it had to. The signal for that was the arrival of the taxi for the WAAF officers at one-thirty.

Everyone gathered outside to see them off amid calls of:

'Have a good leave.'

'See you soon.'

'Great party.'

'Don't do anything I wouldn't do.'

Rick's last word to Carolyn were accompanied by a look in which there was a flicker of hope. 'Only for ever,' he whispered.

Vera was standing close enough to Carolyn to catch her reply. 'Don't keep your hopes too high, Rick, please. Don't tempt fate. You know why I . . .' The rest of her words were lost, but Vera had heard enough.

They piled into the taxi, without worrying about crumpling their dresses, and gave one last cheer as it drove away,

'Sounds like you had a good night,' commented the driver.

'We did,' said Vera brightly. 'We could do no other with a crew like that.'

The happy mood continued all the way back to Wadding-ton where they were checked in by the sergeant and his corporal on guard duty, who smiled as they watched three WAAF officers walk a little unsteadily to their quarters.

'Come in, come in,' said Vera when they reached her room.

'We should get to bed,' said Carolyn.

'Just one more to finish the night off,' insisted Vera.

'I will,' slurred Lucy. She flopped on to Vera's bed. 'Isn't Pete gorgeous? Where's this drink?'

'Right here,' replied Vera, reaching into the pocket of her greatcoat hanging on the back of the door. She got hold of something else as well as a bottle. 'What's this?' She peered at the envelope in her hand. 'Oh, hell!' She raised her head and looked sheepishly at Carolyn. 'It's for you.' Vera thrust it at her.

'Where did you get this?' she asked indignantly. 'It's from my mother.'

'I'm so sorry, Carolyn. It was in the mail I picked up when I went to the Mess mid-morning. I stuffed it in my greatcoat pocket and forgot about it in all the excitement. I am sorry. A pity I wore my raincoat tonight and not the greatcoat.'

Carolyn ignored her explanation, opened the envelope and drew out a single sheet of paper. She scanned the writing quickly. 'Oh my God!' she gasped. Her face paled as she stared at the paper. Then, her face clouding with anger, she glared at Vera. 'You clot! You damned stupid clot! That letter is from my mother telling me my grandmother has been taken into hospital. It might be serious . . . I should be there!' Her voice rose in panic. 'I could have been but for your stu-pidity.'

Vera took a step back in distress. 'Oh, Carolyn, I'm so sorry.'

'A lot of good that does,' she snapped.

Vera looked at Lucy in a plea for help.

She responded with, 'Vera didn't do this on purpose, Carolyn. It was an accident in all the excitement. Anyone could have done the same.'

'Don't you defend her!' snapped Carolyn in disgust. 'You've met my gran. You know how close we are. I should be there for her.'

'You will be tomorrow,' said Vera lamely.

'That's not now!' Carolyn yelled.

Vera sank down on the bed beside her and put one arm round Carolyn's shoulder; a comforting, sympathetic, please forgive me gesture, but Carolyn shrugged it off.

'I know how you feel . . . ' Lucy's words were cut short by Carolyn.

'No, you don't. How could you. You're as stupid as she is!'

'Calm down!' said Lucy firmly. 'You're only making matters worse for yourself, speaking like this. We'll get you to the station in the morning. Get yourself to bed now and have some sleep.'

'Sleep? How the devil do you expect me to sleep, knowing my gran might be suffering, might even be . . . ' Carolyn's voice faltered. She swallowed hard. The tears came and then sobs racked her body.

'Let her cry,' said Vera, her tone gentle. 'She'll sob the immediate hurt out, then we can think seriously about tomorrow.'

They sat with her until the sobbing subsided and Carolyn slept.

Vera and Lucy dozed but were both woken by the early light filtering through the thin curtains. Lucy crept quietly into Vera's room and they made a plan.

'We have these next two weeks to use as we see best,' she said. 'I think we all intended to do some preliminary organizing here and then take a few days off. Let's reverse that. We'll accompany Carolyn. See she gets home as quickly as possible. My parents are in Ripon, not far from Middlesbrough. You and I can go there, keep in touch with Carolyn, and work out the rest of the leave as we receive news of her gran.'

'That's a good idea,' agreed Vera. 'But do you think Carolyn will agree? She was pretty hostile to me last night.'

'That was just shock,' said Lucy. 'Sleep will have done her good. She'll see things in a better light this morning.'

'Will I?' The question startled them. A dishevelled, bleary-eyed Carolyn was standing in the doorway.

'Yes, you will,' said Lucy, going to her friend. She took hold of her arm and gently eased her round to return to her room. 'Come on, let's get you dressed and smartened up. We've a journey to make.'

'I don't want her along,' said Carolyn, with a nod in Vera's direction.

'Well, I do,' returned Lucy firmly, and glanced back to see regret and concern etched on Vera's face. 'Take no notice.' Lucy mouthed at her.

While helping Carolyn to get dressed, Lucy outlined the plan. When she'd finished, Carolyn said, 'I repeat, I don't want *her* with us.'

Lucy immediately said, with a firmness that would not be denied, 'I *do* want her with us. And I won't let you jeopardize the team that Kate has established. We have an important part to play in this war and nothing must upset that. Get it into your head Carolyn. After all, Vera did nothing deliberately. It was just forgetfulness. Anyone can make a mistake.'

143

Carolyn scowled. As much as she knew Lucy was right, she was not yet ready to forgive Vera's lack of care. 'All right,' she muttered reluctantly, then added, 'I only hope we can trust her not to forget information that could be vital to our aircrews.'

14

Though no one commented all three girls were thankful that the next train for Doncaster was leaving in eight minutes. The less waiting about there was for them the better. Carolyn flopped herself down in one corner of the compartment, thankful the seat was against a window so she could look out. Not that she wanted to see anything; it just meant she did not have to converse with the other two.

Lucy knew all about the love between Carolyn and her gran. She also knew about Carolyn's strained relationship with Rick; she could not remember them dancing together after the meal and their parting at the taxi had been very brief. Now, on the train, with tension still emanating from Carolyn, even conversation between Lucy and Vera was stilted. Though neither of them voiced their opinion they sensed they both thought the same: the sooner they had deposited Carolyn at her home in Nunthorpe the better, and hopefully it would be without any more disturbing news.

When the Middlesbrough taxi stopped outside the Maddisons' home, Carolyn was out of the vehicle in a flash and dashing into the house.

Startled by the sudden intrusion, her mother rushed into the hall. 'Carolyn!'

'Where's Gran? Is she all right?' Carolyn bustled towards the stairs.

'Yes, yes. Wait, Carolyn! She's fast asleep. Don't wake her. Calm down . . . '

Lucy and Vera appeared in the doorway.

'Oh, Lucy, hello,' said Sally.

'Hello. Mrs Maddison, this is Vera, a new friend.'

'What happened, Mum?' asked Carolyn

'Your gran tripped over the carpet, couldn't save herself, hit her head and knocked herself out. Your dad and I were outside and didn't find her for maybe half an hour. The doctor was concerned, had her into hospital for a check up, and it was decided to keep her in that night. She was allowed home yesterday, provided she stayed in bed until the doctor thought otherwise. Your dad and I were worried for her and thought it best to get in touch with you and Alastair. We managed to contact him but my attempts to reach you met with failure so I wrote a letter. You must have just received it.'

Carolyn made no comment, but asked with a note of excitement in her voice, 'So Alastair is here?'

'Yes, but he has to be on duty the day after tomorrow. When do you have to go back?'

'I can be here a few days, Mum. Tell you all about that later.'

'We'll be going, Mrs Maddison, we told the taxi to wait until we saw how Carolyn's gran was faring.' Lucy pointedly used the plural to include Vera, and knew that had not been missed by Carolyn. 'Give her our love and tell her we are pleased to hear she is recovering.' As she embraced Carolyn, Lucy whispered, 'Everything will be all right.'

Though Carolyn stiffened as Vera touched her, the other girl said quietly, with genuine feeling, 'I'm sorry I forgot the letter.' There was no reaction from Carolyn.

146

A bell rang upstairs.

'Gran's awake!' said Carolyn, and ran to the staircase without looking back.

Lucy and Vera made their goodbyes to Mrs Maddison in the hall, and left the house. They were halfway down the path when the gate opened and Mr Maddison and Alastair appeared.

'Lucy!' Alastair hurried forward to embrace her. 'Good to see you again, even though it looks like we are ships passing in the night,' he said, indicating the taxi.

'We brought Carolyn. This is Vera.'

The other girl, who had been astonished to see Lucy in the arms of a handsome squadron leader with DFC and bar on his tunic, didn't know whether to spring to attention and salute or flutter her eyelashes. He saw her embarrassment so held out his hand and said, 'Hello. Pleased to meet you. Any friend of Carolyn's is a friend of mine. Is she all right?'

'Worried about her gran,' replied Vera, who had quickly got a grip on her own reaction.

Mr Maddison briefly welcomed them and hurried into the house.

'It was good of you both to come with Carolyn. She'd be glad of the company,' said Alastair. 'Is it back to base for you now?'

'No. We have some leave to play with, but Carolyn will fill you in about all that. We're off to see Mum and Dad in Ripon for two or three days,' explained Lucy.

'A pity I'm not going to be around,' said Alastair. 'I could have taken you both out to dinner one evening.' He winked at them and said, 'Be good.'

'Dishy,' said Vera as they settled in the taxi. 'It'll be no good me making a play for him, though. After the fiasco of the letter, Carolyn wouldn't let me anywhere near her brother.'

Lucy chuckled. 'Maybe not.'

'I enjoyed dancing with Rick. I think he's a nice guy,' said Vera. 'I can't understand why Carolyn is so cool towards him. I thought they might get together. Have you a clue what's happened between them?'

'At the start of the war her gran was bombed, out and when Carolyn was joining up she met a Spitfire pilot, a flight lieutenant, who was kind and attentive to her. They were going to keep in touch but he was killed before they could meet again. Both incidents made her worry about Alastair, her brother. Then, while training at Swinderby, she witnessed a Stirling crash on take-off, killing all the crew.'

'Thanks, Lucy,' Vera said thoughtfully. 'Now I understand why she's cautious about getting too involved with Rick, and why she was so angry about the letter.'

'I've tried to tell Carolyn that we cannot live fully by being ultra-cautious. But she is scared of being badly hurt again.'

'If she's playing it cool, why not apply for a transfer to a job that would take her away from an active station?'

'She would feel she was letting everyone down. Her brother, who persuaded her to go for a Commission, and the people who singled her out for this role, especially Charlie, the flight lieutenant.'

'In other words, Carolyn has loyalty and a conscience, two demanding bed-fellows,' observed Vera.

She pondered on this during the rest of their leave, which they voluntarily ended with one more week left to go. It was time to get organized.

Relieved that her grandmother was up and about again, Carolyn gave thought to returning to Waddington. She contacted Lucy and they agreed a time and day to meet at York station.

'You know Vera has been with me?' Lucy tested her friend. 'She'll be travelling back too.'

'I thought that would happen. It was obviously the best thing for her to do. I hope you both had a good time.'

When they met, Lucy sensed that the grudge Carolyn had felt was gone, though she was still a little peevish with Vera. That lessened once they were resettled at Waddington and had set about organizing it's Intelligence section along the lines that Group Officer Pearson had indicated. Knowing that reports would be passed to her by Squadron Officer Newbauld, they made sure that their individual input left nothing to be desired. Their work soon became all-consuming and the incident of the letter was buried in the past. Rick was never mentioned openly but as on all RAF stations rumours abounded and some had an element of truth in them. The handsome Flying Officer Rick Wood stationed at Swinderby and the vivacious Flight Officer Vera Williams from Waddington had been seen together in Lincoln on several occasions, apparently.

The days drifted into September. The alterations to accommodate more personnel, the laying of solid runways and the extension of such areas as the fuel and bomb dumps, indicated to 'those in the know' that new and bigger bombers would be coming in, but as yet this remained unofficial.

Then, one day in mid-September, an unfamiliar aircraft flew in. Officials were tight-lipped about it, which caused speculation in some quarters, while others took a 'we've seen it all before' attitude.

No one was more surprised than Carolyn and Lucy when, after sitting down in the Mess for lunch, they both felt a tap on their shoulders and heard someone say, 'So this is where you've been promoted to. Well done!'

'Jim Ashton!' they both gasped.

'Is someone sitting opposite?' he asked

'No.'

He went round the table and pulled out a chair.

'Have you brought that strange four-engine plane in?' asked Lucy,

'Yes, my co-pilot and I. When I left Swinderby I was sent to a testing station for new aircraft. I've been working on that one. I'm here today to see if the facilities here are capable of handling its requirements. I can't tell you any more than that. Now, what about you?'

They gave him a brief rundown on how they had fared since they had last seen him, and he was pleased to know that Carolyn had settled into RAF life and had got over the trauma he had feared might unsettle her.

Jim did not linger over his meal and excused himself as soon as he had finished. 'Please forgive me, there's a lot more to do this afternoon.'

'How long are you here?' asked Lucy, as he rose from his chair.

'I'm hoping all the necessary investigations are done so I can get away later today. I'll be extremely busy so I can't bank on seeing you again, but if anything brings me back to Waddington, I'll be in touch.'

Later the sound of aero-engines took Carolyn and Lucy outside their office to watch Jim take off.

'If that's the new aircraft the RAF are pinning their hopes on, I reckon it has nothing much on the Manchester except for a couple more engines,' observed Lucy.

'I suppose the boffins know what they're doing. But we shall see,' said Carolyn.

All thoughts of the mystery aircraft were pushed aside by news that not only rocked Waddington but the whole world as well.

'The Japs have bombed Pearl Harbor!'

'The US main fleet was in port.'

'There have been big losses.'

'They were caught napping.'

'It will be a World War now.'

'December the seventh 1941 will go down in history.'

'What will happen now?' Vera asked when Squadron Officer Newbauld walked into the Intelligence section.

'We carry on as usual. This news won't affect our job here.'

With work at Waddington speeding up and, orders for all construction to be completed by the middle of December, speculation was rife that it was connected with the commissioning of the new bomber. That was compounded when crews without aircraft started arriving.

Carolyn and Lucy were busy helping Vera sort out a large batch of photographs of German installations in France, and defence sites associated with the Ruhr industrial region, when one afternoon the door opened.

'Tra-la, tra-la, and here we are!'

Startled by the carefree entry, the three WAAFs looked up and gasped.

'Good heavens!'

'Rick!'

'Pete!'

'What are you doing here?'

'Flying without an aircraft!' joked Pete as Lucy flung her arms around him.

'Looking for you three,' said Rick.

'Are you are joining 44 Squadron?' asked Vera hopefully.

'Yes, they need the best crew in Bomber Command.'

'When are they flying in?'

'They're already here, in the Intelligence section.'

'Big heads!'

'Are the rest of your crew in good form, Rick?' asked Carolyn.

'Yes,' he replied. 'But getting restive for something to happen.'

'What gives here?' asked Pete. 'It's obvious there's been a lot of construction going on. Rumour has it that a new plane is in the offing, That could be true, seeing the shortage of planes out there and not a Hampden in sight. Come on, tell us.'

'You know as much as we do. We can only corroborate the rumours. But with all Christmas leave cancelled, it looks as though something big is happening. I don't think crews will be languishing here long when there's a war to be won.'

'Christmas leave cancelled?' queried Peter in disbelief.

'We've only just heard this morning,' said Carolyn. 'No doubt you'll be told when the CO welcomes you to the squadron later today.'

'Well, that's war for you,' said Rick with a shrug of his shoulders. 'But Christmas is Christmas and we've already had an advance present – meeting up with you three again.'

'We must get to the adjutant to report we are here,' Peter reminded him.

'OK.' Rick touched Vera on her shoulder as he headed for the door. 'See you in the Mess at six.'

After they'd eaten together Rick asked, with a twinkle in his eyes as they left the Mess, 'Have you any leafy lanes around here?'

Vera laughed, recalling their previous walks. 'I don't know, let's find out together.'

Their fingers linked when they left the station and they fell into an easy companionship, as if they had never been parted.

'It's a small world that's brought you to Waddington,' commented Vera.

'No, my love, it was your magnetism.' Rick placed his hands on her shoulders and drew her close. He looked deep into her eyes. 'I felt lost without you.' Although his kiss was gentle she felt his desire kindle hers.

The pounding of her heart told her she was falling love with him. Rick's feelings, as ever, were impossible to determine.

Vera gave a little shiver and tugged her jacket closer to her when she looked out of the office window early the next morning.

'What is it?' asked Carolyn.

Diverting her thoughts from the previous evening with Rick, Vera said, 'It's eerie. Airfields are usually throbbing with activity, but they take on a different air when they are quiet. Today the silence has a strange atmosphere. It's as if we are waiting for something momentous to happen.'

'I don't know how you can feel that,' said Lucy. 'We're only expecting an aeroplane.'

'It is a new one,' Carolyn pointed out.

'Maybe, but it seems that's the cause of us losing Christmas leave,' countered Lucy.

'I would think there's more to it than that. We'll find out when the CO decides we need to know. In the meantime enjoy the atmosphere that's settling on Waddington. Look, the hoar frost has given even our mundane buildings a sort of charm.' Carolyn glanced at the clock. Half an hour to go. The CO had said to expect the arrival of the new planes at eleven.'

As the hands of the clock drew nearer and nearer to the arrival time, more and more men and women of all ranks appeared, gathering in groups in the technical area and close to the Control Tower.

With five minutes to go Carolyn spoke up, 'Come on, I got permission for us to go on the tower balcony. Keep to the right-hand end – we'll be out of the way of the big wigs from Group.'

'There's Rick and Peter and the rest of the crew,' pointed out Vera as she waved energetically towards the aircrews who had chosen to stand close to the Control Tower. The buzz of excitement had even got to Lucy.

The final moments passed.

'There. Listen!' someone shouted.

The distant sounds of aero-engines brought the expectant crowd to silence. All eyes turned in their direction, eager to see the new additions to Bomber Command, to 5 Group and to Waddington. Everyone was feeling proud to be chosen as the first squadron to be equipped with the new bomber.

'There!' Someone had spotted a silhouette and in a matter of moments there wasn't one person who hadn't fixed the new arrivals in their sight. They watched, entranced by the sight of the three bombers flying in V-formation. They were coming closer and closer.

The planes circled the airfield then passed in front of the Control Tower. They climbed, two of them taking up position to follow instructions for landing while the leader rose another five hundred feet above them. Once the way was clear he turned to pass in front of the Control Tower again, but this time brought gasps of astonishment from the watchers as one by one he closed down three engines.

'Good God, he's flying on one engine!'

'I can't believe it!'

'A plane that size capable of doing it!'

'Amazing!'

The engines started up again one by one. The pilot took the lead plane on its landing circuit, made a perfect touch down, turned off the runway, and finally taxied to a stop alongside the other two aircraft near the Control Tower. When the pilot emerged a great cheer rang out.

'Gosh, it's Jim!' cried Carolyn.

Waddington's CO held up his hand to silence the crowd.

'You have just seen the capabilities of the wonderful new bomber which has been named the Lancaster. Our squadron is proud to be the first to be equipped with her. I am sure you will all come to love and cherish her. May she serve us well.'

A great cheer resounded across the Lincolnshire countryside, and then RAF Waddington and 44 Squadron settled down to prepare to resume their roles in a war that was now global.

15

The Officers' Mess was buzzing with talk about the new acquisition throughout the lunch-time break and beyond.

Though in conversation with a group of senior officers, Jim noticed Carolyn come into the ante-room. He gave her a smile which she interpreted as 'Nice to see you again', but the helpless shrug of his shoulders told her 'I'm tied up. See you later'.

It wasn't until after the evening meal that he was able to do so as they collected their coffee.

'At last,' he said with some relief. 'Let's bag that corner over there.'

When they had settled she asked, 'How long will you be here?'

'I have no set time at the moment. I am staying on, along with the other two pilots who brought the Lancs in. We will be introducing pilots to the new bomber – the more experienced pilots first, then the squadron's most recent intake. We are establishing a Lancaster Finishing School at Syerston, where all new pilots will go for a very short conversion course before posting to a squadron.'

'What will happen when you finish here?'

'Nothing is decided yet, but whatever it is won't happen

until the system is well established. But that's enough about me, what about you? Any regrets about losing out on Flying Control?'

'None,' she replied. 'I'm near enough here to be almost a part of it. Our set-up allows Intelligence to work closely with Flying Control. The officer in charge of FC is very understanding about co-operation between the two departments, so I have no regrets. And I will always have you to thank for seeing me through that difficult time when I nearly threw everything in.'

'It was you who had to make the final decision, but if I helped a little I am pleased everything has turned out well for you. No more traumas?'

'None. You steeled my mind.'

'So how about you and I celebrating that by having dinner in Lincoln?'

Caught by surprise, Carolyn left a slight pause before she said, 'That would be lovely, but won't it lead to gossip that would make your superiors frown?'

'They are your superiors too.' Jim smiled at her.

She gave a little laugh. 'I suppose they are.'

'Let the gossips gossip, if that's what they want. You and I know that everything is above board. If it eases any qualms you may have, let me add that I would also like you to meet my wife. I'll arrange it with her when we spend Christmas Day together tomorrow. She will be coming to Lincoln two weeks today, when I am taking three days' leave that are due to me. I think it would be good for both of you to meet. Bring along a boyfriend if you like.'

'There is no one.'

'What are all those officers at Waddington thinking about?'

Carolyn smiled at the inference. 'Maybe I'm not up to scratch.'

'Or they're blind! I'd better have the MO check their eyesight. Maybe they aren't fit to fly the Lanc!' Jim laughed. 'That would make for talk. "Superb New Bomber Grounded by WAAF Officer!" Please keep the day free two weeks today. You may have found a nice young man to bring by then.'

'Thank you. Now, you'll have had a tiring day and I have an early meeting with Squadron Officer Newbauld tomorrow. She has called it then so it doesn't impinge too much on Christmas Day, so I'll say thank you and good night.'

'It is I who should thank you, for being such pleasant company.'

Carolyn had gathered her hat and greatcoat and was crossing the hall when Rick walked in.

'Hi,' he said as he threw his hat on to the table among the others.

'Hi back,' said Carolyn.

'Flying high, aren't you?' he said with a nod towards the ante-room door. 'I saw you hob-nobbing earlier. I hope you have a head for heights and that you enjoy the flight.'

She eyed him without blinking as she replied levelly, 'Rick, I've had a pleasant evening, please don't spoil it with your sarcasm. And don't mar our friendship with such a petty attitude.' She left him looking at the closed door as she strode away from the Mess.

Throughout Christmas Day and Boxing Day the station relaxed but still retained an atmosphere of excitement at being the proud owners of the new Lancasters, albeit only three of them. A book was run on which crews would be allocated the new aircraft.

During the next two weeks Jim was involved in the initial stages of training pilots who had a considerable operational experience, who in turn could extend the training to new crews as more Lancasters were brought to the squadron. As with all new aircraft there were teething troubles but these were soon ironed out and all aircrew and ground-crew had nothing but praise for it as the new plane proved its worth over enemy territory.

Squadron Officer Newbauld was a regular visitor to the office occupied by the three WAAFs under her command and was always ready to suggest ways in which their Intelligence section could become more efficient and expand their information base. She would listen to suggestions, which they amicably shared before putting them to her. This development pleased her for she had sensed the tension that had arisen briefly between Carolyn and Vera.

Carolyn counted the days to her meeting with Jim's wife, and sought a late night pass from Kate.

'Doing anything nice?' she asked casually as she signed the form.

'Having dinner with Squadron Leader Ashton and his wife.'

Kate raised an eyebrow but sought no further explanation. 'Splendid. A very nice man. Enjoy yourself.'

Carolyn was waiting in the guard-room when the taxi she and the others usually used arrived. She scrambled in quickly, straightened her uniform and settled down with her thoughts. She came out of her reverie when the car drew to a halt.

'Sorry I haven't been talkative tonight, Jack.'

'No matter, miss, I thought you must have something on your mind.'

'I suppose I had.'

'Usual time for your return, miss?'

'Can I ring you? I don't know what my host and his wife have in mind.'

'Of course. I'll wait to hear.'

Carolyn stepped out of the taxi and stood for a moment as it was driven away. She took a deep breath and then walked briskly into the hotel.

Jim was waiting and, with a welcoming smile, came quickly over to her, took her coat and hat and handed them to the receptionist.

'This way.' He indicated a door. 'You know, a uniform suits you. Or should that be, you wear a uniform well?'

The question put Carolyn at ease. She laughed. 'Whatever. Put on a uniform and it does something for anyone.'

They walked into a lounge. A variety of chairs, placed conveniently by low round tables, were occupied by military personnel, Army, Navy, but as she expected, because of the nearness of so many airfields, there were more RAF uniforms in evidence. Carolyn was more than surprised when Jim led her over to a young woman dressed in the uniform of a Chief Officer of the Women's Royal Naval Service.

'Jean, this is Carolyn who I told you about. Carolyn, my wife Jean.'

Jean Ashton rose gracefully from her chair. Her smile was warm. Her dark blue eyes, sparkling with friendliness, had a touch of curiosity in them. She sensed immediately that Carolyn was a little embarrassed. Jean chuckled. 'Did my dutiful husband forget to tell you about this?' she asked, making a gesture towards her uniform.

Jim grinned as he explained, 'I thought if I did it might scare Carolyn away.'

'I think she would have taken some scaring,' Jean laughed, extending her greeting with, 'Do sit down.'

'I'll order us some drinks. I know what you like after a shock,' said Jim, teasing Carolyn as he glanced at her. 'Will it be the same for you, Jean?' he asked. indicating her glass.

'Thank you. Another reviver will be splendid. It's been a tiring day; the last of a recruiting drive I've been initiating in Lincolnshire. It will be good to relax now. I managed to organize three days' leave after it and it was wonderful that Jim could manage the same while I was in the county.'

Jean's easy personality was draining away any embarrassment Carolyn had felt on first meeting her. The evening passed pleasantly as they got to know each other. They were relaxing in the lounge after dinner when Jim spotted someone come in with whom he wanted a word. Carolyn took the chance she'd hoped she might get when the evening had first been mooted.

'Jean, may I ask you a personal question?'

She smiled. 'It depends how personal. I reserve the right to say no if it is *too* personal. So, on those terms, fire away.'

'How did you cope when your husband was on operational duties?'

'Ah, do I sense romance behind this question?' When Carolyn hesitated Jean added, 'I believe I do.'

Carolyn gave a little nod. 'I became attached to a pilot, Rick, during his training, not knowing where he was going or where I would eventually finish up. I suffered several traumas, one of which your husband helped me through. I witnessed my first horrendous crash. Wondering how I would deal with it if Rick suffered the same fate, I decided that I would not get involved deeply with him or anyone until after the war, so I cooled my relationship with him.'

'How did he take that?'

'He didn't like it.'

'I'm not surprised! You are an attractive girl, pretty and fun to be with. If I am not mistaken, you asked to remain friends and he didn't want it on that level.'

'Yes.'

'How far did he want to go?'

'He never suggested . . . ' Carolyn blushed then added, 'He has someone else now.'

Jean nodded thoughtfully and said, 'Carolyn, the first thing you must remember is that these young men dice with death every day. Tomorrow has little meaning for them. They find solace and comfort in relationships with females. They are sustained by them, especially if love is the prime mover. Oh, yes, we suffer too wondering what is happening to them – hoping they are surviving all the brutal sky hurls at them. They need us to help them keep their minds off those horrors. Remember, we too can draw much from a relation-ship forged in the sky.

'Only you can know what you want, and that knowledge might be slow in coming, but when it comes . . . if it does . . . you have to be prepared to grab it and make the love between you work.' Jean paused. 'Oh, my goodness, I've gone on, haven't I? Carolyn, I'm no expert, I can only offer observations drawn from my own experience. You are the only one who can decide how to deal with what lies ahead for you.'

Carolyn saw Jim shaking hands with the man he had been talking to. 'Thank you, Jean. Your experience in this is more than appreciated.'

'Hello again, you two.' Jim's quiet voice broke in at just the right moment. Unknown to him, Carolyn had been left with much to ponder.

16

'Rick's crew are on tonight!' Vera rushed into the Intelligence room. 'Names have just been chalked on the ops board.'

Although 44 Squadron had taken part in three raids during the past fortnight it was only tonight that it was at full strength now the last two Lancasters had been delivered. The plane allocated to Flying Officer Rick Wood's crew, and lettered LM–U, was immediately referred to affectionately by them as 'Uncle'. There was a rush to get the new aircraft operational. Now the bombers stood silent in the late afternoon gloom awaiting their crews, who were thronging into their Messes for the usual pre-op meal of bacon and eggs, all plans for a night out forgotten.

Banter in the two Messes was a little subdued, conversation fitful, minds elsewhere. As soon as they had finished eating the men drifted away, seeking some way to occupy the two hours before briefing time.

Rick came into the billet to find Peter with feet up on his bed reading a novel. 'I don't know how you can do that,' commented Rick.

'What else would you have me do?'

'Well, I'm going to check with the ground-crew that Uncle's OK.'

'What?' said Peter, somewhat surprised. 'How many times have you done that already? Settle down; do something else. You'll have enough checks to do before we take off.'

Rick said nothing. He opened the top drawer of his chest of drawers, took out the little porcelain black cat that Vera had given him two days ago and slipped it into his battle-dress breast pocket. He headed for the door, 'See you at briefing,' he called over his shoulder.

In a hut on the sergeants' site, Don Westwood took out a photo from which a pretty face smiled out at him. His heart and mind sped across Lincolnshire and into Yorkshire until they hovered over a detached house with a sea view in Redcar. Here we go, Beth, he said silently. Your love will see me through. He kissed her, formed the words 'I love you', and placed the photograph in his breast pocket. He looked round the hut, grabbed his flying helmet and headed for the door. It opened before he got there and Uncle's two gunners came in.

'Are you going somewhere?' asked Mark jauntily.

'Haven't decided yet,' replied Don, putting on a puzzled expression. 'It might be France, could be Germany.'

'Well, wherever you go, can I come along and give them a noisy reception?' asked Tim.

'Sure. Good to have you along. Have you seen Phil and Gordon?'

'Gordon said he would see us at briefing. I reckon he'll be chatting up the WAAF parachute packer he brought to the party,' said Mark.

'She was a bit of a humdinger, all right,' said Tim. 'That was a sassy dress she had on; I didn't recognize her at first.'

'Nice lass,' put in Mark. 'Told me she had a chance of a Commission but turned it down to stay as a sergeant in charge of the parachute section here, rather than be separated from the girls she had trained with.'

'And Phil?' asked Don.

'He'll see us at briefing. He said he was going to write to his wife.'

'Myrna's a pretty girl,' commented Don. 'She obviously adores him. She'll be a worrier but she'll do more than her best to keep that from him; she won't want anything to detract from his efficiency. I think he knows how nervous she is and writes to her every day to try and help her through. Well, fellas, I'm off to draw a few lines on a chart. See you.'

When Rick reached the briefing room fifteen minutes before the allotted time he found the rest of his crew already there with Don in a central position at the crew's table, one of twelve facing the podium situated at one end of the room.

The air was filled with the banter crews unconsciously used to ease their trepidation about what could face them in the night ahead.

A side door near the podium opened. The Station CO and Squadron CO walked in, followed by the three Intelligence officers accompanied by the leaders of the squadron sections concerned with tonight's mission. The crews scrambled to attention.

'Sit down, chaps.' The Station CO took off his hat and laid it on the table. After the shuffling of chairs and benches stopped, a hush settled over the room.

The Station CO stepped forward. 'Tonight you will be taking part in an historic event: the first attack on an enemy target by a squadron with a full complement of this new and wonderful bomber, the Lancaster – a plane that I predict will help alter bombing policy and, ultimately, the course of the war. I know you don't want me to go on eulogizing her merits. You have already embraced many of them in training and no doubt you will learn of others tonight. So I will only add: treat her kindly and trust her to bring you home safely. I'll hand over to your Squadron CO. Good luck to you all.'

He moved to one side and let the squadron's Commanding Officer take centre stage.

'I realise you are anxious to know the target for tonight but first I want to tell you that you will be seeing much more of our three flight officers from Intelligence.' He gestured in their direction. 'They will be involved in briefing and debriefing.'

A cheer went up around the room.

A shout came from the back, 'How much more, sir?'

Laughter and whooping swept through the crews.

Carolyn gave a little smile; Lucy and Vera shared her amusement as the CO called out, 'All right, settle down. We have a briefing to get through. Flight Officer Williams, show them where they are going.'

Vera undid the cord that was holding a rolled map in place on the wall and carefully lowered it allowing it to unroll until it was fully in view.

Every man at the tables strained to see how far into Europe the red tape traced their route. It reached as far as Munster.

There were some moans and groans among the more experienced crews but the crew of U–Uncle, ignorant of the reasons, did not bother to ask why; sometimes it was better to remain in ignorance.

One by one, officers from the various sections were called to make their reports. The met officer predicted good weather throughout the whole flight but warned there might be some thin fog across Lincolnshire by the time they were over base, so they should be prepared for a diversion to a

166

fog-free airfield. The bombing leader talked about the load they were carrying, one 4,000-pound bomb known as the Cookie, some 500-pounders, and incendiaries. So the briefing went on. When it came to the Intelligence section's turn Carolyn stepped forward, receiving wolf whistles as she did so. They were quickly silenced when she started to inform them of the reason for the attack, and what was known of the defences in the target area and en route. The navigation leader had held a briefing with the navigators half an hour before the main briefing and now updated and rounded out that information for them quickly, so they could include it when plotting their route and use latest wind information to calculate arrival times at various points on their route. A last word came from the Squadron CO who then left his crews to make their final preparations.

Carolyn exited the briefing room quickly but paused to wish U–Uncle's crew, 'Good luck and a safe return'. As she turned to leave, Rick caught her eye. He winked. She nodded and smiled back weakly. When she stepped into the night, she was arrested by the sight of Rick's Lancaster around which danger would hover until it rested once more in its dispersal. He could be ... She tried to thrust the possibility from her mind but it lingered. She shivered. Jean's words came back to her. Have I really been fair to him? She wondered. Oh, Rick, why can't you be satisfied with my friendship? She started to turn back then stopped and hurried away, needing the security of her own room.

The brief exchange between Carolyn and Rick had been noted by Vera but she made no comment; instead, conquering her own fears of what might happen to him, she said, 'Come back safe, Rick.'

'I will.' He tapped his breast pocket. 'Felix will see me home.'

Lucy did not hold back. 'I'll be waiting, Pete.' She gave him a quick kiss that brought a few ribald remarks from nearby flyers, who were leaving their tables with no outward sign that they feared what might face them over Germany.

'Ignore them, Lucy. They're only jealous. See you soon,' he told her.

'Take care.'

'I will.'

Lucy and Vera, quelling the urge to look back, headed for the Intelligence section.

'Are we going to wait in the Mess until the return?' Vera suggested.

'Four a.m. Estimated time of arrival,' said Lucy.

'Would you sleep?' Vera asked.

Lucy pulled a face. 'Doubtful. Crew's first op, I think I'd be too anxious to get much sleep.'

Vera nodded. 'Me too. Uncle is nearby. How about we watch them leave from here and then go to the Mess together?'

'OK, we'll do that.'

Crews streamed from the briefing room, made some final checks in their individual sections, wrote a last-minute note to hand to a mate who wasn't flying tonight, with a request for him to post it if they didn't return, or went outside for a smoke or merely to breathe in the clear Lincolnshire air before heading for the confines of their Lancaster. But whatever they chose to do to fill in time, they all kept an eye on their watches.

Then, in ones and twos, they headed for the locker room, which soon became a bustle of activity as they dressed to combat the cold at 12,000 feet, the height from which they had been instructed to bomb their target. Earlier, knowing they would be flying tonight, most of them had put on extra underwear; now they hauled thick jerseys over their heads and pulled them down to the top of their legs. They shrugged over this newly issued electrically heated flying suit, and dug their feet into fleece-lined flying boots. Settling comfortably into these layers, they sat down on benches to check the contents of their pockets. There were compact medical kits and escape kits that might be required if they were shot down, chocolate, sweets, plus things of a personal nature that might help them – a religious medal, a lucky charm. Pete tied one of Lucy's silk stockings around his neck, a talisman for every flight from now on. They collected their parachute, exchanging a final quip with the WAAFs in the parachute section, took their flying helmet from their locker and looked around for a final check.

The time came. Trucks, driven by WAAFs, were waiting to convey them to their aircraft dispersed on hard standings around the airfield, but the crew of U–Uncle had no need of a truck; she was near enough for them to walk to her. Their light-hearted exchanges faded as they neared the aircraft that was to take them into the unknown, but no one would admit to the gripping pains in their stomach. The ground-crew were waiting with reassurances that the aircraft was as ready as she could be for her first operation.

Peter chatted to the armourers as he checked the bomb load held snuggly in the bomb-bay. Tim and Mark exchanged words with the armourers responsible for arming their guns. Phil, satisfied with the report that the engines had passed their ground checks, informed Rick, as did Gordon about his radio equipment.

Time then drifted by uneasily until Rick gave a final glance at his watch. 'OK, everyone, let's go.'

Good wishes from the ground-crew were taken with them as they climbed on board.

Tim had expressed a desire always to be the last man to board ... 'Then I'll not only know the door is secure but if I have to open it to bail out I'll know I'll be able to do it and won't find some bloody fool hasn't closed it properly.'

They took up their positions and made their final checks. Having done so, Peter, who was not allowed to be in the nose for take-off, came to stand behind the engineer.

'Pilot to Navigator.'

'OK, Skip, Navigator.'

'Pilot to WOP.'

'OK, Skip, WOP here.'

Rick checked on everyone, and slid back his window.

The silence that lay across the airfield was uncanny. There was no movement to signify that death and destruction would soon be taking to the sky. The Lincolnshire country-side lay at peace.

Girls across the county would wait in vain for their evening date tonight.

They would retrace their steps home, or continue on to the cinema, regretting they weren't sharing a double seat on the back row with a member of a Lancaster crew. They would listen to the roar of aero-engines as the black bombers took to the sky, and send special messages to their crews as they crossed Lincolnshire towards their targets.

The pubs would open as usual, but there would be fewer customers tonight. Regulars would chatter less and let their thoughts join their RAF friends who flew with death hovering at their wings. They would fall silent as the roar of the bombers grew louder, shattering the calm of the evening sky. When these flyers filled the pubs instead the locals did not begrudge them their high spirits; they knew it was men's way of trying to forget the war; to blot from their minds an empty bed on the opposite side of their billet. Tomorrow night the local pub-goers will anxiously watch the door, hoping to see all the familiar faces of the young men they had welcomed into their midst.

The pointers on the crews' watches moved closer with every second. The crew of U–Uncle could not halt the passing of time.

17

Carolyn had pedalled ferociously to her billet as if, in its security, she could blot out the consequences of this night in which she had played a part: there would be deaths in a German city and in the sky above it, and death to flyers even within sight of home. She could not still her racing thoughts. Would it have made any difference to her tonight had she not held Rick at a distance? Would it have made any difference to him? She shuddered and convinced herself that it wouldn't. But, remembering Jean's words, felt doubt sneaking in again.

Annoyed, Carolyn reprimanded herself. This is no way for an officer to behave. I'm on a bomber airfield, where I wanted to be. I've no cause for regret. I shouldn't feel any doubt. There's a job to do, and I will do it to the best of my ability by keeping my personal feelings at bay.

Then the uneasy peace was torn apart by the cough and splutter of a starting engine. Another started up, to be answered by another, and another, and another, until the airfield was filled with the roar of engines that heralded death and destruction in distant Munster.

Carolyn, alone in her room, tried to disassociate herself from the noise. She clamped her hands over her ears but it did nothing to stop the roar of aero-engines and Jean's words blurring together. Carolyn sobbed.

Lucy and Vera stood transfixed by the noise and spectacle of what was happening around them.

'She's moving!' Vera's sharp voice reached Lucy's ears amongst the chorus of engines and they both stared as U–Uncle started to move off.

They watched, fascinated by the slow movement of the huge bomber, as Rick eased her from her site on to the perimeter track to join the line of Lancasters heading for the end of the runway being used for take-off.

The first Lancaster turned on to the runway and stopped to await the signal to take off. A green light flashed from the control van. The noise from the plane's engines rose and rose; the Lancaster began to move, faster and faster. Lucy and Vera held their breath willing the bomber to rise. When it did they let their breath go too. A wave of relief swept over them. But Uncle still had to take off.

One by one the bombers took to the air.

Then it was U–Uncle's turn.

Rick held her at the end of the runway. Beads of perspiration stood on his forehead. He felt his hands tighten on the control column. His mouth was dry. Relax, relax! The words pounded in his mind. The green light flashed. Automatically he started to open the throttles. The movement drove everything from his mind except for the take-off. He sensed his engineer standing by to open the throttles, increasing the power needed to take Uncle and her load of destruction into the air. Faster and faster. It seemed as though the end of the runway would be upon them any moment. Phil took responsibility for the necessary power; Rick, with two hands on the control column, judged the right moment and eased Uncle off the runway. They were airborne. Now they needed height. Orders were called and acknowledged as pilot and engineer settled the aircraft. Rick took her into a climbing turn to port.

'Undercarriage up.'

'Undercarriage up,' checked Phil.

'Pilot to Navigator. Course?'

'One, nine, nought, Skip.'

'One, nine, nought,' Rick repeated.

He settled Uncle on that direction, checking the designated airspeed and the rate of climb.

Peter signalled that he was going down into the nose. Once there he immediately plugged in his intercom and reported that he was in position. Then Rick contacted every crew member.

Seven men settled down to the jobs for which they had been trained, each determined never to be the weak link in the crew. The gunners tested the movement of their turrets and were already surveying the sky, ready to shout a warning should the darkness conceal another Lancaster that was drawing too close for comfort – a reminder that their course to the target would be teeming with unseen aircraft. Don pored over his charts, constantly checking his calculations were correct, but found time to look up and wink at his wife who smiled back at him from the photograph he had secured conveniently at eye-level. Gordon had tuned his wireless to the designated wave-length, checked reception and was ready to pass on information broadcast to the bombers. Phil kept a constant check on the performance of the four engines, and at intervals would sweep his sharp eyes across the dark sky. Peter lay down in the nose of the aircraft, kept a watchful eye ahead and passed on any relevant sighting that would help the navigator steer their course. He had already checked the movement of the front turret, which he would man if necessary, and at the appropriate moment would make everything ready for dropping the bombs, when he would take over guiding Rick on to the target.

U–Uncle droned steadily on, carrying a crew that had settled quickly on their first operational raid into enemy territory.

'Bomb Aimer to Navigator. Enemy coast coming up.'

'Do you see an estuary?'

'Yes.'

'Good, we are on track.'

A few minutes later bright fingers of light searched the sky. Two picked out and settled on a Lancaster, but there was no anti-aircraft fire.

'Eyes alert,' Rick called out. 'No flak could mean fighters.'

The Lancaster coned by searchlights was attempting to escape the probes, but too late. Tracer streamed across the sky, followed immediately by a wall of flame that carved a passage of light through the night.

'That Lanc's a gonner!' shouted Peter.

'Alert everyone. We could have been spotted in the light from that blaze,' Rick warned.

Her crew was shaken by the sight of one of their own bombers, ablaze in an inferno from which no one could escape, plunging helplessly to earth. There would be empty beds tonight and grieving wives and sweethearts, but no one commented on the fact that it could easily have been them.

They went about their jobs methodically until:

'Fires ahead, Skipper,' called Peter.

'Got them,' Rick replied.

'That'll be our target,' Don confirmed. He took a piece of paper from Gordon who had just received information of a change of wind direction and velocity. Don read the information and gave the WOP the thumbs up as a gesture of thanks.

As that was happening Rick had quickly made an initial line up on the target. He kept it like that for ninety seconds then called out, 'Bomb Aimer, she's all yours.'

'OK, Skip,' replied Pete. He took a sighting. 'Hold her there, Skipper.' Peter took a quick look around his instruments. All were ready. He looked through his bombsight and would remain there until the bombs were dropped. Now he was in sole charge of the operation. What he said had to be done. Rick must follow Pete's orders and calibrate the necessary degree of alteration by the tone of his voice; something they had practised hard on solo cross-country training flights. They reckoned they were a good team. Now, as anti-aircraft guns opened up ahead of them, they realized this would test just how good they were.

'Steady, Skipper. Hold her there.'

Uncle flew on.

'Bomb doors open, Skipper.'

Rick pulled a lever. The Lancaster shuddered then settled.

'Bomb doors open,' said Rick.

Silence except for the engine noise.

'Left ... left. Hold it. Steady ... stea ... dy. Steady. Steady. Left, left.' Rick made the slight alteration. 'Steady ... Steady ... Steady.'

The line on the sighting head of the bombsight showed Peter that they were dead on line for the target. Shells burst around them. Uncle rocked. Rick steadied her.

'Steady. Steady.' Peter pressed the bomb tit, saw the release mechanism sweep across all its contacts and felt Uncle lift as the bombs left her. 'Bombs gone!' he shouted.

Rick kept the aircraft steady for a few moments longer to allow the camera to automatically take a photograph of the point of impact.

'OK, Skip,' called Peter. 'Let's get out of here!'

Rick banked to port, pushed Uncle's nose down and opened up the power.

'Yippee, we're coming home!' shouted Mark.

Cheers rang through the aircraft.

But then came the warning as Rick dampened down their enthusiasm. 'Calm down, calm down. We aren't home yet. Keep alert.'

The crew knew he was right.

Carolyn stirred, coming half-awake to the sound of the alarm clock she had placed beneath her pillow. Sleep called to her but the ringing continued. She turned over with the urge to go back to sleep but the alarm clock would not let her. She reached out and switched on the bedside light she had brought from home. Grasping the alarm, she silenced it and focused on the clock face. Three a.m. In forty-five minutes she should be ready to debrief the crews returning from Munster. She swung out of bed, shrugged herself into her dressing gown, grabbed her toilet bag and hurried to the bathroom, pleased to find it unoccupied. She did not linger in the sharp morning air, which reminded her of how cosy she had been in bed. A door opened as she stepped into the corridor.

'Good morning, Carolyn.'

'Oh, hello, Kate. When did you get back?'

'Near midnight. Wanted to be back for your first debriefing. Crept in quietly and dozed on my bed. I'll catch up on my sleep after the crews are back. I don't hear Lucy and Vera?'

'They were still in the briefing room when I left. I didn't hear them come in. I'll give them a knock.'

Carolyn got no answer so peeped into their rooms only to discover the beds had not been slept in. 'Not here,' she called. 'Must have decided on using a chair in the Mess.'

'OK,' Kate acknowledged. 'Be with you in a few minutes. We can cycle down together. That's if my bike is still there.'

'I think it is,' replied Carolyn, smiling at the thought of how cycles here were often regarded as public property if someone was desperate to avoid being late.

Within a few minutes Squadron Officer Newbauld and Flight Officer Maddison were pedalling through the sharp morning air, leaving puffs of breath floating white behind them. Carolyn was glad of the company; it kept her mind off what might face her at her first debriefing.

18

Lucy shuffled in the easy chair and groaned. She felt scrunched up, stiff, and didn't want to move, but a warning sounded in her mind. Bleary-eyed, she realized the lights were on. Her eyelids flickered and she became aware she was in the ante-room of the Mess. She creaked her neck round, focused on the wall clock – three-thirty. That brought her sharply awake. Debriefing! She stretched her legs and then sat up. Vera was still asleep in the chair beside her. Lucy reached over and shook her. A protesting groan was the only answer but Lucy shook her again.

'Wake up! Wake up!' she urged, as she looked round and saw that they were the only ones in the Mess. Why hadn't they chosen the more comfortable option of their own beds to await the returning aircrews? Had they been afraid they might sleep in? Well, they nearly had. She pushed herself out of the chair and headed for the Ladies.

'Don't think I'll do that again,' muttered Vera as she joined her.

'Nor me.'

'I'll have to rely on my alarm in future, but when it goes off, and I'm hardly awake, I have a habit of switching it off and going straight back to sleep.'

'Is that a hint you're going to rely on me?'

'That's right. Come on, hurry up! Let's hope our bikes are still outside.'

They pedalled quickly, without exchanging a word, and were thankful they reached the briefing block before they heard the first distant drone of an aircraft. They dumped their cycles and hurried inside, to catch a buzz of conversation. Three WAAFs from the parachute section were exchanging words about their recent dates; one of the four WAAF drivers was recounting, unsympathetically, some news she had received from home; leaders of the bombing, navigating and gunnery sections were in discussion about the influence of Air Marshal Harris since his appointment as chief of Bomber Command in February 1942. But under it all lay their concern for the returning bombers.

The noise of the aircraft grew louder. The waiting personnel wandered outside, listened and watched.

Two aircraft neared but flew on west of Waddington.

In the dim light of the morning two more were seen.

'Ours,' someone said, noting that they were joining the circuit. They would be in contact with the Control Tower from where they would be guided down by the officer in charge and the WAAF radio operators.

WAAF drivers left the admin block for their vehicles, ready to bring crews from their planes for debriefing. Others stood by to relieve the flyers of their parachutes; two WAAFs arrived with two LACs bringing urns of coffee. Anxious section leaders were there to welcome the crews back, hoping they had lost no one, eager to know if the raid had been successful. Carolyn, Lucy and Vera settled down at their tables and prepared to interview the returning crews, while Kate stood by ready to help her team with their first debriefing.

The outside door opened; footsteps seemed hesitant, more of a shuffle than a brisk step; words were subdued and spasmodic. Then the door to the briefing room opened. Seven men came in, their faces solemn, strained, tired. Kate directed them to Lucy's table. They collected mugs of coffee and flopped on to the wooden folding chairs that had been set out for their arrival. One man gave a weak smile, five looked as if they were thinking thank goodness that's over, and the last managed to wink at her.

She picked up her pencil and lined up a sheet of paper. She looked at the pilot. 'Flying Officer . . . ?' She felt awful for not knowing his name though she had seen him in the Mess.

'Stubbs,' he said.

She smiled and nodded.

So the interrogation started. The target was identified and bombed? How much ack-ack over the target and en route there and back? Fighter activity? Weather conditions? Visibility? Radio communications? So it went on, with Lucy making notes, until finally, 'Anything else to report?'

As soon as the pilot said 'Nothing', the crew pushed themselves to their feet and went to their lockers, got out of their flying clothing as quickly as possible then sought a vehicle with a WAAF driver to whisk them to their Messes where their usual fry-up awaited them. They made a few exchanges with other crews who had arrived but did not linger. They wanted their beds.

Carolyn felt some sense of relief when the first crew went to Lucy though she knew that was only postponing the inevitable. As more and more men came in she was jolted by the sight of their haggard faces, deeply etched by their recent experiences. Some tried to make light of them, others said little, and some could not disguise their emotions when they made their reports. 'Fighter took some pieces out of our wings.' 'Saw two bombers shot down.' 'A collision over the target – no one bailed out.' Carolyn had to concentrate to record and note the position of the incidents recounted to her by the navigators. Throughout the debriefings she found herself glancing anxiously at the door every time it opened to reveal another returning crew. Where were Uncle's men? Where was Rick? She looked across at Vera who, like herself had just finished debriefing a crew. They were wearily making their way to the locker room.

Vera raised a questioning eyebrow; Carolyn shrugged her shoulders. With no other crew awaiting debriefing, she left her table and went outside. She shivered as she met the chilly air. She strained to catch the tell-tale drone of an aircraft, but there was nothing. Her thoughts soared to the loneliness of the night sky. The door behind her opened and Vera came to stand beside her.

'It's too quiet,' she murmured, a catch in her voice.

'Oh, God, let them be safe.'

The door opened again. Lucy joined them.

'Two not reported,' she said reluctantly. 'U–Uncle and Z–Zebra. First op and twenty-third.'

'Makes no difference how many, they can still buy it.'

They continued to watch and wait.

'It's getting cold standing here.' Carolyn started to turn back to the hut. Her hand closed on the door knob but she did not open it. 'Listen!' There was an excited note in that one word.

'Nothing,' moaned Vera as the hope Carolyn had raised in her was dashed by a mocking silence.

'Shush!' snapped Lucy.

'You're both wishful thinkers,' commented Vera.

'No, we're not! There is a plane!' said Carolyn, her tone rising hopefully. 'You'd better get your hearing seen to.'

A distant hum, rising and falling on the night air, was getting louder with every second.

The three friends took in each note, hoping that the plane was theirs and not heading for another airfield.

'I can't wait here,' Carolyn said, and started for the Control Tower where the plane's identity would first be confirmed.

The other two were close behind her. They climbed the stairs to the Control Room. Carolyn stopped at the door, half turned and signalled to Lucy and Vera to be quiet. She gingerly opened the door. The officer in charge saw them and, knowing their relationship with the crew of U–Uncle, waved them in. He came over to them and in a low voice, so as not to interrupt the WAAF who was talking the crew down, said, 'It's Uncle. We couldn't get a report earlier, flak had destroyed their wireless.'

'Is anyone ... ?' Lucy's query trailed away; it did not need completion.

'WOP has facial and hand injuries, but nothing life-threatening.'

'Z–Zebra?' queried Vera.

'Nothing as yet,' replied the control officer. 'Now off with you, let's get Uncle down.'

Three relieved WAAF officers scurried away and took up position outside the door to the briefing block. They watched the black outline against the night sky join the circuit and then land successfully. They waited until the Lancaster had been brought to its hard standing and the engines shut down.

Returning to the briefing room, they added two more chairs to the eight that were already at the table they were going to use.

'You are going to give Rick Wood's crew high priority,' commented Squadron Officer Newbauld with a knowing smile.

'I think they deserve it after completing their first trip,' said Lucy brightly. 'Any news of Z?'

As if on cue the telephone rang. Kate picked up. She nodded. 'Thanks for that.' She gave the thumbs up for all to see and, as she replaced the phone, said, 'Zebra's safely down at Manston; made it back on three engines. There was a fighter attack. Some damage to fuselage and tail-plane, but crew OK.'

Relief saturated the briefing room. They awaited the arrival of Rick's crew. When they walked in a few minutes later, they were accompanied by the MO who had met the plane at its hard standing.

'Wireless Operator Barton has insisted on walking in, but now I'm whisking him off to hospital for a thorough check,' he announced. 'He's insisting he's OK, but that shoulder and arm need looking at and his facial cuts need attention. I'll probably keep him in for a couple of days.'

'Make the most of your chance for a bit of luxury,' called Tim, 'and keep your hands off those two pretty nurses. You won't be able to manage them, but you can save them for me. We gunners can cope.'

The hoots that followed that statement lightened the atmosphere, but the crew still showed the after effects of their night's work.

'Was it bad, Rick?' asked Carolyn.

'Not so bad as I thought it would be, but we had Uncle. She did everything I asked of her. She's a wonderful plane to fly. Didn't turn a hair when she was spattered by ack-ack fire.' Carolyn caught the note of deep feeling in his voice. 'A pity Gordon caught some of it. But he'll be OK.'

Details of the raid were related as the debriefing proceeded.

The next morning, with the weather over Western Europe deteriorating rapidly, all crews were stood down. Knowing the signs from experience, the people of Lincolnshire got ready to receive and welcome their RAF friends.

The two married men in Rick Wood's crew, Don Westwood and Phil Stevens, decided to have a meal in Lincoln, maybe take in a film, but primarily they wanted to phone their wives. When the RAF transport dropped them near Lincoln railway station, they found the telephones. Knowing they had to be careful about what they said, both men had devised a phrase that would tell their wives they had completed a raid into enemy territory safely. Don slipped in casually, 'By the way, Beth, you can cross one off your list.' Phil and Myrna had decided on, 'I've been into town again.' Both wives would now know their husbands had twenty-nine more missions to complete their tour of duty. Twenty-nine more operations filled with danger, and that took no account of training flights between missions. Peril stalked an aircraft whenever it took off.

19

The late May sun had warmed the spring air, encouraging the crew of U–Uncle to lounge on the grass close to their beloved Lancaster. She had brought them through four further missions safely and resisted all German efforts to tear her from the sky. The only evidence of this were some small holes in the fuselage, where spent shrapnel had only just managed to penetrate. Two fighters had broken off their attack to escape the fire from Tim's and Mark's guns and the raking fire from Pete's front turret. Rick's handling of the heavy bomber had been impeccable, reacting instantly to any instructions received from the two gunners and the bomb aimer.

Now they lay in the sun, waiting to learn if ops would be on tonight. They read books, chatted with each other and with their ground-crew, but every minute or so one of them cast an enquiring glance towards the group of large Nissen huts housing the various sections.

A door opened; two officers appeared. They paused, exchanged a few words then one returned inside while the other mounted a bicycle and rode away.

Don, on noticing this slight activity, laid down his book and sat up, eyes fixed on the door that had just closed. He was about to pick up his book again when he saw the door open once more. Three officers appeared and got into a staff car, to be driven away by a WAAF driver. Don reached out and shook Peter.

'What's up?' he asked drowsily.

'Something's happening,' replied Don, running his hand through his hair as he nodded in the direction of the huts.

Pete sat up, alert now to the activity. 'Here comes the skipper.'

With his announcement, aircrew and ground-crew scrambled to their feet and watched intently as Rick cycled towards them. All of them were now on tenterhooks.

He gave nothing away, keeping his face expressionless as he pulled up in front of the little group.

'Come on, Skip, are we on?' urged Pete.

'Yes. On leave,' he replied.

'Pull the other,' countered Pete.

'No. We go on a week's leave tomorrow which means we don't fly tonight.'

'Great!' 'Whoopee!' They all gave a cheer of some sort and Don added, 'Couldn't be better, I'll be home for Beth's birthday.'

'What about Uncle, is she stood down too?' asked Gordon.

'No,' replied Rick. 'The new crew that came in ten days ago will be taking her. Hey, Tubby,' he called, signalling to the sergeant in charge of the ground-crew. 'Make sure they don't mistreat her.'

'They'll have me to answer to if they do,' Tubby replied seriously. 'She's not to be meddled with, by them or by Jerry. The lads and I will look after her and have her in fighting trim for your return.' He turned to his fellow ground-crew. 'You heard that. Now let's see she's in trim for tonight.

187

I know you've all done your jobs, but let's make doubly sure everything's OK.'

They went off to do so, leaving the aircrew to themselves. Each of them felt they didn't want to leave their beloved aircraft in the hands of strangers.

Rick broke the uneasy quiet. 'We can pick up our passes from the Orderly Room in the morning.'

They started to head for their Messes and billets. No one suggested it but each sensed the others would be at the end of the runway later on to see U–Uncle take off without them.

'What's everyone doing during their leave?' asked Rick. 'I expect our two married men will be heading home.'

'Sure will,' they both chorused.

'I'll get in touch with Zoe,' said Tim

'I'll be around,' said Gordon. 'I might be able to persuade that pretty nurse who used her magic touch on my wounds to check them out again.'

'Joan and I are no longer seeing each other, so I'll head for home,' said Mark.

'I must do that too,' said Rick. 'Dad hasn't been well for a few weeks. I know Mum will appreciate my being there. Pete, I know things aren't easy with you and your aunts. I'd ask you to come home with me but as my dad isn't ...'

'No! No,' cut in Pete. 'I wouldn't consider it, under the circumstances. I appreciate your thinking of me but I'll go to my aunts'.'

'But you've told me you and they don't get on especially well?'

'I'm the nephew who was thrust upon maiden aunts who weren't too keen on children. They've done their best. I'll ring them.'

'I'm going to the Mess now, to call Mum and see how things are at home,' said Rick.

'I'll come too and try the aunts.'

'Let's call at the Intelligence section on the way and tell the girls we won't be around for a week.'

'A good idea,' agreed Pete.

They found the three WAAFs busy assembling maps and information.

'Are they for tonight?' asked Rick.

'Yes, but don't expect us to tell you where you are going,' said Vera.

'We wouldn't dream of asking you,' he replied. 'Besides, it doesn't matter to us, we aren't going.'

At that moment the door to the office used by Squadron Officer Newbauld opened and she walked in. 'There are you are.' She handed each of girls a small chit.

'Thank you very much, Ma'am,' they chorused, smiling broadly.

'What's going on?' asked Pete.

'They are on a week's leave as from tomorrow,' said Kate. 'When I got the information that you weren't flying, I made enquiries and was told you were going on leave. My three officers are due some leave soon too so I thought it might be a good idea for them to take it tomorrow, starting at the same time as you. I hope I haven't misjudged matters?'

'Not at all, Ma'am,' put in Rick. 'We appreciate the thought.'

'Well, sort yourselves out but don't be late back,' said Kate as she headed for her office.

'Ma'am, may I ask what is going to happen to the Intelligence section while they are away?' asked Rick.

'The girls know, as I'm sure you do, that there have been reorganizations within 5 Group, some of which have been my responsibility, especially those relating to the efficiency of Intelligence. I am pleased with the way they have taken shape and now have two back-up teams ready and waiting, whenever and wherever they are required. The present situation gives me the opportunity to study them at work and see if this back-up system is effective within an actual operation. One of those teams will be moving in permanently shortly. My three girls here will supervise the new arrivals, only interfering if there is any need to. Enjoy your leave.' She left them to return to her own office.

As the door closed behind her, Rick said, 'What are you going to do, Pete? I still have to go, to be with my mum and dad. I'm sorry.' He detected the disappointment on Vera's face, as she heard him speak.

'OK,' Carolyn said. 'It can't be helped and we hope your father is soon better. Lucy has told us her parents will not be at home so I have extended an invitation to her to come home with me.' Turning to Pete, and knowing a little of his situation, she added, 'Why don't you come too?'

'That would be splendid, but I can't impose on your mother and father.'

'You won't be doing that. They love having young people around, especially if they are in the Forces. That leaves Vera. Have you any plans?'

'None. With family all tied up with the war I'm faced with an empty house in Cornwall.'

'And a long journey,' added Carolyn, 'so I won't take no for an answer when I ask you to come with us.'

'But I can't add ... '

'I said, I won't listen. You are coming. Mum will just love having you all. So will Dad.'

'Thanks, Carolyn. I do appreciate your kindness.' Vera stepped forward and kissed her on the cheek.

'I'd better ring Mum, though I'm sure she will give the OK.' Carolyn glanced at her watch. 'She'll more than likely be at home so I'll ring now. Hang on here, I shan't be long.'

Ten minutes later she was back. 'All fixed. Beds are no problem. Mrs Gibson who lives next door has two rooms we can use. So it will be welcome to Nunthorpe for you all.'

Anxious for their aircraft, U–Uncle's crew were together to see her take off. Their anxiety whilst watching her roll down the runway faster and faster was relieved only a little when her wheels left the tarmac. They remained anxious until she was safely airborne and climbing steadily.

Now came the long wait for her return from Germany. The crew would experience the feeling of being left behind, not knowing what was happening, and wishing, in spite of the risks, that they were part of the bomber force tonight. Total relief came only when they saw Uncle, safe and unmarked, back in her dispersal. As they returned to their billets they thought of the coming week's safety, overlaid with the hope of seeing Uncle waiting for them when they returned to Waddington.

With debriefing over, Carolyn, Lucy and Vera cycled back to their billet, talking excitedly of tomorrow and their escape into tranquillity.

Rick said goodbye to them at Lincoln station; though he let his kiss on Vera's lips linger a little longer than usual, it did nothing to ease her thoughts. Why didn't he ask me to go with him? He hardly talked about his parents. Didn't he want her to meet them? Had he someone else at home he hadn't mentioned? She pushed these suspicions to the back of her mind, determined to enjoy her time at Nunthorpe. Maybe she could find out some more about Rick from Carolyn.

Seeing the romance between Lucy and Pete grow stronger, Vera realized she had become just as closely attached to Rick, while ever aware of the uncertainties of war and the dangers he faced. She hoped his return from leave would bring about a more settled state of affairs between them.

They were given a warm welcome by Carolyn's parents and her gran. Sally quickly had their bedrooms allocated, leaving them to settle in with the words, 'Tea and cake in twenty minutes.'

No one was late, even though by common consent they had all changed into civilian attire, leaving their uniforms on hangers in the wardrobes.

Guy and Sally got to know a little more about each of them while they enjoyed their tea, at the end of which Guy said, 'Make yourselves at home. Come and go as you please. You are most welcome. It is a delight for us to have you here, escaping the war for a few days.'

Peter stood up. 'I know I speak for everyone when I say, thank you, Mr and Mrs Maddison, and you, Gran, for your kindness and hospitality.'

'Don't be too hasty, young man. Enjoy? There are dish cloths, tea towels, spades and garden forks, and after that there are . . . '

'Quiet, Dad,' rapped Carolyn, 'don't frighten my friends away as soon as they've got here.'

Guy pondered for a moment and then laughed. 'Ah, well, maybe not. I should hate to miss my regular gardening stints.'

A little cheer went round the room and everyone relaxed; the stage for their leave was set. Guy capped it with the announcement, 'I'll book us in for an evening meal at the Quacking Duck in Marton on your last night here.'

20

It was a happy group who spent the rest of the day lazing at the house in Nunthorpe.

The following morning, awake at six, Carolyn was unable to go to sleep again. She got out of bed and slipped on her dressing gown. In the kitchen she made herself some tea and immersed herself in solitude. She became so absorbed in recalling Jean's advice to her that she was unaware of her father coming quietly into the room.

'You lost?' he queried.

She started.

'Is a father's opinion any good to you?' he asked. 'It used to be when you were troubled. You have that worried look I remember.'

She gave a little smile, which told him he had triggered her memory.

'Is this about a young man?' he asked gently.

It was the same persuasive tone he always used when offering his help, an assurance it would go no further. It could not be resisted. She told him about the crash; of her feelings for Rick and the fear she had of being irreparably hurt. She also told him about Jean's advice.

Guy listened without interruption, sensing he might miss something vital if he broke in on her revelations.

'There you are,' Carolyn concluded, 'your stupid daughter, taking life's troubles on her shoulders when there are so many more people facing far worse situations than I.'

'Yes, there are,' he agreed, 'but these are your problems. First of all, you must recognize the wisdom of Jean's words and bear them in mind. Secondly, you must try to forget that crash. It happened, unfortunately. It was terrible, and close to the start of your career. But I know you can be strong and overcome its effects. I know you believe so too. If you didn't, you would not have pursued your desire to serve on an operational station. You would have walked away from it and sought a mundane job in some other RAF department. You didn't do that, so I think you are close to letting memories of that crash fade away into the deeper recesses of your mind. That can be helped by the way you manage your feelings for other people.'

Carolyn rose quickly to her feet and kissed him on the cheek. 'Thank you, Dad.' The catch in her voice told him all he needed to know; she had been helped and comforted.

Two days later the early morning promised a fine day. As plans were being made, Guy came in with the morning newspaper.

'I see the Allied stranglehold in North Africa on Tunis and Bizerta is tightening. They could fall any day,' he announced.

'Good,' commented Peter. 'Nice to have better news. The tide seems to be turning.'

'And there's a piece here, Sally, that will interest you. It is compulsory now for British women between the ages of eighteen and forty-five to do part-time work.'

'About time too,' she said. 'The war effort should benefit.

Doesn't affect me by two years, but I am already doing three days' voluntary work in Middlesbrough. I'm free today so, if it suits, we'll eat at six. That won't cut into your time too much. Peter has been asking me about train times, I think he has something in mind for Lucy and himself, so Carolyn, why don't you and Vera take the Great Ayton bus and walk to Captain Cook's monument? Pack yourselves a light picnic.'

'That'll be fun,' both girls agreed.

'Your father has to go into Middlesbrough, and Gran and I will have a leisurely day at home.'

'So what have you in mind?' Lucy asked Peter when Carolyn and Vera headed for the kitchen.

'I thought we might take the train to Redcar, have a walk there, get some sea air and call on Don and Beth.'

Ten minutes after Peter and Lucy alighted from the bus close to the railway station in Middlesbrough they were on their way to Redcar.

'This is exciting, heading into the unknown,' said Lucy, moving closer to Pete in the compartment they had to themselves.

He smiled and slipped his hand into hers. 'This is nice,' he said. I hope no one gets into our compartment when we stop.'

'So do I. Are there many stations?'

'A few small ones, nothing the size of Middlesbrough.'

Have you any idea where Don lives?'

'No, but I have his address.'

Their first enquiry hit the target. An elderly lady eyed them suspiciously, obviously fearing she might be giving information useful to the enemy, but then she gave them directions. They thanked her but as they walked on they heard her chunter, 'Should be ashamed of himself . . . should be in the Forces.' Lucy and Pete suppressed the giggles that threatened to turn into full-blown laughter.

'Let's find a birthday present for Beth,' said Lucy.

A jeweller's presented some possibilities and a helpful elderly man produced an RAF brooch he thought might fill their requirements. While he was wrapping it up suitably for a birthday present, Peter held a whispered conversation with the shop owner, who quickly realized what Peter was about. A second purchase was secretly made and disappeared into his pocket.

'Your stocks must be low because of the war?' commented Lucy.

They are, miss, but I still have my contacts in the trade even though their supplies are curtailed. I do some local buying of second-hand items too. I must try to keep going. There are always people wanting a piece of jewellery or a similar item for a special occasion even in troubled times.'

'I think we should call on Don and Beth now. If they aren't in, we can go for a walk and call back later,' Lucy suggested.

They followed the directions the suspicious lady had given them and found their goal in a row of ten detached houses facing the sea.

'This is a lovely position,' said Lucy as they walked up the path to the front door.

'Looks great today but what about it when there's a howling storm blowing?'

She was pressing the doorbell and did not have time to comment.

A few moments later they saw a figure, blurred by the glass, approaching.

'Pete! Lucy! What . . . ? This is a surprise. Come in, come

in!' Don moved to one side and, as they stepped into the hall, called out, 'Beth. Visitors!'

She appeared, patting her hair where she had disarranged it taking her apron off. Her greeting was as warm as Don's. They were all soon seated in a comfortable lounge enjoying tea. Don and Beth were quickly told what had been happening on their leave. In turn they described the excitement of Beth's birthday, when close family who lived in Redcar had come together for a party.

'We'll make that last a little longer,' said Peter, as he produced a package from his pocket and handed it to Beth. 'Happy Birthday.'

Embarrassed but excited, she opened the package to reveal a light blue box. When she opened it her eyes widened. She sat there in shocked surprise and then, with a trembling voice and tears trickling down her cheeks, gasped, 'Thank you, thank you. Oh, it is so appropriate,' she added on seeing the etching of a Navigator's Wings. 'I'll treasure it for ever. This will always remind me of the men Don flew with on ops.' She jumped up to show it to her husband.

Don's voice choked as he expressed his thanks too on seeing the brooch.

'What are your plans for the rest of the day?' asked Beth.

'To have a walk and just enjoy the day together, then catch the afternoon train back.'

'Good, that will fit in perfectly. Don and I are asked to some friends in the late afternoon. You are invited to have lunch here with us first,' said Beth.

'No, no,' said Pete. 'We don't want to impose on you. That wasn't the idea at all.'

'You must stay. Please,' she said. 'They should, shouldn't they, Don?'

'Of course. We won't listen to any refusal.'

'But are we putting you to any trouble?' said Lucy.

'No, you're not. It will be pot luck but we'll manage something. Please stay.'

'All right. Thank you.'

They chatted for a while then Beth rose from her chair. 'I'll start lunch. Would you like to help, Lucy?'

'Of course.'

'It will give those two a chance to talk,' said Beth as they went into the kitchen, 'and we can have a good natter.'

'This is a nice room,' commented Lucy, 'spacious and so much light.'

'We are very fortunate. Don's father is a builder. He speculated before the war, bought this land and built these houses. But he kept one, believing Don would want it. He and I met at school and, well, the rest is history.'

'So you married early?'

'Yes, probably earlier than we intended, but the war propelled us into it. And I'm so glad it did.'

'You have no fears of . . . '

'Of course, but we all have to deal with them. I believe the love there is between Don and me sustains us and helps us both to cope. It certainly helps me. What about you and Pete? He paid you a lot of attention at the party.'

Lucy smiled. 'Was it that noticeable?'

'I'd say he was falling in love. How about you?'

Lucy smiled. 'I think so.'

'Don't dally if you think it's for real. Time may run out before you expect it. But that's enough of me acting as your adviser. Let's go and enjoy lunch.'

After Peter and Lucy left Don and Beth they had plenty of time to enjoy a walk away from the main part of Redcar. They walked along the sea front with the sun shining brightly. The sea broke in small waves, running up the beach until they could advance no more but only return to the vast North Sea.

Talk flowed between Lucy and Peter then faded until it drifted into a shared silence that drew them closer. Without any suggestion from either of them their hands came together in a touch that said more than words. Before long they were alone. Peter stopped and turned Lucy to him.

His eyes dwelt on hers as if he was seeking confirmation of what was in his mind. Her eyes held his, desiring him to say what she thought she saw.

Confirmation came when he kissed her. Her desire was fulfilled when he said, 'Lucy Gaston, I love you.' They kissed again but this time their lips lingered. As they finally parted she said, 'I love you too, Peter.'

He put his hand in his pocket and drew out a package. 'A memento of our visit to Beth and Don.'

She quickly opened it and stared at the brooch. It was identical to Beth's except that this one had a B etched on it, marking Peter's role in the crew. 'Oh, it's lovely,' gasped Lucy, and gave him a quick kiss. 'I didn't know you'd bought this. I was in the shop all the time, how did you manage it?'

'The shop-keeper cottoned on to what I was doing and played along when you were looking around after we had decided on Beth's gift. A good job he did otherwise I wouldn't have managed this.' As he was speaking Pete withdrew another box from his pocket and gave it to her.

'What's this?' asked Lucy.

'Open it and see. I'll hold your brooch while you do.'

Puzzled, she did as she was told. Then gasped, staring wide-eyed at the contents: a ring set with three diamonds.

'Marry me, Lucy?'

She looked up at Pete. There was a moment of silence.

'Yes, please,' she said.

She came into his arms then, into a moment she would always remember, and a kiss that would remain for ever sweet.

They strolled to the station in a world of their own, but once they were in a carriage reality intruded.

'I would like us to keep this to ourselves until I have broken the news to Mum and Dad,' Lucy said.

'Let's make that until *we* have told them.' Peter grinned. 'Your father might like me to ask his permission to marry his daughter!'

'You'll tell your aunts?'

'Of course, they deserve that. After all, they did bring me up. But I don't think it will bother them, I think they'll be only too delighted to relinquish any involvement with me.'

'So that's settled. Not a word to anyone until we've seen my mum and dad.'

'Agreed. You are going to have to keep that ring out of sight.'

'I think I'd better try it on. It might not fit. You put it on for me.'

He slipped it neatly on to her finger.

'The jeweller who advised me said he was sure it would be all right. His experience has paid off.'

'I'm going to wear it until we get to Middlesbrough,' said Lucy with great delight, and snuggled closer to her fiancé.

'Why is there a monument to Captain Cook on this hill?' asked Vera as she and Carolyn started the climb.

'He was born close by here at Marton, went to school in the area, and worked for a shopkeeper in Staithes on the coast. He got a taste for the sea and served as a seaman under

200

a Quaker ship-owner whose ships sailed out of Whitby. He later went into the Navy and used Whitby built ships for his voyages of exploration. He has a lot of associations with this area.'

The climb made them puff and pant but they enjoyed it even though it kept interrupting their chatter. It wasn't until they reached the top, examined the tall memorial, and found a hollow on the hillside where they could sit to enjoy the sunshine and their picnic, that conversation flowed more easily. Gradually it turned to the serious side of their lives.

'Are you enjoying being at Waddington?' Vera asked.

'Yes,' replied Carolyn. 'I've got settled. The job is interesting and I think it will become more so when 5 Group is able to attack more targets on its own.'

'I wish they would get on with it. They brought me up here as an expert photographic interpreter. That hasn't materialized as I expected.'

'Give it time, Vera, there's a lot of organization to iron out first.'

'We weren't even involved in assembling information for the Dams operation.'

'March 1943,' mused Carolyn. 'Such raids can't be created overnight. We couldn't have coped. We were still getting our Intelligence section organized along the lines Kate envisaged. The Dams raid was in mind long before that, and there were specialities that had to be assembled by Intelligence which we weren't ready to deal with. Our turn will come as 5 Group's role becomes independent of the main force.'

'I hope you're right, I want to get my teeth into something.'

'Have you sorted all the photos that were landed on you?'

'Oh yes. They're all filed and indexed. They're standard

items; we need something new to make us into a top working unit.'

'As I say, that will come, I'm sure. Kate has put a lot of thought into what she sees as the right direction for us as the main Intelligence section in 5 Group. She's not going to let that founder.'

'It will be interesting to see if there have been any new developments while we have been away,' said Vera. 'Incidentally, thank you once again for inviting me. It has made a lovely break ... and still is, of course. I wonder how Rick is getting on?'

'Are you missing him?'

'I suppose so, but not as much as I expected. I thought he might have invited me to go with him.'

' Maybe it's not the right time, when his father is ill.'

'As you know, we have been seeing quite a lot of each other but never once has he mentioned his parents to me. He talks more and more about flying. I think he is becoming obsessed with it, and that plane.'

'I think that's only natural for a person of his temperament. Something new catches his attention and it's all or nothing for Rick.'

'Do you think that applies to his personal relationships?'

Carolyn hesitated, wondering how far she should go. She still had feelings for him. 'To be frank, Vera, it's a possibility. He would not consider my terms of a casual attachment only, which I didn't think too onerous. So we remain on cool terms.'

Vera nodded thoughtfully. 'Maybe I should take that route too, given his attitude to that Lancaster. It's becoming like a love rival.'

'That's a strange analogy. Surely it's not so bad'

'It could get that way, or am I just being stupid?'

21

Their leave came to an end with regrets that it was over.

Carolyn arrived back at Waddington still wondering if she had been wrong in her attitude to Rick.

Vera, refreshed by the break, was now determined that if flying meant so much to him, she would try to be more understanding.

Lucy and Peter came back with their secret. The bomb aimer brooch was admired but the diamond ring lay in her suitcase, kept secret for the time being.

'See you in the Mess later,' called Pete as the three girls headed for their billets, after the taxi had dropped them at the guardroom.

'I suggest a quick settle in and then off to see Kate to find what has been happening while we've been away,' said Carolyn.

Before they came to their section they had an unhindered view of the whole airfield. They stopped as one and for a moment remained speechless.

'Spitfires!'

'Three of them.'

'What are they doing here?'

'Must be visiting.'

'If they are, they aren't in the usual place for visiting aircraft.'

'Kate will know. Come on.'

There was no one in the two main rooms of their section but when they knocked on Kate's door they received an answer.

'Ah, you are back!' She rose from her chair to greet them. 'Did you have a good leave?'

'Wonderful,' they all agreed.

'So, ready for the fray again?'

'Yes, Ma'am,' said Vera, thinking she should sound more official because of her next question. 'What are three Spitfires doing here?'

Kate gave a little smile. 'They're ours.'

The girls looked askance at her. 'The Squadron's? Waddington's?'

Kate kept up the formality. 'Ours. Well, to be more precise, Flight Officer Vera Williams's. She'll have the most to do with them.'

The inference was beginning to dawn on Vera. 'High-flying Spitfires of the Photographic Unit?'

'Exactly,' Kate confirmed. 'Seconded to us until further notice.'

'Great!' whooped Vera. 'Come on, you little beauties. Get some nice photos for your Auntie Vera.'

When the laughter and excitement died down, Kate said, 'This is a great step forward for us. It marks the agreement by the top dogs at Bomber Command that 5 Group can now operate independently whenever a target needs the Group's special attention. The Dams raid proved it.

'Now, àpropos of that, whatever developments there are, whatever raids are planned, they are strictly not to be mentioned to anyone ... and that means *anyone*. Understood?

I'm telling you this because there are already rumours flying around within the group. You know how it is when unusual things appear to be taking place. So you know nothing, OK?' She paused to let this sink in. 'Our aim of being the main Intelligence section in 5 Group is strengthened by the evidence that stands outside – three Spitfires.'

Lucy tightened her lips. Will I be able to keep this from Peter until it is generally known? she wondered.

Vera interjected into the silence, 'How long have they been here, Ma'am?'

'Only two days. The pilots are sounding the place out. We were scheduled for four Spitfires. I presume that still stands. I have not been told otherwise.'

The three friends and Peter were having their evening meal together in the Mess when Rick walked in. The quick glances the four of them exchanged confirmed their opinion that he did not look good. His face was drawn, his colour gone, and his eyes dull, lifeless almost in spite of his effort to present himself otherwise.

'How were things at home?' Vera asked as he slid into the seat beside her and she surreptitiously squeezed his hand.

'Not good,' Rick replied. 'In fact, bloody awful!'

'Your father?' Carolyn raised their concern. She studied him for his reaction.

Rick gave a little shake of his head. 'The doctor gave him nine months ... a year at the most.'

His shock was evident and they all offered their commiserations.

Rick thanked them and gave a little shrug of his shoulders. 'It can't be helped. It is just one of those things we can do nothing about, but it's so hard when you think he's not even old. And there's only going to be me there for Mum.'

'You'll have to see if you can get extended leave,' suggested Carolyn.

'I don't want to do that. I'd lose my crew, I'd lose Uncle and I'd miss flying, just when I feel they are a vital part of my life. So I would rather you kept this to yourselves. Promise me you'll tell no one? But, Peter, you'd better tell the crew.'

The passion with which Rick made that request was not lost on Vera. 'If that's the way you want it, then we promise.'

'But if things don't pan out then see the CO,' added Peter. 'He's an understanding man and might have some ideas to help you get through this.'

'That's possibly the best way forward,' agreed Lucy. 'Now, after your travelling, I think you had better have something to eat.'

Vera agreed.

Rick pulled a face. 'I don't feel like anything.'

'You should try something,' put in Vera 'You've got to eat to keep up your strength and concentration. On your feet, come and choose what you want.'

He knew they were right, especially as he hadn't eaten all day because of the final arrangements he had had to make: getting his father to hospital, then arrangements for his mother's two sisters to be on call, especially when his father would be allowed home after more checks and assessments.

Lucy urged him on to his feet and with Peter to cajole him Rick set about making his choice at the hot-plate.

Watching from their table, Carolyn said, 'This has hit him hard.'

'It has,' agreed Vera. 'I hope it doesn't affect his flying.'

'Surely it won't,' said Carolyn firmly.

'He hasn't mentioned the Spitfires and he must have seen them.'

'He's just paid no heed to them.'

'Do you really think that's like Rick? He should be enthusing and wanting to know all about them.'

'We'll test him out when he's had his meal.'

He ate without enthusiasm.

When he laid down his knife and fork, Vera said, 'Did you see the three Spitfires, Rick?'

'Spitfires?'

They saw his eyes brighten as they told him about them. 'I've got to see these!'

Turning to Vera, he touched her arm and they both rose from the table, to be followed outside by the others. They were glad that looking at the three aircraft seemed to have taken Rick's mind off his troubles, if only for a short while.

The next morning, as the early-morning mist was dispersing from the Lincolnshire countryside, the crew gathered by Uncle and Pete told them about Rick's father. Immediately they all rallied in support of their skipper.

He seemed pleased by their concern, but after a while said, 'I'll go and see if there's likely to be any flying,' and headed for the flight office.

'He's too early,' commented Tim. 'Word won't be through for another hour.'

'It'll give him something to occupy his mind,' said Gordon.

They chatted amongst themselves about their leave, and with the ground-crew about Uncle and how she had fared in their absence. They fell silent when they saw extra activity taking place at the admin buildings.

'Here he is!' called Mark.

They fell silent as they watched the approaching figure, trying to read the likely outcome for them from his manner.

Rick shook his head. 'We aren't going tonight.' Disappointment was obvious in his tone. 'We have to do a test flight with Uncle now. An hour's cross-country flight.'

'All of us?' asked Tim.

'Yes. Flight Officer said he likes to send a crew that's just back from leave on a test flight. Gives them a chance to gel again and pick up where they were.'

'So, is Uncle operating tonight?' asked Phil.

'No, she's stood down too.' No one commented on this; they could sense Rick's feelings about doing this check, and no one wanted to stoke a fire.

'Rick and his crew are not on the battle list for tonight,' commented Vera when she arrived at the Intelligence section. 'They have to take Uncle on an hour's test flight. Rick doesn't like that at all.'

Carolyn, busy with material for tonight's raid, kept an ear open for nearby Uncle starting up. When she heard the familiar sound of the Merlin engines she asked, 'Are you coming to see her taxi out?'

The three friends waved as Rick took the Lancaster to the perimeter track, and he gave a desultory wave back.

'He doesn't seem very enthusiastic about flying,' commented Lucy. 'That's not the Rick we know. He's always so keen to be airborne.'

They watched him take off safely. As they went back into the building, Vera said, 'I'll slip into Control, ask them to let us know when Uncle is sighted.'

'Bomb Aimer to Skipper, base straight ahead.' Pete, from his position in the nose of the aircraft, was pleased to report the sighting. This had not been the best of cross-country flights; Rick had seemed reserved, his replies clipped, without the usual ease of delivery. Pete had detected no enthusiasm in his flying either. It was as if he was finding this checking of Uncle a useless irritation.

'Where?' There was a note of irritation in Rick's reply.

'If you keep on this course you'll fly straight over it.' Pete was surprised that Rick had not seen the airfield immediately. He was usually so quick about locating it, often managing it before Pete.

A WAAF who had been on the balcony of the Control Tower came in and placed her binoculars on the desk.

'U–Uncle's in sight. Should be calling in any moment.'

The two WAAF s in the Control Room, who occupied their time knitting when there was little flying, put down their needles and prepared to talk U–Uncle down safely.

The WAAF who had made the sighting went quickly to the Intelligence room. 'Uncle's on her way.'

'Thanks,' called Lucy, pleased that Peter was nearing home.

'I'll bet they've enjoyed flying again,' commented Vera, as the three friends went outside to see the Lancaster land. 'I hope this has put Rick in a better frame of mind.'

'There she is!' Lucy pointed excitedly. Welcoming Peter home today seemed like a special occasion to her, but she had to be careful to keep her enthusiasm toned down; they still had to make an official announcement about their engagement.

Rick called base seeking permission to land, but got no reply. He tried again, still without success, and cursed under his breath.

'wop, I can't raise control,' he snapped.

'OK, Skipper. I'll try them,' replied the wireless operator.

'Be bloody quick about it!' rapped Rick.

Gordon pulled a face; this was so unlike the Rick he knew, who would usually have sympathized with his difficulty.

Minutes passed. Rick seemed anxious. His hands felt hot. He tightened his grip on the control column. 'Come on, come on,' he hissed, then exclaimed loudly, 'WOP, what the hell are you playing at?'

'Everything's dead, Skipper. I can't . . . '

'Try harder!' Rick yelled.

The WAAFs in the control tower tried in vain to raise U–Uncle.

'Can't get any response,' one of them called out.

'Keep trying,' ordered the officer in charge as he moved to a better position to view the Lancaster. 'Keep the incoming line open.'

'Line open,' another WAAF responded.

'Still no contact, Skipper,' Gordon reported. 'Everything is dead.'

'Damn!' fumed Rick. 'I'll have to go in without permission.' As if to relieve his frustration he immediately banked the Lancaster into a tight turn, cutting a corner of the circuit and losing height at the same time.

'Ruddy hell, Skipper, take it easy!' yelled Peter, who was now standing behind the engineer, his position for landing. The two crew members exchanged glances of alarm.

Don, who had left his position to look out of the astrodome, glanced down at Gordon, still trying to make contact with the Control Tower. Unease came into their eyes as Rick banked the Lancaster even further. The gunners, alone in their turrets could do nothing but hope that Rick would recover from a position that was edging them towards disaster.

*

'What the hell's he doing?' Unease laced the Flying Control officer's voice when he saw Rick bank the aircraft steeply to cut the corner and take a slice out of the circuit he should follow. While still keeping their contact lines open, the WAAF radio operators stared disbelievingly at what must be a disaster unfolding before their eyes.

Carolyn, Lucy and Vera were frozen to the spot by the antics of Uncle.

'What's Rick doing?' gasped Carolyn, seeing the aircraft bank more steeply. As if in answer the pilot pulled the control column. Uncle straightened but was in no position to make a successful landing.

'Oh my God!' gasped Vera, thinking Rick was going to try. Her face paled; she didn't want to lose him!

Lucy stood frozen in fear, but her mind brought Pete vividly before her and she kept repeating to herself, 'I want to get married. I want to get married. I want to get married.'

The Lancaster dropped. 'You won't do it!' yelled Peter when he saw how close they were to the ground. He looked at Rick and was shocked by the set expression on his face, My God, Peter thought, he's snapped! So he did the only thing he could – he had to assume authority.

'Get her up! Get her up! Go round again!' he yelled, in a tone that demanded instant obedience.

The bomb aimer's command reached Rick through the roar of the engines. He eased the control column to take the hurtling Lancaster away from the airfield. Pete remained silent, watching his skipper carefully. He saw that the insanity he had glimpsed for a moment had disappeared. Rick's hands were relaxed, caressing the control column to make the Lancaster do his bidding. He levelled out in the proper manner on rejoining the circuit.

With tension draining away everyone one breathed more easily. They watched Rick straighten the Lancaster at the start of his circuit and follow the usual procedure towards the final part of his approach.

'Undercarriage!' Carolyn's shout drew everyone's attention back to Uncle.

No undercarriage was showing! Was it aircraft trouble or pilot error? The questions racing through their minds were forgotten in the anxiety that gripped them again.

'Undercarriage!' yelled the engineer.

Rick grabbed at the lever and pulled. The plane jolted as the wheels started to lower.

The final turn had to be made; Rick banked the aircraft to line U–Uncle with the long finger of the runway, but she was close to the ground. Sizing up the danger, Peter yelled, 'Up, Rick! Up!'

Like a thunderclap in his mind, Rick realised Pete was right! Rick pulled at the control column. The nose came up. Too much. He corrected. The heavy machine sank. The wheels hit the runway. The Lancaster bounced. Sank. Rubber met tarmac. Uncle bounced again. She dropped once more. Tyres screeched but gripped. The Lancaster tore down the runway. Rick started to apply the brakes. He kept the aircraft steady and gradually she responded to the resistance and finally came to a stop where the runway met the perimeter track. Only fields lay beyond.

Every member of the crew breathed a sigh of relief. The watchers on the ground, silent with exhaustion, felt a lifetime had passed before their eyes.

Carolyn cradled her head in her hands, trying to expel the vision of a Stirling unable to clear some trees. She felt a gentle touch on her shoulder, saw Vera's ashen face and heard her friend whisper, 'I thought I'd lost him.'

Lucy stood unmoving, staring at the Lancaster shivering with shock. Tears streamed down her face.

Carolyn shook herself and said, 'Come on. I'll get you both a cup of tea.'

The suggestion sounded so ludicrous that the three WAAFs started to giggle and they didn't stop until the tea was ready.

The telephone rang in the Control Tower. The officer picked up.

'Adjutant here. Who was flying that plane?' he demanded.

'Flying Officer Rick Wood.'

'Tell him to report to me immediately.'

'Can't do it. All communication with him was lost before he reached base.'

'All right. I'll contact him myself when he gets to his dispersal.' The adjutant hung up.

'Rick is taxiing,' commented Vera, looking out of the window of the Intelligence section. Carolyn and Lucy joined her. Steadily Rick brought Uncle to her dispersal.

'I'm off to see Pete,' said Lucy.

'Better keep out of the way,' replied Carolyn. 'The adj is heading there and his stride spells trouble.'

22

Rick brought Uncle to a halt and closed down the engines. He left his seat and exited the plane quickly without a word to any of his crew. He had seen the adjutant waiting and had guessed what was coming.

His feet had barely touched the ground before the adjutant said, 'CO wants you immediately, Wood.' He turned to Peter who had just got out. 'Bring the rest of the crew to my office immediately and wait there.' Rick fell into step beside the adjutant who said brusquely, 'Don't ask questions. I can't give you any answers and I've to make no comment.'

The adjutant knocked on the CO's door and entered at his terse, 'Come in.'

'Flying Officer Wood, sir,' announced the adjutant.

Rick came smartly to attention and saluted. The adjutant turned to go.

'Wait, Jack, I need you to hear this.'

The adjutant nodded and closed the door. He knew his CO wanted a witness to Wood's answers.

The superior officer let the silence charge the atmosphere as he eyed Rick critically but without final condemnation: he had not heard Wood's explanation yet.

Judging the moment to be just right, he snapped, 'What the devil were you doing, Wood? You could have created a devilish disaster.'

'I'm sorry, sir.'

'Sorry? People could have died. There could have been carnage – and all because you wanted to show off.'

'No, sir, I didn't.'

'Well, what other reason can you give me?'

'All communication with Control was lost, sir.'

'That's no excuse for flying as you did. Cutting a corner of the circuit is inexcusable. It caused confusion as to what was happening but, worst of all, it took you into a situation that could have become impossible to counteract. You were lucky. I'll not say skilful because you should never have got into a situation where lives were jeopardized. I made a quick study of your records while waiting for you. Up to now they've been exemplary. I don't know what got into you today. Have you anything else to say?'

'No, sir.'

'Nothing else to mitigate what you did?'

'No, sir.'

'Very well. You are dismissed for now, but I will want to see you again.'

Rick saluted smartly and left.

'I think there's more to this than we have heard,' said the CO. 'If the crew are waiting, wheel them in one by one.'

Peter, as the other officer in the crew, was first in.

'Just give me the facts about what happened up there,' said the CO.

Peter did just that, passing no opinions. In their answers to the same question, the crew were all guarded in their replies. When the adjutant had seen them all he dismissed them except for Peter, whom he asked to wait outside.

'Jack, what have you gleaned from those reports?' the CO asked, eyeing his adjutant with a searching look.

'They were all a little reticent in their replies. I felt they were fearful they might give something away ... something that would go against Wood who they regard as an excellent pilot and a good fellow. I did not detect any disharmony among them. I think there is something we still haven't heard about.'

'Exactly my feelings,' agreed the CO. 'Obviously what happened in the plane cannot be assessed in the same way by every crew member because of their location within the Lancaster. The breakdown in communications must be investigated and the cause put right, but whatever happened it's no excuse for Wood's flying behaviour. Jack, let's have Pilot Officer Wilkins in again.'

Peter saluted and looked straight ahead, controlling his feelings while waiting for his CO to speak.

'Sit down, Wilkins.' The senior officer indicated the chair on the opposite side of the desk and gestured to the adjutant to sit at the end of the desk.

'Wilkins, I have interviewed your crew. Everyone is in agreement on what actually happened. Nobody seems to be hiding anything in that respect, but I get the strong feeling that there is something else that I am not hearing, something that might have affected Flying Officer Wood's judgement. If you know of anything that may have adversely affected that, I urge you to tell me. If you tell me that Wood's irresponsible action today was caused by a private matter, it will go no further than this room, I promise you.'

The adjutant nodded his approval.

Peter hesitated. How much should he tell, if anything? Would Rick even admit he had allowed a personal problem to influence his flying in a way that had endangered lives?

How much did he value his privacy? Peter battled with his thoughts until he decided that he could not let his friend face a ruined career by holding back the truth.

Still waiting for an answer, the CO said, 'From your hesitation I deduce that this has something to do with Wood's private life. It would be best if you told me what it is.'

'Sir, my skipper asked his three closest friends and the crew to say nothing about the trouble he encountered when he went on leave.'

'What was that?' asked the adjutant when Peter paused.

'His father is seriously ill. The doctor told Rick his father has no more than a year to live.'

The CO's lips tightened. He gave a little shake of his head. 'Terrible, terrible.'

'He is an only child, sir, and has his mother to consider. The only support appears to be from two aunts, but they don't live nearby and of course have their own families.'

'It is tragic news for Wood, and not a problem that will be easily solved.'

'He has become engrossed in flying lately,' Peter continued. 'I think he sees it as balm for his troubles, especially flying on ops. He was very disappointed not to be on the Battle Order tonight, with a cross-country test flight as the only consolation. I think the shock of the news about his father, coupled with the frustration of missing out tonight, got to him and he flipped. I was near him in the plane, I saw it happen.'

Looking Peter in the eyes, the CO said, 'And from what some crew members told me, your speedy and precise actions saved you all from disaster. I want to thank you myself for preventing a needless tragedy. Wilkins, you must not believe you have betrayed the trust of a friend in speaking to me. After I have had a quiet word with Wood, I am sure he will see it that way too.'

217

'I know he's strong enough to do so, sir, and from now on I believe his flying will be beyond reproach.'

'I am sure you are right, Wilkins. Thank you for being so frank with me. That will be all. Find Wood and send him to me. There's a lot happening with ops on tonight, but I'd like to put this matter to bed at once.'

'Yes, sir.' Peter saluted and marched out.

He found Rick eyeing the Spitfires.

'CO wants you now, Rick.'

He gave a little smile. 'Walk back with me?'

'Sure.'

'I was a fool, Pete. I've let myself down, the crew down, the girls down, the squadron down. I deserve what's coming to me.'

'Don't be too hard on yourself, Rick. What's done is done. It could have been worse.' Peter was thankful that Rick did not press him to say anything about his interview with the CO.

They stopped just short of the admin block.

'Pete, thanks for what you did up there. Your reactions saved us from complete disaster.' Rick did not give him chance to reply and in a few moments was saluting his CO.

'Sit down, Wood.'

Surprised, Rick did as he was ordered. He had expected a stripping down leading to some form of punishment. Maybe, just maybe, he would be lucky. He shot a quick glance at the adjutant who was sitting quietly on one side.

'Wood, I have spoken with your crew. They are a fine, reliable bunch. You had confided in them on a private matter, which they were guarded about divulging. Pilot Officer Wilkins eventually saw the wisdom of sharing this with me and explained he saw it as the reason for your behaviour. I am sorry you did not come to me with your problem in the first place, but it is no good harking back to that. I have weighed everything up and believe that such an occurrence will not happen again. I think today will have made you strong enough to cope with your father's illness and not let it affect your flying.'

'Yes, sir.'

'I am going to overlook this misdemeanour. From now on I look for great things from you and your crew.'

'Thank you, sir.'

'One thing more, Wood. If you have any further problems, come to the adjutant and he will judge if it is something for us to deal with. We are both here to solve any problems that might interfere with the smooth running of the squadron and the station.'

'Yes, sir.

'Oh, there is one other thing ... give my best wishes to your father, won't you?'

'Yes, sir. Thank you, sir.'

The CO nodded. Rick sprang from his chair, saluted and walked briskly out. He felt overwhelmed with joy at his reprieve, and vowed that henceforth flying would be first and foremost in his mind. There was a spring in his step as he headed for the Intelligence section. He wanted to break the good news to Vera whom he knew would have been on a knife edge too.

The three WAAFs were putting the final touches to their information for the crews engaged on tonight's raid on Dusseldorf when Rick walked in.

'Vera jumped to her feet when she saw him, her face filled with concern.

'Everything's OK. 'The words were accompanied by a broad smile. 'I just got a ticking-off.'

Vera rushed over to Rick and flung her arms round him. 'Oh, I'm so glad! What a relief.'

'Thank goodness,' sighed Carolyn.

'That's good,' agreed Lucy

'The CO had high praise for Pete, Lucy.' When Rick saw her puzzled expression, he explained, 'Pete saved the day. Thank goodness he had done the rudiments of a pilot's course and recognized the danger when I flipped. He blasted a command at me, which I automatically obeyed. He's precious metal, Lucy. Look after him.'

Still somewhat bemused, she said, 'I will. I didn't realize ... Pete, a hero?' She choked and her eyes dampened.

'I think we'd better get this job finished or the CO will be ticking *us* off,' broke in Carolyn.

'I'll get out of your way,' said Rick, his fingers still curled around Vera's. 'What time is take-off?'

'It's been put back an hour to give an unpleasant weather front over Germany time to clear.'

'So it will still be light at take-off?'

'Yes.'

'Shall we wave them off together?' he asked.

They all agreed.

One by one Merlin engines started up around the airfield. Crews carried out their last-minute tests, making sure everything was as it should be. A small group began to gather at the end of the runway, among them the crew of U–Uncle wishing they were preparing to take off for Dusseldorf, yet thankful they would be spared the hell of the night sky that awaited the men in these Lancasters. There would be another chance for them. Tomorrow? Two days' time? Not for a week? But they knew it would come.

Three WAAFs watched plane after plane line up at the end of the runway, heard the roar of the engines and witnessed the ever-increasing speed needed to get each Lancaster and its heavy load into the sky. Were their arms raised in farewell a comfort to these men off to face death in the skies? How many of them would be waving an acknowledgement in the morning? At least they had Uncle's crew safe tonight.

The last Lancaster rose from the ground and soon became a fading dot against the darkening sky, its engines sending back one final note of farewell.

The watchers each made their personal wish for the crews' safe return and then walked back towards their Messes and billets. Their talk was stilted, as if they saw it as sacrilege to be trying to lead a normal life while their friends were risking death.

Vera slipped her hand into Rick's.

Lucy linked arms with Pete.

Carolyn hung back, finally setting off over the deserted airfield on her own.

Don and Phil walked together, bemoaning the phone restrictions. 'I wish we could let Beth and Myrna know we aren't flying tonight. Then they could sleep easy,' Don was saying.

Tim thought of the news that had thrilled him earlier that day. His step lightened and he caught up with Gordon and Mark. 'I've something to celebrate,' he said. 'Buy you a pint in the village pub?'

'Thanks,' they both agreed.

'Mine will have to be a quick half, though,' said Gordon. 'When I knew we wouldn't be on ops tonight, I got word to Wendy to meet me outside the pub. Said we'd get the bus into Lincoln and go to the flicks.'

'You don't lose any time!' chaffed Mark. 'So you're getting Wendy to nurse you in the back row now instead of in the camp hospital?'

'Well, that leaves you and me to continue the celebrations

when he's dumped us for Wendy,' said Mark. 'What are we celebrating anyway, Tim?

'Zoe has had her application for a transfer approved by the Land Army. She will be moving in two weeks from North Lincolnshire to a farm three miles from Waddington.'

'Hey, do you realize that makes me the only member of Uncle who hasn't got a girl on hand?' complained Mark.

'You'd better get organized then,' Tim suggested.

'I sure will.'

'Maybe we could help him,' said Gordon. 'Fix him up with a blind date.'

'We'll give him a choice, Land Army or nurse?'

'I'll do my own choosing,' grunted Mark.'

'Spoil-sport!'

'Coward!'

'You'll see. One day you'll be asking me, how did I reel that glamour-puss in?'

'That'll be the day!'

23

Carolyn sank on to her bed, her thoughts in confusion. She felt in need of company, but did not want to intrude on Lucy and Vera. Where her thoughts led her and for how long she did not know, but suddenly she found herself looking in the mirror and getting ready to visit the Mess. She knew it would be quiet tonight and harbour the special atmosphere it held when ops were on.

She paused outside the billet. Darkness was closing in. Recalling the Met report that the crews would have a 'bomber's moon' before the attack started, she hoped U–Uncle would escape the attention of the German night fighters.

She entered the Mess, discarded her hat and greatcoat, and was walking to the ante-room when the outside door burst open behind her. She hesitated and turned to see three young flight lieutenants laughing at something one of them had just said.

'A shilling you can't do it!'

'Get your money ready,' ordered one, who was holding his hat.

Carolyn waited to watch the outcome.

The officer made a few sweeping gestures with his hat

towards the pegs on the wall. Then with one deft movement he sent it skimming through the air. It spun in its trajectory.

Carolyn held her breath and watched it spin, dip and fall on to a peg.

There was a peal of laughter and several cheers from the three pilots. A smiling Carolyn clapped.

The officer who had thrown his hat moved quickly to her side and took her arm. 'A drink with my winnings for my lucky charm!' he cried, and led her to the bar.

'Greg Saunders,' he introduced himself with a broad, endearing smile, his flashing eyes revealing how lucky he considered himself to have beaten his two fellow officers to getting her attention. 'Ignore these two,' he added, trying to edge them out.

She laughed. 'I can't do that! I must welcome all new-comers to the Mess and to Waddington. Carolyn Maddison, Intelligence section,' she said, and held out to him her hand. 'Greg, welcome.'

'Thanks. These two no-goods are Merv Harris and Allan Carson. That's Allan with two ls.'

She shook hands with them. 'And I suppose you fly those Spitfires parked out there?'

'Bright girl,' commented Allan.

'And pretty with it,' said Merv, assuming a serious tone of voice. 'It's a prerequisite for Intelligence work, you know.'

Carolyn laughed and said, 'And the DFC ribbons you're all sporting tell me you aren't new to those planes.'

'One hundred per cent accurate, miss, go to the top of the class.'

'These two are the jokers in the pack,' explained Greg. 'Now I'd better keep my promise about my winnings. What is it to be?'

'A malt, please.'

Greg chose to accompany her in a whisky and, knowing what their choice would be, ordered beer for the others.

When they had collected their glasses, Merv and Allan went off to play darts.

Carolyn finished her drink. Greg drained his and said, 'Should you and I go and eat?'

'What about those two?' she asked, nodding in the direction of the darts players.

'Don't bother about them, they're happy enough. They'll grab something when they're ready. We are the best of pals but we don't hang out together all the time. We go our own ways.' He paused and shot her a charming smile. 'So should we go?'

'Yes, why not?' she replied brightly, thinking her evening had taken a better turn.

As she and Greg started for the dining room she noticed Vera and Lucy glance curiously in her direction and saw that Rick and Pete were also showing interest. She paused, introduced Greg to them, but did not linger.

'Are you settling in?' Carolyn asked Greg as they sat down at a table for two.

'Yes. Can't say any of us were pleased when we were told we were going to be attached to a Bomber Station. But when it was explained that we would be acting only for 5 Group, and therefore be independent of the main Photographic Reconnaissance Unit, we realized we would have more freedom and be able to put forward suggestions ourselves about the way to tackle assignments.'

'That sounds good for you.'

'We think so. We've only just arrived so are still finding our feet here.'

'When will your Senior Officer be arriving?' asked Carolyn.

'We don't know when and we don't know who. We probably won't get any notification. Your CO may know. Should be any day now; the powers that be will want those Spitfires in the air playing their part rather than parked idle on the tarmac.'

'You will certainly make our job in Intelligence easier and be able to supply information for the bomber crews of 5 Group more quickly, particularly for Vera, the WAAF you just met. She has trained especially in assessing and interpreting photographs.'

Greg raised his eyebrows. 'An expert then?'

'Yes.'

'Are you off duty now?'

'Only until the squadron returns then we three WAAFs will be debriefing the crews. It will be pandemonium for a while – organized pandemonium. We try and get some sleep first, but it doesn't always work out that way. Tomorrow we'll be analyzing all the info we've acquired. Then it begins all over again.'

'When do you get time off?'

'Depends on the schedule and which operations are on.'

Greg studied her for a moment and smiled. 'Being born in Ireland but brought up in Hampshire, I don't know this part of the world. How about you?'

'I know it reasonably well,' Carolyn replied. 'I was born and bred in Middlesbrough about a hundred and twenty miles north of here. I did all my training in the north, mostly in Lincolnshire, and eventually came to Waddington.'

'I like exploring new places. Will you be my guide?'

She gave a little smile. 'Are you asking me for a date?'

'As many dates as you like.'

Deeming it wise not to let this attraction develop too fast, she said, 'We shall see. It has been nice spending time with you this evening, Greg. I have enjoyed your company. I think now I would like to get some sleep before the crews return.'

'Of course,' he said. 'You must be wide awake for them. May I walk you to your billet?'

'Thank you, you may.' Then she added with a teasing twitch of her lips, 'As far as the door.'

He met her playful glance with one of equal amusement. 'Opening it might be a pleasurable experience but I hadn't dreamed of doing that. To stray further could mean court-martial and neither of us would want that.'

Carolyn's four friends, who were still eating, noted what seemed to be a growing rapport between her and the Spitfire pilot. She was amused by their attempts to disguise their interest and knew that before long she would be answering their questions.

Lucy caught Vera's eye and mouthed, 'We'll find out later!'

As they stepped outside the Mess, Carolyn felt Greg's hand slip into hers. Not a word was spoken as they walked to her billet; each sensed that the other wanted to enjoy this closeness without words.

When they reached her billet, Carolyn said with a trace of humour in her voice, 'The door.'

Greg said, 'Ah, so it is.' He slid his hand around her waist and drew her gently to him. She did not resist, and returned his kiss for a moment. As she broke it off, she said, 'Good night, Greg.' He drew hope from her tone of voice.

'Good night, and thanks.' He walked briskly away.

She listened to his fading footsteps for a few moments and then walked thoughtfully to her room. When she had seen her four friends together she had felt a pang of loneliness but Greg's offer of friendship had eased that. She felt wanted, and found she enjoyed the feeing.

She tidied her room and had just picked up a book to read when she heard the outside door of the hut open. She smiled, knowing who this would be.

'There's a light under her door ... '

'Good. She's still awake.'

Before the expected knock, Carolyn called out, 'OK, come in.'

The door opened. Vera and Lucy walked in and plonked themselves on her bed.

'You've lost no time,' said Vera.

'Quick to latch on to a newcomer,' added Lucy.

'Spitfire pilot, no doubt?' Vera suggested

'Come on, tell all,' pressed Lucy.

'He's a nice friendly guy, new to this part of the world. He wants to explore it and wants me as his guide.'

Vera looked impressed. 'Sounds as though it has all the makings ... don't you think so, Lucy?'

'Every indication,' she agreed. 'Tell us more.'

'No. That's all you're getting.'

'Aw, come on!'

'No.'

'Spoil-sport.'

'Off with you. I need some sleep before debriefing and so do you.' Carolyn crossed her arms and stared them down.

'All right,' they muttered reluctantly, getting up off the bed.

'Night,' said Vera, sliding out of the room.

Lucy gave Carolyn a smile and paused to whisper, 'I'm pleased for you.'

'Thanks,' Carolyn mouthed back silently.

When she closed the door she stood with her back against it and smiled to herself. Though amused by her friends' curiosity, she appreciated their concern for her love-life.

Maybe this was the time to think more positively about her future, and reconsider her attitude towards having a man in her life.

'We're on tonight,' Rick informed the crew two mornings later. 'A full complement of 5 Group operating independently of the main force.'

Before midday they had checked their aircraft and equipment while all across the airfield bombs were being taken to the waiting Lancasters; tonight they would be carrying a Cookie, ten 500-pounders and incendiaries. Petrol bowsers delivered enough fuel to every Lancaster to see them to the target and back.

Though everyone on the station tried to ignore it. they felt tension settle over the airfield. No one mentioned it; they accepted it as part and parcel of the job they had chosen and had trained to do.

The pre-raid routine was followed as normal, even down to the individual quirks that superstitious aircrew followed.

The three WAAFs completed their briefing of the aircrews and returned to their section, to stand by in case there was any change of plan.

'I'm off to the locker room,' called Lucy. 'I won't be long.' Without another word she was gone. She knew the aircrews would be there, putting on their flying clothing to protect them from the cold at 15,000 feet.

'Don!' she called on seeing Uncle's navigator heading for the large Nissen hut that housed the various sections and the crews' lockers.

He stopped and turned round to see who had used his name. 'Hi, Lucy.'

'That's convenient, I needn't go in there,' she panted, nodding in the direction of the door.

'Something wrong?' he asked.

'No, no. Please give this to Pete.' She handed over a small package wrapped in brown paper.

'Sure.'

'Thanks. Tell him it's a good luck charm to keep his neck warm. Have a good trip.' With that Lucy hurried away.

Don glanced at the item she had pressed on him, shrugged his shoulders and entered the hut. A cacophony of sound hit him. He dodged bodies in every direction, at various stages of pulling on electric flying jackets, white pullovers, battle dress, fleece-lined flying boots, and checking their silk gloves and outer leathers were at hand.

'Hi, Pete,' he called, 'Lucy was coming to find you herself but asked me to give you this when we bumped into each other.' He handed over the package and passed on Lucy's message to a surprised and curious Peter.

'Thanks.' He ripped the paper off and was left holding a single silk stocking.

The whoops, cheers and comments from those nearby spread quickly through the hut, but Peter took little notice of the chaffing that followed. He tied the stocking round his neck, knowing that this way Lucy would always be with him whenever he was flying.

'You'll all wish you had one when you see how it keeps the gremlins away.'

'Have you seen one?' someone shouted, a contemptuous note in his voice.

'That sounds like a query from a sprog,' he countered, believing only someone new to operational status could doubt the presence of the mischievous unseen imps that meddled with equipment. His statement raised cheers from the believers.

'Well, have you?' someone pressed.

'I've not seen one, but I've had them play havoc with my bombsight.'

There were some derisive calls.

'You doubters will find out one day,' he answered, as he stuffed his gloves into his flying suit pocket. 'I am meticulous in carrying out my checks as soon as we have entered enemy territory, in particular making sure my bombsight is switched on. One night I was lining up the target when I realized something was wrong. Quick check of everything and I found the bombsight was off. I had followed procedures as usual, but it was off. Only a gremlin could have done that.'

There were a few hoots and catcalls.

'Must have been Hitler's special agent gremlin!' someone laughed.

'Aye, could have been,' said another seriously, backing Peter's statement. 'And that was another failure for Adolf.'

The door opened; an LAC poked his head in and shouted, 'Transport!'

The aircrews started to move, leaving the locker room one by one.

Uncle's crew let them go. They had no need for the transport. As they walked towards their Lancaster, standing silent in her dispersal, the chatter between them drifted away, leaving only the tap and shuffle of feet on the tarmac to remind them of where they were going.

The target was Karlsruhe.

The Met report was good again.

Take-offs were on time and all aircraft were safely airborne. The three WAAFs, among others waving the bombers off, gave special waves to U–Uncle and especially to Rick, silently wishing him well on this his first 'real' flight since their return from leave and feeling sure that his flip would not be repeated.

The crew of U–Uncle, once they were safely airborne, sensed from the tone of Rick's voice and the way he handled the aircraft that all was well with him; he was happy to be flying again.

Apart from some 'welcoming' anti-aircraft fire when they were crossing the Dutch coast, the crews were experiencing a quiet approach to the target. They believed the planned route, which took them east of Karlsruhe, must have fooled the Germans into thinking the target was to be further south. The Germans tried to react quickly when the bombers swung east and then north, on a tack that would carry them over the target and be on a direct course for home.

They were only partially successful but a large number of bombers got through before the defences became really active. The thin layer of cloud over the town did nothing to upset the attack; the marking aircraft were successful with their target marking. Soon fires were raging below but this had an adverse effect for the bomber force; the light from the fires was spread, by the thin cloud, over a wide area of the sky. The Lancasters stood out against the intense glow. German fighters moved in for the kill and cut down the bombers like a reaper cutting corn. Tracer from the hunters marked the sky. A glow appeared; continued on its course, flared, brightened, then plunged on a downward path from which it could not escape.

'Keep alert, everyone.' Rick's voice was quiet but firm over the intercom as he urged Uncle away from the glow and towards the darkness that could give some protection to the crew.

The Lancaster roared on. The crew began to breathe more easily but were vigilant; death still stalked the skies.

Over the coast, across the sea, England, Lincolnshire, permission to join the circuit granted. Then came each phase of landing: downwind, cross-wind, up-wind, funnels, the runway, touch-down. Relief spread through their Lancaster. Rick brought her to a halt. Solid ground beneath their feet again, and the ground-crew joyously celebrating their safe return. Tim knelt and kissed the ground.

'Are you going to do that after every op?' asked Mark.

'No,' replied Tim. 'But I thought this one was special.' There was no need to explain further; they knew he was celebrating Rick not flipping as he had done on their previous flight. 'The next time I do it will be when we finish our tour.'

They plodded off to the debriefing. Lucy and Vera were already interrogating two crews, but Lucy managed to give a wave to Pete and Vera gave Rick the thumbs up before he slid on to a chair opposite Carolyn.

'Good to see you back,' she said.

'Thanks. It's good to be welcomed by three charming WAAFs,' replied Rick. He leaned forward and said, 'Maybe I should say four.' He inclined his head towards the door.

Carolyn saw that Squadron Officer Newbauld had just walked in. Carolyn gave a little smile and said, 'Maybe you should.'

The rest of the crew, armed with mugs of coffee, found chairs or gathered round and the debriefing began.

24

An hour before the squadron was due back Carolyn's alarm woke her. She stuck her tongue out at the clock as she switched it off. Knowing that to rest her head back on the pillow would be fatal, she rolled sleepily out of bed and staggered to the mirror, where she came properly awake on seeing dull skin, crumpled hair and dreary eyes that sparked off the thought: I wonder what Greg would think to me now? She shook her head to clear it and got ready to meet the cold morning. When she stepped into the corridor she heard Lucy and Vera moving in their rooms. She knocked on their doors and, wary of waking Kate, called quietly, 'Hurry up, you two.' Vera and Lucy appeared just as Kate opened her door. 'No need to be quiet,' she said. 'I'm ready.'

'Thought you might be staying in bed,' ventured Vera.

'And not be there to see our boys coming home?' Kate said a little frostily.

They cycled briskly, eager to be out of the sharp air that always seemed to be coldest just before dawn.

They were pleased that a thoughtful LAC had brought a small urn of coffee for the section leaders, medical staff and those engaged in the debriefing. Urns for the returning crews

234

would be transported from the cookhouse when the first returning aircraft was heard.

'That's good,' commented Lucy after her first drink, with its warmth seeping through her.

They waited. Conversations were muted. Uncle's crew came in, anxious to know how the squadron had fared.

'Any news?' asked Rick.

'Sightings over the South Coast but we don't know who yet,' replied Vera.

The clock ticked on.

The door opened. Carolyn was surprised to see Greg walk in. He spotted her and came straight over. Vera and Lucy exchanged knowing glances while Rick raised an eyebrow.

'I didn't expect to see you here,' said Carolyn with a smile.

'Thought I'd see what went on in this alien bomber world. Besides,' he lowered his voice, 'it meant I'd see you again.'

Her lips twitched in reply to the compliment. 'Greg, I think I'd better introduce my friends properly this time. This is Lucy who I met when I joined up and we've managed to stay together ever since. Vera, our new recruit, who will be interpreting all the photos you bring back. And our favourite crew, who fly U–Uncle.' With pleasantries exchanged, she added, 'Come and meet Kate, our boss.'

She saw them heading in her direction and excused herself from the four officers to whom she was talking.

'Greg, this is Squadron Officer Newbauld who is in charge of our section and is one of our liaison officers with 5 Group Headquarters. Ma'am, this is Flight Lieutenant Greg Saunders.'

'Pleased to meet you, Ma'am,' he said with an engaging smile as he took Kate's hand.

'And I am pleased to meet you. I must also say we are

delighted to see you here and have our own Photographic Reconnaissance Unit in 5 Group. I will be pleased when your officer in charge arrives and we can make full use of you.'

'Have you any notification when that will be, Ma'am?'

'None. I was hoping you might be able to tell me.'

'Sorry, I don't know. I don't think it had been decided for one reason or another before we left. We were told to get here and be in readiness for his arrival, so I think it will be soon.'

'Good, the sooner the better, then the final piece of the jigsaw can be fitted.' She glanced around. 'You'll have to excuse me, Greg, but welcome to Waddington.'

'Thank you, Ma'am.'

Kate gave him a little smile. 'And, Greg, off duty it's Kate ... well, I'm sure you know the etiquette.' She glanced at Carolyn and then back at Greg to say, 'And be sure you look after her.'

Ears were straining to catch the first sound of an aero-engine.

When it came the atmosphere in the briefing room changed. Their anxiety for the returning crews was accompanied by a determination to do all they could to make the return as easy as possible.

One by one the Lancasters reported in.

A – Apple, no damage
Z – Zebra, ack-ack fire – holes in tail-plane
P – Peter, engineer – shrapnel wounds
Y – York, fuselage holed by fighter attack
C – Charlie, fire in main fuselages put out by mid-
   upper gunner and WOP. Report to medical officer.

So they came home until, thankfully, all were accounted for.

Some crews were buoyed up by their success, some merely pretended to be. Others said little, trying not to remember the hell they had faced over the target. 'Heaviest concentration of anti-aircraft fire we've encountered.' 'Ack-ack bad over the coast.' 'Fighters had picked up our exit route and were waiting for us.' So the reports from tired, weary and dishevelled aircrew were made, until they were transported to their Messes for a meal before they hit their beds to sleep and await an uncertain tomorrow.

25

Mid-morning the following day word came through that 5 Group had been stood down, giving the squadrons that had operated the previous day time to heal the battle-scars that had been suffered by the crews and their Lancasters.

An aircraft sound, different from that usually heard on a bomber station, drew everyone's attention as it grew louder.

'Spitfire,' said Vera.

'I wonder if it is coming to join the three we already have?' said Lucy.

'Let's go and see,' suggested Carolyn.

Eyes turned skywards, located the plane and identified it.

'Hope it's ours,' said Kate as she joined them.

'Could be,' said Vera. 'It looks as if he's going to join the circuit.'

The words were no sooner out of her mouth than the pilot took his aircraft on a climbing turn to starboard, heading away from the airfield. As he levelled out and climbed a little higher he gave his engine more power. He levelled out again then swung round in a wide arc that brought him heading towards the main runway.

'He's going too fast to land!' called Lucy.

'His undercarriage isn't down!' cried Vera.

'Get up! Get up!' shouted Carolyn, alarmed by the Spitfire's closeness to the ground.

With a booming roar that shattered across the airfield, the Spitfire zoomed past the Control Tower, did a sharp climbing turn and made another low-level pass, leaving the whole station admiring the pilot's skilful display.

They continued to watch as the pilot eased the power, side-slipped and then levelled as he joined the circuit to make a perfect landing and finally bring his Spitfire to a halt close to the Control Tower. The pilot slid back the canopy and was heaving himself out of his cockpit by the time three of the station's ground crew, who had been nearby, were there to help.

'Fantastic piece of flying, sir,' one of them ventured.

The squadron leader smiled. 'Thanks. Maybe I'd better not do that too often, your Station CO might not like it.'

'He might not, sir,' a corporal agreed with a grin; he liked the friendliness of the newcomer.

'My bus is here to stay, Corporal. Don't know who'll be looking after her but see she's OK until she's assigned a place.'

'Yes, sir.'

'I'd better report in.' The pilot headed for the door to the Control Tower.

The four WAAFs, whose view of the pilot had been blocked by the plane, were making for their section when he appeared.

Carolyn stopped dead in her tracks; her eyes widened in disbelief. 'Alastair! Good heavens, that was you!'

'Hi, sis!' He held his arms wide and Carolyn flung herself at him, with tears of joy streaming down her face. He held her tight. With a broad smile, he said, 'Come on, sis, wipe those tears away and introduce me properly – though I can see a

239

few familiar faces.' He swept his gaze across the onlookers who were trying to grasp the significance of this reunion.

Carolyn wiped away the tears but none of her joy. She gave a little laugh as she said, 'They look gob-smacked, don't they? Here goes: Squadron Officer Newbauld, Head of our Section and much more. Kate, this is my brother Alastair.'

She smiled and shook hands. 'I am pleased to meet Carolyn's brother. I've heard quite a bit about you but I think not all.'

'Ah, you never tell sisters everything.' A smile twitched his lips.

'Well, will you tell me if there are pieces missing and if so what they are?'

'I don't think my sister would like me to tell all but you certainly deserve an explanation of my reason for dropping in on you without warning.'

'I'm hoping it concerns that Spitfire you've just flown in. We were promised four but only three have arrived so far.'

'Now you have four!' he said. A ripple of excitement ran through the group. 'I didn't know myself until the day before yesterday that I was coming to take charge of the newly formed Photo Reconnaissance Unit here. I see my arrival hasn't raised the interest of my three pilots.'

'We've had no explanation of what was happening about your unit so they've probably gone into Lincoln,' explained Kate.

'Right. So what about Carolyn introducing me to the rest of this gathering and then, Squadron Officer, you can take me to your adjutant so I can officially announce my arrival and I'll take it from there.'

Carolyn did the honours and enjoyed basking in the glow of admiration Lucy and Vera showed towards this tall, fair-haired handsome fighter pilot, who seemed to have dropped into their laps from heaven.

Alastair crammed his hat on his head and was about to suggest to Kate that she should take him to the adjutant when he saw two flying officers pedalling furiously towards them. 'And who might these two be? They seem eager to meet me,' he added with a chuckle.

Before Carolyn had time to reply they were off their bikes and letting them clatter to the ground. They were starting to rush towards the group when they saw the rings on Alastair's battle-dress. They pulled up sharp and saluted. Alastair saw that his sister was amused by their embarrassment and managed to give her a sly wink.

Carolyn put on a formal voice. 'Squadron Leader Maddison, this is Flying Officer Wood and Flying Officer Wilkins.'

They both gulped. 'Maddison?' said Rick. He glanced at Carolyn, 'Your brother?'

'Yes,' she replied. 'He just brought the fourth Spitfire in. That completes the photo unit.'

'Look, I'll see you later in the Mess,' said Alastair. 'I must get off now or the adjutant will be after me for not reporting in immediately.'

'Very good, sir,' replied Rick. 'I admired that flying.' He turned to Carolyn as her brother walked away with Kate. 'You didn't tell me he was being posted here,' he complained with a feeling of hurt.

Alastair spent the rest of the day settling in. His aim of meeting up with Carolyn and her friends in the Mess that evening was thwarted by the demands of the Station CO, the Squadron CO, the adjutant, section leaders and senior WAAF officers, who all wanted some of his time for one reason or another.

The following morning he managed to say hello briefly to his sister as they crossed in the Mess dining room, which he was leaving with his three pilots. 'Take off for us in forty-five minutes,' he explained to her, and was gone.

Greg hung around to say, 'Just learned he's your brother!' he sounded surprised.

'I didn't know Alastair was posted here until he flew in yesterday. You were out late.'

'Yes. We'd been in Lincoln.' He gave a little grin. 'With a big brother looking after you, I'll have to watch my step.'

'Alastair's not my keeper, Greg. He respects my privacy.'

'That's good to know.' He started to move off.

'Greg, look after him when you're flying together won't you?'

He smiled and winked at her. 'Will do.' Then ran from the Mess.

26

Alastair settled in at Waddington. He and his three pilots soon familiarized themselves with the Lincolnshire countryside from the air, finding the cathedral a useful landmark. He was pleased to have his sister serving on the same station and to reacquaint himself with Vera. Over the next two months he established a good working relationship with the Intelligence section in which he cultivated a light-hearted banter to keep their minds off the exacting trials of war and the bomber crews that did not return. He was pleased that his mum and dad knew of, and supported, Carolyn's attachment to Greg.

'Good morning, Vera.'

She recognized the voice, so had no need to look up from the photograph she was studying, but she did, and gave Alastair a broad smile. 'Good morning, sir,' she said, emphasizing the 'sir' with a teasing twinkle in her eyes.

He looked round. 'You know my rules for you three WAAFs serving in Intelligence when there's no one else here. So we'll begin again. 'Good morning, Vera.'

She laughed. 'Good morning, Alastair.'

'That's better.'

'So, is this an official visit or social?'

'A bit of both,' he replied.

'And which is first?' she asked, smoothing a photograph.

He watched her hands with interest. 'You have beautiful fingers,' he said, with a catch of admiration in his voice.

She gave a little smile. 'I take that to mean it's a social call?'

'Well, I was hoping it might soften you up for a date.'

'Rick . . .'

He accepted the inference but added with a cocky smile, 'You'd rather have a plodding bomber pilot than a fighter pilot, a knight of the skies?'

'Hey, you! Don't belittle the role of the majority of pilots on this station. And don't forget 44 Squadron was in action from the very beginning, before you lot got going.'

He put his hand on his heart and bowed. 'I give way to your greater knowledge,' he said humbly.

'So you should.'

'OK, I'll admit you have a point. But I'll say again,' Alastair went on in a tone that rapidly became serious, 'Don't forget there's a guy here waiting for a certain girl to tell him she's disillusioned by her present romance.'

Vera's expression was similarly serious. 'Don't bank on that. And don't wait for it to happen; it may never turn out that way. Alastair, we get on well. I like you a lot. You're great to work with and nice to have around. Don't spoil that.' She laid a hand on his arm. 'Please try and understand.'

He nodded. 'You're a great girl, Vera. But remember what I said.'

'How could I not? You flatter me. Now, social visit over, what about the official angle?'

He nodded and adopted a different tone of voice. 'Before I came to see you, 5 Group HQ got in touch with me. I can't disclose all the details about the places they want my Spit-fires to cover. HQ has long-term objectives that at present they can't disclose to me. I was warned that my unit might be called on at any moment. If that happens it will be all go on an operation that will need speedy delivery. But please. Don't disclose any of this conversation to anyone until I give you clearance.'

'My lips are sealed.'

'Good. Gen up on the defences at leading French ports concerned with Atlantic shipping.' Seeing she was going to ask a question, he raised a hand. 'No more!'

When he left Vera considered both sides of the visit and then set them aside and got on with her work for the bombers. During the next weeks she helped in briefing the crews for two targets in the Ruhr.

Then she saw the four Spitfires take to the air together and knew something connected with Alastair's visit to her was about to happen, especially when they operated as a team again on the two following days. Nothing was forthcoming from them. Alastair made no comment to Vera and brushed aside Carolyn's and Lucy's observations that the Spitfires had obviously been busy with something.

Then, after two quiet days, Greg made a lone flight.

'Photos are in,' he announced as he came breezily into the Intelligence room, his flying helmet swinging from his fingers.

'Good,' returned Vera, looking up from the photo she had been studying with a satisfied smile. 'Any trouble?' she added.

'None,' he replied. 'It was a piece of cake.'

'Good,' said Vera with a sense of relief. 'It's always a worry to us when you are flying alone.'

'I was flying too high for the Luftwaffe to trouble me.'

'But you have to come down sometime.'

'With no armament, we're too fast for Gerry's fighters.'

'But there's always a ...' Vera's response was cut off when the door opened and Carolyn came in.

'Hi, Carolyn,' called Greg brightly.

'Hello, Greg.' Her thoughtful expression was replaced by a smile of pure pleasure. 'I was relieved when I saw you coming in to land.'

'I had a nice feeling too, knowing there would be a charming WAAF waiting for me,' he quipped with a twinkle in his eyes.

'I bet you never gave me a thought when you were high in the sky,' countered Carolyn.

'Do you know, I found an angel up there who danced in and out of the clouds with me. She promised to dance with me in Lincoln this evening as well.'

'Did she now?' Carolyn paused and tilted her head as if listening to something. She gave a little nod of agreement. 'Greg, she's just whispered to me, telling me to go instead.'

'That's my angel! Five o'clock. Transport at the gate.' He made for the door, pausing only to give her a peck on the cheek. He went out, deliberately leaving the door open, so that his whistling of 'You Are My Sunshine' drifted back into the room.

'You've made a hit there,' commented Vera.

'He's a nice guy ... fun, full of life. We enjoy each other's company.'

'From what I've observed he's in deeper than that.'

Carolyn gave a little shake of her head and changed the subject. 'Did he think the photographs would be good?'

'Yes, he said conditions were ideal.'

'Any idea where he's been?'

246

'No. You know Greg. He's tight-lipped on such matters.'

'I reckon the way the war is going, it will be to do with oil, shipping or canals. From all the activity we've been seeing with the Spitfires, there's something big afoot.'

'We'll learn about it in good time,' said Vera lightly, to get the subject dropped. 'In the meantime, you've a date for a dance.'

'What about you? Have you any plans with Rick?'

'I haven't seen him since we knew there would be no ops tonight.' Vera sighed and gave a little shake of her head. 'He's too tied up with that Lancaster and flying. He's becoming obsessed by them. You would think after ten ops in the last eight weeks he'd want to relax and have some fun but ... ' She left the inference hanging in the air.

'You'll have to use a bit more charm,' said Carolyn.

'I've tried just about everything I have,' countered Vera. 'I won't go the extra mile. I've seen too many girls do that and get left on the shelf. Not that Rick has ever suggested it,' she hastened to add, 'he hasn't, but he is getting a bit fanatical about flying and that can be boring. There's more to life, after all. We should make hay while the sun shines, who knows what the next flight will bring?'

'Oh, dear, that sounds as though someone isn't too happy.' Alastair's voice coming from the doorway startled them both. 'Sorry,' he apologized, 'I wasn't eavesdropping. I only heard the bit about Rick being absorbed in flying and his plane. I've seen this happen before. In one instance it broke up a marriage.'

'Well, it can't do that in this case,' countered Vera.

'So maybe we should do something about it?' Alastair let the question hang a moment before he asked another. 'As I was coming here I saw one of my pilots leaving. I would say he was in a happy state. The tune he was whistling seemed to be making a statement, and he gave me a smart salute without dropping the smile from his face. I think, Carolyn, you were the cause of that.'

She laughed. 'So Greg was still whistling? He's always such a happy chap.'

'I would hazard a guess that you are seeing him later?' her brother said.

'Yes. Nothing planned except we're going dancing in Lincoln, maybe having a bite to eat somewhere.'

'Good. How about Vera and I joining you to make it a foursome? Stirring up a little bit of jealousy in Rick might work in your favour, Vera.'

She chuckled. 'Fine by me.'

'Right, that's settled,' said Alastair, rubbing his hands together.

'I was meeting Greg at five by the gate,' said Carolyn.

'Let's make that four,' said Alastair. 'I'll get word to him.'

'Thanks,' said Carolyn. 'How do we dress this evening?'

'Uniform,' replied Alastair. 'I find it helps sometimes.'

They had the appearance of four people ready to enjoy themselves when they came together at the gate to find the taxi ordered by Alastair awaiting them. Conversation flowed smoothly, spirits were high, and the taxi driver joined in with advice on the best place to eat, the cosiest hostelry for a quiet drink, where the best band would be playing. He was pleased to make an agreement to pick them up at midnight when the strains of the last waltz would be bringing the dance to a close.

The jovial atmosphere continued throughout the evening. Apart from mixing in the Mess, this was the first time Vera had been in the company of Alastair socially.

He was pleased to see his sister enjoying the evening and content that she had found someone she liked in Greg, whom

248

Alastair knew to be a sound person and a skilful pilot, who viewed his present job as a duty to be completed before he could return to helping his father run their estate. Alastair thought his sister could do no better than fall truly in love with Greg.

As the evening drew to a close, with the band playing the last waltz 'Who's Taking You Home Tonight?', they knew the answer. Greg drew Carolyn a little closer. She snuggled into his arms and let her mind drift to what could be. Alastair, respecting Vera's relationship with Rick, was silent as he took the last dance with her.

'We must do this again,' he suggested when, back at the base, they watched the taxi disappear into the darkness.

'A good idea,' Carolyn and Greg readily agreed.

'I'd like that too,' said Vera. 'I've enjoyed this evening. Thank you very much.'

'So did I. I'll look forward to the next time.'

She made no comment and he drew hope from that.

Greg and Carolyn wandered on their own path, seemingly in no hurry to part, enjoying each other's company. Greg stepped into the deep shadows and turned Carolyn to face him.

'You know that angel who danced with me in the clouds?'

She nodded.

'I think I've fallen in love with her.'

Carolyn tensed. She had heard words she wanted to hear, yet didn't. Greg offered the prospect of happiness, which seemed even more precious when they were living with death close at hand. Her mind whirled. She didn't want to make any firm commitment, yet to disillusion him might have disastrous effects; she would not be able to bear that.

Her thoughts were interrupted by Greg's next question. 'Will you marry me?'

'Greg, please don't ask me that. I like you a great deal and I think I could fall in love with you ... '

In the momentary pause she left he stepped in with another question. 'So what's holding you back?'

'I've been hurt by this war before and fear what else it might bring. I couldn't bear another loss. There are things I need to sort out. I don't know what the outcome will be.'

'May I cling to the hope that you might decide in my favour?'

'Yes, you may, but don't press me into making decisions now. Maybe at the end of the war.'

'Then I'll wait until then, angel.'

She sensed Greg's love for her in the way he held her and in the depth of his kiss, which she did not resist.

The following morning Vera was having breakfast with several WAAFs from various sections that made up the active bomber base when she saw Rick come into the dining room, pause and survey the occupants. His eyes settled on her for a moment, then seeing she was occupied with other WAAFs, he turned away to join Peter.

Not in a good humour, she thought, and guessed what was coming next.

She lingered over another cup of tea while the other WAAFs gradually left the dining room, but was quickly on her feet when the last one rose from the table. Vera followed her out but was halted by a sharp question. 'Where were you yesterday evening?'

She swung round to face Rick. 'I was in Lincoln with friends,' she said tartly.

'So I heard this morning,' he said, with an equally cutting edge to his voice.

'Then why ask me?'

Rick ignored the question and said, 'I looked all over for you, but when I enquired of the corporal on duty at the gate, I was told you'd left camp in the company of Squadron Leader Maddison.' Rick gave a contemptuous little grunt and added scathingly, 'Moving in higher circles now, I see, forgetting lowly flying officers.'

'Don't be ridiculous, Rick. You sound like a spoilt brat. I was invited to make a foursome. You hadn't made any arrangement with me so I jumped at the chance to have an enjoyable night out. And so it proved to be.'

'But I thought we had an understanding?'

'You know what thought did?' she retaliated. 'I'm not here just to be at your beck and call, Rick.'

'I suppose you'll be seeing him again?' Rick's tone indicated he had already worked out the answer to this.

Vera was annoyed and bit back, 'More than likely. He paid me attention. He was interested in me, and didn't bore me stiff with talk of flying and aeroplanes all night. Why don't you behave more like him, Rick, or you'll lose out every time?' Vera swung on her heel then and walked away, leaving Rick in confusion. He stood for a few moments glaring after her, then with a shrug of his shoulders dismissed her complaint and headed for Uncle. If Vera were not around he'd have more time with the Lancaster and her ground-crew. And there were plenty more pebbles on the beach if he wanted a new one.

27

'Morning, Skip,' called Phil who was lounging on the grass in the morning sunshine with Tim and Mark, close to Uncle's dispersal.

'Have you done your checks?' growled Rick.

'Sure have,' replied Tim.

'You know us, Skip, the most efficient crew on the squadron,' quipped Mark.

Walking towards the open door of their Lancaster, Rick did not slacken his pace as he muttered, 'You'd better be.' He thought he had kept his comment low but it was caught by the two gunners and the engineer, who exchanged glances and pulled faces at each other as Rick climbed into the Lancaster.

'He got out of the wrong side of bed,' muttered Tim.

'Or else he's had a bad night,' suggested Mark.

'Maybe he's been stood up by Vera,' added Phil.

'Could be,' Mark agreed.

Their conversation was caught by Pete as he joined them. He pointed out, 'We shouldn't let personal problems become an issue. We don't want our efficiency as a unit to be affected.'

'No, and it won't be, but Rick was a bit snappy this morning. Not like him at all.'

'Let's drop it,' advised Pete. 'It's Rick's affair, he'll sort it.'

'OK, Pete,' they readily agreed.

'Has Zoe settled in her new posting, Tim?' Pete asked to direct their thoughts away from Rick.

'She has. Loves it. The farmer and his wife have really taken to her. They lost their only daughter in the London Blitz so they think the world of Zoe.'

Rick climbed out of the Lancaster. 'I'm going to see if there's likely to be anything on tonight,' he called.

They raised their hands in acknowledgement. They had their answer before he returned. Activity began to pulse across the airfield. Petrol bowsers headed out to fuel bombers, armourers stood by to receive the bombs while others checked the Brownings in each of the three turrets: the bombers' defence against enemy fighters. Then, as if to confirm that ops were on, a staff car sped across the airfield to the Intelligence section. A flying officer, holding a folio tightly, jumped out of the passenger seat and rushed into the building.

'Hot from the press!' he cried, thrusting the package at Vera.

'Expected this when I saw things erupt,' she commented as she took the package from him.

'Photographic section was on to it as soon as Flying Officer Saunders brought it in yesterday. The pictures were pored over by the CO and his gang. He's told me what he thinks these pictures reveal but he wants your expertise to confirm his opinion. If you agree with him I am to signal him immediately from here and then he will approve "operation on". Group will be told and every airfield within it will burst into action. Only this group will be involved in the attack.'

Vera was opening the large folder as he was speaking. She saw a coastline, rivers, towns, and closer views of dockyards and quays. Now she knew the relevance of Alastair's suggestion that she should study anything she had on file about the French coastline.

'Brest,' she said thoughtfully. She peered closely at two other pictures using her own personal magnifying glass. 'Unbelievable,' she gasped. 'Six U-boats on the surface!' She looked up at the officer who was keenly awaiting her assessment.

'That confirms the CO's interpretation, but he wanted an expert opinion.' The officer grabbed the phone and within a moment was speaking to his superior. 'Flight Officer Williams agrees.' He replaced the receiver and turned to Vera. 'Ops are on. Everything was on stand-by until your confirmation. Briefing will be at two, take-off three-thirty.'

'That's a tight schedule,' she commented.

'That timing will enable the bomber force to make a daylight attack. With the weather report as it is, they'll have a clear view of the target before escaping into the gathering darkness. Now, I'd better get back or the CO will be doing his nut.'

As he reached the door it opened and Carolyn and Lucy hurried in.

'Looks like panic stations out there,' said Lucy. 'What's on?'

Vera gave them the rundown on what she knew and concluded with, 'We must give the crews all the help we can, so let's get them the most up-to-date gen we can.'

'I saw Alastair's Spitfire was missing when I came in this morning,' said Carolyn. 'Maybe he's been out on a final reconnaissance.'

Half an hour later they saw him return and hurry to the

254

Photographic section. Before long Vera was in possession of the latest photographs of Brest and she lost no time in comparing them with the previous ones.

'Oh, my God,' she gasped. 'The Germans have been busy during the night. They've moved in about twenty mobile ack-ack guns. They sure don't want those submarines harming. They must be part of a bigger plan.'

A little more was revealed when the CO made his summing up at the briefing. 'We believe, on the authority of agents working in the Brest area, that the Hun is planning either an intensive operation against convoys bringing vital supplies from America or they want to use them as defence for their battleships, which they could be moving from their Baltic ports to operate in the Atlantic. Whatever their intention, those subs in Brest are a menace so get out there and destroy them!'

It sounded like a battle-cry to the crews and stirred in them a determination to succeed. They checked over their flight plans, knowing that because the attack was scheduled to be from different heights accurate timing over the target would be essential.

With her job completed Vera found her thoughts returning to Rick. She had been hurt by his attitude and had reacted instinctively. Now she wished they had not exchanged harsh words. She wanted to take hers back but couldn't. What had been said had been said. She hadn't the time to try and make amends, and would not see him again before take-off; crews were already on their way to their Lancasters. But she did not want Rick to face the brutal sky without peace between them being restored. All she could do was to be at the take-off, wave, and hope he saw in her presence an offer of love. She grabbed her hat and hurried from the building.

She stepped into the roar of engines. A brief glance told her that Uncle was already on her way around the perimeter track to the runway in use.

Vera hurried there and joined Carolyn and Lucy, who were standing apart from the other onlookers. As she did so she saw Alastair in the company of the CO. Seeing him gave Vera a little jolt of pleasure at the recollection of the evening they had spent together in Lincoln.

'Rick's third in line,' shouted Lucy, as the noise from the engines of the Lancaster at the end of the runway soared. It rolled forward until it reached take-off speed. The pilot eased it from the runway, banked and went on his mission to attack the submarines and shipping in Brest's heavily defended harbour.

Uncle's turn came soon enough. Rick halted the aircraft and slid back his side window. He saw the three WAAFs and waved, and then Vera sensed his eyes on her alone. She saw his expression change into a smile for her, as much as to say, 'Thanks for being here.' Then it was gone but she held on to the memory as he took the Lancaster faster and faster down the runway. She watched intently until relief swept over her as the huge plane, with its lethal bomb load, took to the air.

One by one the squadron onlookers left. Silence settled on the airfield.

The three WAAFs walked to the Mess without exchanging a word, each dwelling on their own thoughts, not wishing to share them.

Lucy prayed for Pete as she always did. She was aware of an aircrew's estimated life-span, but blanked her mind against that and concentrated on her plan to introduce him to her mum and dad and reveal their plans to marry.

Carolyn too was thinking of the crew and hoping they

would return unscathed from the hell they would soon be facing.

Vera felt she had made her peace with Rick, but there was a doubt at the back of her mind. She was still not sure that he preferred her to his plane, and was that the best basis for a loving relationship?

The seven men settled into their jobs as their Lancaster flew on. No one voiced it but each of them thought the same thing: they were flying into a heavily defended area to reach a target that the Germans greatly prized. All hell could break loose soon. No one cared to dwell on the fact that they might not survive. They were there for each other and not one man contemplated becoming a weak link in the chain of trust that existed in U–Uncle.

'Bomb Aimer to Navigator.'

'Go ahead, Bomb Aimer.'

'Coast clearly visible ahead, about five miles to starboard.'

'Thanks, Bomb Aimer.' Don checked the chart on which he had drawn the course they should follow. 'Hold that course, Skipper, we're bang on track.'

'Thanks, Navigator,' called Rick.

They flew on, everyone with the exception of the navigator and wireless operator aware of the number of Lancasters flying beside them; a stark reminder of how at night, in the pitch dark, they could be close to colliding with one of their own.

'Pilot to Mid-upper.'

Tim flicked his microphone switch. 'Mid-upper here, Skipper.'

'Position in the stream, Mid-upper?'

'We are about a third of the way. Two-thirds well strung out behind us.'

'Good.' Rick was satisfied that they were holding their alloted position in the stream for them to approach the target.

'Plane going down ahead,' called Peter from his position in the nose.

'Got it,' replied Rick. He watched it, hoping to see someone bail out, but any hope was lost when the plunging bomber suddenly blew up.'

'Sharp look out!' Rick announced sharply. 'No ack-ack. Must be fighters about.'

As if in answer tracer flashed across the sky ahead, but missed its target. The bomber force flew on.

'Twenty degrees port, Skipper.'

Rick made the alteration, bringing the Lancaster on to its new course.

'Navigator to Bomb Aimer. This should bring you over the coast south of Brest in a few minutes. You should be able to see the town when we do, then pick up the docks and our target. So you take over when we cross the coast.'

'Bomb Aimer to Navigator, understood. Will let you know when we reach the coast.'

They flew on.

'At the coast now! See that church tower starboard ahead, Skipper?'

'I see it, Bomb Aimer.'

'Fly straight over it directly from where we are now.'

Rick made the adjustment and levelled the aircraft.

'Hold it there, Skip.' Peter made a quick assessment. 'Right, right,' he called. Rick altered the flight path accordingly. 'OK, Skip. Submarines ahead.'

'Got 'em,' replied Rick.

So strongly had they been concentrating on perfecting their attack that they had been oblivious to the ack-ack shells exploding along the track of the bomber force.

A Lancaster reared under a direct hit and plunged from the sky; another peeled away on fire. Only two parachutes opened before it to fell to earth.

Peter got the target lined up in his bombsight. 'Steady, Skipper, steady.'

Rick knew from his tone of voice that his bomb aimer had got a perfect line on the target. 'Steady, steady, ste ... ' The rest of the word was torn away when the Lancaster was rocked by the shells exploding around them. Rick grasped the controls tighter, steadied the plane, quickly checked his course and made the necessary slight adjustment.

'OK, Skip. Steady, steady.' Peter pressed the bomb release. The crew felt the aircraft jerk a little as the bombs fell away. He made a quick check. 'Bombs gone!' He craned forward and saw them falling away towards the inferno that was already engulfing Brest's harbour area.

Rick held the Lancaster level for the short time required for a photograph to be taken automatically, then he checked the sky around him, banked sharply to port and dropped the nose to get clear of the defences bent on bringing down as many Lancasters as possible, but, almost at the same moment Uncle rocked violently. Shell after shell burst around her. She bucked, her nose dropped and she hurtled downwards.

Rick hauled at the control column but it seemed to have little effect. 'Engineer! Help!'

Phil pushed himself quickly up from the floor where he had been flung by the violent descent and grasped the control column. They both heaved with all the strength they could muster, and slowly, ever so slowly, Uncle responded. Between them they brought her back on an even keel.

Only when Rick was certain that the plane was steady did he give Phil the thumbs up.

Phil, still breathing hard from the terrific strain, nodded.

Rick checked with every member of the crew and was thankful to receive no casualty reports, but expressed concern about the hole that had been made in the fuselage, reported by the wireless operator.

'Give it a closer look, WOP.'

'OK, Skipper.'

Gordon left his position and a few moments later reported, 'It should give us no trouble, Skip, as long as we have no more violent action. Then it might be another story.'

'Thanks, WOP. We're nearly clear of the ack-ack. It will be fighters now, so keep a sharp lookout. Let's seek the cover of darkness.' Uncle seemed to discover more power in response to his suggestion.

Find it they did but even the night-time could bring disaster if their concentration slipped in the haste to reach base safely. Their determination to do that only added to their exhaustion, which they felt become almost overpowering as they eventually climbed out of the aircraft. Even then another shock awaited them; the radar equipment housed under the bottom of the fuselage was completely missing.

'Bloody hell,' commented Mark. 'Ack-ack was far too close for comfort.'

'We did bounce a bit near the target,' added Tim dryly.

'Another foot or two and we wouldn't be standing here,' said Phil.

'That's a mighty big hole in the fuselage,' said one of the ground-crew, all of whom had made a quick assessment of the damage sustained by their beloved Lancaster. 'It's fixable. We'll soon have her fully fit again.'

'Make her as good as new,' said Rick, patting the side of his Lancaster affectionately. 'You got us through, old girl.'

The weary crew, exhausted by the strain of a difficult mission, headed for their debriefing.

Vera, Carolyn and Lucy showed concern when they saw the drawn, pale faces of the returning crews. They knew instantly that it had been a trying operation and did all they could to make the debriefing as short as possible and let the aircrews get away to their beds. All the time they waited anxiously for Uncle's crew.

Lucy's heart lurched when Peter came slowly into the room and looked around as if he was not sure where he should be. Gordon bumped against him, then grabbed his arm and guided him to the nearest vacant table.

'Excuse me for a moment?' she asked the crew she was debriefing.

Knowing she was sweet on Rick Wood's bomb aimer, they nodded.

Lucy sprang to her feet. 'Thanks, only be a second.' She was beside Peter in a flash. 'Are you all right?' she asked, her face creased with anxiety.

Looking up, he smiled weakly. 'Yes. It was a bit rough, but I'll be OK.'

The rest of the crew flopped down on the chairs around the table where Carolyn was ready to debrief them. She cast her eyes over them. They looked so weary, as if all their youthful energy had been drained away. Her eyes met Rick's with concern. He read their meaning and nodded back at her. 'I'm OK.' He grimaced. 'Let's have this over with and get them off to bed. They're whacked.'

28

With the squadron stood down for two days, the airfield seemed unusually quiet. It was as if everyone, without voicing their thoughts, was mourning the loss of their two Lancasters, part of a total loss of twenty throughout the Group. Every squadron was licking its wounds.

A lone engine started up. Alastair eased his Spitfire into motion and taxied to the runway. A last quick check and a few minutes later he was making a climbing turn within sight of Lincoln Cathedral, to take a south-westerly course. He flew high and fast. The results of yesterday's raid on Brest, when the Lancasters had taken a mauling, needed to be documented. The photographs he would take would enable the head of Bomber Command to make a decision about the effectiveness of the attack and whether Brest required another immediate raid or not.

The port was clear of cloud and the weather ideal for his photographic sortie. Alastair felt comfortable in the knowledge that he was too high and too fast for German attention. They would know he was there and what he was about so he would have to keep alert when he was losing height heading for home. Prowling fighters might be waiting then, hoping to spring a surprise on him.

As he crossed the English coast he saw two German fighters but a quick manoeuvre took him into some cloud cover and there was no sign of them when he re-emerged into cloudless sky.

He knew, once he had been sighted by Flying Control at Waddington, everything would be put in place for the moment he landed. Film would be rushed off to be processed, prints would be made. One set would be dashed to Vera, who would appraise the evidence of success or failure. Then contact would be made with Bomber Command HQ to which a copy would be rushed by a light aircraft, brought in for the express purpose of getting the photographs there as quickly as possible.

When Alastair finally reached the Intelligence section, after shedding his flying gear, he found several officers anxiously awaiting Vera's assessment. She perused the photographs carefully, taking her time, wanting to avoid any error of judgment. Finally she straightened up.

'Well?' asked the CO anxiously.

'Comparing the photographs of before and after the raid, I see one U-boat has survived with only minor damage. I think that is because it had been moved from its earlier position. I don't see anything to indicate that move was of any major strategic importance. Support vessels for the U-boat fleet appear to have been heavily damaged, with three vessels listing badly and two others with heavy structural damage. Dock sides are in a mess, with cranes and other equipment badly damaged. All in all, sir, I would judge the raid to be successful.'

The CO smiled, and sighed with satisfaction. 'The Air Marshal will be delighted with this result but he'll be aching at the cost in lives. He hates to lose any crew but is even more put out if the losses are heavy, as they were with this raid. Thank goodness the results are excellent. Flight Officer

Williams, when he rings through, as I am sure he will, you speak with him.'

'Oh, sir, not with Bomber Harris . . . '

'Yes, you must, Williams,' he said firmly. 'That's an order. Tell him exactly what you told me. He'll have the photographs in front of him by then. He won't bite your head off.'

'Yes, sir.' Vera could do nothing but agree. The minutes ticked by. The phone was silent. She kept glancing at it as she walked round the room, nervously rubbing her hands together. Her mouth was dry. Five minutes later she was startled when the piercing ring tone shattered the silence. The CO grabbed the phone.

'Wing Commander Costaine . . . Yes, sir . . . Flight Officer Williams is here, sir.'

As she took the telephone from her CO, she saw it had been linked to a special secure line.

'Flight Officer Williams speaking, sir.'

'Good day to you, Flight Officer. You and I will be looking at the same photographs, but after you give me your assessment of them, I want you to do something for me.'

'Yes, sir.'

'I want you to congratulate the pilot who took these photos. I can see, and it is borne out by my experts here, that he has done a thoroughly good job. Congratulate him from me, won't you?'

Pride surged through Vera; Alastair would be delighted to receive this personal message from the Commander-in-Chief. 'I will, sir,' she replied, more confidently.

'Now, tell me what you see in them.'

They spoke for twenty minutes, with Vera's self-assurance growing by the minute.

'Your assessment tallies very much with mine and my so-called experts here, but I must tell you that you have spotted

264

several aspects that we haven't, which, because of what we know of the U-boats and their base at Brest, might prove invaluable in the future. Thank you, Flight Officer Williams. I am indebted to you for your judgment that the raid was successful. I believe it will have helped this country towards a final victory. It is only regrettable that the crews suffered such heavy losses.' Vera detected genuine regret in his voice. 'But those are the wages of war, sadly.' He paused then drew their exchange to a close. 'Thank you, Flight Officer Williams. Please put your superior officer on.'

The CO took the phone, made himself known, and, after listening for a few moments, said, 'Yes, sir. Thank you, sir,' and hung up. He looked round the room where everyone was waiting expectantly. 'He's delighted with the results, sorry for the losses, and the stand down for the Group still stands.'

Shortly after breakfast of the second day, Rick received an order to see the adjutant in his office within the next half-hour. Without a clue what it was about, he lost no time in reporting there.

'Wood, last night I was working on leave rosters for the crews.' The adjutant glanced at the two sheets of paper laid on the desk in front of him. Rick could see pencil marks struck through some names on one sheet while the other had pencilled notes scrawled across it. 'The loss of two crews, who were due to go on leave before you, means you have moved up the roster and therefore can go on leave the day after tomorrow. Pick up passes as usual.'

Rick hesitated slightly before he said, 'Thank you, sir,' and then added with a note of regret in his voice, 'It seems we are stepping into dead men's shoes.'

The adjutant leaned back in his chair, steepled his fingers together and looked Rick straight in the eye. 'I know exactly how you feel, Wood, but you mustn't think that way. This is the life we have chosen to live so we must accept the rough with the smooth. You and your crew go off on leave and enjoy the smooth.'

'Yes, sir. Thank you, sir.'

The adjutant watched the door close and sighed. Now he must attend to the dead men's belongings, see that everything was packed neatly by the WAAFs assigned to the task, with orders to have the items ready to be dispatched three days after the CO had sent a letter of condolence to the next-of-kin.

Rick, realizing the adjutant was right, made his steps brisk, hoping Peter would still be there.

'Ah, Pete, glad I've caught you. We can go on leave the day after tomorrow.'

Pete's face lit up. 'Great! Why not before then?'

Rick shook his head. 'Don't know. I'm only telling you what the adj told me. Accept it and don't ask questions.'

'That's easy to do. If we're going to be here this evening, we'll celebrate our leave in the village pub.'

'Right, let's tell the crew.'

They soon found them and, in their delight, agreed they would make tonight in the local pub the unofficial start of their leave.

'Wives and girlfriends too, if you can round them up,' said Rick as they reached the door.

'Intelligence section now?' asked Peter.

'We'd better. Otherwise we'll never hear the last of it!'

'You two look to be in a good mood,' commented Vera when Rick and Peter rushed into the Intelligence section.

'Leave, leave, glorious leave!' they both chanted, doing a little jig.

'Since when?' asked Lucy.

'Day after tomorrow,' returned Pete.

'So we celebrate tonight in the village pub,' Rick added. 'All are welcome.'

'We'll be there,' said Vera, speaking for the others. 'Then what? You'll be out of our clutches!'

'So we must make hay while the sun shines,' quipped Pete. He caught Lucy's eye and knew what she was thinking. They casually left the room together.

'Looks as if Pete wants to be straight off,' said Rick.

'Leave the lovebirds alone,' said Vera, sharply.

'Sorry,' said Rick, surprised by her reaction.

'You men, blind as bats!' said Carolyn.

'Only two things on your mind, Rick, that aeroplane and the sky,' Vera snapped, a touch of real annoyance in her voice.

'Do I detect jealousy?' he mocked.

The uneasy banter was broken when Peter and Lucy returned.

Pete cleared his throat and looked a little embarrassed when he announced, 'I've asked Lucy to marry me and she's said yes.'

For a moment there was a stunned silence at the unexpected announcement, then congratulations, hugs and kisses were exchanged.

'You are the first to know,' said Lucy when the uproar subsided a little. 'Pete asked me a few weeks ago and I said yes, but we decided to say nothing until we had seen my parents. We've changed our minds, though. We're telling you and the crew now. We didn't want you to hear it from anyone else. But we're asking you to keep it to yourselves until we have seen my parents.'

'Our lips are sealed,' said Rick.

'It's a pity we aren't getting leave as well now,' said Carolyn,

'I'm going to see Kate, explain the situation and see if she can push my leave forward,' Lucy explained.

'She's pretty understanding. I'm sure she'll play ball,' Carolyn encouraged her.

'I can but try.'

'Right, let's away, Pete, and tell the crew – leave *and* an engagement. Couldn't be better news for them.' The two men departed, leaving the WAAFs to themselves.

Amidst their chatter Vera's mind turned to the exchanges she had just had with Rick. She balked at the idea of being jealous of an aircraft, but as much in love as she was with Rick, she was not going to play second fiddle to his growing obsession with flying.

Marriage. The word rang in Carolyn's mind when she saw the radiant joy lighting Lucy's face. She put a question to herself: Have I been stupid in allowing the worst of war to dominate my judgment, and mar the happiness that might have been mine for the taking?

At the party that night Vera asked Rick, 'Are you heading for home?'

His fingers twined around hers as he replied 'Yes, I must. Dad hasn't been too good lately. He's up and down, as I told you, but I fear the letter I received yesterday from Mother was really despondent. Though she didn't spell it out, I could read between the lines. I'm not sure what I am going to find when I get home. Mum tries to spare me any worry because of what I'm doing, but I think it's only flying that stops me from worrying. It keeps my mind focused.'

Those words bit into Vera's mind and she wondered: Why flying and not me?

'I wish I could come and help in some way,' she said lamely.

'Oh, we'll be all right,' Rick replied, and picked up his tankard.

A surge of exasperation ran through her, but she stifled it. He didn't even say, 'Thanks, I wish you could too,' she thought.'

'I've phoned Mum,' said Lucy, taking her place beside Pete again when she rejoined the party. 'She's over the moon that she's going to meet you at last.'

'You didn't say anything about us?'

'No, of course not. That's up to you.'

'I hope I come up to expectations,' he replied a little warily.

Lucy pursed her lips thoughtfully. 'I don't expect you will.'

'Oh, my goodness. If you're doubtful, what am I in for?'

She laughed. 'This is going to be fun!'

'It's all right for you but ... '

'Oh, drink up and live for now. Let tomorrow take care of itself. And don't look so serious!' She leaned against him and kissed him on the cheek, collecting a cheer from the rest of the party.

Alastair and Greg had joined them at Carolyn's invitation and no one was holding back on enjoying themselves, but at one point Carolyn, sitting next to Greg, said, 'You're looking thoughtful. Want to tell me about it?'

He grinned. 'I was just thinking, two Spitfire pilots, two WAAFs on their own ... we can't leave it like that for a week, so how about we four go dancing in Lincoln the evening the others go on leave?'

'Good idea,' agreed Carolyn. 'I'll have a quiet word with my brother and Vera. Leave it to me.'

The opening of the pub door brought renewed cheers from their group. Faces wreathed in smiles, Myrna and Zoe walked in, beaming.

'Where have you sprung from?'

'How did you know we were here?'

Zoe explained, 'Tim rang to tell me the crew were starting leave the day after tomorrow, so as I was due a week's leave, I asked the farmer if I could take it now. When I explained everything, he said he couldn't deny any flyers ...' she hesitated then stuttered ... 'well, you know what I mean. So I got in touch with Myrna and she agreed to come with me, so here we are.' The new arrivals accepted the drinks that were thrust on them.

The evening continued with great merriment until the landlord announced, 'Time, ladies, gentlemen, please.'

The crew of U–Uncle went on leave.

29

'No ops tonight.' Carolyn made the announcement as soon as she entered the Intelligence section.

'Great,' responded Vera. 'A free evening means the pictures or dancing. Which shall it be?'

Carolyn pondered the question for a moment. 'Pictures,' she decided.

'What's on?'

'I don't know, but we'll find out from the paper when we go to the Mess for lunch.'

'Right. Now back to work. Concentrate. The name Harburg has been cropping up as a likely target. Let's get on with sorting the latest information we have on the port and its installations,' Vera suggested.

'Keen again,' commented Carolyn, aware that Vera's instincts had stood them in good stead in the past.

'It always pays to get ready.'

'True,' agreed Carolyn, already reaching into a cupboard to the row of files on the shelf marked 'North German Ports'.

Vera unlocked one of the six filing cabinets that held the photographs of those same ports.

The girls extracted the files marked 'Harburg' and took

them to their desks. They studied them without speaking until Carolyn made an observation.

'Harburg could be a tricky target. It's just across the River Elbe from Hamburg, which is one of the most heavily defended areas in Germany.'

'Even if my instinct is right, the crews won't be scheduled to fly over Hamburg. It will be up to them to see they don't stray in that direction.'

'I suppose so,' replied Carolyn. 'Let's go and get some lunch.'

They locked everything away and headed for the Mess.

When they walked into the dining room they found it only moderately busy; some crews had taken the opportunity of the stand down to go into Lincoln or take lunch in one of the nearby villages as a change from RAF food.

Carolyn, making a quick survey of the room, caught sight of Greg at the same time as he saw her. He waved and pointed to two places at his table. She signalled her acceptance.

When she and Vera reached him, he stood up. 'Good to see you both. I hoped you might be in for lunch but with the stand down for the bomber boys I thought you might be taking the chance of some off-site entertainment.'

'We don't always get the same time off duty as they do,' countered Carolyn. 'There's always preparation work for us to do. But we have got that done this morning.' They made themselves comfortable at the table.

'So, have you any plans for tonight?'

'We're going to Lincoln later, to the flicks. How about joining us?'

'Can't say yes, can't say no.'

'Hey, come on, don't talk in riddles,' chaffed Vera.

'Well, Alastair was on to Group HQ when I left our site, trying to find out what might be in store for us.'

'For likely reconnoitring?'

'Yes. He said he would join me here, so I'm keeping that place for him.' Greg nodded at the chair he had tipped over to lean against the table, a signal to newcomers that a place was taken.

'I'll keep my fingers crossed that his news will be of a stand down for you too,' said Vera, 'then you and he can hit Lincoln with us.'

'I'd like nothing better,' enthused Greg, winking at Carolyn.

They were enjoying their soup when Alastair joined them. He realized why the three of them had stopped eating so kept them on tenterhooks while he sat down. He took a spoonful of his soup. 'That's nice. But the rest of today, Greg, could be made much nicer for us by two WAAFs.'

Vera's face broke into a broad grin. She gave a little. 'Yippee' and, glancing at Carolyn, said, 'We can see to that, can't we, Carolyn?'

'Nothing more certain,' she agreed.

During the rest of the meal they made plans, which resulted in a late-afternoon visit to the cinema, an evening meal, then a dance and a late taxi back to Waddington.

As they strolled towards the WAAF quarters, Vera peered up at the sky. 'This beautiful night is the perfect end to a perfect day,' she mused, looking into the cloudless darkness from which the moon bathed the land in its silvery sheen. She felt the closeness between her and Alastair intensify. His fingers moved against her palm, sending a shiver through her, and she stepped a little closer to him.

Carolyn was bewitched by the stars. Their twinkling reminding her of Greg's earlier wink at her. He had been so attentive tonight, without ever making her feel pursued.

When he held her fingers in his she knew everything he was trying to tell her.

Nearing the WAAF quarters the two couples automatically drifted apart and found shadowy places of their own in which to exchange their goodnight kisses.

'I hope the crew are all having a good leave,' said Carolyn when Vera arrived at the Intelligence section the next day.

'I'm sure they will be, but I do wonder about Rick,' said Vera.

'I hope the news about his father won't affect his flying,' said Carolyn.

'I don't think it will. When he steps into that plane nothing and no one matters but his aircraft and the op. There are times when he can talk of nothing else. I have known whole evenings ruined because of his obsession. So unlike yesterday – Alastair and Greg never mentioned flying once. They were there to enjoy themselves and take their minds, and ours, off flying and the war.'

'You seemed to be getting on well with Alastair?' commented Carolyn.

Vera made no reply to this but answered with her own observation, 'I could say the same about you and Greg.'

The conversation went no further. Squadron Officer Newbauld walked in then. She chatted amiably with them for a few moments before coming to the reason for her visit. 'You'll have Section Office Pearl Givens with you for a month. She's still under training and will eventually be posted to one of the other stations in the Group, provided she comes up to standard. I want you to see that she does. Her home, as it happens, is in Lincoln. She has to report in here every morning at eight but I have given her permission to sleep out, unless of course there is an op on when she will have to be on duty.'

'Very good, Ma'am,' both WAAFs said.

'We are in a position of authority,' laughed Vera marching across the room.

'It might be a test for us,' warned Carolyn.

'How can it be?'

'Well, Kate might be testing our ability to handle authority, with promotion in mind.'

'What? You can't be serious?' queried Vera.

Carolyn pulled a face. 'Maybe not. I can't see us as squadron officers.'

'Nor can I, but I can imagine Rick's face if it was to happen,' chuckled Vera. 'That really would be one in the eye for him! He'd even have to salute us. Imagine that!'

Both girls roared with laughter at the thought.

Their merriment faded when they heard two aero-engines start up. They looked at each other.

'Spitfires,' said Vera.

'Must be Greg and Alastair,' said Carolyn. 'The other two were away early this morning.'

They grabbed their hats and hurried outside. The Spitfires were already taxiing out of their dispersals. Alastair and Greg saw them and waved from their open cockpits. Then Greg, with his right hand held up, performed a little dance with his fingers. The girls laughed and waved back enthusiastically. The Spitfires moved forward. One last salute and the two pilots closed their cockpit covers.

The aircraft reached the runway in use; then, with a roar, they took off, circled the airfield and climbed high and out of sight.

'I wonder where they are going?' said Vera.

'We'll get to know all in good time if their photographs are destined for your eagle eyes,' returned Carolyn.

'Bring them back safely,' said Vera, almost to herself.

275

But Carolyn caught the words and added, 'Amen to that.'

They watched for a while, locked in their own thoughts, then turned inside without a word.

Half an hour later Squadron Officer Newbauld appeared again, to introduce Section Officer Givens.

She finished by saying, 'I'll leave her in your charge. See that she turns out well.'

'I didn't expect a posting to a squadron so soon,' said Givens when Newbauld had left. 'I'm a little shell-shocked by the speed of it all. I hope I won't let anyone down.'

'Squadron Officer Newbauld must see potential in you and wants to make proper use of it. She's an understanding person. Keep on the right side of her and you'll be fine.' Carolyn and Vera had been weighing up the newcomer. They saw an attractive red-head, with searching eyes full of curiosity and eagerness. Her slim figure was enhanced by her officer's uniform. 'We'll show you our department, introduce you around the Mess to whoever's there, but with stand down there won't be so many in for lunch, and this afternoon we'll show you some of the things we have been doing lately. The other WAAF in our department is Lucy Gaston but she is on leave with Pete Wilkins, Uncle's bomb aimer.'

They were about to leave for the Mess when the sound of approaching aircraft interrupted them. Carolyn and Vera hurried outside. Wondering what this was about, Pearl followed them, to find the two WAAFs waving enthusiastically as two Spitfires came in to land and taxied to their dispersals.

'Come on, we'll see them at lunch,' said Vera enthusiastically. 'Maybe find out where they have been.'

'You know very well you won't do that. They're too tight-lipped about their ops until they are official,' Carolyn pointed out. Seeing Pearl was a little bemused, she explained about the role of the Spitfires and the Photographic section.

They had no need to introduce Pearl around the Mess; the Lancaster boys were soon making themselves known, keen to share her table for lunch.

Vera and Carolyn did not mind; they became fully occupied when Alastair and Greg arrived. Once they were settled Vera tried her best to get them to make a slip of the tongue and learn where they had been, but met with a blank wall of silence about their mission.

In the afternoon Section Officer Givens was attentive to everything, asked probing questions, not only about the work she would be doing but also about the squadron and the men who flew the Lancasters.

'I'm sure you'll have your pick of them, as we saw at lunch,' said Vera, then gave her a little smile, 'but keep your eyes off the crew of U–Uncle. They're on leave at the moment, but when they get back, they're ours.'

'I'll bear that in mind,' said Pearl, 'but I thought, from the way you two reacted earlier, those two Spitfire pilots were special to you.'

Vera looked at Carolyn, cocked her head, and with a smile asked, 'Was it that obvious?'

Bad weather over Continental Europe gave Alastair and Greg more opportunities to date Carolyn and Vera, a situation the pilots made the most of.

On entering the Mess on the third morning, after another stand down had been announced, Pearl saw Carolyn and Vera having breakfast alone so joined them. After their initial exchanges, Pearl commented, 'This persistent bad weather seems to be giving you every opportunity with your Spitfire pilots?'

'Why not?' said Vera.

'Make hay while the rain falls!'

'You mentioned the crew of U–Uncle. I thought you ... '

'When the crews are away, the WAAFs will play, 'interrupted Vera lightly. 'What about you? How are you making out?'

'I'm biding my time,' came the reply. 'Casting my eye over the talent, sussing it out.'

'Applying the fruits of your training?'

'You could say that. It's surprising what you learn if you do.'

Carolyn eyed Vera. 'We'd better keep our eyes on this one and watch our step.'

The weather cleared on the fourth day and that night the squadron flew to Harburg.

'You must have a sixth sense,' said Carolyn to Vera, when they learned the target.

'No, just putting two and two together and making four.'

'Harburg must have been Alastair's and Greg's destination the last time we saw them take off. The photographs have just come from the Photographic section and they're good.'

Pearl slotted in extremely well and both Carolyn and Vera were impressed by her enthusiasm and astuteness.

It was still daylight when the squadron took off and Pearl had her first experience of seeing the beginning of an operational sortie.

'See you later,' called Vera, hurrying away.

Carolyn raised her hand in acknowledgement.

'She's in a hurry,' commented Pearl. 'I didn't see the Spitfire pilots here. Don't they bother to watch?'

'Oh, yes, but not every time.' Carolyn sensed that Pearl was fishing for more so diverted the subject. 'Now it's the awful wait,' she said as the final Lancaster took to the sky.

'What do you usually do while you're waiting for the bombers' return?' asked Pearl.

'Bed down in the billet, with the alarm set in time for us to be ready to do the debriefing. Or doze in a chair in the Mess, gossip or read the time away ... whatever works best. But, no matter what you do, it's advisable to be ready in the briefing room half an hour before the first plane is due back.'

'What do you usually do?'

'Depends on the length of the trip; this one's just over five hours so I think I'll have something to eat in the Mess and then doss down in an easy chair. The steward will give us a call if necessary.'

'Do you mind if I join you?'

'Of course not. Vera didn't say what she was doing but I guess she'll be along sometime.'

So the die was cast for the evening and into the early hours when the Lancasters would once again limp home.

'Ma'am.'

Carolyn stirred.

'Ma'am.'

The word was clearer this time. It penetrated more easily. There it was again. A man's voice. The steward's. Carolyn sat up.

'Oh ... ' She blinked. 'Thank you, Steward.'

'Would you like a cup of tea, Ma'am?'

'Heaven.'

'I thought so, Ma'am. The kettle is on. Be with you in a minute.'

'Thanks. I expect Section Officer Givens would like one too,' she said, indicating Pearl's sleeping figure.

When the steward moved off, Carolyn shook Pearl awake. 'Time for up.'

She was wide awake instantly.

'Gosh. Do you always wake as quickly as that?'

'Generally, if I have slept well. And I just have.'

Within twenty minutes they were heading for the briefing room where they found Vera already there.

Fifteen minutes later Pearl quietened them with, 'A plane!'

'You've a sharp ear,' commented Vera. 'I'm usually the first to pick up the Lancaster sound.' She went to the door, opened it and then called over her shoulder, 'You are right.'

One by one the Lancasters returned. With Carolyn beside her, Pearl watched the first landings by bombers after an operational sortie. She marvelled at the skill of the pilots in bringing their planes down, with only the WAAFs in the Control Tower to ensure an orderly landing and a flare path marking the runway. But that did not prepare Pearl for some of the sights she witnessed later after the first crew had arrived for debriefing.

Exhausted faces were etched by the terror they had faced and the strain of avoiding destruction in the skies. The men's flying clothing was often ripped, exposing flesh wounds clotted with blood, yet these young crew members acted as if that was an expected, everyday occurrence. Then Pearl began to realize that a full complement of crew members did not always appear at her table. The missing person had been dealt with immediately the aircraft landed, rushed to hospital or, worse, the morgue. Pearl was beginning to feel the strain of caring for the crews even though she did not know them well.

The debriefing went on.

'Z–Zebra's not back yet,' someone shouted across the room.

'Only one of the squadron missing,' someone confirmed.

'Could have been the one I saw go down,' said a mid-upper gunner who was just about to complete his debriefing by Carolyn and Pearl.

'Where and when was this?' asked Carolyn.

'The navigator will have that info. I gave it him. But I can tell you the plane was over Hamburg, silly B. You WAAFs told us to keep clear so it was his own stupid fault. They threw everything at him, and I can tell you that was pretty fierce. He was lit up like day by the searchlights. He couldn't get out of them, weave as he tried, but it was no good. The ack-ack was too fierce. It blew him out of the sky.'

Revulsion hit Pearl then. Her stomach churned. She jumped to her feet and rushed outside where she retched and was sick. A hand gently squeezes her shoulder. Looking up, she saw Carolyn.

'Oh, I'm sorry, but it got to me,' sobbed Pearl. Her words poured out. 'How can they be so casual about it?'

'It's their way of dealing with it. They know if they dwelt on it they would go out of their minds so they treat it offhandedly. "It hasn't happened to me, thank God for that."'

'But ... oh, I feel so ashamed about ...'

'There is nothing to be ashamed of. We have all been through this. It happened to me when I saw a Stirling crash on take-off.'

'But those poor young men ...'

'They wouldn't want our sympathy. They knew the risks. They were trained to do a job they wanted to do. Come on, take a few deep breaths, grit your teeth and finish the briefing. Don't walk away. It's the best way to cope.'

Pearl gave a weak smile, brushed the tears from her eyes, squeezed Carolyn's hand in a gesture of thanks and reassurance that she would cope, and walked back into the briefing room. Carolyn, knowing it was for the best, let her go in alone.

30

Uncle's crew had cast away all thoughts of war as each man had set off to spend his leave.

'You're quiet,' Lucy commented to Peter after they had settled in their carriage. 'Are you getting cold feet?'

'Wouldn't you if you were me meeting my prospective in-laws for the first time?'

Lucy laughed. 'They won't eat you! Besides, the walk after we leave Ripon station will settle your nerves.'

'That sounds ominous.'

'It's not meant to be, as you'll find out.'

Peter knew he would get no more out of her so settled back and commented on all the sights that were new to him.

'We've half a mile to walk,' said Lucy once they reached Ripon.

'Just a couple of strides then,' said Peter, teasing her by taking wobbly steps as if he was weighed down by his suitcase.

'Step it out and we'll soon be there,' countered Lucy, marching off.

'Hold on,' he called. 'Do you want me to meet your mum and dad in one piece or not?'

'Maybe I'll settle for one piece, otherwise Mum will wonder what I'm bringing home.'

They steadied their pace and enjoyed the walk to Lucy's street.

'These houses were built in nineteen thirty-six,' she informed him when the row of six detached houses came in sight. 'Dad bought the end one on the right because it had a bigger garden.' She cast Peter a wry glance. 'I hope you can talk gardening?'

Pete screwed up his face, expressing doubt. 'I did a bit at home for my two aunts, kept it tidy, but I had no aspirations to being a good gardener. I just did what they said and that was it.'

They had reached the gate when the back door opened and Lucy's mother bustled out then made a quick about-turn to throw her apron out of sight. She re-emerged, smoothing her skirt and jumper.

Lucy smiled at her mum's attempt to be prim and proper and winked at Pete, who grinned in return. The exchange had made him feel at home; there would be no standing on ceremony here, he realized. As if verifying that, Mrs Gaston held out her arms to him and said, 'Welcome home, son.'

'Thank you, Mrs Gaston. It is so nice to be here.' He went over to her and received a hug.

'You all right, love?' Sylvia asked, holding out one hand to her daughter and drawing her closer.

'Fine, Mum. Couldn't be better.'

'Come on in. Oh, where's your dad? He's never around when he's wanted. Kevin!'

Almost at that moment he came round the side of the house. 'Here, love. I was just casting an eye over the garden before those clouds open.' He gave Peter a quick glance. 'Hello, lad. Seems as if we'll have to introduce ourselves.' Kevin Gaston held out his hand, and when Peter took it he felt a hard grip and knew he had met a man's man but one who doted on his beloved wife and daughter. 'Come on in, lad. I expect you'd like to shed that uniform and relax. I know I'd like to get out of this collar and tie,' Kevin chuntered.

Seeing Sylvia raise her eyes to heaven in despair, Peter turned his smile on Kevin and said, 'Then let's do it!'

'Aye, all right, lad, we shall.' Kevin beamed and tugged at his tie.

Lucy was relieved. The tone had been set. These initial moments augured well for the news they had to break.

The time came after Peter had thanked Lucy's mother for an enjoyable meal and they had all settled down in the comfortably furnished drawing room. He glanced uneasily at Lucy, who gave him the encouraging nod, the signal they had arranged for her to give when she judged the moment was right.

Peter shuffled in his chair and gripped his hands tightly together. 'Mr and Mrs Gaston, I ... er ... I ... I would like to marry your daughter.' The words tumbled out, not in the way he had planned but nevertheless they were out, hanging in mid-air awaiting an answer.

Kevin gave a little chuckle. 'I thought that was coming, didn't you, Sylvia?'

She smiled. 'I believed the signs were there.'

'Hm.' That wary tone and the serious expression that had come to her father's face told Lucy he was about to make a pronouncement. 'Have you thought this through, Pete? Considered what the result of your dangerous trade might be?'

'Yes, Dad, we have,' put in Lucy. 'The future is unknown. We want to grab happiness while we can.'

Kevin smiled knowingly and glanced at his wife, who gave a little nod in a way that only he could interpret.

'Have you approached your parents, Peter?'

'Regrettably, I lost them when I was only young. Two maiden aunts took me in. They're quite well off. They gave me a good home, saw I had a decent education. The only thing I lacked was love. Oh, they treated me well enough, gave me stability, but it was short on love. I think secretly they are proud of my role in the Air Force, though.'

'And so they should be, lad.' Kevin gave a nod of approval, which pleased his daughter.

'To answer your question, Mr Gaston, I haven't mentioned Lucy to them but I intend to, now that you know about our relationship. I hope to take her to meet them during my next leave.'

'Very well,' said Kevin. 'That sounds fine.' He did not voice his thought that by that time more operations hopefully would have been completed and Peter would be nearer to completing his tour. Maybe even have completed it, and the dread news been avoided. He looked at his wife and, with a teasing twitch of his lips and a serious expression in his eyes, said, 'I think we might say yes to this young man's request, don't you, Sylvia?'

'I think we might,' she replied, as she got to her feet and held out her arms to her daughter.

'Oh, Mum, thanks!' cried Lucy.

They held each other tight and laughed and cried. Lucy turned to her father then, who had been accepting Peter's effusive thanks with a firm handshake as he said, 'Look after my little girl, son.'

While the rest of the crew, with their wives and girlfriends, were making the most of the precious days allotted to them, Rick was wishing he was back with his beloved Lancaster, to take his mind off his father's slow deterioration. Not that

285

he regretted being at home; his mother needed him and was touchingly grateful for his presence. Inevitably, though, the day of his return to Waddington arrived.

'Be strong, Mum. I'll ring you each day if possible. I've had a word with Auntie Cecilia and she'll come when she's needed but, as you know, it's not easy for her with an invalid youngster.'

'I know, love. The district nurse is a great help to me, and your father is holding his own. You know he wants to be here when you finish your ops.' His mother looked up, patted Rick's cheek and added, 'Now, you be careful in that aeroplane of yours.'

'I will Mum.' They walked arm in arm to the gate where Rick kissed her goodbye and gave a final wave before he was out of sight.

In their shared happiness, Pete and Lucy made the rest of their leave idyllic. They walked in nearby fields, strolled by the River Ure, spent a while in Ripon buying presents for her father and mother in memory of this special time, and enjoyed the autumn peace and tranquillity amidst the ruins of Fountains Abbey. They were lost in their love for each other, far from the world of war.

When Peter returned to his billet he saw Rick's case lying unopened on his bed and his greatcoat thrown beside it. He dumped his own things and hurried over to the Mess. There was no one in the ante-room so he guessed Rick might be in the bar. He was right but surprised to find there was no one else there except for the steward.

Rick looked up when the door opened. A flutter of relief crossed his face. 'Hi, Pete. Thank goodness someone's arrived.' He looked at the barman. 'Give him a whisky, Walt.'

'Yes, sir, coming right up.'

Peter felt a charge of concern. Rick looked tired even after his leave.

'Thanks, but don't match his double,' Pete said, having noted, with surprise, the quantity in Rick's glass. 'Something brewing?' he asked.

'Ops are on. Briefing is taking place now,' explained Rick.

'How was your leave?' Peter queried.

Rick pulled a face. 'My father wasn't too good, but better than I'd expected. It's what I've heard on my return that's upset me.'

'What's that?'

'Vera's been seeing Alastair again and from what I hear they seem to be getting pretty close.'

'You can't believe all you hear,' Pete warned.

'It's a pretty reliable source. She could have had more thought for me at a time like this, when my father . . . I can't cope with more bad news just now.'

'Oh, come on, Rick, be fair. Vera will always want some fun in her life. Her vivacity attracted you when Carolyn held back. Now it seems to me that you expect Vera to head for a nunnery or jump to your wishes, which at the moment seem only to be constantly talking about Lancasters and flying.'

'Why shouldn't I talk about them? They're my life.'

'Rick, a girl needs a bit of fun. She doesn't always want to hear about planes and ops and your love of flying. Like all of us she wants to forget the war for a while, at least when she's off duty.'

'But if she thought anything about me . . . '

'Aw, come off it, Rick,' Peter interrupted him sharply. 'If you can't cope with her having some fun, give the girl her freedom. Don't hold her back.'

287

'That's drastic advice!' snapped Rick. It was not what he'd wanted or expected to hear.

Pete shrugged his shoulders. 'Take it or leave it.'

Rick was about to protest again but thought better of it; he did not want the camaraderie of his crew undermining. He took a sip of his whisky instead and asked, 'What about you? Did your leave go well?'

'Yes. Couldn't have been better. Lucy's mum and dad made me feel at home straight away.'

'Good. Have you fixed a date?'

'Not yet. We aren't doing that until after I've seen my two aunts and that will be on our next leave.'

'So we await developments?' said Rick.

'Yes.'

Uneasy with wedding talk, Rick continued, 'The squadron will soon be airborne, then we'll entertain our Intelligence section in the Mess. Just a meal, a quiet get-together and a chat.'

An aero-engine broke the silence of an airfield on the edge of war. It was joined by another and another until the whole squadron was filling the air with its sound as if each Lancaster was eager to fulfil its purpose.

'I'm going to see them off,' said Rick. 'Are you coming?'

'Sure.' Pete was on his feet and in a matter of moments the two officers were pedalling their way to the end of the runway in use. Pete saw a gleam in his skipper's eyes that told him Rick was where he really wanted to be and his domestic troubles had been pushed to the back of his mind.

By the time they reached the end of the runway a small crowd of well-wishers had gathered, among them their three favourite WAAFs.

Vera moved straight to Rick's side. 'Hi, how was your father?'

'Not good. It was hardly the leave I wanted, but that's life. How about you? No trouble while I was away?'

She became aware of his darkening expression. 'Should there ... ?'

Rick interrupted her. 'Of course, there would be no trouble with Alastair by your side would there? I've heard you're still bent on escaping from us lowly ranks,' he added scathingly.

'Oh, please don't be like that, Rick!'

'How do you expect me to feel? As soon as I go on leave, you're out hunting!'

Not wanting this to turn into an open row Vera turned away, putting his reaction down to his home troubles, but the sharpness of his words troubled her.

She asked the rest of the crew about their leave and was pleased their reports were all upbeat, especially Lucy's.

The Lancasters were taxiing around the perimeter track, making for the runway in use. U–Uncle was brought into position by her replacement crew.

'She's done one other trip while we were on leave,' Rick informed Mark, raising his voice above the noise of the engines.

'Hope they bring her back in one piece,' shouted Mark.

'They'd better!' yelled Rick. 'Or I'll want to know why. She's my favourite girl.'

Vera's reaction was lost in Uncle's roar as the Lancaster started down the runway, drowning out any further exchanges. Rick held his breath and only let it go easily when the Lancaster was airborne and set for its flight. One by one the squadron took to the sky, with every spectator hoping that they would see all the crews return safely. The watching

289

group broke up when the final Lancaster took off, and in place of the deafening engine roar silence began to engulf the airfield.

'Rick and I are planning to eat together this evening. Why don't you three join us?' said Peter. 'We can have a drink and a chat afterwards.

'Good idea,' agreed Carolyn.

'I suppose *you'll* settle for no less than a squadron leader?' muttered Rick to Vera.

'At least he wouldn't talk aeroplanes and flying all night, if he were here.'

'Ah, so has he deserted you? Where is he?'

'No, he hasn't deserted me. He was called to 5 Group HQ yesterday and won't be back until tomorrow.'

'So he's hob-nobbing with the higher-ups again!' commented Rick contemptuously.

'You're insufferable,' snapped Vera, turning away from him.

He grabbed her arm and swung her round to face him. Contrition was written all over his face. 'I'm sorry, Vera.'

'You should be, Rick. I had a pleasant time while you were away. Now you are spoiling things with your petty jealousy.' She saw he was about to speak so pre-empted him with, 'And don't use your sick father as an excuse. You should be man enough to rise above that. And another thing . . . I am not going to sit around like a nun just waiting for you. Oh, and a final reminder . . . I am *never* going to play second fiddle to aeroplanes and flying. NEVER.' She broke away from him then and hurried off to ask Uncle's gunners about their leave.

When Vera entered the Mess that evening the silence seemed uncanny. With the squadron operating at full strength, it was only natural that the Mess would be quieter than usual in the absence of the exuberant young men whose lives were a contradiction – within a few hours they could be plunged into a world of violence and death.

Carolyn and Rick were already in the bar enjoying a pre-dinner drink. He jumped to his feet. 'The usual for you?' he asked Vera.

'Thank you but no, I think I'll have a whisky,' she said.

'Water?'

'A dash.'

He nodded, ordered the drink at the bar and signed the chit.

Lucy and Peter had just joined them when Greg came in. Carolyn waved him over and said, 'Join us for the evening, Greg. We're waiting for the bombers to come back.'

'Thanks.' He smiled and sat down beside her.

Five minutes later the phone rang. The steward took the call and nodded as he said, 'Yes, sir, she's here. I'll fetch her.' He came to their table and, looking at Carolyn, said, 'An outside line for you, Ma'am.'

Surprised, Carolyn went to the phone. She listened and her face broke into a huge smile. She spoke, nodded, spoke again and hung up. Then she had a word with the barman and returned to her seat. Though the others looked at her expecting some explanation, there was none. The chatter started again. It faded when the barman appeared with a tray full of drinks, which he just managed to slide on to their table.

'With the compliments of Flight Officer Maddison,' he said and handed a chit to Carolyn which she signed. As he returned to the bar her friends looked at her askance.

'A celebration,' she said. 'That phone call was from Alastair to tell me that the C-in-C Bomber Command has recommended an immediate award of his second DFC.' There was surprise and an outburst of congratulations flashed from the table. 'Apparently it was one of the reasons for the CO of 5 Group wanting to see him at HQ. The other was to discuss the Photographic section.'

'Immediate!' said Greg. 'That sounds as though it's connected to the Brest attack.'

'That is so,' replied Carolyn. 'The photographs that the section took beforehand were good enough to prompt the attack, but those Alastair took afterwards were extra-special apparently. The C-in-C also praised Vera for her interpretation of them and for spotting what nobody else had: the position of extra submarines. That led to their destruction too. A vital blow against the U–boat menace.'

Cheers rang out then. This had all the makings of a good evening and they were ready for it. But Vera had noted the sullen expression that had crossed Rick's face when Alastair and she had been heaped with praise. It made her wonder what he wanted from life. Would it always be lived on his terms only, and if so did she want to stick around?

31

Three days later the squadron took off into the evening sky, with the rest of 5 Group's flying force.

Some final words from the CO at the end of the briefing summed up their mission. 'The Dortmund-Ems canal is one of Germany's important waterways, vital for transporting wartime supplies and cargoes. Breach the banks and you'll drain it. Waterborne transport will be disrupted and the German war effort will suffer . . . so press home the attack. Make it successful. Good luck to you all.'

As the Group's aircraft climbed, Peter, keeping lookout from his position in the nose of the Lancaster, marvelled at the array of changing colours as the setting sun was sent spinning into whirling pools of red by the rotating blades of the propellers. It seemed as if aircraft were chasing the last of the daylight before the inevitable onset of night.

Uncle's crew went about their jobs efficiently. The tension of not knowing when they would be under attack was always there, but pushed aside so they could concentrate on the task ahead.

'Looks as though we're going to run into cloud,' Rick called over the intercom. 'Sharp look out.'

'Met told us there would be no cloud below nine and a

half thousand feet,' said Don from his position at the navigator's table.

'They got it wrong,' said Rick tersely.

Uncle flew on.

'Markers going down,' called Pete from the nose.

'I see them,' confirmed Rick, noting the glow on the cloud ahead.

Then, with the target area a little more than ten miles away, the Master Bomber controlling the attack, gave his assessment of the developing situation to the bombing force over the intercom. Misunderstanding had arisen with the marker force, delegated to mark the target, leaving the main force uncertain whether to attack visually from below cloud or make their sighting on sky markers above the cloud.

'That's bloody confusing,' snapped Rick. 'What do you make of our instructions, Pete?'

'Not clear. I'm for a better sighting – below cloud!' said Pete without hesitation, knowing the whole crew would back him whatever his decision.

'Okay, here we go!' called Rick.

He put the nose down. Uncle responded. Cloud tried to swallow her but Uncle was defiant. She burst out into a clear sky.

'Four and a half thousand feet!' yelled Rick.

'Target dead ahead!' shouted Pete, who had rapidly summed up their position.

'Bloody hell, it's like daylight out here,' called Tim from his mid-upper gunner position.

Flares from the marker force were still falling, lighting up any bomber below four thousand feet. Streams of shells from light anti-aircraft guns streamed across the sky.

'Aircraft ahead hit and going down!' shouted Pete.

'I'm levelling out,' called Rick

'OK, Skipper, hold this course. Bomb doors open.'

'Bomb doors open,' responded Rick.

Peter glued his eyes on the two red target markers that had been dropped accurately close to the canal's sides. He lined them up in his bombsight. Almost perfect. 'Left, left.' His order was sharp and clear. Rick knew exactly what his bomber aimer required: a slight adjustment. 'Left, left.' Rick obeyed. 'Steady, steady.' Everyone in the aircraft knew from Pete's voice that he had got a perfect line on the target. Shells burst around them. 'Steady ... steady ... steady ... ' Peter watched the progression of the target in his bombsight. He pressed the bomb release. Then, 'Bombs gone!' He craned forward into the nose of his compartment to try and look back; this was the first time he had bombed from such a low altitude on an actual raid. He saw bomb bursts along the canalside. 'Got it!' he shouted.

'You sure have,' confirmed Mark from his rear turret, which was giving him a perfect view of the target as they left. 'Water's pouring out!'

Cheers rang through the aircraft but Rick quickly quietened them. 'We're heading back into cloud.' They all knew the extra threat that brought – unseen aircraft; collisions.

Their spirits rose with every mile they travelled towards home.

'What time are they due back?' asked Pearl, cradling a cup of coffee in her hands.

'They took off at seventeen-forty-five and it should be about a five-and-a-half-hour flight if all goes well,' said Vera.

'Not worth hitting the sheets then,' said Pearl.

'When it's a short trip like this one we generally stay put

in the Mess until they're due back. Reckon we'll do that tonight?' Vera's querying glance at Carolyn and Lucy received nods of approval.

They settled themselves in easy chairs, chatting quietly so as not to disturb the few other occupants of the Mess also awaiting the bombers' return. They read a book, skimmed through a newspaper, played darts, dozed, or tried to ward off sleep with endless cups of coffee, until someone announced, 'The first one is here.'

'Trust Fosdyke to hear the first plane back,' muttered the young flying officer in charge of the transport that would be collecting the returning crews at the dispersals around the aerodrome.

'Lost your bet again? Thought you'd be wise to Fozzy's exceptional hearing by now.'

The Mess became alive with activity as its occupants rushed to resume their duties.

The Intelligence section WAAFs quickly shrugged themselves into their greatcoats, crammed on their hats and headed outside. The cold air had just started to cloud their breath when a car pulled up beside them.

Squadron Officer Newbauld wound down the window and called from the driving seat, 'Room for four if three of you don't mind a squeeze in the back.'

'Thanks, Ma'am,' they chorused as they quickly sorted themselves out, Carolyn being urged by the others to occupy the front passenger seat.

'Been at HQ today. I have this car for twenty-four hours so thought I might as well use it now and keep out of the cold,' the Squadron Officer explained.

'Lucky for us. It would have been rather nippy on the bikes. There's frost in the air.'

The first aircraft was touching down, with others on the

296

circuit, when the WAAFs piled out of the car and hurried to get out of the cold. Vera paused at the door to the hut and looked towards the runway in use. Everything seemed normal. She watched two planes land; a third was making its final approach to the runway. Then the roar of its engines was lost in the noise of a tearing explosion, the blast sending Vera hurtling to the ground. She was aware of a huge flash lighting up the runway for a moment.

'Oh my God! What the ...?'

Her words were lost as the door of the hut was hurled open and a cacophony of alarm competed with other noises from every part of the airfield.

The pilot of the Lancaster making its final approach pushed his throttles open and sent his plane climbing, hoping he could escape what he imagined was a bomb exploding at the near the end of the runway. Carolyn burst out of the hut to find chaos developing, but she had no time to assess it before the airfield was plunged into darkness when all lighting was extinguished.

'Intruders!' yelled the flying control officer who had just had time to see an alien aircraft zoom past the Control Tower. 'Get a message to HQ *now!*'

Two WAAFs obeyed and were lucky to get connections immediately.

'Yes, that's what I said ... we've been attacked by intruders!' one reported.

The other WAAF was also having trouble convincing the operator at the other end of the line about what she was reporting. 'A bomb has been dropped. It probably hit our runway. I can hear machine-gun fire ... must be a fighter-bomber strafing ... Yes, that's what I said!' She cast a helpless glance at the control officer.

He took the telephone from her. 'We are being attacked!

There are intruders about, so get your finger out and alert Group. Our returning Lancasters are in danger.'

'March Tune calling, March Tune calling.' Waddington's call-sign crackled in U–Uncle's headphones. 'Scram procedure. Scram procedure. Intruders about! Intruders about!'

Rick banked the Lancaster. 'Skipper to crew, sharp eyes now. There'll be a lot of aircraft milling around.' He started to fly on the course designated for such an emergency, though no one at 5 Group had ever thought it would happen – German fighter bombers must have infiltrated the bomber force and flown home with them, to catch them at their most vulnerable when going in to land.

U–Uncle flew on, the crew tense, awaiting the next instruction which they hoped would be one signalling the danger was over.

'Aircraft on fire, ahead to port,' Peter reported.

Tension mounted.

The sky ahead was suddenly bright with leaping flames, far enough off not to worry them but a significant reminder that war had come to their own doorstep. 'Must have hit a petrol dump at some airfield,' commented Rick.

Ten minutes later they were given the all clear but received the news that Waddington was out of action. They were diverted to Bitteswell, a training unit further inland.

'The all clear has been given,' Squadron Officer Newbauld informed her WAAFs, who had sought cover in a small filing room off the main briefing room when the unexpected attack had brought chaos to the airfields of South Lincolnshire.

They emerged looking bewildered and dishevelled, uniforms askew, stockings laddered.

'Report,' Kate called out.

'Maddison, Ma'am.' Carolyn was the first to answer. 'I'm OK.'

'Gaston, Ma'am,' Lucy called. 'Bashed my arm when I hit the floor, but I think it will be all right.'

'Good enough to cuddle Pete when he gets back?' Vera asked, trying to lighten the mood. But her question only aroused concern for the crew of U–Uncle.

Emergency lighting came on, enabling a quick assessment to be made of the damage to the airfield.

Kate's attempts to get any news were thwarted by blocked telephone lines. 'No good. I'll go and see what I can find out,' she said. 'You girls sort yourselves out and bring some order back in here,' she added, glancing at all the files and paper that had been scattered by the bomb blasts. 'And try and block those broken windows.'

Four anxious WAAFs, not wanting to express their concern for the squadron's crews, set about trying to restore some order to their section.

When Kate returned everyone looked anxiously at her.

'Uncle's been diverted to Bitteswell and the news is she is safely down.'

There were audible sighs of relief, but Kate continued, 'Our squadron lost one over the target and two were shot down by the intruders.'

A silence fell, charged with sorrow for the lost crews. Kate knew she should break it quickly. 'Two of the Spitfires have been badly damaged also. Complete write-offs. The bomb crater on the main runway is already being dealt with. There is damage to the main hangar, mainly to the doors. Around the station, windows have been blown out, doors blasted off their hinges, and some transport vehicles put out of action. So much for how we fared. I am loathe to tell you that the Group as a whole lost eight over the target and fifteen to the intruders,

299

some of the losses from training units.' She paused to let the gravity of this sink in then added, 'All sections have been called out to deal with any problems concerning them. Breakfast is being served in the various Messes from now until ten o'clock. From then on normal mealtimes will apply.'

'Ma'am,' Carolyn spoke up, 'I think it might be a good idea if we all went to breakfast now, I know it would help settle my stomach, which has been churning ever since the attack started.'

The others added their approval.

'Very well,' said Kate. 'Let's be back in an hour and a half. If I am waylaid by authority, you all know what is required here. I'll see you later.'

The four WAAFs were putting on their greatcoats when the door opened. Alastair and Greg walked in and they set off for the Mess together.

'We heard you had lost two Spitfires,' said Carolyn as she fell into step with her brother.

'Yes,' he replied. 'Thankfully Greg and I were not parked close to the other two. I'm having ours thoroughly checked now so we can be fully operational as soon as possible.'

'Will you get replacements immediately?'

'Not for a fortnight. The replacements will have to be adapted for photographic work – cameras installed and armaments stripped out to make the planes lighter. Greg and I will continue to operate for 5 Group from here. Merv and Allan have leave due so will use the time to fit that in. They'll be on leave for two weeks from tomorrow.'

'Two weeks?' Carolyn was surprised. 'It's an ill wind that blows nobody any good. Lucky them.'

'More work for me and Greg.'

And more danger, Carolyn realized. Her eyes met Greg's.

*

Bitteswell had quickly adapted to receive the diverted air-crews and to get everything ready for a departure the next day, as soon as the availability of their home airfields could be confirmed.

After an uneasy night spent in an armchair in the Officers' Mess, Rick left Pete still blissfully asleep and wandered into the dining room. Apart from a pilot officer with full Wings above his breast pocket, and a WAAF section officer, the only other people there were the WAAFs standing by to serve breakfast. Rick's choice was quickly assembled. As he took it he was aware of being stared at as if he was a god newly arrived from the heavens and realized that these inland WAAFs had probably never before met anyone from an operational aircrew. It made him feel rather special, a pilot who had flown a Lancaster on an operational mission and survived. He gave them a broad smile to send their hearts fluttering. He turned to decide where he would sit, but that was resolved for him.

'Come and join us,' call the pilot officer.

'Thanks,' said Rick, and slid into place opposite the two other diners.

'Did you manage any sleep?' asked the section officer. Oh, I'm Jenny, by the way, and this is my boyfriend Roy.'

Rick nodded, introduced himself then replied to her question. 'Not much, I don't like armchairs for sleeping. My bomb aimer is still in there, though, out like a light.'

'Was it a rough op?' asked Roy.

'Roy! Rick won't want to talk about it . . . ' Jenny's retort was sharp.

'Sorry,' Roy apologized.

Rick brushed this away.

'Well, can I ask what the Lanc is like to fly?' Roy enquired.

'A dream,' replied Rick, eyes shining at the prospect of being able to talk to someone who had showed interest in his beloved aircraft.

The questions were asked and answered, the two pilots pleasantly absorbed in them until Jenny had finished her cup of tea.

'Well,' she said testily, 'thank you for forgetting I'm even here and replacing me with a Lancaster!'

'Sorry,' both men replied sheepishly.

'Roy can talk about nothing else. All he's looking forward to is getting behind the controls of a Lancaster. At times I wonder why I bother with him.' Jenny stood up. The two men rose with her. 'Oh, sit down and carry on,' she told them, then looked at Rick. 'I hope you don't bore your girl-friend with constant talk of flying. There is another life out there and it can be full of fun, you know.'

Rick held up his hand in a gesture that told her he under-stood it was meant as a friendly observation. 'Goodbye, Jenny. Nice to meet you.'

'Safe flying,' she replied. 'See you later, Roy.'

After the short flight from Bitteswell, U–Uncle touched down on the repaired runway at Waddington, where the ground-crew were overjoyed to have their aircraft safely back in their hands.

After a quick debriefing and changing out of their flying clothes, Rick and Pete hurried to their billet, shaved and washed.

'Where are you heading?' asked Rick.

'Where do you think?' replied Pete.

'Well, I'll accompany you.'

They were both joyfully greeted by the WAAFs in the Intelligence section.

Vera answered Rick's smile with one of relief.

Lucy took Peter by the arm and led him outside. 'Will you marry me sooner rather than later?' she asked without any preamble. He showed surprise. 'I mean it,' she insisted.

'But your parents expect ...'

'Never mind what they expect. I'm asking you.'

'Well, yes,' he spluttered. 'If that's what you want.'

She pulled him to her and kissed him. 'It is.'

'What's brought this about?' he asked.

'Last night's intruders. I always knew there was danger whenever you were flying, but last night planes were being shot down over their own bases. I want to grab my chance of happiness with you while I can.'

'Your parents are expecting us to wait. I'll have to write ...'

'No, Pete, I'll do that.'

He nodded. 'Very well, but when do you want us to marry?'

'Your next leave. I'll ask Mum and Dad to make arrangement with the vicar and anybody else who needs to be notified, so that they are standing by when we know your leave date.'

'All right. I'll write to my aunts. I'm certain there'll be no objections there, though I would have liked them to have met you first so they could see for themselves the wonderful girl I want to marry.'

'You are so sweet! I love you,' said Lucy, and kissed him.

They went back inside where they found Rick finding out what had gone on at the airfield last night.

'It's tough when trouble lands on your doorstep,' said Vera. 'It was hairy enough down here. It must have been hell when you found out what was happening.'

'It wasn't pleasant but I had every confidence in my crew

and in Uncle, who all behaved magnificently. Uncle responded instantly when I needed to take evasive action to avoid another Lancaster. We were at the same ... '

Sensing she was going to receive a lengthy account, Vera diverted the subject with, 'And what was Bitteswell like?'

'Crowded with diverted aircrews. I was awake early so I went in for breakfast and got talking to a pilot officer and a WAAF section officer. He was quizzing me about the Lancaster and what it's like to fly.'

'Just up your street,' said Vera, a little sarcastically.

'The conversation went further than that. I'd like to tell you about it sometime.'

Vera thought it might be better to get this out of the way as soon as possible. 'I'll be finished here in a few minutes. I'll walk with you to the Mess, you can tell me on the way.'

While tidying her desk, she observed Rick was deep in thought. His mood had not lightened by the time they stepped outside.

'Well, what did you tell those two that I haven't heard before?' she asked.

'It was not what I told them that was important; it was what they said that set me thinking. I'll not go into the details of the conversation but it's made me realise that I am being unfair to you, Vera. I am bound up in my Lancaster and in flying, and I think I owe it to my crew to stay that way. Besides that, in my off-duty time, there are the worries about my father. I think it only fair to you to say that those two things preclude me from giving you what you want from life, whereas Alastair is ready to put you first. Please don't hold this against me, but I think we should stay as friends without any other obligations to each other.'

There was a long silence while she weighed up what he had said. Vera hesitated before she spoke but kept her eyes fixed firmly on Rick. She saw a man who had come to terms with his life, one who would always turn it his way. Anyone else who wanted to come along would have to do so strictly on his terms.

'Rick, thanks for being so honest with me,' she said, choking back tears. 'I have loved being with you, but now I see that we have both changed and want different things.'

He took her hand and pressed it. 'I'll leave the way clear for Alastair. He's much more suitable for you.' He gave a little smile, turned and walked away.

Vera watched him go for a few moments, her dreams dissolving. The tears started to flow then; her lips moved silently. Fly safely, my love.

32

'Should be an easy one,' commented Pearl as they watched the bombers take off on a daylight raid to destroy German oil plants near Homberg. 'Short too, four and a half hours. They should be back late afternoon.'

'Nothing is ever easy,' said Lucy. 'There's danger on an op from the moment they take off, and you've seen what can happen even after they reach home.'

Pearl made no comment to this but thought, That's put me in my place.

One by one the Lancasters returned from a raid in which they had flown in loose formation – a gaggle, as it was known.

As the crews came in for debriefing Carolyn remarked quietly to Vera, 'They seem a bit subdued. I hope they're all back.' But as the debriefing unfolded the reason for the air-crews' low spirits became obvious.

The gaggle had been flying just above thin cloud cover through which the target markers were visible. Anti-aircraft fire greeted the bombers, and intensified the closer they drew to the target.

'The bombers ahead of us were clearly visible to me as

we ran into the target,' reported Peter, 'and our squadron was holding its place in the gaggle.

Then I saw a plane hit, ahead and to port. It veered and dropped away from the stream like a wounded bird, smoke streaming from two of its engines. I saw no more as we were on to our bombing run. Rick kept Uncle steady on our line of attack, obeying my directions. I had a good sighting on the glow from the markers on the clouds but could not see the results.'

'Did you see any more of the aircraft that had been hit?' Lucy asked.

'No, but it didn't look good. Planes are still coming in. There's still hope, I suppose.'

That faded as time passed, and was finally extinguished when the other squadrons in the Group reported all their Lancasters were safely back, leaving 44 Squadron with the only loss, G–George.

Gloom settled over them all. Lucy sensed that Peter was particularly upset.

'Want to talk about it?' she asked when they left the debriefing together. 'It might help.'

He gave a grim smile. 'Somehow seeing an aircraft, especially one of your own squadron, shot down in daylight creates a different reaction from observing losses at night, when it's not possible to identify if the plane is from your squadron or not.

'G–George's bomb aimer was on the same course as me in Canada, but we were separated when we got back to England. We next met here on the squadron. We were never close friends, but now I can't help thinking about the times we had together.'

'Pete, you can't dwell on it. You mustn't. It could affect your concentration and that might endanger your crew. You're just back from a raid, you're weary. Get some sleep and I am sure you'll cope. And you always have me, remember.'

Pete squeezed her hand. 'You're a lovely lass, Lucy. I'm lucky to have you.' They had reached her billet. 'I'll see you later,' she said, and kissed him goodbye.

Concerned by his reaction to the raid, Lucy flopped on to her bed wondering how to take his mind off it pondering the situation, she realized he needed to focus on something outside his operational flying. She swung herself off the bed, sat down at the table and started to write her second letter to her parents in as many days.

Dear Mum and Dad,

You will have received my letter re the wedding. I am sorry to press you for an answer so soon but I do need it for Peter's sake. He had a rough ride this morning. I can't write about it here, but we need your answer soon. Please let it be yes.

Love,

Lucy

Leaving the Mess after breakfast three days later, Lucy saw there was a letter for her. Recognizing her mother's handwriting and seeing the date-stamp, she knew it must be an answer to her request. With shaking hands she tore the envelope open and extracted a folded sheet of paper. Her eyes scanned the familiar writing. Relief swept over her.

Dear Lucy,

Your two letters arrived this morning. The first one must have been delayed. Probably just as well in view of the second one. I hope Peter is feeling a bit better now.

Your dad and I want nothing but happiness for you both. If that means holding the wedding before the time we originally agreed, then so be it.

Your dad is away to see the vicar now. Hopefully he will have the all clear when he returns and I can add it to this letter ...

He's back now. The Vicar was very sympathetic and helpful. He will fix a date immediately we know Peter's next leave.

Love,
Mum

Four days after their break-up Vera did her best to keep out of Rick's way, but she could not avoid him continually. The Mess was a close knit community; she knew their paths were sure to cross. As she got ready one evening her thoughts turned to past times with Rick and tears flowed until she chided herself. She looked in the mirror, frowned, and rubbed her eyes with a damp flannel and a dry face-cloth. Then she combed her hair and fluffed it with her fingers. A quick tug at her uniform and she looked presentable and composed again. She headed for the Mess.

'Hello, there!' a familiar voice called out as footsteps quickened behind her. She faltered. Alastair! This wasn't the right time – or was it? Was this how it was meant to be? 'Hello,' said Vera, attempting a smile.

'That's slightly better,' he said. 'You were looking a bit grouchy when I first saw you. Is something bothering you?'

'Rick broke up with me.'

A quick glance around told Alastair that they were alone. He took her in his arms.

Vera realized that it would not look good for either of them if they were seen like this. She pulled away from him gently. 'I'm sorry, I shouldn't burden you with my troubles'.

'Don't be,' he said gently. 'I'm glad I am here for you.' He looked deep into her eyes. 'This may not be the right time to say it but I would like you to remember the times we have spent together. Can we build on those? You know I think a great deal of you. Let's start right now and have lunch together in the Mess.'

Vera nodded and said, 'Thank you. I'd like that.'

They kept the conversation light until they saw Carolyn and Greg come in. Vera went over to ask them to sit with Alastair and her.

'A quick word with you both first,' she said, and quickly informed them that she and Rick had split up. They both expressed surprise and sympathy.

As they moved towards the table where Alastair waited, Carolyn said, 'And my brother? Where does he fit in?'

Vera smiled. 'Alistair and I have enjoyed each other's company, and he's a kind and generous man, but it was Rick's love of flying that broke us up. My rival was a Lancaster.'

The four of them had a pleasant meal together. Alastair then suggested that, as there had been a stand down, the four of them should spend a quiet evening in one of the local pubs. This was approved by all. 'Good,' he said. 'Meet at five o'clock here then. A two-mile walk to the Greyhound will give us an appetite.'

It was a cheerful group who set off later on the two-mile walk. Alastair, Carolyn and Greg were bent on keeping Vera from fretting about the end of her relationship with Rick.

'What a beautiful night,' she commented afterwards, when they stepped out of the pub into countryside bathed in brilliant moonlight. Alastair moved nearer and took her hand.

He was pleased when he felt her fingers twine around his. Their walk became slower and gradually their chatter stopped and both felt the strong draw of shared silence.

Carolyn and Greg had lagged behind until it no longer mattered that they had split up the foursome. He slid his arm round her waist and drew her closer. They too said little, not wanting to spoil the dream-like quality of a night in which the stars seemed to be smiling down.

Greg stopped and held Carolyn, saying nothing. She made no objection when he turned her to him but met his searching gaze, knowing what he was about to say.

'Greg, please don't ask me again. I promised I would give you an answer when the time was right.'

'And what better time than on a magical night like this?'

'It certainly is spellbinding and I might so easily ... '

'Then why not?' he urged. 'Say you will marry me?'

'Oh, Greg. You and I have something special. I don't want that to change just yet. If I say yes now it might alter everything.'

'It wouldn't.'

'So easily said.' The moonlight revealed the disappointment in his eyes. 'Greg, I do love you, and one day the answer you want could well be given to you, but I need more time, to see this war over.' She pulled him close then and silenced his protests with a sweet kiss.

Alastair glanced down at Vera as he linked arms with her. 'I hope tonight has helped,' he said.

'You have all been wonderful to me, especially you, Alastair. You have been very considerate and I appreciate that. You accepted what I told you without a hint of triumph.'

'I don't believe in kicking a man when he is down. I know Rick will be suffering too because he has pushed away a

311

wonderful girl, but that was of his own choosing. I have always had a high regard and special affection for you. May I hope that one day I will be allowed to declare them to you?'

She told him, 'Of course. All I ask at this moment is, please don't rush me.'

'I won't. And in the meantime here is something to remember me by.' He kissed her gently.

'Thank you,' whispered Vera. 'I'll remember tonight always.'

Three days later Lucy and Peter were able to tell their friends that they had decided to bring the wedding forward to the crew's next leave. Now all they could do was pray that it would come soon and without anything happening to cloud their happiness.

33

When Peter and Lucy broke the news that the wedding was to take place during the crew's next leave, the crew and the WAAFs of the Intelligence section all started to make provisional plans for their attendance, assuming it would take place on a day when the squadron would be stood down for one reason or another.

Kate Newbauld came to discuss some ideas with her WAAFs but found Alastair already making some suggestions.

'Kate, it's providential you should come now. I was just telling the girls that I am friendly with one of the local farmers, who slips me a drop of petrol from time to time. I'm sure he will oblige for the wedding. If we all squeeze into my old jalopy we can make it there and back in the same day. I'm assuming Lucy will have been granted leave the day before, so she and Peter will already be in Ripon. That would leave me as driver, and four passengers, you, Carolyn, Vera, and Greg.'

'This is great,' enthused Carolyn. 'The crew will have started their leave the day before and will have made their own arrangements to stay overnight before the wedding; maybe even afterwards but that is up to them.'

The buzz of excitement continued throughout the day

and Carolyn found it was still in her mind when she closed her billet door for the night. Lucy's words still rang in her mind

As Carolyn laid her head on the pillow she wondered if she was doing the right thing, keeping Greg waiting. Was she perhaps being selfish, thinking only of herself? Hadn't the scars of what she had witnessed healed by now? She fell asleep still pondering the question.

In the morning she looked at herself in the mirror but her reflection could not help her to decide. 'Only you can do that,' she told herself.

Greg was already in the dining room when she walked in. He shuffled up to make a place for her.

'You're in early,' she commented.

He nodded. 'Alastair gave me an early-morning call. I'm taking off in half an hour.'

'Is it a long flight?' she asked. She knew he could not disclose where he was headed.

'Medium.'

'Well, take care. I'll be watching for your return.'

'Aren't you going to see me off?'

'Of course. That goes without saying.'

He smiled his pleasure; it wasn't every pilot who had the girl he considered 'the special one' to see him off. As he pushed himself from the table, his hand rested on Carolyn's for a moment. 'I'll see you later.' His touch jolted her. It seemed to say more clearly than words, 'I love you.' Her heart beat faster as she watched Greg walk away. She wanted to stop him then, to hold him close and never let him go.

Ignoring her breakfast, she hurried after him but he was out of sight.

Half an hour, he had said.

314

Kate appeared then.

'Ah, Maddison, is Gaston in the dining room?'

'No, Ma'am. I was told she's been and gone.'

'Ah, well, it doesn't matter. Will you tell her to be in my office along with yourself in three-quarters of an hour?'

'Yes, Ma'am.'

Carolyn glanced at her watch. Not much time to find Lucy and see Greg take off.

She had just got Kate's message to her friend when she heard the unmistakable sound of a Spitfire's engine starting up. Carolyn started to run. The Spitfire's hard standing would be the nearest. Hopefully she could reach it before Greg taxied out.

She ran harder. She must be there, she *must*. She had no idea why it was so important to her, but today she knew she must not let him down.

Relief flooded over her when the dispersal came into view. Greg's Spitfire was still there! Gasping for breath, she slowed her footsteps. She saw his canopy slide open and when he raised his hand knew he had seen her. Still breathing hard, she walked nearer then stopped. She saw him smile just for her, and allowed her lips to form the words she knew he could not hear. Yes, I Will, Greg. I Will!

His wide grin and thumbs-up signal told her he had understood. Joy flooded into her heart as she watched him take to the skies.

Carolyn was thankful that the meeting with Kate did not require much concentration and was over in twenty minutes. She was bursting to tell Lucy and Vera her news but wanted to see Greg first. Though it was hard she managed to keep her excitement under control so that it would not be a giveaway. Later, when she heard the drone of a returning Spitfire, she left the office on some other pretext.

Greg made a perfect landing. When he neared the dispersal he pushed his canopy back, saw Carolyn, blew her a kiss and waited for her to blow one back.

He brought the aircraft to a halt, climbed from the cockpit, rushed to Carolyn and immediately took her in his arms. 'You really meant it then?' he asked, searching her eyes. To his relief he saw confirmation there.

'Of course, with all my heart.' She glanced around and added, 'Your ground-crew are wondering about us.'

He laughed. 'I think they've already cottoned on that you are my girl. Let's take the film to the Photographic section and then I'd like us to break the news to Alastair together.' A worried expression crossed his face. 'You haven't told anyone else yet?'

'No.' She gave a reassuring shake of her head. 'I wanted you to be with me, and I wanted Alastair to be the first to know.'

One of the ground-crew approached with film from the aircraft. 'Thanks, Tubby,' called Greg.

'Good flight, sir?'

'As good as it could be. Hope the photographs prove it.'

Greg and Carolyn chatted happily, expressing their hopes they would find Alastair in his office and speculating on his reaction to the news.

They both came smartly to attention when they faced him over his desk and saluted, but they failed to keep their expressions serious, causing Alastair to comment, 'No need to command you to stand easy. You both look like cats sharing the cream.'

'We are, sir,' replied Greg. 'I've been enjoying mine ever since I took off.'

'And I've been doing the same since then.' Carolyn glanced at Greg and gave him a sly wink.

'Sir, can we drop the formalities?' asked Greg.

'They appear to be going out of the window, so yes, permission granted.'

'We want you to be the first to know that Carolyn has said yes.'

'I suppose that was in answer to a certain question you put to her?' Alastair smiled as he rose from his chair and came over to them. He hugged his sister and said quietly in her ear, 'Be happy, you've got a good man here.'

The words of approval brought tears of joy to her eyes. 'I will, Alastair, and thanks.'

He turned to Greg then. 'I'll be proud to have you as a brother-in-law.' They shook hands. 'Look after her, Greg.'

'I will.'

'Come on,' said Carolyn, grabbing Greg's hand, 'let's break the news to the others!' She was already propelling him towards the door.

'You two, behave in an orderly manner when you get outside!' barked Alastair.

Lucy and Vera were delighted for them.

'If we had known sooner we could have had a double wedding,' said Lucy.

'But separate weddings might keep the ball rolling for others,' jested Carolyn, with a meaningful glance at Vera.

The crew was equally enthusiastic. They had come to know Carolyn well, and had no hesitation in organizing a celebration for her and Greg in the local pub when they heard that there would be no operations that night.

'There's only Rick to notify,' said Carolyn as she and Greg headed for the Officers' Mess. 'I hope he hasn't gone to Lincoln since there's a stand down.'

They were nearing the Mess when they saw him come out of the building.

'Rick!' Carolyn called.

He stopped on hearing her familiar voice.

'Can we have a word?' she called. 'We have something to tell you,' she added when they reached him. 'We have just announced that we are to marry and wanted to tell you before you heard it elsewhere.'

Rick was startled but masked his reaction with a smile. 'I wish you both well,' he said, and kissed Carolyn on the cheek. Turning to Greg, he exchanged a warm handshake. 'All the luck in the world,' he said. 'You've got a great girl here, look after her.'

'I will,' promised Greg.

'There's a celebration in the local pub tonight,' Carolyn told Rick.

'I'll be there.' He walked away, recalling how close he and Carolyn had once been. Had his attitude even at that time been too selfish? Had he expected too much of Carolyn, as he had done of Vera? Would he ever be able to give himself to a woman completely or would there always be a rivalry between her and his love of flying.

After their evening meal in the Mess, Greg and Carolyn headed for the village pub.

'I haven't seen anything of the others,' commented Carolyn, as she slipped her hand into his.

'Nor have I,' said Greg. 'They'll be along no doubt.'

At the front of the pub they manoeuvred their way through two sets of doors that the landlord had had specially erected at the outbreak of war so that no light could escape to contravene blackout regulations.

When they stepped into the bar the low buzz of conversation broke into a roar of greetings. Cheers lifted the rafters; congratulations thundered around the room. Locals and regular customers at the inn turned their heads and were pleased to join in, seeing the young men and women in blue, whom they had taken to their hearts, coming together in this joyous occasion in spite of the shadow of war that hung over them.

Rick, pint in hand, drifted over to Greg and Carolyn. He raised his glass. 'To you both,' he said. 'Look after each other.'

'We will,' said Carolyn.

Someone started to tinkle with the piano keys. When they moved into a waltz, Greg took Carolyn to a space in the centre of the room. Cheers broke out and a party mood filled the building. Songs sweet and bawdy rocked the area and beer flowed until the landlord called, 'Last drinks, please.'

The squadron operated three times in the next fortnight. Though the first two raids saw all aircraft return, four Lancasters had sustained substantial damage due to considerable anti-aircraft fire over the heavily defended Ruhr. The third raid, however, took its toll on the squadron with the loss of two aircraft. One of the crews involved had hardly had time to adapt to squadron life, being only on their second operation. The other loss was Commander of A Flight and his crew who were on their twenty-eighth operation with only two more to do. The Reaper seemed oblivious to a crew's experience or length of service.

The following day Rick was called to the CO's office. Wondering about the reason for it, he came smartly to attention and saluted his superior officer.

'Stand easy, Wood.'

Rick did so, relieved that the CO sounded to be in a good mood.

'In fact, sit down.'

Rick was aware that the CO was observing him with a watchful eye.

'We lost a good man last night. Ginger Barton used his considerable experience to run a tight but relaxed flight, to the benefit of the squadron. He will not be an easy man to replace but I have no doubt that you will do your best to uphold and continue to build on the sound foundation he established.'

Rick, completely taken by surprise, gasped, 'Me, sir?'

'Yes, you, Wood.' A twitch of a smile at the flying officer's reaction touched the CO's lips. 'I have kept an eye on you. I think you can handle being a flight commander. You will need to work hard to win the respect of all aircrew members of your staff. That does not mean you must take part in every operation. In fact, it is desirable that you don't, which will mean your tour will be time-extended. That will also apply to your crew, but if any of them do not wish to face a longer tour by time then they are at liberty to make that known to you and can operate with other crews, as and when that is necessary.'

'I feel certain that they will all want to stick together, sir, but I will give each of them the choice.'

'Very well. By the way, I have been studying their individual records. I see Flying Officer Wilkins is due for promotion to Flight Lieutenant in two months' time. I will recommend that promotion as of now, and will also recommend your navigator, Sergeant Westwood, for a Commission, with effect as soon as possible.'

'Thank you, sir. Am I at liberty to break this news to my crew?'

'Of course. I would be surprised if my recommendations are not granted immediately.'

'Thank you, sir.'

'Very well, Wood. Off you go and take charge of your flight. The adjutant will already have posted notices in the flight offices and the Mess so it will more than likely, have become general knowledge while you have been here with me. Good luck, Wood. If ever you meet any problems, remember, I am always ready to help solve them.'

'Yes, sir.' Rick rose from his chair, put his hat on, saluted smartly, turned and strode from the office.

As he headed down the corridor he saw the adjutant's door was open. When he reached it a voice called out, 'Flight Lieutenant Wood.'

Rick deviated into the adjutant's office. 'You want me, Adj?'

The adjutant smiled. 'Congratulations, Rick.' He held out his hand, and when he took it Rick felt he had accepted an important trust. 'Keep faith with the CO. He's the heart of this squadron.'

'I will,' Rick promised.

34

Rick assumed a serious expression as he entered the billet.

'Good grief!' exclaimed Pete, swinging off his bed. 'What on earth did the CO want?'

'It affects the whole crew.'

'Oh, hell. What now?'

'A-flight has a new flight officer, and you're not going to like it.'

Peter stared at him, awaiting the revelation. 'Come on, tell me. It isn't Moaning Manners, is it?'

Rick shook his head. 'No, worse than him, I'm afraid.'

Pete groaned, 'Who could be worse?'

'Me.'

It took a moment for the truth to strike home. 'You're in charge of A-flight? '

There was disbelief in Pete's eyes until Rick grinned, saying, 'You'd better get used to it.'

Peter let out a whoop then. 'Great! And well deserved!'

'There is more news,' added Rick. 'You're promoted to flight lieutenant as of now.'

Peter gaped at him then punched the air. 'A fine wedding present?'

'And there's more,' Rick went on. 'Don is to get a

Commission as soon as possible, which I think means immediately.'

'Is that it then?'

'I think so, but this is a very good reflection on the crew. There could easily be more promotions by the time we finish our tour.'

Rick's news pleased the whole crew and if there was any jealousy it was soon dismissed. The crew had decided long ago to work as a solid unit in which everyone acted to the best of their ability, whatever the circumstances.

Rick had judged his crew correctly; they all wanted to stick together until the end of their tour of thirty operations, even though this meant the remaining fifteen might take longer to complete. Though they showed no outward signs of it, they basked in the honour of being regarded as one of the most experienced crews on the squadron.

Rick's WAAF friends also were eager to express their congratulations.

'Well done, Rick. I'm pleased for you. Keep safe,' Carolyn told him.

'I'm so happy for you, Rick, and I'm sure the crews of A-flight will be delighted,' said Vera. 'Your father will be thrilled too.'

He gave a little smile. 'He will,' he agreed.

After four weeks and two operations in which Rick and his crew took part, Vera announced that two days later they could start their leave.

Lucy was immediately on the phone to her mother. 'Leave starts on Thursday. Can we get married on Friday?'

After her initial gasp, Mrs Gaston said, 'It will be arranged.'

That was reassurance enough for Lucy

The telephone lines out of Waddington and neighbouring

villages were red-hot as Uncle's crew made arrangements to attend the wedding of their bomb aimer and the likeable WAAF officer from the Intelligence section.

No one opted out. Wives and girlfriends had already made tentative arrangements for accommodation and travelling.

Alastair's farmer friend gave him the nod and the wink and put petrol into the tank, so it was a happy group of guests who headed north from Waddington, eventually leaving the Great North Road to find their way over the final miles that took them to the tiny village of Sharow close to Ripon.

'This is so pretty,' Vera exclaimed. 'It will be even more so in spring.' But the wedding was taking place now and no one regretted the timing, least of all the bride and groom.

The bride, smart in her uniform and holding a small posy of flowers, stepped out of the taxi to take her father's arm.

'All right, love?' he asked.

'So happy, Dad,' she replied with a smile, and just a hint of dampness in her eyes. She gave a little nod to her father and they walked up the path to the church door where her bridesmaid, Carolyn, awaited Lucy.

The two friends hugged each other. 'All the happiness in the world,' said Carolyn.

Lucy smiled her thanks and the small procession started their walk to the altar.

Peter, with Rick beside him, welcomed his bride with a light in his eyes that spoke volumes of his love for her.

She felt great joy as the ring was slipped on to her finger, and afterwards left the church as his wife.

Mr Gaston had managed to arrange two taxis to transport the wedding party to the reception in Ripon where, after the toasts, Peter thanked everyone for coming.

'It's not easy in wartime, so Lucy and I are more than grateful to you all for making this day extra special by being with us. I must give a special thanks also to my crew, who have given up some of their leave to lend me support today. I could not fly with a better bunch. Although I look forward to ending our tour successfully, I don't look forward to jumping out of our Lancaster after our final op as that will mean the crew will be split up, but I am sure our comradeship, in which we have become closer than brothers, can never be destroyed.' He looked at his crew mates and said with a catch in his voice, 'Thanks for putting up with me. And now I must extend my thanks to Mr and Mrs Gaston for handling the arrangements for today so perfectly, and to my aunts, Victoria and Melanie, for all the support they have given me throughout my life. I would not be where I am today without their encouragement.'

Soon afterwards the bride and groom departed for Scarborough on the Yorkshire coast, where Lucy's mother had managed to book four nights' accommodation at a good small hotel that was managing to stay open in spite of the war. The rest of the gathering went quietly on their separate ways. Rick was soon off to catch a train south, to be with his father and mother. Alastair gathered his party for their return to Waddington. Peter's aunts had booked into a hotel in Ripon for an overnight stay and were rather pleased that they were not to be left alone for the evening; Don and Beth and Phil and Myrna by chance had booked in at the same one.

When Don suggested that the six of them should dine together that evening, Peter's aunts, were very grateful. 'It will be delightful. You have all made us feel young again today.'

*

'I hope you will be comfortable here,' said the proprietress, as she took Lucy and Peter into their room. 'You have a view over the North Bay as far as the castle on the right. The evening meal is at seven.'

'Thank you,' they both said.

When she closed the door, Peter turned the key after her. Lucy came willingly to his open arms.

'Happy, love?' he asked.

Her answer was revealed in the joy that shone from her eyes and in her next words as she glanced at her wristwatch. 'You just have time to make me even happier!'

Five days later they walked out of Lincoln station and got into a taxi.

'Waddington village.' Peter informed the elderly driver.

Lucy looked askance at her husband. 'What ... ?'

'Wait and see,' he said with a grin.

Lucy hugged herself. 'I like surprises.' Her eyes sparkled with anticipation. She knew better than to press him and spoil his delight in surprising her.

A quarter of the way to the village Peter asked the driver to stop and wait. The car had no sooner stopped than he was out of the door and holding it open. 'Out, Mrs Wilkins.'

Lucy scrambled out of her seat, looking askance at him as she straightened her uniform. Peter took her arm and led her four paces to a garden gate. He opened it and indicated to her to go up the path to the front door of a small cottage. He fell into step beside her and, on reaching the front door, produced a key. He pushed the door open. 'Welcome home, Mrs Wilkins,' he said with an exaggerated bow and a sweep of his arm.

With a query in her eyes Lucy stared back at him. Then a

gesture of his arm persuaded her to step over the threshold. 'What's all this?' she queried.

'Our bolt-hole. I discovered it a couple of months ago. It belongs to a young couple who had married just before war broke out. He is in the Army, was posted abroad last year. She stayed on but eventually decided she would go to her parents and shut this cottage for the duration. I persuaded her to rent it to us.'

'And here am I, expecting to have to resign my Commission because we can't live on camp as a married couple.'

'I had a word with Kate about that. She thinks highly of your work and regards you as a vital part of the team she has built up. She does not want you to leave, so after consultation with the Station CO, her own admin officer and my CO, she's said you can resign your Commission and still be employed as a civilian, if that is what you want?'

Lucy gasped with joy. 'Oh, darling, that's so wonderful!' She flung her arms round Pete's neck and kissed him. 'I was dreading the thought of leaving our friendly bunch and not being useful any longer. Now I can work near you, and see you here whenever you are off duty. You're a wonder!'

Pete pulled her to him then and kissed her lovingly. 'Come on, we'd better tell everyone we are back.'

He locked the door, presented the key to Lucy, took her hand and hurried to the taxi. 'Main gate,' he told the driver as they got in.

She snuggled up to him and whispered again, 'Pete Wilkins, you are wonderful and I'm proud to be your wife.'

35

'I met your mum and dad at Lucy's and Pete's wedding, it's time you met mine,' said Greg to Carolyn over a final cup of coffee one evening when they had decided to have some time together in Lincoln. 'How about you trying to wangle your leave when I get mine?'

'That sounds really serious,' replied Carolyn teasingly.

'It might be, it might not,' he said, giving her a wink.

'Well, whatever, I would love to meet them and learn all about your past.'

'You'll be disappointed. There's not much to tell except that their son is in love with the most wonderful girl in the world.'

'Maybe they won't think the same way.'

'They may not realize it now but they soon will, so let's plan a time we can get together.'

Greg approached Alastair then to ask when it was likely he could get some leave.

'There are rumours coming out of 5 Group. Things are brewing that may mean we have to hold back on leave. I'm sorry, Greg,' he was told.

He felt Carolyn's disappointment, as keen as his own, when he told her that evening while walking her back to her billet from the Mess. 'Ah, well, It can't be helped,' she said, 'I suppose King and Country has to come before Greg and Carolyn.'

Resigned to waiting, they made the most of any time they could spend together, but that was restricted due to their hours on duty. 5 Group was operating more these days as a single unit, so the Intelligence section was kept very busy and Greg was flying more than usual, but they both looked forward to the day when that meeting could take place.

In his electric flying jacket, grey jersey and battle-dress, Greg went through the routine that, during the last three months, had preceded daily photographic flights for the four Spitfire pilots operating out of Waddington. Naturally superstitious, he would on no account have altered his order of dressing for a forthcoming operation.

Alastair had briefed them: 'Once again you will be photographing a large area of Northern France. Each of you has his own section to cover; you will see that from the maps which have been prepared for you. Merv and Allan will photograph the area to the east of Greg, but thirty miles inland. I will devote my attention to the coast east of Calais. Greg, you will concentrate once again on the coastal area west of Calais to the Atlantic coast.'

'Why the same area again for me?' he queried, feeling miffed. 'Aren't my photos good enough?'

'No question of that, Greg. As you know, these photos have been going straight to the top in Bomber Command, with certain ones being earmarked for 5 Group's exclusive use. The powers that be are definitely pleased with them, I can assure you of that. The repetitive nature of your work at the moment indicates to me that something big is being planned. I've no idea what they expect to find. Just let's carry on doing a good job.'

Greg pulled on his fleece-lined flying boots and wriggled his feet in them, seeking to make them comfortable. He checked his pockets: handkerchiefs, some boiled sweets and mints, a packet of Horlicks tablets, a photograph of Carolyn, and a wallet containing some English and French money. Satisfied, he glanced at his watch – ten minutes before he would leave the locker room to walk to his plane. He spent the time deep in thought; his three fellow flyers knew he wanted to be left alone.

At these times he contemplated home, thanking his mother and father for always being supportive of what he wanted from life. He liked to remember walking in the countryside near his home, running on the beach or standing still in the sea, letting the gentle waves trickle between his toes. And now there were thoughts of Carolyn too and the wondrous life they would have together. If he came through.

He glanced at his watch. Time to go. Greg stood up, a sign that he would now engage in conversation with his fellow flyers.

Their banter was jolly. There was shared enjoyment of a new joke from their devoted ground-crew and then, with a final thumbs-up gesture they climbed into their cockpits.

Greg took the parachute straps from one of the ground-crew who was standing on the wing ready to assist him. He locked them to the parachute on which he was already sitting, making it ready should he have to bail out.

Carolyn was there as she had been every time he had taken off these last three months. With each of those moments he felt their love had grown deeper if that was possible. He raised his hand and waved to her, a broad smile lighting his face. He blew her a kiss. She caught it, then blew it back to him. He waved again and taxied out. She watched his progress to the end of the runway in use, saw him take off and climb into a blue sky. She blew another kiss and whispered her usual words: 'Be safe, my love.'

Greg settled into the flight, alone in the beauty of the vast expanse that never ceased to fascinate him. One day he would show it all to Carolyn. Carolyn! Joy surged through him. He pushed the nose of his Spitfire down, gathered speed, faster and faster, then he pulled his control back, thrilled to its response that took him into a fast climb to his operational height.

He levelled out, pleased he had left the clouds behind and had a clear view of the area he had to photograph. He started his assignment, meticulous to the last detail. This was so different from his combat days when death was ever close at hand. He viewed his job with the Photographic Reconnaissance Unit as more of an office job, evidenced by the notepad strapped to his right thigh and a pencil poised to note when, and at which map co-ordinates, he made his turns. So his flying went on until, checking time and fuel, he knew the moment had come to head for home.

He began to lose height, pointing the nose of his aircraft towards England visible across the Channel. He circled over the sea, lower and lower. His altimeter showed ten thousand feet.

Then, his placid, private part of the sky was blown apart.

Cannon shells ripped through the air. The Spitfire jerked as if it had hit a brick wall but its power carried it on. Greg cursed and sent his aircraft into a diving turn. He twisted to get a view of his attacker, but, even as he got a clear sight of a Messerschmitt 109, more shells hit him from behind. 'Damn. Two of them.' He realized that the regular visits

331

made to the same area of the French coast must have been noted and two fighters had been designated to hunt him down. Unarmed, it would take all his flying skill to save himself and the photographs he was carrying.

He put the Spitfire through manoeuvres he would not previously have considered possible. The aircraft responded, but he knew two against one was an unequal struggle. He twisted and turned, climbed and dived, all the time heading nearer and nearer the English coast. He crossed it with the two German fighters still determined to bring him down. They closed in. Greg felt a searing pain tear through his right arm and a lesser one in his right leg. Sweat poured from him. He must get the plane down as intact as possible and save the photographs; bailing out was not an option. He pulled the nose up; the unexpected change of direction caught the Germans out. He confused them even more when he immediately put the Spitfire into a steep diving turn. He twisted and turned, trying to sight them, but there was no sign. The sky was peaceful. One moment hell, the next moment heaven; but the latter had been only partially achieved.

The Spitfire began juddering badly; Greg was aware of the pain in his arm and leg, and of blood oozing from cuts in his face. Cannon shells had done their damage. Fighting the pain, he searched for a suitable landing place. He wrestled with the controls. Lower and lower. He tried to ignore the hurt ripping through his leg and the pain pounding in his arm. He eased the Spitfire down. Closer, closer . . . the urge to put the aircraft on the ground had to be ignored for a little longer otherwise there would be utter disaster. Try as he might to lower the undercarriage it would not respond. He would have to make a belly landing.

Suddenly the field he had chosen was rushing up at him. Easy, easy, the instructions thundered in his mind. He held the plane up with the little control he had over it. It touched earth, bounced, hit the ground again and slid fast forward on its belly. It slewed round, tilted its starboard wing tip into the ground. Amidst a ripping of metal and earth it came to a sudden stop, pitching Greg forward against his disintegrating instrument panel and into unconsciousness.

The sound of a Spitfire! Carolyn hurried outside. This must be Greg; it just had to be. Merv and Allan were already back. Her heart sank. No, it was Alastair's plane. Despair struck her. She had not felt like this before when Greg had come in after the others, but now she sensed something was wrong. She tried to control her anxiety as she rushed to her brother, who was getting out of his plane.

'Where's Greg?' she cried.

Alastair saw how worried she looked 'Hey, come on, he'll be back.'

'Did you see anything of him up there?'

Alastair could not ignore the anguish in her voice but he had to be truthful even though he knew it would be of no help. 'No. I didn't expect to. We were working different sections.'

'But where *is* he? The rest of you are back.'

'It might have taken him longer for any number of reasons.'

'There's something wrong, Alastair, I know it.'

'Hey, come here.' He took her in his arms.

She shook her head. 'It's not right, it's not right, it's happening to me again!'

'No, it's not! Don't think like that. There are a thousand reasons why Greg is not here now. He'll be all right. Wipe those tears, straighten yourself up and come with me. I'll get in touch with Control, see if they have heard anything.'

He saw that the ground-crew were going through their usual procedures when any of the Spitfires returned from photographic duty and everything was being taken care of. Alastair signalled his approval and thanks to them, then said, 'Come on, Carolyn, I'll see if there is any news of Greg,' and hurried her to his office.

'Thanks,' she said as she slumped on to a chair. She watched him intently as he picked up the phone. In a matter of moments he was through to Control.

'Squadron Leader Maddison speaking. Who's on duty now?'

A WAAF gave him the information and added something else.

He nodded. 'I see. I'll hold this line then. Put him on as soon as he has finished his present call.'

Carolyn looked questioningly at her brother but he gave nothing away.

A few minutes later Alastair heard a familiar voice. 'Hi, Al, you must have sixth sense. The call I was taking concerns you.'

'Right, Hugo, what was it?'

Carolyn saw him try to hide the concern that came into his expression then but she knew her brother well and felt certain that what he was hearing concerned Greg. The conversation went on. At one point Alastair picked up a pencil and wrote something on a sheet of paper. Carolyn was itching to know what that was but her brother had turned the paper over.

'Thanks, Hugo, if you get any more news, let me know at once.' He put down the phone slowly as he took in what he had just heard.

'I know that call was about Greg. What's happened?' demanded Carolyn, fearing the worst, her face twisted with concern.

334

Alastair knew it was no good smoothing over the facts as he knew them; his sister would only recognize his attempts to spare her. 'Greg has had to make a crash-landing near Oxford.'

'Oh, no!'

'Sis, medical teams were soon on the scene. He was found alive and was rushed to St Hugh's College, Oxford, which is now being used as a hospital. I have directions – that's what I wrote down. I've been told Greg is in a coma. I have no further details than that.'

Carolyn was on her feet. 'I've got to go! I must.' Seeing her brother step towards her, she held up her hands. 'No, no, don't try to stop me. I must be with him, I must!'

'Steady on, Carolyn. I know that's where you want to be but it's not as easy as that. You can't just rush off.' He was picking up the phone while he spoke. 'Leave it with me, I'll see what I can do.' Then he said into the phone, 'Squadron Leader Maddison here, put me through to Squadron Officer Newbauld, please.' Carolyn watched her brother anxiously. 'Ah, Kate, it's Alastair here. Could you come to my office immediately, please?' A slight pause, then he added, 'There's a crisis that needs dealing with now.' As he put the phone down, Alastair looked at his sister. 'Kate is on her way.'

'Thanks.' She gave him a weak smile and dabbed at her tears.

Kate immediately sensed trouble when she walked into the office. Alastair lost no time in telling her the facts.

'You must go, Carolyn,' said Kate immediately. 'Stay here while I see what can be arranged.'

When she had left them, Carolyn said quietly, 'I want to talk to Mum, Dad and Gran.'

Alastair saw all the strain his sister was under and knew

she wanted comfort from those who were dear to her. 'You'll have to use the outside line from the Mess. Come.'

They breathed a sigh of relief when they found the phone not in use. Within in a few minutes Alastair was telling his father the reason for the call. 'Carolyn wants a little reassurance from you, Mum and Gran. It must be brief though because, as I explained, she is getting a lift to Oxford soon.'

Carolyn spoke to her father and her mother and finally her gran. 'Remember what you said about a miracle early in the war, Gran?' she asked finally.

'I do, love.'

'I want another one, please.' Carolyn choked as she made the request.

'I'll do my best, love.'

When they returned to the Mess, Kate had just arrived. 'Arrangements have been made. Carolyn, you and I are off to Oxford together.' Kate saw the relief dawn in Carolyn as she heard this. 'I was due at a one-to-one meeting three days from today with my counterpart at Bicester.'

'Close to Oxford,' put in Alastair.

Kate nodded and continued, 'I have just spoken to my counterpart about your situation and she sends you every sympathy. She says she will see me tomorrow instead. I have cleared everything here to enable you to have some compassionate leave. The CO is in agreement. We can get ready now and leave as soon as you like. The transport department has brought forward the use of a car. So, is that OK for you?'

'Wonderful,' gulped Carolyn, choking her thanks.

'OK. Off you go. Meet me at the transport section in half an hour.'

'Thanks, Ma'am.' She turned to her brother then. 'Thanks, Alastair.' Carolyn gave him a hug and was gone.

'Do you have any more news than you have told her?' asked Kate as the door closed.

'Broken right arm and bad wound in his right leg, but that is all I know. There hadn't yet been a full assessment. I got the sense I was not being given every detail, though I was told the signs were reasonably good for him to pull through. I kept that bit from Carolyn.'

Kate nodded. 'I'd better go and sling a few things into a suitcase.'

'Thanks for all your help, Kate.'

'No need for thanks, Alastair. I'll phone you when I can.'

Twilight was heralding the dark when Kate drew the car to a halt in front of St Hugh's. They quickly entered the building where a nurse sat at a desk checking through the latest reports.

'Squadron Officer Kate Newbauld from RAF Wadding-ton, and this is Flight Officer Carolyn Maddison from the same station. She is the fiancée of Flight Lieutenant Greg Saunders. We have been told he was brought here after a flying accident near Oxford.'

'Yes, Ma'am. He is here and is in theatre at the moment.'

Carolyn gasped. 'Is it that serious?' She bit her lip anxiously.

'I am not able to say, I'm sorry.'

'Is he likely to be in surgery long?' asked Kate.

'I am sorry, Ma'am, I don't have that information either. Maybe I should bring Matron to see you?'

'If you would, please.'

In a few minutes the nurse reappeared alongside the formidable-looking figure striding towards them. Carolyn quaked a little, thinking she would not get much information from this martinet. The assessment proved to be wrong when Matron spoke to them.

'I am Felicity Adamson. I believe you are here about Flight Lieutenant Greg Saunders, who was brought in earlier today.' Her voice was gentle, belying her appearance.

'Yes, we are,' replied Kate. 'We have come from RAF Waddington in Lincolnshire. This is Flight Officer Maddison, the fiancée of your patient, and I am Squadron Officer Newbauld.'

'You must both think a great deal of Flight Lieutenant Saunders to have come all this way at such short notice. Shall we go into this room?' Matron indicated a door to her left, glanced at her companion and said, 'Thank you, Nurse.'

Carolyn was determined to get the first word in. As they sat down, she said, 'Ma'am, I don't want you to hold anything back from me. I want the truth from the start.'

Matron nodded. 'Very well, I will respect your wishes. The flight lieutenant's crash was a bad one but the major damage had been done before that. Immediate examination of the wreckage revealed he had been hit by cannon fire, so it was assumed he had been engaged in combat with the enemy and had come off worst.'

'He is with a photographic unit and flies without armament,' explained Kate.

Matron nodded. 'Fortunately his plane did not catch fire otherwise that would have been the end for him. He had been thrown forward in the crash, hitting his head so hard he only recovered consciousness after he arrived here.'

'That's a long while,' commented Kate.

'Too long, really, but he has spunk and fight.'

A cold chill ran down Carolyn's spine. 'The truth, Matron, please.'

'Very well. As I say, he suffered a severe blow to the head. There were also two deep cuts as well as minor ones. It is the head injuries our surgeons are dealing with at this moment.

338

It is fortunate for him perhaps that he crashed where he did. We are a hospital that specializes in head injuries and have great experience in this field. Some of the ambulance crew who went to the crash recognized the seriousness of those particular injuries and directed the driver to bring him here immediately. If it hadn't happened that way, I doubt he would have survived thus far.'

'Are you implying that there are other serious injuries?'

Matron nodded. 'Yes, I am.'

'Oh, my God!' gasped Carolyn.

'They are not as threatening as his head injuries but nevertheless they are serious in their own right as well as adding more shock to his system. His right arm is badly shattered, we believe by a shell or bullets, and there is also damage, though not as bad, to his right leg.'

Carolyn had lost all colour. She sat with her hands gripped tightly together as if to control the feelings that were churning inside her, while her mind cried out: Not again! Not again!

'How long is he likely to be in surgery?' asked Kate.

'I don't know.' I have told you what I do know and can assure you he is in the best of hands. He has our finest surgeons with him now. May I make a suggestion? You have come a long way to see this young man. I have two rooms I can put at your disposal until we see what the outcome will be. Please feel free to use them.'

'That is most considerate of you,' replied Kate. 'We certainly will accept your kind offer. I had a meeting at Bicester later in the week but managed to switch it to tomorrow so that I could bring Flight Officer Maddison here today.'

'Let me show you the rooms I have in mind.'

'Matron, I am most grateful to you,' said Carolyn, 'and to you, Kate. It means a great deal to me to be able to be close to Greg. And, hopefully soon to be with him face to face.'

'We are all here to help. Now, your rooms and then I'll show you our Mess.

'Won't that be shut down for the night?' asked Kate. 'We don't want to be any trouble.'

'There is always someone on duty in the kitchen. We never know what might be wanted during the night. On the way I'll introduce you to Sister Pam Pendle. She's on night duty. Should there be anything you need, call her.'

'Is it all quiet on your wards, Sister?' Felicity asked once introductions were over and they had reached the Mess.

'Yes, Matron.'

'Good. You stay with our guests while they have something to eat, and then see them to their rooms.' She turned to Kate and Carolyn. 'I'll look in on you both later.'

They were nearing the end of their meal when Kate saw her opportunity to carry out her promise to Alastair.

'I have some phone calls to make. Can I do it from your switchboard?' she asked Pam.

'Yes. The switchboard is just off the main entrance. Whoever is on duty there will put you through.'

'Good,' said Kate rising to her feet. 'I'll leave you here with Pam, Carolyn. This shouldn't take too long.'

Kate soon had the use of a phone. She made two short calls regarding her meeting the next day and then put a call through to RAF Waddington. She gave Alastair the news about Greg so far as she knew it.

'Not good then,' he commented.

'They're doing all they can for him, but it could be touch and go.'

'Tell Carolyn we are thinking of her and that I have informed Greg's parents of the accident. I warned them

340

about rushing to Oxford immediately, explaining that Carolyn was there and it would be better if they arrived tomorrow. She can expect them then.'

Carolyn was thankful when Kate explained this. 'I have never met his parents. We intended to make the introductions the next time we had leave. Greg has talked so much about them that I feel I already know them, but it's not going to be easy meeting for the first time under these circumstances.'

'I'm sure you will cope,' Pam comforted her. 'I'll look in on you from time to time during the night.'

'And I'm only next door,' said Kate. 'Come on, let Pam go back on duty. I'll see you settled.'

The room was spartan but adequate and, thankfully, warm. Though she felt she could not sleep, Carolyn knew she must not cling to Kate any longer. Hiding her reluctance to let her friend go, she bade Kate good night and closed the door. Despondency seized her then. With a great sigh Carolyn sank down on the side of her bed. Her ability to cope seemed to have disappeared. 'This bloody war has brought me nothing but heartaches! Why? Why? What the hell is the point of them? What has happened to my life?' she asked herself.

There was a knock on the door. It opened and Matron walked in. 'I've brought you a drink of Horlicks and a sleeping pill.'

'Thank you, Matron.' Carolyn watched Felicity place them on a small table close by but she made no move to take them.

'I'm not leaving until I see you have had them both,' said Matron firmly. When she had she said, 'Right, now into bed with you.'

Carolyn gave a wan smile and automatically obeyed. She was asleep within a few moments of her head hitting the pillow.

341

36

Carolyn was drawn out of her sleep by a tapping sound. Slowly consciousness returned and she realized she was not in familiar surroundings. Then she remembered why. Carolyn slid out of bed and went to answer the door.

'Good morning, Carolyn,' said Sister Pendle, in a gentle tone of voice.

'Hello, Sister.' Carolyn moved to one side to let Pam enter.

'Did you have a reasonable night?'

'I suppose so. I did wake several times but the sleeping pill helped.'

'I'm sorry to have to wake you but ... '

Alarm struck Carolyn then, bringing her fully awake. 'Is everything all right? Is Greg OK?'

'Yes, yes,' answered Pam quickly in a reassuring tone. 'I had to wake you because the surgeon, Mr Western, wants to see you in a few minutes.'

'Oh.'

'Don't be alarmed. This is routine. I'll straighten things here while you get ready.'

Ten minutes later Pam showed in Mr Western, who greeted Carolyn pleasantly and then said, 'I am going to see Flight Lieutenant Saunders to assess his condition. I am told he has had a good night, though of course he was heavily sedated and may continue to be so for several days.'

'Are you telling me Greg might be in a coma for that long?'

'It is not possible to be more precise. It is just a matter of waiting to see how his condition develops. I want to explain a few things to you, but first tell me a little about your relationship with Greg.'

'I am stationed at Waddington and got to know him when he came there as part of a photographic unit of four Spitfires. As it happens the CO of that small unit is my brother. Greg and I fell in love and were planning to get married.'

'Were?' There was no mistaking the inference behind the surgeon's question.

Carolyn was immediately confused. 'Er, I didn't mean that what has happened makes any difference.' She gathered her thoughts, met the surgeon's gaze firmly. 'How can I judge at this stage? I do not know your assessment of Greg's injuries. I do not know what his chances of recovery are. I do not know his reaction to what has happened, and above all I do not know what Greg's attitude to marrying me will be now that he has been badly injured. Mr Western, I want you to be straight with me.'

'At this stage it is difficult to judge how he will recover. I see in you a young woman is in love and will do all she can to preserve that. I hope I read you right because Greg's recovery will depend on the support and love of the people around him. As I see it, that means you and your family as well as his own. All of you have a part to play. And, of course, ongoing contact with fellow flyers could be of great importance to him too.'

Carolyn nodded. 'I understand.'

'I will take you to him shortly, but first you must be aware that he has suffered greatly.'

'Tell me,' she said firmly. 'I must know what I face. I have witnessed the horrors of war before.'

'He has lost his right arm.'

Carolyn gasped, but held back the words that wanted to pour out.

'His right leg has sustained bad wounds also but they will mend. He has cuts and bruises all over the place, but they will heal with attention. His head injuries gave us more cause for concern, but we were relieved to find no swelling on his brain.'

'Oh, thank God.' Carolyn felt weak but stayed focused on the surgeon as he continued talking.

'With care and attention, I believe those head injuries will not lead to any permanent damage.' He stopped talking, his eyes fixed firmly on her. He saw the initial shock being replaced by acceptance. 'My advice to you is to return to Waddington, where I have no doubt your work will keep you occupied and will help to ease the worry until we know more about Greg's likely progress. As I have said, we do not know yet when that will be.'

'Can I see him?' she asked tentatively.

'For a few moments, but don't expect to receive any reaction from him.' He glanced at his watch. 'The timing is about right. I sent word to Squadron Officer Newbauld to meet us in my office. Now I'll take you to see Greg. But, remember, don't expect any reaction from him.'

Carolyn felt apprehensive as they walked along the corridor.

'Here we are,' Mr Western said on reaching a door. 'Flight Lieutenant Greg Saunders,' announced a card attached to it.

Carolyn felt her stomach tighten and her body become cold. She knew she could turn and run out of Greg's life, never need to see what the war had done to him, but loyalty and love made her see that was impossible. How could she refuse him her help when he most needed it?

The door swung open. Mr Western stood into the doorway and stopped to make a quick assessment of the situation. He looked back at Carolyn and saw the doubt and hope in her face. He nodded and stepped to one side, a signal for her to enter.

She dampened her lips. When she went in a nurse rose from the chair from which she had been carefully observing Greg. Carolyn glanced at the bed and leaned towards him. When he made no movement she realized he did not see her. Sheets and blankets were drawn to his neck in such a way that they put no pressure on his legs and hid his injuries. Tears began to flow down Carolyn's cheeks and her lips silently said, 'Oh, my love.'

A gentle touch on her arm was a signal from Mr Western that they should leave. She smiled wanly at the still figure on the bed and, as she turned to go, mouthed a silent 'Thank you' to the nurse. When the door closed behind them it seemed as if Greg was being taken from her.

'This way,' said the surgeon.

When she stepped inside an ante-room she saw how meticulous the surgeon's arrangements and timing had been. A WAAF rose from behind a desk, saying, 'Squadron Officer Newbauld is in your room, sir.'

He escorted Carolyn into his office where he greeted Kate warmly. 'I'm sorry if I have kept you waiting.'

'No, your timing is impeccable,'

'Then I'll leave you to it. I'll be in the filing room, just across the passage, if you need me.'

Kate acknowledged this, and as he left them turned an anxious gaze on Carolyn. 'How are you?'

'Pleased to have seen Greg, Ma'am, but he looks so

helpless.' Anything else she was about to say stuck in Carolyn's throat.

'Mr Western has told me about the coma. I think it's best you return with me to Waddington and resume life there until we know more about Greg's situation.'

'But, Ma'am, I'd rather be near him so I'll . . . '

'Carolyn, may I remind you that you still have a job to do at Waddington? These last couple of days were granted as compassionate leave. Now we know the situation, you cannot expect the authorities to spare you from your duties. When we have further news of Greg we will act accordingly.'

'I want to be here,' said Carolyn with a touch of defiance, and added, 'I'll renounce my Commission, leave the WAAFs and be here for him.'

Kate's eyes narrowed. 'That may sound very commendable but you need to think this through carefully. Other people are involved in your decision, most notably Greg. You should hear what he has to say. Whatever decision he makes, I'm sure it will be with his parents' participation. If you and Greg are to make a life together, it will have to involve them too. The same applies to your parents. And what about Alastair, and the team I have built up to serve this country in a time of war? I don't want to see it weakened, as it would be, if we lost you. Lastly, please remember that you are a serving officer, and don't do anything hasty to mar the trust that has been placed in you.'

She left Carolyn no time to comment. 'You will pack your things now, say goodbye to the people here and come with me to Bicester. If my meeting is short enough we will head for Waddington immediately. We'll deal with that situation as it arises. But you will leave this place now.'

Though the rebel in her wanted to defy Kate, Carolyn knew it was wiser not to. What lay ahead of her now would be her biggest test in war-time.

37

As they drove away from Oxford, Kate informed Carolyn that she had spoken to Alastair shortly before leaving. 'I have told him of the situation here and he is in full agreement that the best place for you to be is among your friends at Waddington. She went on to explain. 'The purpose of my visit to Bicester is to explore the possibility of developing a back-up photographic unit in 5 Group. I don't know how long the discussion will take; I certainly don't expect to be finished until mid-afternoon, so we'll have to play with time as it develops. We'll take lunch in the Officers' Mess. I suggest you make yourself comfortable in their ante-room. I'll find you when I'm through.'

Carolyn found she did not lack company; there was always someone willing to chat to a pretty WAAF who appeared to be on her own.

Kate proved right in her estimation of the time when the discussions would be over. 'We'll have a cup of tea and then be on our way,' she said when she rejoined Carolyn.

The further away they drove, the more Carolyn regretted leaving Greg behind but it gave her more time to compose her thoughts and herself before reaching Waddington.

'I estimate we are about half way back. Night is drawing

in and I could do with something to eat. It might be a good idea to find somewhere to stay overnight and arrive at Waddington fresh tomorrow morning,' Kate decided.

'I am in your hands,' replied Carolyn. 'I appreciate all you have done for me and are doing.'

'This looks a likely place,' commented Kate as she stopped in front of a pub facing on to the square in the centre of a small market town.

A buzz of conversation was filtering from a room to the right of the entrance. It only faltered for a moment when they walked in, but in that moment Kate and Carolyn knew they had been inspected and approved.

They were greeted by a smiling landlord whose girth indicated good living despite rationing. 'Good evening, ladies.'

'Good evening, landlord,' returned Kate. 'Would you have two rooms for the night?

'I think that can be arranged but I will fetch my wife. She takes care of that side of our business. May I get you a drink while I fetch her?'

'I think a whisky each would be in order after our trying day.'

'Very good, Ma'am. If it is going to revive you and it is your first visit, it is on the house.'

'That is very generous of you.'

'Not at all. We must look after our girls in blue.' As he had been speaking he had been getting the glasses of whisky. Placing them on the bar in front of them, he said, 'I'll fetch my wife.'

A few moments later he returned with a woman who exuded the same air of friendliness. Her eyes shone with interest as the introductions were made and within a few minutes Kate and Carolyn were being shown into two almost identical rooms, neat, comfortable and welcoming, reflecting the approach of the pub's owners to any customers who sought their hospitality.

'I am Selina Whitworth,' the landlady introduced herself. 'My husband is Gordon. Am I right in presuming you would like a meal?'

'You're not wrong,' replied Kate.

'Good, I'll see what I can rustle up. It's not easy these days but I'll manage something. Come down to the bar when you're ready. I'll set you a table in one of the cosy corners. You'll be all right there, we aren't a rowdy pub.'

So it proved, and even though Greg was never far from Carolyn's mind she tried to join in.

They reached Waddington mid-afternoon the next day. When Carolyn visited the Intelligence section she found Lucy and Vera gathering up their notes and photographs ready for a five o'clock briefing of the three crews designated to drop mines in the Kattegat off Denmark's east coast.

Once Carolyn had reassured them that Greg was in good hands but that they faced a wait of indeterminate length, and they had expressed their full support, she was able to ask which crews were operating.

'Sergeant Edmonds, Pilot Officer Starkey, and Rick,' Vera informed her.

'Rick?' said Carolyn in surprise. 'I thought he regarded mining operations as the most dangerous?'

'That's why he chooses to do them himself,' said Lucy. 'He believes a full Group or full Bomber Command operation offers more protection to individual aircraft, whereas with only a few mine-layers operating, individual targets are easier for enemy aircraft to pick off.'

'I reckon there's no difference,' said Lucy. 'Whatever the

objective is, every op is dangerous. I fear for Pete but I don't let him see it.'

'Do you mind if I sit in on the briefing?' asked Carolyn. 'It will keep my mind off Greg.'

'Of course we don't,' said Lucy. 'If we can do anything to help, you only have to ask. I know that will go for anyone on this station. I hadn't really realized how highly the Spitfire pilots were thought of here until this happened.'

The door opened and Alastair walked in. 'Hi, Sis, heard you were back.'

'I called on you on my way here but you weren't in.'

'We'll see you later,' said Lucy as she and Vera headed for the door.

'Did Kate tell you of my arrangements?' said Alastair.

'She did. Thank you for all you have done and are doing.'

He brushed her thanks aside. 'Greg's one of my pilots. Naturally I'm concerned for him.'

'What were you told this morning?'

'He's still in a coma. No signs of any change. Only time will tell.'

'It's the waiting that's hell.'

'I know. We all feel so helpless. Everybody here is rooting for you and Greg.'

'Thanks.' Carolyn choked on the word and tears began to trickle down her cheek.

Alastair hugged her. 'I'm here for you. I've kept Mum and Dad and Gran informed. If you want them to come down, they'll get somewhere to stay nearby.'

'That's kind but I think I'd rather lead as normal a life as possible here. You think it's best, and Kate does too. That's what I'll try and do, beginning now. I'm going to sit in on the briefing for this mine-laying operation. Walk back that way with me.'

350

'Sure.' He left her at the briefing room. 'See you later.'

Crews were beginning to filter in to take their seats at one of the three tables that had been arranged near the front. Carolyn saw Rick come through the door, laughing at something his engineer had said. His expression changed when he saw Carolyn and he immediately came over.

'Carolyn, I'm so sorry about Greg. What is the latest?'

'He's in a coma, badly injured. Six-hour operation on his head.'

Rick blanched at the thought.

'He's lost his right arm.'

'My God. What . . . ?'

'We shan't know until he comes out of the coma. I would have stayed in Oxford but everyone thought it would be better if I came back here. Alastair will be in touch with the hospital every day so I'll always have news.'

'I'm glad of that. If there is anything I can do, please don't hesitate to ask.'

'Thanks, Rick. It's nice to know I have your friendship.'

'You'll always have that. I only wish . . . '

Anticipating what he might be about to say, she stopped him with, 'Please don't say any more, Rick.'

He saw the rest of his crew were coming in and, from their glances, knew they were wanting to have a word with Carolyn. 'Here they come, the best Lancaster crew there is.'

One by one they sympathized with the WAAF who had been and still would be an important part of their lives. She was grateful for their kind words.

Carolyn listened to the briefing. On the surface this looked as if it should be an easy operation.

Though the plight that Greg was facing hung over her, Carolyn felt she was slipping back into Waddington life

351

again. So much so that, knowing when the crews were due to return, she went to spend the intervening time in the Mess with Lucy and Vera. They talked, dozed and slept, but six and a half hours later Lucy's bodily automatic clock kicked in and she roused her friends.

By the time they reached U–Uncle's dispersal they could hear the drone of an approaching Lancaster. It circled and made a straightforward landing.

'S–Sugar,' commented Lucy, tension in her voice; there was no sign of another aircraft. The minutes ticked on. Unspoken tension filled them. We'll have to go and debrief Sugar's crew. The three WAAFs had no need to voice their thoughts; each knew what the others would be thinking. They headed for the debriefing.

They sat down at a table. S–Sugar's crew padded in, faces strained.

'That was bloody rough,' said the rear gunner as he flopped on to a chair.

The skipper went on, 'We were jumped by fighters as we left the target. Saw a kite go down. We were lucky to escape.'

A chill struck Lucy but she sternly reminded herself two other squadrons in the Group had also sent Lancasters on mining runs in the same area.

The debriefing was short with the crew having nothing much to say except that they had dropped the mines at the designated point. The WAAFs strolled outside again, hoping to pick up the sound of returning aircraft. Time dragged.

Then: 'Listen!' Lucy's voice cut through the silence that by now covered the airfield.

'Nothing,' commented Vera.

'Hush, listen,' demanded Lucy.

Tension heightened.

'Yes – there,' confirmed Carolyn.

'Only one,' said Vera,

'No, there's another but he's in trouble,' said Lucy in a tone that held both terror and hope.

Two aircraft appeared, black against the lightening sky, flying close together; one was airborne on only two engines.

'Oh, God help him!' Holes in the starboard wing, part of the tail sliced away and one part of the undercarriage dangling helplessly, mocked Lucy's cry. She found some measure of relief when she saw the letter U on the other aircraft as it peeled away from its stricken companion.

'Rick's been escorting him home,' said Carolyn.

They watched, taut with fear, willing A–Apple to get down safely.

'He's coming straight in!' But they could tell the pilot was having difficulty in doing that because of the battering his aircraft had taken. Lower, lower. Then the aircraft protested; the pilot pulled it to port, taking it away from the runway until he could no longer influence its progress. Then, near to the edge of the airfield, its nose reared up, it stalled and plunged to the ground where it exploded.

Carolyn watched the final throes of the Lancaster, thinking of Greg and his crashing Spitfire. She grabbed hold of Lucy's arm and held on tight. Lucy, recognizing what witnessing this crash must be doing to her, held Carolyn close. Vera slid her arm round Carolyn's shoulders.

Tears for the aircrew who would never fly again streamed down her cheeks. 'Why me? Why do these things happen to me?' Carolyn sobbed.

'It's the tides of war, love,' whispered Vera. 'We are all helpless in them. We can only be thankful that Rick and his crew are back safely.'

As if in answer, U–Uncle was coming in to land on the

runway that the pilot of the stricken plane, knowing he would not be able to land there successfully, had left free from debris for the flight officer who had escorted him home.

'And I believe Rick's survival is a sign to you that Greg will be OK,' whispered Lucy.

38

Carolyn shuffled uneasily in her bed, trying to get more comfortable, hoping if she did she would find the sleep that was eluding her. She shivered, not with cold but from remembering the Lancaster in its death throes. Helpless to do anything she had watched, clinging to the hope that a miracle would unfold before her eyes. That explosion! It echoed still in her mind. She sprang up in bed, drawing in her knees, tightening her arms around them.

This was the fifth night since the crash that she had been woken in this way. Then, as always, her mind drifted from the horror she had witnessed to the helpless figure still in a bed in Oxford.

'Oh, Greg, I want you back with me.' The words always came out quietly, so as not to tempt fate.

Carolyn faced another day when she poured her energy into her work to prevent any fears that she might never hear Greg speak words of love to her again.

Each day at twelve Alastair rang the hospital in Oxford only to receive the same answer to his query: 'Sorry, sir, there is no change in Flight Lieutenant Saunders's condition.' Every time he passed on this information to his sister he sensed the helplessness she felt.

Carolyn recalled Charlie jumping into her railway carriage on the day she set out to become a WAAF. She wished she had seen him again, but only the memory of his kindness had stayed with her. A Stirling failing to clear trees was the first horror she witnessed. The kindness of Squadron Leader Jim Ashton had saved her from walking away from the career that beckoned. Then she saw again weary aircrews, the wounded and traumatised men returning from their battles over Germany. The kaleidoscope of horror whirled and reformed before she forced it from her mind and embraced a new day.

'Sorry, Sis, no change in Greg.' How much longer would Alastair repeat the same message?

Time moved on. Her brother continued to lead the Spitfires on their reconnaissance duties, returning with photographs and information that was interpreted by the three WAAFs and their civilian counterpart and passed on to the bomber crews whose attacks on the enemy helped to bring the war closer and closer to a decisive victory.

Then, ten days after Greg's crash: 'Thank you, Matron, we're on our way!' Alastair said. He jumped to his feet, dropping the phone back on its cradle. He spent a few hectic minutes before bursting into the Intelligence section, startling. 'Oxford here we come!' His words, full of joy and hope, resounded from the walls.

'Greg has shown signs of revival. Matron says it's good news and Mr Western believes it could be beneficial to Greg if you are there, Carolyn. I have seen the CO and Kate and cleared leave for you. So come on. We can be away as soon as you are in the car the CO has authorized for our use. Ostensibly I am heading for a conference with one of my counterparts near Oxford.'

Carolyn was beside her brother, flinging her arms round him in excited appreciation of the news.

'Forget work, we'll see to that. And I know Kate will get more help or very likely step in herself,' said Lucy with an excitement that was matched by Vera's. She still found time to offer some advice.

'You need only concentrate on one thing, Carolyn. Give Greg encouragement to see there is still a good life ahead for him.'

Half an hour later Alastair drove a Humber Hawk out of Waddington and headed for Oxford.

Greg's eyelids flickered but his mind remained unaware of where he was. Boom! Boom! Boom! His thumping head left him with no desire to move. He was oblivious of time passing. Eventually he sensed something trying to poke into the dullness that surrounded him but could not make out what it was and gave up trying to fathom it until he became conscious that he was bathed in brightness. His eyes opened wider. White walls! Where was he? Why was he here? He moaned with the effort of trying to focus his attention.

'Ah, so you are awake? Good day, Flight Lieutenant Saunders.'

Flight Lieutenant? That sounded familiar. 'Where am I?' The question came quietly.

'You are safe and in good hands.'

He felt reassured by the voice and the way in which the words were delivered. At the same time he realized he was in bed. He turned his head slowly and focused on the pretty nurse standing beside him.

'Am I in heaven with an angel hovering around me?'

She smiled. 'I am no angel and you aren't in heaven. That place is reserved for you many years ahead. I am Sister Pam Pendle'

'Then tell me where I am.'

'You are in St Hugh's, Oxford.'

Greg struggled to recall why he was there. 'But I shouldn't be. I have to report back with the photographs I have taken. They will be wanted.' He lifted his left arm slowly as if to move the bedclothes.

She stopped him. 'That has been taken care of. Just lie still and we'll have the doctor in to take a look at you,' she added, carefully avoiding using the word 'surgeon'.

She pressed a bell and in a matter of moments Matron appeared accompanied by a nurse. She acknowledged Pam Pendle as she came in and went straight to the bed. 'Good day, Flight Lieutenant,' she said brightly. 'I'm Matron Adamson. You've met Sister Pendle and this is Nurse Nicola Carrick. While we three have other duties too, you have been assigned to us as our special patient.' A little smile curved the corners of her mouth. 'We expect you to carry out our instructions at all times, but now you must rest.'

Greg gladly obeyed as he felt an overwhelming desire to sleep.

Sister Pendle was left in charge. Three hours later Greg woke to find her by his side, though he had no recollection of her name.

'Bloody well get me out of this bed, get my uniform and take me to my aeroplane,' he said weakly.

'All in good time, Flight Lieutenant. First you must see the doctor. You have been unconscious for a few days and certainly can't leave hospital just yet.' She glanced at Nicola. 'Nurse Carrick, fetch Mr Western.'

The nurse hurried from the room and in a few minutes was back with a middle-aged man whose dark hair was beginning to grey at the temples.

'Good morning, young man,' he said breezily to Greg.

'I'm Mr Western, a surgeon at this hospital. I'm here, together with all these charming ladies, to put you right.'

'I don't know why I'm here or who brought me. There's nothing wrong with me. Just take me to my Spitfire and I'll be out of your hair,' Greg insisted.

'We'll attend to that for you, but first I think you and I should have a little chat.' There was something in this man's tone that made Greg realise he should listen. 'You were brought in here for us to heal you and that is what we will do.'

'Heal?' The word had jolted something in Greg's memory.

Mr Western realized what was happening. He had decided in the few moments he had spent with this young flyer that withholding information from him would not be a good idea so he dealt the blow at once, 'You crashed your Spitfire. You were badly injured and I had to amputate your right arm.'

For one moment there was a deathly silence. In that instant every aspect of his last flight flashed before Greg. Everyone in the room waited for the outcry, the curses, the shouting, the ranting and raving, but none came. There was a slight movement of bedclothes. Nurse Carrick automatically started forward but stopped when she saw the surgeon shake his head.

Greg looked straight at him. 'You are right, it isn't there!'

The plain, factual statement relieved everyone by its frankness, but they recognized the drugs speaking. When the full realization hit Greg, and the initial effect of the drugs wore off, they understood it would be the shock as well as the medical aspects of his condition that would really test their capabilities.

His eyes swept around the people gathered by his bed. Sensing they cared about him, he felt drawn to them, but for now he wanted to digest the terrible news he had been told.

'Right, we'll start,' said Mr Western. 'I will ...'

'Just a moment, sir,' Greg cut in, and then hesitated. 'This is a lot to take in. May I have some time on my own to think about it?'

Appreciating what Greg needed, Mr Western said, 'Very well, I'll return tomorrow. Nurse Carrick will be in attendance if there is anything you need.'

It wasn't long before a deep sleep took hold of Greg. When he eventually awoke he was aware of the figure of Mr Western entering the room.

'Hello, young man, your long sleep will have done you good. Now, can you remember what I told you yesterday?'

Greg slowly recalled the words of the previous day, and automatically felt for his right arm.

'Yes, sir.'

'Good, then let me go into a little more detail.'

'I don't want you pulling any punches. I want the truth, the whole truth. My head is bandaged too?'

'You sustained multiple injuries. You had several cuts to your head. Fortunately there was no brain damage, but you were left unconscious. However, your right arm ... well, sadly, it could not be saved. Your left arm has been gashed but nothing was broken so you will have full use of that before long. You were badly wounded in your right leg but that will mend, as will all the other cuts and bruises you suffered.'

'My left leg?'

'By a miracle it's OK. A few lacerations but they have been dealt with and will give you no trouble.' The surgeon was looking hard at Greg as he made this last statement. He had seen no adverse reaction so far to what he had told him. 'Any questions?'

There was a long pause before Greg replied, 'No. You have been frank with me and I thank you for that.'

'If you work with the nursing staff, who have been assigned to look after you, I have every confidence that you will make a full recovery.'

Except for my arm, Greg silently screamed inside.

'But that needn't hold you back. I believe you will make the most of your situation, and that starts now. A charming young WAAF officer is on her way here from Waddington ... '

'Carolyn!' Greg's expression became one of utter dismay. 'She can't see me like this! She mustn't! Tell her I won't see her! Send her back!'

Mr Western shook his head slowly as he said, 'I can't do that. She originally arrived when I was operating on you. She saw you briefly afterwards but I advised her to return to Waddington. She has kept in touch, through her brother, during the last ten days while you have been unconscious. She has been waiting for the moment she could see you again. You can't throw that loyalty back in her face. I think she must love you very much.'

'Then please, send her away, spare her from seeing me so helpless.'

'She knows what I had to do to save your life.'

'Better you had let me die and spared her then.'

'She doesn't believe that. She insisted I should tell her everything and did not regard you as a lost cause.'

'She knows how useless I'll be?'

'I have never told her that because I don't believe it is true, but only you can prove me right. I can tell you how you can do that, but only you can do it. If I judge her correctly she will want to help you by giving you her love and support. In the short time I saw her, I judged her to be a wonderful girl and you will make the biggest mistake of your life if you reject her now. I will say no more about that. It is up to you how you receive her when she arrives.'

361

39

'Visitors for you,' said Sister Pendle brightly.

Greg scowled but then looked surprised. 'Mum! Dad!'

'Hello, son.' Mr Saunders tried to make his greeting sound casual but could not disguise the worry in his eyes. 'How are you?'

Mrs Saunders was at the bedside, failing to stop the tears that spilled down her cheeks. Greg took her hand. She hadn't dared to touch him for fear of giving him more pain.

'It's good to see you both,' he said.

'We've kept track of you,' said his father. 'Squadron Leader Maddison has been in touch every day. We were told that you were up to seeing visitors now. He also said we might see him later as he is coming down from Waddington and bringing the WAAF you have mentioned in your letters.'

'I am looking forward to meeting her,' added Greg's mother.

He frowned. 'I don't want Carolyn here.'

His parents exchanged shocked glances.

'Sadie . . .' started her husband, only to stop talking when she demanded, 'Why not? I sensed from your letters that you and she were . . .'

'Not now. How can I expect her to take a broken man?'

Sadie Saunders glanced anxiously at her husband.

He knew he had to take a grip on things otherwise his son would lose any ability he had to fight this situation. 'Greg, it is not for you to dictate what Carolyn should do or should not do. In the end it is her choice, not yours. If she didn't love you, she would not have constantly wanted news of you, nor would she have made two journeys from Waddington to be at your side.'

Greg gave a resigned shrug of his shoulders and tightened his lips. His father knew his words had been noted and that the topic must rest.

'We have booked into a nearby hotel,' said Sadie, to divert him from any further discussion about Carolyn.

'How long for?'

'We've no time limit. We'll see how things develop.'

They fell into talk about family and friends, and passed on all the enquiries that had been made about their son.

Sister Pendle and Nurse Carrick came in then.

'We need to check the dressings,' said Sister. 'Nurse Carrick will show your parents to a waiting room. It shouldn't take us too long.'

'I'll get someone to bring you a cup of tea,' said the nurse when she had seen them settled.

Twenty minutes later Sister Pendle took them back to their son. 'There you are, all straightened up and refreshed.'

'We had better not be too long,' Sadie said. 'He's probably had too much of us already.'

'No, I haven't,' Greg protested, welcoming some semblance of normality.

His protest was short-lived because at that moment the door opened and Nurse Carrick looked in and with a smile announced, 'Two more visitors.'

Eager to see Greg, Carolyn hurried in but pulled up short

363

when she saw he already had visitors. She quickly composed herself and said, 'You must be Greg's mum and dad.'

Sadie smiled and said, 'And you must be Carolyn. We've heard so much about you.' She held out her arms and was pleased that Carolyn accepted her embrace.

'I'm so pleased to meet you,' the girl returned with genuine feeling. 'And Mr Saunders. Oh, Greg is so like you.'

Dan swelled with pride..

Carolyn quickly introduced her brother to Mr and Mrs Saunders, who expressed their pleasure at meeting their son's commanding officer.

As soon as these exchanges had been made Mrs Saunders, sensing they were intruding on moments that should be exclusively Greg's and Caroline's, diplomatically suggested, 'Maybe we should give these two a few minutes,' and ushered everyone out of the room, Alastair taking the opportunity to say quickly to Carolyn, 'I'll ring Mum.'

She nodded. 'Thanks.'

She had been tense about seeing Greg and had tried to steel herself against being shocked, but she had found that the presence and attitude of his mother and father had eased her feelings somewhat.

'Now, my love, what silly thing have you been doing?' she said lightly as she crossed the room.

'You already know,' said Greg, without any greeting. 'I'll be no good to you now. Leave and forget me.'

She had reached the bed. 'How can I forget the man I love?'

'I'm no longer that man and you know it.'

'I don't know it,' said Carolyn firmly while giving him a stern look. 'Physically you may be different, but the man I love is still there inside. Don't you dare try and discard him. If you do, you will be killing me too. You and I will marry as soon as you can step into the outside world. You can

364

achieve that sooner or later, depending on your determination to cope with a new life. Out of that challenge we can forge a wonderful life together. You have told me you love me – don't deny me that love now. I need it as much as you need mine, even if you won't admit it.'

'But I'll be a hindrance to your life, a burden when you could still have much enjoyment. Forget me, Carolyn. Find someone else.'

Carolyn's anger flared. 'I don't want anybody else; don't you ever think that. If I had I would have walked away from you before the crash. She folded her arms and fixed him with her eyes, 'So, Flight Lieutenant Greg Saunders, will you marry me?'

Taken aback by her forthright admission and question, he hesitated.

'Well? Do you really need time to consider a proposal from the girl you have said you love?' she demanded.

He gave a slow, sheepish grin. 'I thought we'd decided on marriage some time ago.'

A radiant smile lit up her face. She leaned over him and kissed him.

'Better bring them back in,' said Greg. He adopted a serious expression and when the others were back, said, 'I want you to know that I have got to conquer any disability I may be left with because I'm going to marry a lovely girl called Carolyn, so now I must make the formal introductions. Mum, Dad, meet Carolyn Maddison, your future daughter-in-law.'

Expressions of delight rang out. Alastair's eyes danced as he hugged his sister. 'I'm so pleased. He's a great guy. Talking to Mum on the phone, she said they were coming to see you both. This latest development will be a surprise but one I'm sure they'll heartily approve of.'

Mr Saunders beamed proudly as if to say how glad he was to have a daughter.

Mrs Saunders took Carolyn in her arms again. 'I'm so thankful that you didn't walk away. I know my son. When he wants something important he'll do all he can to get it, but not at the expense of someone's feelings. I have no doubt he tried to persuade you to end your relationship. That you are still here, and planning to marry, tells me how strong your love for him is. Carolyn, his dad and I welcome you to our family. I know your love will give Greg the strength and determination he needs to cope with whatever lies ahead for you both.'

The following day, when Alastair arrived at the hospital, he requested that he be informed when his mother and father arrived. This happened sooner than anticipated.

'I didn't expect you and Gran until later. This is wonderful,' he told them.

'We left soon after your call yesterday but arrived in Oxford too late to visit last night. Gran insisted on coming too,' his father explained.

'Carolyn will be delighted.'

'How is she?' asked his mother.

'Fine, Mum. In very good spirits. They're both determined to make light of Greg's injuries. Knowing them, they will. Come on, you'll love your prospective son-in-law.'

As they walked along the corridor his mother squeezed his hand. 'Thanks, Alastair.'

'Gran!' Carolyn exclaimed when they all came in. 'Are you here to perform another miracle?'

Her grandmother chuckled then added seriously, 'I think you have already done that with this young man.'

Carolyn drew a great deal of pleasure from seeing her mother and father and gran welcome Greg into the family.

40

The four Merlin engines roared with the power needed to free Lancaster U–Uncle and its bomb load from the constraints of earth and allow her to embrace the twilit sky.

The seven-man crew settled to their various tasks. This was the final operation of their tour. Everything hung on it.

One by one the rest of the squadron took to the sky, every crew wishing the popular Flight Lieutenant Rick Wood and his crew a safe return.

The same sentiments were coming from the three WAAFs who silently watched U–Uncle seek the cover of darkness as she headed for Germany, not knowing what awaited her.

'A nine-hour trip,' commented Lucy as they walked back to the briefing room. 'Rick could have chosen an easier one for their last operation,' she added, a little peevishly.

'You know he would never do that,' said Vera.

'The crew wouldn't want him to,' said Carolyn. 'They'd fly through hell for him if he asked them. There's never an easy op. There's always danger, no matter how long they're gone.'

'I know,' answered Lucy. 'It's just that I want Pete back safe and sound with his tour completed.'

*

Eight hours later Vera woke. Quietly, so as not to waken the others, she got ready for the day. She tiptoed along the corridor but when she stepped outside was surprised to find Carolyn and Lucy already there.

'Couldn't you two sleep either?' she asked.

'Off and on,' replied Carolyn.

'I had a restless night,' admitted Lucy.

'There's hardly a sound,' commented Vera. 'A wonderful, peaceful start to the day.'

'And soon that will be shattered by returning aircraft,' put in Carolyn. 'Let's go and get something to eat, while we have the chance.'

They were leaving the Mess when a distant sound reached their ears.

'Only one,' said Carolyn.

'Oh, please, please let it be Uncle,' whispered Lucy.

'Could be,' commented Vera, 'if they're following the tradition of a crew completing their tour being the first home.'

The speck in the sky was getting bigger and bigger.

'It's Uncle! It's them! They're back!'

Rick circled the airfield, called Control and heard the WAAF give them permission to land. She then added, 'Well done, U–Uncle, we are happy to have you back.'

'Thanks, it's good to be back,' he replied. A cheer from all the crew resounded through their head-phones and was loudly received in the Control Tower.

Rick took Uncle on her customary circuit and concentrated on bringing her down safely. There was a screech of rubber touching runway. They were down! Relief surged through the bomber and every member of the crew yelled their delight at each other.

The power of the engines was silenced in the dispersal. A

grinning, back-slapping ground-crew greeted everyone as they tumbled out of the Lancaster. Then Tim dropped to the ground and kissed it to fulfil his vow. Rick's gaze swept across his Lancaster as his thoughts sped to his father. That last one was especially for you, Dad. Now you can rest in peace.

They were cheered when they entered the briefing room and all received a special welcome from the three women who had taken Uncle's crew to their hearts.

41

The crew of U–Uncle returned from their end-of-tour leave to learn what fate had in store for them. They met up in the local pub, exchanging news about their leave and their families, but overall there was the strange feeling that they were in limbo, not wanted at the briefing for that night's operation. They watched the squadron take off, regretting they were not participants yet experiencing some measure of relief at not having to face the dangerous skies again.

As they had been instructed they reported to the adjutant's office the following morning at ten o'clock.

'I have your postings here,' he said when they were all settled. 'They are all for ten days' time so it is up to you what you do in the meantime. Officially you will still be on the strength of this squadron, so stay if you want or, if you prefer, travel warrants for home and then on to your new base will be issued tomorrow.' He looked down at the paperwork on his desk. 'Right, here are your postings. Flight Lieutenant Rick Wood, your application to do a second tour has been accepted. I will give you details after I have dealt with the rest of the crew.'

'Thank you,' said Rick. 'May I say one thing?'

'Go ahead.'

He had noticed the glances exchanged by his crew. 'Sorry not to have expressed my intention to you before we went on leave, but now you know I will say it: if any of you want to join me, I will be pleased to have you.'

The adjutant gave a little nod of agreement. 'That gives you something to think about, but you must make the decision before you leave this room so that I can activate any changes immediately. Right, I will carry on. Flight Lieutenant Peter Wilkins, you will be going as an instructor to Swinderby.'

Peter felt relief surge through him. This posting meant he could still share the cottage with Lucy.

'Pilot Officer Don Westwood, you too are posted to Swinderby as an instructor.'

Don glanced at Peter who gave him a thumbs up and received a wink in return. It meant their wives could share the cottage and the two men would still work closely together.

The two gunners, Tim and Mark, had exchanged meaningful glances, and when they voiced their desire to continue flying with Rick he was delighted to accept them.

'Sergeant Phil Stevens, you are posted as an engineer instructor at Bitteswell OTU.' This suited him because the move was not far away and he knew he and Myrna could easily avail themselves of the dance halls in Nottingham.

'Last but not least,' went on the Adjutant, 'Wireless Operator Gordon Barton, you are posted to RAF Yatesbury in Wiltshire.

Gordon screwed up his nose. He didn't like this posting which seemed to be moving him away from the crew, who were otherwise still based close together. But he shrugged his shoulders in resignation. What would be would be.

As they left the adjutant's office, Rick called to them all,

'Party tomorrow night before we split up. Get in touch with wives and girlfriends and the Spitfire boys. Make this party happen!' He didn't use the words 'final party'; that would be tempting fate.

The party was soon in full swing. Everyone had made a special effort to look their best. Carolyn regretted that Greg could not be with them; he was making good progress but was likely to stay in hospital for another six weeks. She was not going to let that spoil the evening for anyone, however.

She glanced at her watch and turned to Lucy. 'It's nearly an hour since we all got here and there's no sign of Rick. Where is he?'

'Just what I was wondering. Pete, have you seen Rick today?'

He shook his head. 'No, but I do know he left the station early.'

'Going where?' asked Lucy.

Pete shrugged his shoulders. 'I don't know. I thought he'd be here before any of us.' He reached for his glass of beer.

No one was holding back on celebrating the end of their tour.

Ten minutes later the door swung open. The girl on Rick's arm brought a hush to the room, charged with surprise and admiration.

She looked at Rick and her face broke into a broad smile. She winked at him when someone's 'Wow!' summed up everyone's reaction. Her laughter rang out, encompassing a room full of strangers. Her friendliness was unmistakable. She was tall and slim with a figure that was accentuated by her uniform. The central lettering in the Wings above the left-hand breast pocket told everyone that she was a member of the Air Transport Auxiliary.

'All right, everyone. Thanks for the reception for Maddie. I know her from way back. I didn't even know she was flying now,' Rick explained. 'I heard there was a Lancaster being delivered to us so I waited to meet it. Surprise, surprise, Maddie stepped out.'

'Sorry I held Rick up,' she called to them. 'My navigation was a little rusty today.'

'I'll navigate for you any time.' Someone's shout brought rival offers from around the room.

The course of the evening was set. Maddie blended in as if she had always known the crew of U–Uncle, and was ready to talk about her missions delivering aircraft to RAF stations around the country.

'She seems as mad about flying as Rick is,' commented Carolyn to Vera. 'Maybe he's found his soulmate.'

'I hope so,' agreed Vera. 'He deserves that.'

EPILOGUE

Alastair rang the small handbell that had been placed on the table before him and rose from his seat. A hush fell across the room and all eyes turned to him.

'I would like to thank everyone for being here today to see this wonderful girl marry this brave man. Courage tests us all in one way or another. Carolyn and Greg have faced their test with boldness, confident now that they can cope with anything. I hope they can deal with what I am about to reveal.

'There was something about Greg's crash that puzzled not only me but also my senior officers in the Photographic Unit and all the way up to the Head of Bomber Command. Greg was engaged in an important survey. Meetings took place, information was gathered, and conclusions were drawn that answered the question that had puzzled us from the start of our enquiry. That question was, why hadn't he bailed out? From what we had gleaned we realized he could have done, and before the final attack that caused the loss of his arm.'

All eyes turned to Greg, who was looking mortally embarrassed by Alastair's words.

He continued, 'I can tell you the reason Greg did not bail out. His mission that day was a vital one. He had previously photographed that same section a number of times, but when he was engaged in doing so again he realized something had changed; at the height he was flying he could not be sure what it was. He went lower to get better photographs and that was when he was spotted by two Messerschmitts. They were armed, Greg was not. The result you know, but the question is still: why didn't he bail out?

'Greg realized the photographs he had taken could provide vital information to those in command and that information was still in the cameras he had been using. If he'd bailed out those cameras and the information they contained would have been lost. He chose to make a controlled crash landing and save the vital photographs. In choosing to do that he left himself open to further attacks and paid heavily for it.'

Alastair allowed a small pause to lengthen then said, 'Contrary to all normal procedures I have been given permission, because of today's happy event, to announce that his bravery and courage have been recognized by the award of the DSO.'

Congratulatory shouts rang out amongst the thunderous clapping. Everyone rose to their feet, leaving an embarrassed Greg sitting in his chair. Carolyn held out her hand and drew him to his feet then took him in her arms and kissed him, setting another rousing cheer echoing round the room.

Greg held up his hand for silence. 'I thank you all for being here. I thank you for your congratulations, which I don't deserve. After all, I was only doing my duty. I think there are those here who more richly deserve your praise. They have completed thirty gruelling operations against our enemy, helping to bring us nearer victory and peace. Please raise your glasses to the crew of U–Uncle!'

ACKNOWLEDGEMENTS

There are many people involved in the production of a book, from the germ of an idea until the finished copy reaches the bookshelf. They cannot all be named, but I thank all those at Piatkus and Little, Brown who assisted with the publication of this book. I must make special mention of Caroline Kirkpatrick, Assistant Editor, who has looked after this novel from the start. It has been a pleasant relationship, as has that with Anna Boatman, Senior Editor.

I thank Peter Murton, Research and Information Officer at IWM Duxford, Cambridge, who confirmed facts re the employment of WAAFs and Traffic Control that had faded from my memory with the passage of time.

I also thank my four children: Judith Gilbert for her research work and advice as the novel proceeded; Geraldine Jones for medical information and for checking the completed manuscript; Anne Hudson and Duncan Spence for their continued support and interest in my writing.

Lynn Curtis has been a brilliant copy-editor for all of Jessica Blair's novels. I am most grateful for that and for her friendship throughout.

And thanks to all my readers.